THE
DUSK GATE CHRONICLES
BOOK FIVE

CANES
OF DIVERGENCE

BREEANA PUTTROFF

FIRST EDITION
ISBN 13: 9781940481012

~~~~~~~~~~~

Cover Design: Mallory Rock

Formatting & Layout: Mallory Rock

~~~~~~~~~~~

Thirteen Pages Press
P.O. BOX 350944
DENVER, CO 80035

Canes of Divergence: The Dusk Gate Chronicles Book 5 is a work of fiction. Names, characters, places and incidents are products of the author's imagination, or the author has used them fictitiously.

EMPTY CHAIR

Bristlecone, Colorado

"YO, CUNNINGHAM. Are you coming?"

"What?" Zander looked up, confused for a second. His friend Adam Lamos was staring at him impatiently.

"Uh, lunch?"

"Oh." He glanced around, becoming aware of his surroundings again. Everyone was packing up their things. He hadn't even heard the bell, but the clock read 12:00.

"What are you working on, anyway?" Adam asked, eyeing Zander's notebook.

Snapping the black-and-white cover closed, he shoved the notebook in his backpack. "Nothing. Just an extra-credit assignment."

"Dude, it's almost the end of senior year – you've already been accepted into, what? Four colleges? It's cruise time. Didn't you get the memo?"

Yes, Zander had gotten the memo – about a thousand times. Adam – like half the senior players on the football team – believed nothing he did at school mattered now that the college acceptances had come in.

Even if they were right, Zander wasn't personally taking any chances. Although, to be honest, his "extra-credit assignment" wasn't exactly for school.

Adam didn't wait for a response. He headed for the door, anxious – as always – to see his girlfriend, Abigail. Those two had been together for over two months now, which was some kind of record for both of them.

Zander, on the other hand, was finding the cafeteria harder to tolerate with each passing day. Like every day, he got his lunch tray and followed Adam to their usual table, and like every day, the empty seat beside him was a black hole, threatening to suck him in.

Of course, the chair wasn't always empty. Over the last month, others had begun sitting there. For a week or two after Quinn had left, it was Melanie Fisher, Adam's first attempt to get Zander to "move on." Once he'd finally ended that, the seat had been used on a sort of rotating basis by different people. Today, though, nobody was there and he found himself glancing at it a few more times than he should.

"It's time to get over her, you know." Abigail's voice, too close to his ear, made him jump.

"Excuse me?"

"She's been gone for over a month, and she hasn't even bothered to call or text anyone or anything. She isn't coming back."

He nodded. "I know that, Abigail…but don't you think it's weird? That isn't like Quinn – to just take off without a word to anyone."

"I wouldn't have thought she would cheat on you, either, Zander, but…"

He flinched. Yes, that still stung; not as badly as it had at first, but it still hurt. He didn't let it stop him, though. He looked straight into Abigail's eyes. "Do you know that for sure? I mean, if she left to go with Doctor Rose because he was really her uncle, then doesn't that make William her cousin or something? I don't know that she cheated on me."

"She broke up with you."

"Yeah. At the same time her mom told her she'd been lying to her about her family for her entire life. Don't you think she might have been upset about that?"

"How would I know? She never told me – she never even told any of us any of that. She just picked up and went to *Europe* with them without telling anyone anything. And now she can't even be bothered to call."

"Maybe she doesn't have a phone."

"Maybe she just doesn't give a rip about us. Last I checked, there are computers in Europe. But has she e-mailed? Anything?" Abigail's short hair – newly dyed an impossible shade of purple – bobbed back and forth in emphasis.

By now, everyone at the table was staring at them, but Zander decided he didn't care. He'd had enough of everyone pretending that nothing was going on here. "Or maybe she didn't tell us anything because we were all so mean to her that last week before spring break. She was your best friend, Abigail. Don't you care? Aren't you worried about her?"

Abigail rolled her eyes. "We weren't mean to her. She was lying and keeping secrets from us then. Now, she's off running around Europe with her rich doctor of an uncle. Obviously she's not worried about us. It's time for you to accept that. If she really ever cared about you, she would have at least called before she left."

A sudden fierce anger rose inside him, and he knew that if he stayed here, something – *not good* – was going to happen. He stood up, shoved his chair in and walked off, not even bothering to throw away his untouched tray of food.

He didn't stop walking until he was outside in the parking lot, staring at the front of his little black pick-up truck. After only a moment of considering, he climbed inside, turned the key, and drove off.

Everything Abigail had said was true – Quinn had broken up with him. She was the one who hadn't called anyone, who wasn't returning calls, or texts, or e-mails, or anything.

At first, he had to admit, he'd been hurt, and he'd been angry with her. The last time he'd talked to her had been the last day of school before spring break, and he'd seen her standing in the hallway, talking to William Rose, after she'd just broken up with him the night before…yes, that had been like a knife in his gut. He hadn't *wanted* to talk to her or see her.

Then, over spring break, on the day that Adam had convinced him to go and hang out with him and Abigail and Melanie Fisher, he'd run into her. Sort of. She'd been eating breakfast with her mom at the café, and he'd seen her through the window. Her eyes had met his for just a second, though she'd looked down as soon as she saw Melanie. He'd taken some satisfaction from that – her seeing him with another girl after what she'd done to him.

But then there had come the night, the last day of the vacation, when Quinn's mom, Megan, had come over to Zander's house for dinner, alone. When Megan had told them the news.

There were a lot of parts to the story – Doctor Rose being offered a prestigious research position somewhere in Europe, Quinn finding out that Doctor Rose was really her uncle and that Megan had been lying to her. Zander hadn't really been able to listen to it – he'd missed most of the details because they weren't important. All that mattered was the news that Quinn was gone.

Megan didn't even know when – or if – her daughter was coming back.

For the first week or so, the anger had been overpowering. She'd just up and left without saying anything to anyone – as if they didn't matter to her at all.

Gradually, though, other thoughts had occurred to him. She had been fighting with everyone before spring break. Zander and Abigail, especially, hadn't exactly been nice to her. If Quinn *wasn't* cheating on him – if she'd broken up with him because she just didn't know how to deal with finding out about her mom lying to her – now he felt guilty that she'd seen him with Melanie.

Had they really been *that* awful, though, that Quinn would think they wouldn't even want to know she was leaving? That they wouldn't even want to hear the details or say good-bye?

And really, he'd started to think later, wasn't it all just plain weird? The more time passed, the harder he was finding it to believe that Megan would just allow her daughter to run off to *Europe* with her dead father's family.

It wasn't like her uncle had custody of her. Quinn had been legally adopted by Megan's new husband, Jeff, when she was eight years old. Megan didn't *have* to let her go anywhere.

In fact, the more he thought about it, the more things just didn't add up, and all of it caused a sick twisting in the pit of his stomach.

As he drove, he tried to clear his thoughts, tried to remember everything that had happened with Quinn before spring break.

She'd been acting weird, even before any of this had happened. One of his most vivid memories was the night she'd gasped when he'd touched her arm. The look on her face when she'd pulled up her sleeve to reveal painful-looking bruises and stitches still haunted him.

That was the first time he realized she was keeping secrets from him. And right after that – the same night even – she'd disappeared for the entire weekend, without telling anyone, not even Megan. He'd found out later that she'd spent that weekend with William Rose.

Only a few days later, she'd broken up with him, right before spring break. And right after that, she'd disappeared.

There had to be more to it, didn't there? Maybe she'd known she was going to be leaving, and that's why she'd broken up with him in the first place. But why not tell him?

Something was wrong here. But what? Nothing seemed to add up, and each possible answer only led to more questions.

Thinking that a drive up into the mountains might help clear his mind, he flipped on the radio and headed toward the highway.

Of course, in Bristlecone, it was always difficult to drive the way he wanted to right now. The light at River Road turned red just as he was approaching, even though there were no other cars in sight.

Mumbling under his breath as he pulled to a stop, he looked around the intersection, noticing that the county still hadn't repaired the guardrail on the other side after that tourist had crashed there back in January.

He remembered the incident well. He hadn't seen it, but Quinn had. Megan had called Zander's mom the night it happened; apparently it had freaked Quinn out quite a bit. Not that Zander blamed her; he found out later that she'd actually stopped and administered first aid to the banged-up tourist. A situation like that would probably have bothered him, too.

Maybe it was selfish, but he'd been glad for the excuse to talk to her. At the time, the two of them hadn't been close for quite a while, and he'd been feeling like a jerk about it. He'd realized how much he regretted not making the effort with her earlier this year, after that disaster of a homecoming date with Adrianna Marrs.

Working up the courage to talk to her had been hard – he'd worried that Quinn probably wouldn't want to have anything to do with him after the way he had been ignoring her, and it never seemed to be the right time. After the accident, asking her if she was okay had seemed like a good way to break the ice.

Now that she was gone, he didn't know what the right thing was anymore. Maybe she wanted him to just ignore her again, to pretend the whole thing hadn't happened. But what if she *wanted* him to reach out to her?

For the past month, he'd fought that battle, alternately writing a letter to her in his notebook and then closing it, shoving it under his mattress for a few days. He didn't know if there was any way to send it to her even if he did ever finish it. Today in class had been one of the days the letter came back out again.

The light turned green and, without really knowing why, instead of driving straight ahead, he turned left on River Road. There was a little picnic area a little way up the road with a parking lot. Maybe he'd park there and then walk up to look at the damaged rail.

It was stupid, he knew, but he just couldn't shake the idea that he'd find answers there. A couple of weeks ago, Abigail had said something about Quinn starting to act strangely after that incident. Nothing else was helping, anyway – what did he have to lose?

He drove down into the picnic area and parked.

Although the spring day had been warm enough to leave his letter jacket in the truck during school, here, in the shade of the trees down close to the river, it was cooler, and he wanted to wear it now. Pausing for a moment, he took a deep breath of the mountain air, allowing it to calm him a little.

Birds chattered in the nearby trees, and from here the rushing of the river, overflowing with spring melt, was loud – almost loud enough to drown out the confusing jumble of his thoughts.

Wanting – needing – that distraction for a while, he walked down to the edge of the water, watching as it pounded against the rocks and swirled in waves. He stood there for a long time just staring at the river, trying not to think, to erase the questions and thoughts from his mind.

More than anything, he wanted to be able to talk about all of this – with *Quinn*. She was the one who could have talked him down from this – even if they'd stayed broken up, he missed her friendship.

The river was nice, though. Calming, clearing his head enough that he might be able to let some of this go for a while and make it through another day. Out in the middle a silvery fish jumped, shimmering in the sunshine before making a huge splash and disappearing again.

Zander smiled and turned to head back for his truck. He'd almost decided not to bother with going up to the guardrail but once he was away from the water, it seemed important again.

Before he got to the parking lot, though, something else caught his attention.

A few feet away from the riverbank, there was an enormous tree. It would have been worth paying attention to all by itself. The massive pine was the largest one he had ever seen – too large, really, to only be a single tree. And, in fact, when he looked closer at the base, he could see where the one tree had started out as two trunks that had grown next to each other and then somehow twisted and become one.

But that wasn't what had made him stop.

The whole area underneath the tree was dark and muddy, as if someone had been digging there. In fact, as he got closer, he found several holes that had been started, but then abandoned.

The mud extended all the way around the trunk, although it was much worse on the north side of the tree, closest to the river. On that side, a big rock had been haphazardly dragged over the center of the muddy patch, leaving a trail in its place. Without stopping to consider what he was doing, he went over to investigate.

The rock was heavy, but not too heavy, and he was able to lift it out of the way and move it without much effort.

The size of the hole underneath startled him; it wasn't very wide, but it was deep.

Someone had gone to a lot of effort to dig it, almost as if they were searching for something. He couldn't see anything inside it, though. Kneeling down on the ground, wondering if he was crazy, he carefully put his hand down in the hole. When his arm was in the ground halfway to his elbow, he hit bottom. There was nothing there, only cold, smooth stone. Almost smooth, anyway.

He felt around some more, running his fingers along the surface of the rock, but then he gasped and brought his hand quickly back up. There was a small cut on his middle finger, just beginning to bleed. He'd run it along a sharp edge where the rock had felt broken, as if there was a chunk missing from it.

"Did you find what you were looking for?" A voice behind his head startled him, nearly sending him face-first into the hole. He spun around.

An older man was standing there – well, Zander assumed that he was older, from the long, white hair that trailed down his back, tied with a leather band. His face looked younger though, except for the bushy white eyebrows under the brim of his hat.

He had no other facial hair or wrinkles, and the gleam in his bright green eyes showed no signs of age. He was decked out in full fly-fishing gear. His dark green waders were wet, and sounds were coming from the creel that peeked around his side, indicating a recent catch.

Recovering from the sudden interruption, Zander shrugged. "I wasn't really looking for anything."

"Ah," the man said knowingly. "That's often when I find the best stuff."

Zander blinked. *What?* He stood up, trying to compose himself. "I, uh … I didn't see you here a minute ago."

The man smiled. "Who said I was here a minute ago?"

"How did you get here, then?"

"How did *you* get here Zander?"

He almost fell back down. "Excuse me?"

The man's bright blue eyes – *had they been that color a moment ago?* – flicked to Zander's jacket and then back up to meet his gaze.

Right. His name was embroidered on his jacket. Zander squared his shoulders and looked directly back. "I'm sorry. I didn't catch your name."

If the man noticed Zander's irritation, it didn't seem to affect him. He smiled brightly, extending his hand. "You can call me Alvin."

Zander raised an eyebrow, still unusually piqued. "Is that your name?"

"You don't like it? I've always been told it suits me. If you prefer, though, you could call me Blueberry – I rather fancy blueberries."

All right then, the man was crazy. He didn't look quite old enough to be having symptoms of dementia, but clearly *something* wasn't right. It was a little harder to hold on to his anger.

"Can I help you with anything, Mr. … Alvin? Are you lost?"

Alvin's smile only grew wider. "I'm right where I'm supposed to be. As are you, I should think."

That made Zander chuckle. "No, Mr. Alvin, I don't think I'm supposed to be here at all."

"Zander, if you're not going to call me Blueberry, you could at least drop the 'Mister' bit. Nobody has called me that in a hundred cycles, at least."

At this point, Zander was certain there was something wrong with the man. His anger had all but vanished, and he was starting to get concerned. "I'm sorry, uh … Alvin."

Alvin's eyes were clear and bright – there was nothing about him that *looked* crazy. "Blueberry was the wrong choice, I see; it's given you the wrong impression *Mister* Cunningham. Maybe Glasberry would have been better – your friend Quinn certainly prefers those."

Zander had been focused so intently on the man's strange behavior, trying to figure out how someone who looked so coherent could sound so crazy, that it took a minute before he registered what Alvin had just said.

The blood in his veins turned to ice water. "Excuse me?"

"Glasberries – you know, little green berries. Shiny. Very juicy. Delicious. I heard the king of Philotheum is having his head gardener build a greenhouse just so the queen can have glasberries in any season." His eyes met Zander's again. "But that's a secret – it's meant to be a surprise for her when they return home."

"I'll be sure not to say anything," Zander answered drily.

"Excellent!" Alvin rubbed his hands together and smiled.

He was no longer interested in the man's odd ramblings, only in one thing he'd said. "What about my friend Quinn? How do you know about her?"

"I thought you said you weren't here looking for anything." The shrewd look on Alvin's face made Zander suddenly sure that there was nothing crazy about him at all.

"Do you know Quinn?"

"Yes, I know her quite well. She's a lovely young woman – more stubborn sometimes than you're being right now."

He ignored that. "Do you know where she is?"

Alvin looked around, going so far as to turn in a circle. "She doesn't appear to be here."

"Obviously."

"Then why are you searching here?"

Frustration welled inside of him again. "I didn't mean to search here! I was walking by the river and I saw that whole area dug up right there. It made me curious, that's all."

Alvin nodded. "But what are you doing here in the first place? Shouldn't you be sitting in your English class right about now?"

"I was having trouble concentrating at school. I couldn't focus on it." He had no idea why he was telling this to Alvin, especially because it was beyond creepy that the man had guessed right – a glance at his cell phone told him that English had just started.

"What were you thinking about instead?"

"I was thinking that it's not normal for a teenage girl to just disappear off the face of the Earth and for her mother to not even care."

"What makes you think her mother doesn't care?"

"Would you let *your* daughter run off to another country to live with an uncle she never even knew about before? A stranger?"

Alvin lifted one shoulder. "I'd hardly call Nathaniel a stranger."

Zander's jaw fell so far that he was afraid he was going to get gravel on it. "How could you know that? Who are you? What do you know about all of this?"

"That's a lot of questions."

"I want some answers."

Alvin cocked his head to one side; Zander felt as if he were being studied. "What do you plan to do with those answers once you find them?"

"Why do you care?"

"Why do *you* care, Zander? What difference does it make to you why Megan Robbins allowed her daughter to go and live somewhere else with her family?"

"She was my girlfriend."

"*Was*, being the operative word. I have it on good authority that Quinn ended that in the best way she knew how."

"She was my friend, too."

"Was she really? Were you treating her the way you would treat a friend?"

"I thought she was cheating on me! She was running around behind my back and lying to me."

"Perhaps." Alvin nodded. "But what does that have to do with what you did?"

"What do you mean? I didn't do anything. Anybody would have been mad if their girlfriend lied and cheated on them."

"Many people would have, yes. Of course, I'm not talking with any of those people. I'm having a conversation with you."

"Are you saying I should have just acted like she didn't do anything wrong?"

"I'm not saying you should or shouldn't have done any particular thing. I was merely asking about what you did."

"Do you think I did something wrong?"

"What does it matter what I think?"

A sudden pain made Zander look down at his right hand. It was clenched into a fist so tightly that the rough edge of his fingernail was digging into his skin. He had to work to loosen it. "What do you know about Quinn? Do you know where she is?"

"Why isn't the answer you were given by her mother good enough for you?"

"Because it doesn't make any sense."

"It doesn't make any sense that Quinn would want to get to know her family after being deprived of them for so long?"

Zander stared at him. "It doesn't make any sense that Megan would just send her child off to another country with people she barely knows. It just feels like there's something wrong. I'm worried about her."

The old man rolled his eyes, which was so unexpected that Zander actually cracked a grin.

"Quinn's a child now?"

"You know what I mean."

"I'm afraid I don't."

"She's still young enough to be at home with her mother – not running off to live in another country before she even graduates high school. I just think that something must be wrong."

"Something you don't think Quinn's mother is able to handle?"

Zander didn't have a response for that.

"Is this because you're really worried about Quinn, or is it about your own feelings? Because you believe you're owed some kind of an explanation that you're not getting?"

He thought about that for a minute. "Does it matter?"

"Do one's intentions matter? I think you know the answer to that."

Zander sighed, more confused now than ever.

"You're very invested in this, aren't you?" Alvin's eyes were gentler now, almost sympathetic, and something about his expression made Zander *want* to answer.

"Yes. I don't know why – I can't explain it, but I just can't let it go."

"I think you need to stop for a moment, Mr. Cunningham, and decide what it is that you're after. There are things you can't unlearn once you've learned them. Quinn learning about her father's side of her family – learning that her mother had been keeping that information from her for her entire life – was such an event for her. While it is not my place to share her story with you, I can tell you this. It changed her life – permanently – in ways she couldn't have imagined, and forced her to make decisions she probably wasn't prepared for."

"And you're saying the same thing will happen to me."

"Everyone is different." Alvin shrugged. "I'm merely warning you that getting involved in things which are not your concern often has consequences. Not the least of which is the fact that Quinn has obviously chosen not to tell you about this – and she has never struck me as the kind of girl who would take that sort of thing lightly."

"And Quinn is not my concern."

"She certainly doesn't have to be. She relieved you of that responsibility, and she did that on purpose."

"Right after she found out that Nathaniel was really her uncle."

"Just before, actually. But at that point, she already knew that her life had changed enough that she'd not be able to offer you what you needed from her."

"So she wasn't lying to me."

"Yes, Zander, she was. In the same way that you're not going to go tell your friends or your family that you ran into me here today – don't look at me like that, I know you're not going to."

"Not telling them something is not the same as lying."

"What if they asked you directly?"

Zander swallowed, remembering a time when he had not only asked, but *pushed* Quinn for an answer she hadn't seemed willing to give him. When she'd begrudgingly shown him the stitches and bruises running down her upper arm, he'd freaked out, and she still hadn't given him a straight answer.

"If you continue on this path, Zander, keep sticking your nose in this issue, you are going to find yourself in the same situation – telling lies to the people you care about."

Who was this guy, anyway? A CIA agent or something? What in the world? Zander was getting a little scared now.

"And you're here to what? Warn me to stay away?"

"Among other things, yes – not to threaten you, Zander. There's no need to be afraid of me. I'm merely asking you to be sure of what your motives are. Quinn doesn't *owe* you an explanation. If you insist on having one, you will be responsible for whatever else it brings into your life."

"Why do I feel like I'm in some kind of weird spy movie?"

Alvin smiled. "It's not a movie, Zander. I merely consider it only fair to let you know that you might get more than you bargained for if you pursue this, and to give you a chance to back out now."

Alvin's face was perfectly kind and friendly now – there was nothing menacing about him at all – but a chill ran down Zander's spine. "Did Quinn have the same warning?"

"No. That's an advantage you have that she didn't – not that she'd likely have taken the warning." Alvin smiled; the look in his eyes when he spoke of Quinn was a fond one – it calmed Zander a little. "But her circumstances were very different than yours. This isn't your family, Zander, and it isn't your concern."

"Unless I make it my concern."

"Unless you do."

"What if I really just want to know that Quinn is all right – that nothing has happened to her?"

"Nothing happening to her and her being all right are two completely different things. I can tell you that she is currently healthy and well. Now, if you will excuse me, today's an excellent day for catching fish."

Zander wasn't anywhere near ready to *excuse* Alvin to go anywhere, but by the time he opened his mouth to respond, the old man was already several hundred feet away from him, down by the riverbank. He wasn't even sure how he'd gotten there so quickly.

Sighing, his thoughts traveling in even more directions than they had been when he'd arrived, he turned to walk back to his truck. Halfway there, just before heading into the trees that would obscure his view, he glanced back, half tempted to chase the man down and demand more answers from him, but when he looked, Alvin was gone. Zander couldn't see him anywhere.

Startled, he turned all the way around, looking up and down the riverbank. Nothing. *Weird.* There hadn't been time for Alvin to leave. He started to walk back down to where they'd been talking, his eyes scanning the entire area.

That's when he saw it. If not for the small movement, he would never have noticed the man. Way up the slope that led to the highway above, and quite a distance downriver, there was a man, just sitting there, right next to a boulder.

It definitely wasn't Alvin – he was too far away for one thing, and for another, this man had the blackest hair he'd ever seen; cropped close to his head, it looked nearly midnight blue. And he was staring right at Zander.

Even at this distance, he knew that the man had seen him, too – but the stranger didn't seem to care. If anything, his posture indicated boredom. He didn't look away, he just continued to watch. Zander was reminded of a hawk, a thought that sent a shudder rippling down from his shoulders to his toes.

Though the spring day was growing warmer, Zander snapped his jacket closed around him as he turned back and headed toward his truck.

SAMUEL

Rosewood Castle, Eirentheos

THE KNOCK ON the door was so soft that at first Quinn wasn't sure she'd actually heard it, but William's head turned at the sound, too. The baby in his arms sighed contentedly; William had just finished changing him and wrapping him up in a clean blanket.

"Do you want me to answer it?" he asked. "I think whoever it is knocked that quietly because they don't want to disturb us if we want to be left alone."

"Go ahead," she said, glancing toward the window at the bright sunlight pouring in through the small crack William had opened a little while ago when the baby had woken them. "They've been patient for long enough, I think."

"You're not too tired for company?"

She shook her head. "Three hours of sleep at a stretch is probably as good as it's going to get for a while. Might as well get used to it. Besides, I'm a little hungry."

"Good." He smiled, leaning down to nestle the baby in her arms and kissing her hair before going out to the sitting room to answer the door.

Nathaniel appeared in the bedroom doorway behind William. "Are you sure it's okay? If it's not, I'll leave this here and go." He nodded at the tray in his hands, loaded down with bowls of hot grain cereal, sweet rolls, fruit, and glasses of juice.

"Oh, come in, Nathaniel. We have something we wanted to tell you anyway."

The answering grin on her uncle's face made her glad he hadn't waited any longer.

William took the tray from him, and Nathaniel approached her. "How are you feeling?"

"Great, actually. I'm not even as tired as I thought I would be."

He smiled again, gazing down now at the baby. "May I?"

Nodding, she tucked the edge of the blanket back over a tiny arm before handing her son to him. Her uncle had come to check on her and the baby last night after William and the midwife delivered him, but he hadn't held him. Nobody had yet, besides her and William.

"Oh," Nathaniel breathed. "He's perfect. He has William's hair, but otherwise…he looks just like you, Quinn." Cradling the baby with one arm, he gently brushed his finger across the little forehead. "This is exactly what you looked like, the first time I held you."

Warmth filled her chest as Nathaniel held her son so tenderly. Her uncle wasn't always expressive, and the two of them were still figuring out what their relationship was going to be like, but watching him now – there was no doubt how he felt about her, and now about her child. Of course, right at the edges of the warm fuzziness was the ache in her chest that never quite went away.

"I'm so sorry that you mother isn't here, sweetheart," Nathaniel said, as if he sensed what she was thinking. "Or the rest of your family. I wish they were all here. And I really wish Samuel was here. This would have been a shining moment for him."

"It's still a wonderful moment," William said, coming to sit on the edge of the bed beside Quinn. He handed her a glass of juice and put his arm around her, squeezing her shoulder gently. "I know wherever Quinn's father is, he's seeing this now, and I still – we still – have hope that Quinn will see her family again, that they'll get to meet our son, even if it's not today. But today is still a pretty great day."

"Yes, it is," Quinn agreed, nodding. And it was. She would always miss her family; it would always be hard, but something had shifted inside her when William had first set the baby on her chest last night. The joy she'd felt then – the same joy she felt now when she saw that sweet little face – outweighed all of the sadness.

"We wanted to tell you we've chosen a name," she said. "I know it's supposed to be a secret until the Naming Ceremony, but we thought you might like to hear it first."

"Oh?"

"We were thinking Samuel…Samuel Owen Rose."

Nathaniel's eyes lit up. "That's perfect." He looked down at the baby. "A perfect name for a perfect little boy," he cooed, leaning down to kiss little Samuel on the forehead.

"So is everyone else pacing the hallway waiting to get in here?" Quinn asked, once Nathaniel finally handed the baby back to her.

He grinned. "Only Thomas. Charlotte and Stephen are anxious to see you, of course, but they've been through this enough times now to be patient. Alice has asked a few times, too."

"Bring them in," Quinn said. "There's no telling how much longer we have until he needs to eat again."

William sat down beside her, resting his hand on Samuel's little head. "If how he's been so far is any indication, I'd give it half an hour, tops."

Almost as soon as Nathaniel went out, Thomas appeared in the doorway, making Quinn chuckle. "You really were out there waiting for an all-clear, weren't you?"

"I only have a limited time to spend with my nephew before you run off back to Philotheum with him." He grinned. "I have to soak up every second I can get."

William rolled his eyes. "You're coming *with* us at first."

"But only for the Naming Ceremony. I'm not staying." Thomas' eyes were on Samuel now. "You two and Linnea and Ben are going to have all the fun after that. Hand him over, Sis. It's my turn."

She thought about teasing him for a second, but then she saw the look in his eyes – behind all of the banter, he was quite serious – and she let William take the baby from her arms and hand him to his brother.

He was so natural with the baby; Quinn was reminded instantly of the first morning she'd ever known Thomas, when he'd so easily taken his youngest sister from his mother. Now, he held little Samuel in front of him so they were facing each other. For several moments he was silent, just studying his nephew, while the baby lay there contentedly. Finally, he bent down and kissed Samuel on the forehead before turning his attention back to them.

"I can't believe you're a father, Will."

"No, neither can I. I always figured you would be the first one of the two of us – I was never sure I'd ever get to be one at all." He sat down next to Quinn again, putting his hand on her knee.

Quinn couldn't help rolling her eyes. "Whatever. You're eighteen, Will. And Thomas, you're sixteen. In my world, people would think you're crazy for even talking about babies. If I went back there now, with him…" She shook her head. Truthfully, she couldn't even imagine it. Her life in Bristlecone seemed like a million years ago now. In some ways it was as if she'd never lived there at all. "What's your rush?"

Thomas shrugged and pulled the baby closer, cradling him against his chest. "If I'd lived as long in your world as I've lived here, I'd be somewhere around a hundred and sixty years old. You'd be a hundred and seventy. Somewhere in there, I think wanting a family is pretty normal."

"Maybe." Quinn still wasn't sure.

"Do you regret marrying Will?"

William's hand tightened on her knee, and she looked up at him. "No. Of course I don't."

"It just doesn't stop you from imagining other possibilities, does it?" William asked quietly.

She shook her head. "It's just…nothing prepared me for this, you know? It's probably still the same school year in Bristlecone."

"Yes," William said, nodding. "It's been less than two months there since the last time we came through the gate."

"I will never wrap my head around that."

"Showing up there now with a husband and a baby would present more problems than just your age." Thomas chuckled.

"Uh, yeah, no kidding. Maybe it's best I *can't* actually go back right now." But even just saying those words set off the ache in her chest again. Although outwardly she was still smiling, William's hand moved from her knee to around her waist, pulling her closer to him, and she leaned against his side.

No, she didn't regret her decision to marry him even a little bit.

"Can we come in?" a voice called from the doorway.

"Of course," Quinn said, smiling at Charlotte and Stephen.

She pushed back the covers to stand up and go to them, but Charlotte held her hand up.

"You stay right there. It's our job to wait on you for a few days."

She sighed, but sank back against the pillows as William stood instead to go and hug his parents. "Will the waiting on me *stop* after a few days?"

Charlotte chuckled, and gave a wry shake of her head. "No."

"You're a queen now, Quinn," Thomas said. "At some point, you're just going to have to get used to it."

"No promises," she grumbled.

"If I can get used to it, so can you," Charlotte said, though her attention was almost fully on the baby now, as she lifted him from

Thomas' arms. Sitting down on the edge of the bed with him, she held him up so she could rest his soft little cheek against hers, and then she cradled him again, kissing him gently on the nose.

"I never thought anything would be as wonderful as snuggling my own babies," she said softly. "But, oh, grandbabies might be even better."

"Gee, thanks," Thomas said, though he was still watching the baby with such wonder that it was obvious he wasn't actually offended.

"Now that," Stephen said, coming to stand beside Quinn, "is a beautiful baby. From an equally beautiful couple."

"Thank you," Quinn said.

"He'll make a wonderful king someday."

Though she smiled, the thought made her breath catch in her throat a little. He was so *tiny* – she wasn't ready to imagine him as the heir to the throne.

"Hush, Stephen," Charlotte said, handing the baby back to Quinn. "You should know better than that by now." She nudged him gently with her elbow, rolling her eyes. "When Simon was born, I had to tell him that, outside of the Naming Ceremony, he wasn't allowed to mention anything about my baby running a kingdom until he was at least walking. He's been pretty good about holding back with Evelyn, but maybe he thinks you're different because you're the ruler."

With the baby safely back in her arms, it was easier for Quinn to smile about that.

Charlotte rested her hand on Quinn's shoulder. "Queen or not, you need time to just enjoy this little one without worrying about his future."

"Sorry sweetheart. I'll go back to my rightful place as doting grandfather," Stephen said, resting his hand on the baby's soft hair. "Thank you for making me one again."

Suddenly, there was a lot of commotion in the doorway. "Oh! He's so cute!" Emma exclaimed, running up to Quinn. "Can I hold him?"

"No, Emma," Stephen said gently, laying his hand on his daughter's shoulder. "You can look, but the baby needs to stay with Quinn for now, okay?"

"It's okay, Em," Quinn said softly. "Just come sit up here by me."

"You too, Alex." William lifted his little brother under the arms and up onto the mattress next to Emma. Both children gently touched the baby's feet and cooed at him.

"Do you want to see too, Alice?" William asked, picking her up and holding her in his arms.

She nodded, but made no move to get down onto the bed. Instead, she laid her head against William's shoulder while she stared at Samuel.

"He is cute," she said.

"I think so," William agreed.

"I love him."

"He's going to love you, too."

"When he gets bigger." Alice's voice was very matter-of-fact.

William smiled. "Yes. He's too tiny to notice very much right now. But he would love you if he understood who you were."

"Can I kiss his head?"

"Of course you can." Quinn shifted the infant up so Alice could reach better.

Alice didn't leave William's arms; he just held on and lowered her so she could lean over and plant a very soft kiss on the baby's hair. "I love you, baby," she whispered.

"Hey, quit pushing me. This is my spot!" Emma shrieked beside Quinn.

"Oops," Stephen said, lifting her down from the bed in one swift motion and then reaching for Alex. "I think it's time to head back to your lessons. Both of you."

Emma gave an indignant huff, but neither of them argued.

Stephen turned back to his new grandson, running his finger gently down the side of the baby's face. "I'll come back another time to enjoy a cuddle with this one who doesn't squabble yet. Congratulations, again."

Then he turned to William, pulling him into an enormous hug, before stepping back and looking at him, tears in the corners of his eyes. "I'm so proud of you, son. I always have been, in everything you've done – but this, William – seeing the kind of husband you are to Quinn, and what kind of father you already are to my grandson…this may be the proudest of you I have ever been."

Quinn saw tears in William's eyes, too, as he stood there with his father; the two of them were nearly the same height – she'd never noticed that before.

Stephen followed his younger children through the door at the same moment Linnea appeared there.

"I wondered when you were going to show up," Quinn teased.

"Sorry," Linnea said, smiling and walking toward the bed. "Nobody told me you were up for company yet – I just heard the stomping through the hallway," she glanced back at the departing twins.

"I think it's time for us to get out of here for a while," Charlotte said, reaching to take Alice from William. She then bent down and kissed Quinn on the head. "Let us know if you need anything. We love you – all three of you."

"We will, Mother," William said, following her back to the door. "We love you, too."

"So do I get to hold the little prince?" Linnea asked, climbing up to sit near Quinn's feet.

William helped transfer the baby from Quinn's arms to Linnea's.

"Yup. Pretty much perfect," Linnea said. "Wow, Quinn."

"I know. I'm still having a hard time believing we made him – that this was what was kicking around inside me. He felt so much bigger in there than he looks out here."

While Linnea was holding the baby, William handed Quinn one of the glasses of juice and set a small bowl of fruit in her lap.

"Where's Ben?" Quinn asked, dutifully taking a bite.

"Working. I think he and Marcus are making a perimeter run of the castle."

Quinn frowned. "He does know that I don't expect him to work every day of his honeymoon, doesn't he?I know I've told him that. This castle isn't even his job anymore."

"He knows. You know him, though – he can't go that long without feeling like he's contributing. Besides, I think he was afraid I was going to ask him to come in here with me."

"Why wouldn't you? He doesn't want to come and meet his nephew?"

"Of course he does," Linnea said, nuzzling her cheek next to the baby's. "It's just…he's still a guard. Even though you're family now, I think the idea of walking into his queen's bedchamber the morning after she's had a baby might be a little too much for him."

"I don't think about it that way," Quinn said.

William rubbed her back. "You may not, but Ben's pretty traditional. Which is kind of the polar opposite of you, Linnea. You two still surprise me with that."

She shrugged. "I don't understand it either, but he's great." The warm glow that lit Linnea's cheeks right then told Quinn that her sister-in-law's happiness was very real.

"Do I intimidate everyone now?" Quinn asked. She looked over at Thomas. "Is that why Mia isn't here, either?"

"Relax, Your Majesty," Thomas said, grinning and walking back over to her. "Yes, you intimidate some people. You're the *queen* of Philotheum. You're supposed to, you know. The guards and servants, yes, are a little more comfortable if they know how to respond to you. You'll get used to it."

"Maybe."She wasn't so sure.

"Anyway, you did just have a baby. Maybe you're all happy and awake about it right now – but give it a few hours, and you might appreciate the privacy a little more."

At that moment, the baby stirred, grunted, and then let out a wail that was shockingly loud. His whole face turned red as he batted at his mouth with his little curled-up fist.

"All right then." Linnea stretched him instantly back toward Quinn. William whisked the dishes from her hands so she could take him. "This one doesn't give much of a warning. I think he's hungry."

Quinn nodded, cradling the little bundle toward her chest. He calmed a little when she held him tightly, but he immediately turned his head, searching for food.

"See what I mean?" Thomas asked. "This, I think, is our cue to leave for a little while."

After William had closed the door behind Thomas and Linnea, he came to sit back down beside Quinn and the baby, who was now happily nursing.

"Since I'm the queen now, do you suppose I can just *order* people to treat me like I'm normal?"

He chuckled. "Warn me in advance before you try it, because I really want to watch."

She picked up a pillow and lobbed it toward his head. He ducked, catching it and grinning. Little Samuel let out another wail, announcing his displeasure at the sudden movement.

Laughing again, William handed the pillow back to her and helped her get him settled. "I have a feeling we're going to find out really quickly which one of us in this room is actually in charge."

"So, Nay…when am I going to get a niece or nephew from you?" Thomas teased, once he and Linnea were halfway down the hallway after leaving Quinn and William.

She turned and stuck her tongue out at him. "You could be a little more patient, you know. Ben and I have only been married for two weeks."

"Yeah, I'm pretty sure Quinn was pregnant by then. You're slacking." He opened a door to another section of the hallway and held it for her.

"*I* don't need to worry about producing an heir. I'm also not sure I'd mind getting moved and settled in Philotheum before I'm throwing up everywhere. I think Quinn would take that back if she could."

Thomas paused in front of another door and tilted his head. "I don't think she'd take anything about that baby back now — he's just about perfect."

"Not that you're biased."

"What? It's not my fault the Maker decided to give all of the best nephews in the kingdom to me. I would kind of like a niece now, though." He opened the door, which led into one of the circular stairwells.

She couldn't help smiling as she followed him down the steps. "Ben said he wants a little girl first."

"See? I knew what I was doing when I chose a brother-in-law."

"Yeah, that was all you, T. I had nothing to do with it at all."

He chuckled, opening the door at the bottom of the stairs. Linnea stepped out, right onto the corner of the main patio. There were still small patches of white in the shady spots, and everything was wet from the snow that had already melted, but the early afternoon was warm, and the sunshine felt good on her face.

"Well, whoever's responsible – it was a good choice."

"I think so."

"You two are awfully happy, aren't you?"

"I don't know about your sister, but *I* am." Ben's voice in Linnea's ear startled her, and she spun around to face him; he caught her under her arms and kissed her on the nose.

"Hey you," she said, putting her hand on his cheek. "How do you always manage to sneak up on me like that?"

"It's my job." He shrugged. "Besides, I took my armor off already."

"You're done working?"

"I told you it would be an hour or two. It's been an hour."

"You mean your father sent you away."

"No, Linnea. I mean that everything looks secure out here for now, and I wanted to get back to spending time with you." He pulled her tighter against his chest with one arm, and with his other hand he ran his fingers down the side of her face, gently tucking a strand of hair behind her ear. "Okay?"

She nodded. "I'll take you however I can get you, Ben. It's okay with me if you want to work, too."

"I know that, sweetheart. But what I want right now is to be with you. I haven't gotten to hear the answer to Thomas' question yet."

"What's that?"

"Whether you're happy."

She looked up into his eyes. "Yes, I am. Very happy."

"Good." He kissed her on the lips this time.

When she turned back to Thomas, he was grinning, but there was also a sort of faraway, speculative look in his eyes. Whatever it was had been weighing on his mind for a couple of days now, but she hadn't managed to get him to spill it yet. She had an idea of one thing that was bothering him, but there was more to this look than just that. "Let's walk down to the stables," she said. "All of us. I haven't seen Snow in a couple of days."

Ben had probably just been *at* the stables, had probably checked every corner of Snow's stall, and fed her a treat, but he just nodded and took Linnea's hand. Though he had removed most of his body armor, he still carried a dagger at his belt.

They were about halfway to the stables when Thomas cleared his throat. "So, Ben … what is going on that has you all worried but you're not telling Quinn?"

"Pardon?" Ben's expression didn't change, and his voice was steady, but the hand that was entwined with Linnea's grew slightly damp.

"All of the extra patrols, the meetings, the birds flying back and forth from Philotheum constantly…"

"Well, with two monarchs under one roof…"

"No. That explains some of it, but not all — and it definitely doesn't explain why it got so much more intense about a week ago. What's going on?"

Ben sighed and looked all around them. Linnea felt her own palms beginning to get sweaty.

"I don't know exactly, Thomas. We've heard some rumors, had some odd things… It's just making us nervous."

Linnea stopped cold in the middle of the path, taking a step back from him. "What kind of rumors and odd things?"

"Nothing definitive right now. We've been dealing with hostilities in some of the villages in Philotheum really since the coronation. You know there are those who were loyal to Hector and Tolliver."

"Right — that's nothing new."

"Well, there's just been a little more activity with that lately. It feels like something's changed."

"In the last week?"

He nodded.

"What else?" she asked. It was obvious that Ben was holding back more.

"There have just been a couple of messages from Philotheum… Last week, my father sent a message to Charles about some business that needs to be attended to at the castle. Charles, of course, has been sending messages here regularly — and none of his messages has acknowledged the one my father sent."

"So what, like he's ignoring the message?"

"Or like he didn't get it." Thomas said.

Ben looked at him. "That … I shouldn't even be talking to you about this, you know. This is treason."

"Quinn's not going to accuse you of treason, Ben. She would tell us."

"It doesn't matter what Her Majesty will or won't accuse me of, *Prince* Thomas – and it doesn't matter what you believe she would tell you. That's her prerogative. I've made an oath, and I will keep my word." His eyes flicked to Linnea. "Even when it comes to my wife and her brother. I'm sorry."

Linnea stepped close to him again and pulled his hand back into hers, squeezing it as pride filled her – this man, her husband, was a good man.

"No, Ben, I'm sorry," Thomas said. "I know I shouldn't be asking you that. It's just…you do *plan* on telling Quinn what's going on don't you?"

Ben almost cracked a grin. "So that you could run to her and ask her to give you the details?"

Thomas shrugged, chuckling.

"Yes, if we had the slightest inclination of real danger, or any better evidence of wrongdoing, then yes, of course we would tell Her Majesty. Right now, we don't believe there's enough to warrant interrupting her and King William in their personal time. I think the two of them deserve to have a few days to rest and get to know the new little prince, don't you?"His posture had relaxed again, and Linnea knew he was talking to Thomas as his brother-in-law again, not as the queen's guard.

Thomas smiled. "I'm still not used to Quinn and William having other people to protect them and look out for their interests. I'm glad they have you, Ben."

They'd reached the stables now, and Linnea could tell that Ben – who was always uncomfortable being praised for his work – was glad to have an excuse to walk away from them to go "check on something," and Thomas and Linnea headed for their horses, Storm and Snow.

"So, what is going on with you and Mia?" Linnea asked, once she was sure they were alone.

The grooming brush that Thomas had just picked up fell to the ground. "What do you mean?"

She narrowed her eyes. "Don't try that with me, Thomas. I may have been a little preoccupied with the wedding and honeymoon, but I haven't disappeared – or gone blind."

Thomas sighed, reaching down to retrieve the dropped brush, taking longer than necessary. "I don't know, Nay. Everything was going so well for so long. And then after Quinn got here – and especially after your wedding. She's just been different – distant. Always busy when I want to talk to her, working late hours, even when she doesn't need to be."

"I've noticed she's hardly ever around you."

"She's not. Not for the past couple of weeks, at all. The few times I have gotten her alone, she's been worried about Quinn, asking about the baby, always thinks of some reason she needs to go check on her or William – something she needs to do in their room or bring to them."

"Have you asked her?"

"I've tried. Like I said, I barely get even a few minutes alone with her, ever. And the one time I outright asked her if everything was okay, she just gave me the 'what are you talking about?' look."

"The one you just tried to give me?"

He chuckled, running his fingers along the bristles of the brush, pulling them back and releasing them in a rhythmic motion. "That would be the one," he sighed. "Except I let her get away with it – unlike *some* people."

She cleared her throat. "You'd have more answers right now if you *hadn't* let her."

"Maybe."

She walked over to him and took the brush from his hands

before he gave himself a rash from rubbing the bristles too harshly against his skin. "But what?"

"Maybe I didn't want to hear the answer."

She put her hand on his shoulder. "I don't think it could be as bad as that, Thomas. I think you should just talk to her."

"I will…when I actually get a chance to be alone with her."

PRINCESS ANNIE

Bristlecone, Colorado

BACK IN THE car, Zander's thoughts were a jumble.

The whole thing down at the river had been so strange … his conversation with the old man, the weird guy up on the slope, and hearing about Quinn… If he'd thought he was confused before, it was nothing compared to now.

Without really meaning to – at least not consciously – he drove down to Bray Street, toward the house where he knew Doctor Rose and William had lived. He wondered if the house had been sold already – probably it hadn't. New people didn't come to Bristlecone very often, and he'd have likely heard rumors of someone new.

Zander's father owned the real estate business that handled nearly all of the home sales in Bristlecone, but he hadn't asked his father if Doctor Rose had listed his house.

When they were younger, sometimes he and his friend Adam would sneak a peek at the list of lockbox codes and use them to go look around the inside of empty houses. Not that he planned on going inside Doctor Rose's place…

When he reached the house, though, he had to check twice to make sure he'd gotten the right address. There was no for sale sign in the yard, no newspapers in the driveway – he wouldn't have guessed nobody was living there.

He pulled his truck right in front of the house and stopped to investigate further. Closed wooden blinds covered the inside windows – nobody had removed those. There were even still chairs on the covered porch. Interesting. Maybe Doctor Rose wasn't going to sell the house. Maybe they were planning on coming back. It hadn't sounded that way when Megan told them about Quinn leaving – but then, he hadn't actually asked her about it, either.

That possibility cheered him a little, and he paused, losing the impulse that had almost made him get out of the car and look around more. He didn't really want to get caught here and have to explain himself to someone.

He started the truck again.

Zander's mother came out of the kitchen when he closed the front door behind him. "What are you doing here?"

He was confused for a second, and then he remembered – he should have still been at school. "Uh…I had this really bad headache. I just wanted to come home for a bit." As soon as the words were out of his mouth, he remembered his strange encounter with Alvin, and his warning – which seemed almost ominous now – about how he was going to find himself lying.

Sort of lying, anyway. The day's events really were beginning to give him a headache.

His mom frowned. "Those absences aren't going to be excused, you know."

"I know."

"Are you doing okay, Zander? With everything? I know it's been kind of hard for you lately…"

"I'm fine, Mom."

"I know she was the first girlfriend you were halfway serious about."

Nodding, he pulled his backpack off his shoulder and shrugged out of his jacket, then turned to hang the jacket on one of the hooks behind the door. "Yeah, she was. But breaking up is normal when you're in high school, right?"

His mom was silent for a long moment, though he felt her come up behind him. Finally, he turned back to face her again. "Is that what this is about, today?" she asked.

He sighed. "I don't know. Kind of."

Closing her eyes for a second, she nodded. "Okay. Do you want me to call it in for you?"

"I don't think it matters much, Mom. There's a month left of school."

"Still, I don't want you to make a habit of this. You're better than that, Zander."

"I know."

"All right. Then I'll be glad you're here. I was hoping to run to the grocery store before I had to pick up Ashley and Owen at school, but the little girls are still asleep. You can stay here with them for me."

"They're going to wake up the second you go."

"Probably."

"Can I go back to the headache story?"

She raised an eyebrow. "There's medicine in the cabinet. Be nice and I won't ask you to chop the vegetables for the salad while you're at it."

"Fine."

"Thanks honey."

"You're welcome." He carried his backpack over to the couch and plopped down.

She was halfway to the chair where she'd left her purse when she turned back, coming to sit on the coffee table in front of him. Zander sighed.

"Look, Zan … I know this is hard for you. It's been kind of hard on all of us, Quinn breaking up with you and leaving like this. Megan and I always sort of secretly hoped… Anyway, whatever any of us hoped, it's still going to be okay."

"I know, Mom. I still have my whole life ahead of me and I'm going away to college anyway, and all of that. I'll be fine. I just … I wish she'd said good-bye, you know? Why did she have to leave so fast without telling anyone?"

His mother shrugged her shoulders. "I don't really know. From what I understand, Quinn was pretty upset when she found out her mom had been lying to her about Nathaniel – I don't know if I can blame her."

Zander fidgeted with the zipper of his backpack. He didn't blame Quinn for that either – he'd seen how tense things had been between her and her mother before spring break, and he'd been there the night her boss had told her that her father and Doctor Rose had been friends. Of course, even that had turned out to be a lie. Megan had been hiding the truth from everyone.

"Even so, Mom – would you just let me take off and go to Europe with someone? If I had just found out they were my family? Don't you think that's a little strange?"

She sighed. "I'm not keeping any secrets from you about your family, so it's not exactly the same. I think Megan has a lot of guilt about that too. I got the feeling it wasn't just Nathaniel. Megan isn't sharing too many details right now, but I think Quinn has a whole set of grandparents and cousins and everything else she didn't know about, either."

"Wow."

"Yeah, and in any case, secrets or no …in a few months, I'm going to have to let you go off to wherever it is you want to go – without an uncle to take care of you. You've been accepted at a college in Massachusetts. I'm sure you could go to one in Europe if you wanted to."

"I could just stay here, though. I've been accepted at Mesa, too."

"You could. And of course, there's a part – a *big part* – of me that would love if you went there. To have you close, and keep you close forever. I love you, you know?"

"I love you, too, Mom."

"But you're not going to go to Mesa, are you?"

An uneasy lump formed in his stomach "I was thinking about it – for a while…"

"But it wasn't because you wanted to stay close to Mom and Dad, was it?"

He shook his head.

"That's okay, Zander. That's normal. Dad and I tried to raise you to grow up and be independent and have a life of your own. I'm not going to say I would have thought it was a great idea to pick a college because of a *girl*, but … you're growing up. And it turns out you didn't need my lecture on the girl thing."

"No."

"I'm sorry about that. There will be other girls, though, and lots of other adventures. I know it's been really hard on Megan to let Quinn go – but I think she also knows in the end she wants her daughter to be happy and fulfilled more than she wants her to be in her house where she can see her every day. I think going with Nathaniel was Quinn's decision, and Megan felt she had to let her make it. Honestly, I hope I can be as strong about it as Megan when the time comes with you – very soon."

Zander was silent for several moments, thinking about it. His mom reached out and took his hand. He squeezed it and looked back up at her. "I just don't understand why she didn't even tell me – why she didn't even say good-bye."

"That's called a broken heart. It wouldn't have been any easier on you – or Quinn – if she had. Maybe she just couldn't face you. If you were the one who had to choose to leave, and you had to break up with *her*, would you have been able to call?"

"I don't know."

"I think this opportunity came up for Nathaniel really quickly, and he just had to take it. And then with Megan and Jeff getting ready to move anyway…"

His head snapped up. "What? Megan and Jeff are *moving?* To where?"

"To Atlanta. Zander, you know this. You were there when Megan told us – the same night she told us about Quinn leaving."

If he hadn't already been sitting down, he would have needed to. How could he not have heard that? "Have I really been that out of it for the last month, Mom? I really don't remember."

She sighed, reaching over and tousling his hair. "You haven't been yourself lately, no. But I didn't realize you didn't even know that. I'm sorry. We've *been* talking about it – I thought you were there for some of the conversations, but maybe you weren't. We're watching Annie and Owen this weekend while Megan and Jeff fly to Atlanta to look at houses. You really didn't know?"

He shook his head.

"Oh, Zander…"

He shook his head, appalled with himself. "No, I know. That's just crazy. I guess I need to snap out of it. I'll work on it, okay, Mom?"

"Okay." She wasn't convinced.

"You'd better go, or you're not going to have time before you have to pick up the kids."

"All right. We'll talk more later, okay?"

Talking with his mother any more about this was the last thing he wanted to do, but he nodded. She stood and kissed the top of his head.

Once his mother was out the door, he had to stand and walk around the living room a few times. He was an idiot – he really must not have been listening at all that night. Was he really such a lovesick *kid* he could miss that much of the conversation? It all made a lot more sense now. Why wouldn't Quinn leave to go with her family, if she was going to have to move to Atlanta anyway?

No wonder nobody at school was as worried about it as he was. This was just him not knowing how to deal with his first broken heart. *Maybe I should spend the weekend watching chick flicks and eating chocolate*, he thought, beginning to chuckle at himself.

Finally calming down, he sat back on the couch and opened his backpack. At least he could get some of his homework done.

At almost the exact second he set his binder on the coffee table, he heard one of the back bedroom doors opening, and then small footsteps coming down the long hallway.

Of course.

"Hey, Annie," he said, when the little girl appeared at the entrance to the living room.

"Zander!" She ran across the room; he barely had time to brace himself before she threw herself into his lap. "You're home!"

"Yep." He ruffled her brown curls. "Did you have a nice nap?"

"I didn't sleep. I wasn't tired."

He chuckled, rubbing the sleep from the corner of one of her brown eyes with his thumb. "All right. What did you do, then?"

"Played with my horse." She reached into her pocket, struggling to extract something from it; when she finally succeeded, she set it in Zander's hand. He held it up – it was a beautifully carved little wooden horse, very detailed.

"That's a nice horse, Annie. Where did you get it?"

"William made it for me."

Oh. William Rose was still the one piece of this he really didn't understand at all. "Your cousin William?"

Annie frowned. "No, he's not my cousin. William is my brother now."

"What do you…" he stopped himself. Annie was four. If he thought all of this was confusing for *him*, he couldn't imagine what it must be like for this little girl who was missing her sister.

"Did you know I'm a princess now?"

He smiled. "I didn't know that. How exciting. What kind of princess are you?"

"Look!" She leapt off his lap and ran across the room to retrieve her little backpack, all purple and white stars. She unzipped the front pocket as she carried it over to him. Reaching inside, she pulled out a delicate silver chain with a round pendant hanging from it; half of it was silver, and the other half was gold.

"Annie, is that something you're supposed to have in your backpack? That looks real." It looked very real – heavy and expensive.

"I can have it if I want it. It's mine! See?" She held it up, setting the pendant in his hand. "It has my name on it."

He held the pendant between his fingers, using the light from the window to study it. There was some kind of design on it – a circular design he'd never seen before.

"The other side, silly," Annie told him.

"You're silly." He flipped it over. There was an inscription on the back: *Love you forever Princess Annie.*

"See? I'm a princess."

"I guess you are. Did your Daddy bring that back from Afghanistan?"

"No. Quinn got it for me in 'Renthos. That's where she lives now. In a castle. And William gave it to me, too."

"A castle, huh?" Annie had always had a great imagination. Or maybe they'd been reading Owen's books about Europe and medieval times, or – who knew – maybe there really was a castle wherever Quinn was living now, and she'd told Annie about it. "Have you been talking to Quinn on the phone?"

"No. They don't have phones in 'Renthos. We have to wait until we can go visit. Mommy said maybe this summer when we can go for a long time, and then I can wear my princess dress again."

They didn't have phones? Maybe they weren't jet-setting around Europe. Maybe Doctor Rose was doing one of those service things in a third world country.

He was relieved when, a second later, his little sister Sophia poked her head out of the hallway.

"Sophie!" Annie shouted. "Do you want to play dogs?"

She jumped off his lap and ran off, the two little girls instantly crazy, pretending to growl at each other and roll all over the carpet.

After everything that had happened today, he was more confused than ever, but also mortified about what kind of impression he'd been leaving on everyone. If he'd missed the fact that Megan and Jeff were getting ready to move – what else had he been missing?

He stared at the pendant in his hand. If Quinn had given this to Annie, it meant she hadn't just run off without any thought. She'd taken the time to say good-byes to her family, to give them gifts. And they were planning on visiting her.

Nothing was wrong here. He just needed to get over this and move on.

PROBLEMS

Rosewood Castle, Eirentheos

THE UNEXPECTED KNOCK on the door of the clinic nearly made Nathaniel drop one of the jars he'd been carefully arranging in a cabinet. He turned in time to see the door opening and Stephen standing there.

"Can I come in?"

"You're always welcome here. It's not even my clinic anymore."

"You built it, Nathaniel. It will always be yours."

"Thank you." He smiled, walking over to greet his friend. "Is everything all right?"

"I can't come and talk to you if nothing's wrong?"

Nathaniel rolled his eyes, and Stephen chuckled, though there was concern hiding in the shadows of his smile.

"You don't come dig me out of the clinic when you don't need something."

"Am I that bad?"

"You're a king with thirteen children, Stephen. And three grandchildren now, too. I'm content when we're able to share a meal."

"One of those is at least as much your grandson as he is mine. You raised William more than I did."

"I could never thank you enough for sharing him with me. I don't think I can take as much credit as you give me. Watching him as a father now … I admire the example you were for him."

"You just like that baby."

"Yes I do." Nathaniel chuckled. "Can't believe he's four days old already."

Stephen smiled. "Time goes fast. You'll see. Both with that baby, and now that you're going to be a father yourself."

"I think I could find a world where time goes by ten times as slowly as *this* one, and that would still be true of children, wouldn't it?"

"Indeed," Stephen said, raising an eyebrow. "Just don't suggest such a thing to Thomas. He's having a hard enough time waiting to be of age right now, I think."

"It's a difficult place for him to be – with both William and Linnea married. It's a lot of changes for him. And he's courting a girl who's of age. It's hard. The brother I was closest to was much older than I was. If we'd have stayed at the castle, been subjected to all of the rules and traditions I *should* have been, I daresay I'd have struggled at Thomas' age as well."

"You had a whole different set of challenges because you *weren't* inside those traditions, though."

"I did. There's not an easy answer to that – but I'm sure you and Charlotte will sort it out. Your children know how loved they are. I only hope I can be half the father to Cammie's children…"

"You will be."

"Thank you…now, are you ever going to stop avoiding telling me the real reason you came to find me? Because, as much as I love talking with you about these things…I know that's not why you're here. What's wrong?"

Stephen sighed. "We've just had a bird from Eli in Cloud Valley."

Nathaniel's heart jumped into his throat. "It's not…"

"No. Cammie and the children are fine."

"I was planning on traveling to Cloud Valley the day after tomorrow."

"I know. But I think you're going to have to change your plans. Eli said that earlier this morning, a man came into the clinic after a raccoon came into his house – right into his kitchen – and attacked him."

"Oh no."

"I know." Stephen reached into his pocket and pulled out the silver tube containing the message, and handed it to him. "It's the third incident in that area in the last two moons."

Nathaniel nodded, unrolling the message and reading it. "Well, luckily they did trap it. Eli hasn't finished testing it, but he's pretty certain…"

"Yes. I'm going to send some soldiers along with you. It's time, I think."

"I think you're right – much as I hate to agree with that." As he talked, he walked over to the small refrigerator in the back room of the clinic. It had been a major achievement to get it through the gate a few cycles ago. After that, they'd brought another one for Jacob's clinic in Mistle Village, which, luckily, had not been destroyed by the fire. None of the other clinics had reliable refrigeration.

As he opened the refrigerator and looked through the vials in the back, his heart sank. "We're running really low on both the vaccine and the immune globulin. Only enough for maybe two more cases – counting this one."

"Can you make more?"

Nathaniel closed the door and turned back to him. "I hope so. At least of the vaccine. We're out of luck on the immune globulin. William and Jacob and I have been working on the vaccine for a long time. Jacob keeps the cultures going at his clinic now that William and I aren't here. Our version is not as safe – we've been grateful to never have to rely on it. But now that we don't have access to the gate… we're going to have to start manufacturing it, I guess. It takes a while to make, though."

"I don't know as much about it as you do, Nathaniel. All I know is this is starting to worry me. We haven't had this many incidents in more than five cycles."

"It worries me too, Stephen. Let's try not to panic, though. We have enough for now, and I will speak to Jacob about going ahead and I need to get this out to Cloud Valley as quickly as I can. The sooner we start treatment, the better. When will you be able to send soldiers?"

"By the end of the day, hopefully. Luke is in the process of finding some men who are willing to do what needs to be done."

Nathaniel closed his eyes and nodded solemnly. "All right. I need to go and talk to William before I go. I'll stop in Mistle Village myself on the way and speak to Jacob about the medicine."

"Thank you."

"Hey, Thomas, Daniel and I were going to go out and work with the colts some more today while it's nice. Do you want to come?" Josh asked

He did; he'd been enjoying the training of the young horses, but there were other things on his mind right now. "Maybe later?"

"Sure." Josh shrugged and then ran down the hall – he was always so laid-back about everything, which Thomas appreciated. Most of his other siblings weren't quite so easy to brush off.

Once Josh was gone, he turned his attention back to the stairs he'd just seen Mia climb, carrying a basket full of laundry.

It took him a minute to find her upstairs, even though she'd only just gone up. She was always so quick with everything. He finally spotted her in Sarah's room, standing next to the couch where she was sorting and folding the tiny socks and shirts.

"Hey," he said.

"Hi." She didn't look up, intent on her task.

He took a deep breath, trying to loosen the little hard lump that had settled in at the bottom of his ribcage. Annoyance wasn't an emotion he dealt with very often, but today… He'd been trying to talk to Mia for weeks now – and failing miserably.

"Laundry isn't really your job anymore, is it?" Now that Mia was not only helping with his younger brothers and sisters, but with Simon's infant son Ryan as well, most of her housekeeping duties had been given to others. "I thought Nicoletta was responsible for this stuff now."

"She doesn't put anything where I can find it. And the way she folds shirts, they don't even fit into the drawer right."

Sure. Time to talk to him, she didn't have, but when it came to the state of a toddler's shirt drawer, she suddenly had all the time in the world. He squeezed one of his hands inside the other. Deep breaths weren't cutting it.

And then there was the undertone in her voice – she was annoyed at him, too. He didn't know why. For asking about the laundry? Either way, this obviously wasn't a good time to talk to her about their relationship.

"All right. I'll let you get back to it, then. Maybe we could go for a walk after dinner?"

"It'll be kind of col…" She paused, checking herself, finally glancing up at him. The distance in her green eyes physically hurt. He wanted to get out of here almost as much as he wanted to cross the room and rub his thumbs over the soft sprinkling of freckles on her cheeks. "Sure," she said instead. "We can take a walk if I'm not busy with anything."

But, of course, she would be. If none of the children needed her, their socks surely would.

"I'll see you later then."

ABIGAIL

Bristlecone, Colorado

ZANDER PULLED THE KEYS out of the ignition and tucked them into his jacket pocket, but he didn't climb out right away. For most of this week, he'd been thinking of excuses why he couldn't go to this party.

The last time there had been a party at Jake Price's house, he'd taken Quinn. It had sort of been their first date.

He hadn't been sure he could face coming here again without her. Jake's house just reminded him of too many things. And this week it would be especially hard – everyone here would be gearing up for prom next weekend, and he hadn't asked anyone.

All of his moping around, though, was making him a little angry with himself.

He knew it was time to stop thinking about her. He had a month left of high school, and he couldn't spend it dwelling on a girl who had dumped him and gone away.

He was going to go to this party – this was going to be the beginning of his enjoying the last little bit of carefree time he had with his friends. At least, that was the pep talk he'd been giving himself.

All of those intentions flew out the window, though, when the first person he saw when he got inside Jake's house was Abigail.

He had managed to successfully avoid her for the last couple of days at school, having decided there was no reason he needed to continue sitting at the lunch table he'd shared with her and Quinn.

But now, here she was, right near the front door when he walked in. She spotted him immediately, and headed right for him. There was nowhere else for him to go.

"What do you want, Abigail?" he asked.

"I'm not even allowed to talk to you anymore?"

He shrugged. "What is there to talk about? You already told me how you feel and what your opinion of me is."

To his surprise, her face fell a little. "Can I talk to you privately for a moment? I'll make it quick."

Sighing, he held up his hand and took a step back through the door, leading her outside onto the front walk.

"What is it, Abigail?"

She raised an eyebrow. "You really don't like me, do you?"

"Why do you care if I do or I don't?"

Her eyes widened, just a little, giving him silent satisfaction. "Look, I wanted to apologize for how I acted the other day, at lunch."

"Did you say something you didn't mean?"

She looked down at the ground and fidgeted with the shoulder strap on her bag. "I shouldn't have attacked you the way I did. I didn't need to be that harsh."

"Abigail, I'm really not trying to be a jerk here, but ... what difference does it make?"

"She was my friend too, you know."

"Really?" Irritation bubbled up inside him — and it wasn't just because of the incident the other day in the cafeteria. "Because, I'm going to be honest here, I don't see that. I haven't seen it for a long time. The whole time Quinn and I were together, you treated her like some kind of pet dog that should be wagging its tail over seeing you whenever you got bored of whatever party you were at or whatever boy you were chasing after."

Her cheeks were cherry red now. "It's not like Quinn wasn't invited to the same parties. And, if you'll remember, *she* had a boyfriend, too."

"You know what I mean."

She stared down at the sidewalk for a long moment, her shoulders rising and falling as if she were taking several deep breaths. Finally, she looked back up at him. "She hurt me, too, Zander. I know you're right. I know I wasn't the kind of friend to her she usually was to me. Maybe I just always expected she would be there when things changed again – when I needed her."

"What about when she needed you?"

Tears appeared in the corners of her eyes, and his stomach flipped. Maybe he had taken it too far. He took a step closer to her, but she backed away. He could see her biting her lip, trying to get herself back together. After a minute or two, she managed it.

"Do you think it's my fault?" she asked, once she was calm.

"That she left?"

"Yeah. Do you think I was such a horrible friend to her that she just couldn't stand to be here anymore?"

Wow. "No, Abigail I don't. I actually don't think it had anything to do with you. I think she had her own stuff going on and, for whatever reason, she just needed to go with Doctor Rose."

"Then why wouldn't she tell me, Zander? Why won't she call me or answer my e-mails?"

"*That* part might be your fault."

She chuckled, though he was pretty sure she didn't find it any funnier than he did. "Would you be able to take off like that – just go away like none of this meant anything to you?"

He shrugged. "Isn't that what I'm going to do in August? Or June, if I take a summer program somewhere."

"You'll tell people where you're going."

"Blake Gunderson was at every party we went to last year. Where did he go to college?"

She paused for a second, but then smiled triumphantly. "CSU."

"Have you seen him since he left?"

"No. I heard he only came home for a few days at Christmas, and then he went back to Fort Collins and stayed with friends or something."

"And what about Carina Nguyen? Where did she go to college?"

She rolled her eyes. "You've made your point Zander. I won't expect you to be sitting in your dorm room in a few months crying over me, okay? And I guess, after the way things were going between me and Quinn for the last year … I should have realized at some point she would get her own life. I just didn't know it would happen like this."

"Yeah, well, it did."

"Yeah. I also kind of expected you to be the one person who was really on my side with this, after she cheated on you."

"She didn't, Abigail. He's her cousin."

"I don't know, Zander. Something about that is … not … *right*."

He held up his hand. "I don't want to talk about that part anymore, okay?"

She nodded. They both stood there in silence for a minute.

"Do you think she's okay?" Abigail's voice was smaller now. The defensiveness had disappeared.

He looked at her. "I hope so."

"Me, too."

IN THE ROSE GARDEN

"IS THE WEATHER always this strange here?" Quinn asked, shifting the baby up over her shoulder and turning to face the sun.

William opened his eyes. He, too, had been basking in the warmth as they watched his younger siblings play on the swings and in the wilting gardens.

"Strange how?"

"Strange as in … it was snowing last week."

He shrugged and held his hands out to her. "If he's finished eating, it's my turn."

"Excellent. I think he needs to be changed soon."

"I can handle it," he said, pointing to the small cloth bag he'd brought outside with them and scooping the baby into his arms.

"You never get enough, do you?"

"No." He adjusted the white blanket over his own shoulder and brought little Samuel's forehead to his lips, kissing his soft, downy hair before propping him on his shoulder and patting his back, working to get the burp he knew was still in there.

He looked at Quinn. She was smiling at them, looking so beautiful it took his breath away. Leaning over, he pressed his lips against her temple. "I could never get enough of this…of both of you."

Still smiling, she turned to him, her lips finding his, kissing him a little longer than she usually did when they weren't alone.

"So…what were you asking me about the weather?" he asked, trying to collect himself after she finally pulled away.

She chuckled. "I was just asking if it's normal for it to be this warm again after it's already been snowing."

Sometimes, he almost forgot she hadn't grown up here – hadn't always lived in Eirentheos with him and that so many experiences would still be new to her."Yes, it's normal. The weather here is a little milder usually than it is in your world – well, in the Colorado mountains, anyway. I'm sure there are other places there that are more like here. It'll do this all winter. You'll get used to it."

"I wasn't complaining."

He smiled. "I like it, too. And so do the kids."

She looked around at the wide area where they were all playing, then frowned. "They are going to destroy those."

He followed her gaze.

Emma and Alice had wandered away from the playground area, and they were climbing into the huge bed of rose bushes that lined the back wall of the garden. In the summer, the area was a huge cascade of blooming flowers that seemed to pour off the stone walls and stretch forever, separating this area from the kitchen gardens.

During the growing seasons, it would have been impossible for the children to even get in there. Now, though, it was slightly more sparse – mostly a tangled mass of sticks and stems; the last of the blooms had finally wilted and been trimmed off the remaining canes by the gardeners only a few weeks ago.

The two children were climbing carefully, but every few seconds, another twig would snap. As he watched, Emma stepped right into the middle of one of the bushes; the leg of her pants caught on the thorns for a second before she pulled it free.

"Yes, they are. Where are Ben and Linnea?"

She nodded toward the swings as he stood and handed the baby back to her. Ben had just picked up Sarah, who was crying, and Linnea was bent down talking to Alex.

"I have no idea what those two think is appealing about playing in those thorny roses, but my mother won't be happy if they kill all of her bushes. I'll be right back."

"I knew you'd get out of it somehow," she teased, chuckling as she reached for the diaper bag.

He raised an eyebrow at her. "Right. Because I haven't changed the last hundred diapers. Do you even know how to do it?"

"Um…" She giggled as she glanced into the bag. "I'm sure I can figure it out."

"I love you," he said, kissing her on the head.

"I love you, too. Now go, before there are no roses next cycle."

He'd only been kidding, of course. Quinn had changed her share of Samuel's diapers, but he considered it only fair that if she had to do all of the feedings, then he could do as many of the changings as possible.

He yelled for the girls before he ever reached the flowerbed, but they were so wrapped up in whatever they were doing that neither one of them even turned at his voice. Sighing, he looked for the clearest route through the thick brambles and climbed in.

Less than ten feet into the flowerbeds, he noticed the girls had stopped moving and both of them were kneeling down. A second later, he saw what was holding their attention so fully.

"Emma! No!" he shouted.

Whether she'd finally heard him, or she was just frightened by the sudden movement of the animal that crouched in the bushes didn't matter. Emma stood up and leapt back in such haste she bumped into Alice, knocking her sideways into the bushes – and right into the path of the startled fox.

In the next instant, Alice was screaming, and William was running toward her, his worry about the plants forgotten.

"Get out of here, Emma, *now*!" he yelled as he reached them.

Before he could grab Alice and yank her out of the way, the fox sprang, closing its jaw around the little girl's forearm.

He reacted without thinking, elbowing the fox's muzzle twice, until it let go of Alice and then shoving her to the side. Immediately, the animal's teeth sank into his arm.

William twisted his whole body in an attempt to get away from the fox, but it wouldn't let go. The girls were both screaming and crying now.

Suddenly, he felt a huge *thud*, and then the fox whined, its teeth finally loosening from his arm.

He scrambled away as quickly as he could, trying to pull himself to his feet at the same time, putting himself between Alice and the fox.

The high-pitched whine that was still coming from the fox made no sense to him until he finally turned around.

Ben was there, brambles and thorns stuck to his pants, beet-faced and breathing hard, kneeling over the fox, which was, William could now see, dying. Ben's dagger was through its side, pinning it to the ground.

He scooped up Alice, pressing her face to his chestas Ben placed his boot over the fox's neck, withdrew his dagger, and then stabbed it again, this time through its heart. The animal fell silent.

"We need to keep it – to get it back to the clinic." Although he didn't really. He knew, from the wild look that had been in the animal's eyes, from the white froth that even now was escaping its mouth, what the test results would show.

Ben nodded. "It's not going anywhere now. Let's get the girls there first." As he spoke he was already walking to where Emma was huddled on the ground. She'd stopped screaming, but tears still streamed down her face.

William could see small cuts on her hands from where she'd fallen in the roses, but he didn't think she'd been bitten.

Ben picked her up, and both of them hurried to carry the girls out of the flowerbeds.

Alice's wound was beginning to bleed everywhere. He pressed his hand against it as tightly as he could. She whimpered, but didn't start crying again.

Quinn and Linnea were standing at the edge of the flowerbeds looking shocked.

"What can I do?" Quinn called as he approached her. Her face was white as she took in his appearance. He was covered in Alice's blood already, and he was sure his own wounds were bleeding, too.

"You can get Samuel and the rest of the kids upstairs. Now, please. They don't need to see any more of this."

"Are you okay?"

He nodded, though he was sure she saw right through him. "Linnea," he said, "please find Mother and Father and have them meet me down at the clinic."

NO CHOICE

Bristlecone, Colorado

ZANDER WAS SURPRISED to see lights still on inside his house when he pulled up to the curb. Normally, his parents would be in bed before he made it home from a party.

He checked the clock. No, it wasn't late enough for them to start worrying. Still, he was wary as he approached the house.

"Is that you, Zander?" his dad called from the kitchen at the sound of the door closing.

He didn't sound angry. "Yeah, it's me."

His dad appeared in the doorway separating the kitchen from the living room, a dishtowel slung over his shoulder. He didn't look upset, either. Zander relaxed. "What are you still doing up?"

"Oh, it was kind of a crazy night here with the extra kids. I told your mom I'd finish cleaning up so we can get out of here at a reasonable time tomorrow."

"I forgot you guys were leaving."

"Yeah, Ashley's performance is tomorrow night. We thought we'd get an early start and maybe take all the kids to the zoo first. Are you sure you don't want to come?"

"Am I sure I don't want to be packed into a hotel room tomorrow night with you and mom and four little kids?"

His dad chuckled. "It's a suite."

Zander raised an eyebrow.

"I know. I don't think I would have wanted to at your age, either. What are you going to do here for the rest of the weekend?"

"I don't know. Maybe hang out with Adam; maybe go through the college catalogs again."

"Still haven't made a decision?"

"No – and I know I'm running out of time." This wasn't entirely true. He knew where he wanted to go – he just wasn't ready to have that conversation with his father.

"Another letter came for you today – it's on the mantel."

"Really?" He was pretty sure he'd heard back from all of the colleges he'd sent applications to.

When he saw the logo on the envelope, he was confused. He hadn't sent his application to DU. As he tore it open, he tried hard to convince himself it was something else, just junk mail, or … but it wasn't. His heart sank when he unfolded the acceptance letter inside.

"So?" His father's voice was gleeful; Zander was surprised he wasn't jumping up and down.

"Didn't you already open it and look? Why wouldn't you take that upon yourself, too?"

"Zander, it's a good school. They have a great business program. Four years from now, you could be ready to become a partner at the office."

"And what if that's not what *I* want to do?" He'd never outright challenged him on this point before, wanting to avoid the battle. When his father had brought out the application for DU, Zander had filled it out dutifully, essays and all. But he'd never mailed it. One afternoon, when he dropped Quinn off for work at the library, he'd stopped in to use their shredder.

But Jack Cunningham was meticulous about everything. He'd made copies of every application before they sealed them up. Most likely, he'd realized that Zander never sent the original when the check for the application fee wasn't cashed.

"Zander, I remember what it was like to be your age, I do. This wasn't what I originally wanted to do, either. I had the same argument with my father. But then, I went to college, I met your mother, and I realized this was going to be a good job – that I would be able to provide for her, to raise a family with her."

"I don't plan on getting someone pregnant in college, Dad."

"Regardless," his father answered, his voice only slightly darker, "you're going to want to marry someone someday. And you're going to want to have a career that can provide for you – and them. I have a business ready to hand over to you."

Zander stared at him, silently contemplating, not wanting to turn this into a fight. He knew his father loved him and that his intentions were good – but Zander wanted no part of running a real estate office in Bristlecone, Colorado. And he didn't want to go to the school his father had gone to. Wasn't he supposed to have some choice in the matter?

"Look, I know DU doesn't have a football team…"

"Is that what you think this is about, Dad? *Football?*"

"Well, I know it's been important to you."

"What else is supposed to be important in *Bristlecone?* Seriously, Dad. It was you who made me go out for football in the first place."

"Made you? I thought it was important to you. You're so good at it."

He wasn't going to be able to stay calm a whole lot longer. "Dad. It's fine. Football was fine for high school. I had fun, and I made some good friends. I might have been okay for Bristlecone

High, but I already knew I wasn't going to be playing football in college. It's not about football, *okay*?"

"Then I don't understand. What is it about?"

"I don't know, Dad. Maybe it's about making my own choices, about living the life *I* want to have, instead of one somebody else picked for me."

"The world doesn't really work that way, Zander. At some point, everyone has to grow up and do the responsible thing."

"Why does it have to be *your* 'responsible thing'?"

"What else are you going to do?"

"Do I have to decide right this second? I've been thinking about computer science…or maybe even pre-med."

His father rolled his eyes. "Those are jobs for really smart people."

The words stung so badly Zander actually flinched. He took several steps backward.

"Oh, don't take it like that, Zander. I just meant the kind of people who go into those are the ones with straight 'As' – the ones who study all weekend and don't have lives. You have a life."

He bit his tongue until he tasted blood, willing himself not to do something he'd be embarrassed about later. It was true he didn't have a straight 4.0, but he'd never made less than a B in anything. And his grades in science and math *were* perfect. Maybe his father had never even noticed that. Or maybe he just didn't care, because it got in the way of his vision of what *he* wanted for Zander. "I don't want to talk about this anymore," he finally muttered through his teeth.

"Well, you can't put off talking about it forever. The deposits are due soon. And, honestly, son, I don't have any intention of throwing my money away. If you're determined to mess around and waste your time chasing after something that doesn't have a future for you, then you're going to have to find a way to pay for it yourself."

Zander stared at him, stunned into silence; his mind had suddenly gone completely blank, and he couldn't focus on anything, except the strange ringing in his ears.

"Someday, when you own a nice real estate business, and you're standing in the kitchen of a nice house with your own son, you'll thank me for this, Zander. Now, I have to get to bed. I have a busy day planned with my family tomorrow, which will be paid for with money from the business I run. Good night."

His father paused on his way out to pat him on the back, but Zander still couldn't respond.

WILLIAM

Rosewood Castle, Eirentheos

THE SOUND OF the sitting-room door closing startled Quinn; she hadn't realized she'd dozed off. At the motion, the baby, who had just finally fallen asleep on her chest, stirred and immediately began fussing again. She didn't know if it was because of her own heightened emotions or what, but Samuel had been a mess ever since she'd brought him inside after the fox attack.

For the moment, though, she ignored the fussing and carried him with her to the other room. The motion quieted him down a bit.

"Will! Are you all right?"

He nodded, though he wasn't the least bit believable. The dark blue of his shirt hid most of the blood spatters, but it was ripped in a couple of places. Most notable was the big white bandage that was wound around his right arm, just below the elbow. Almost white, anyway, a small dot of red had seeped through in the middle of it.

"You're still bleeding."

"It's fine," he said, shaking his head. "We can't close the wound all the way right now. The fox probably had rabies."

Cold, stark horror washed over her. "What? Are you sure?"

"Almost positive. Nathaniel is going to test it."

"Did he give you the shots?"

"No…why is he crying like that?"

Samuel's fussiness had now exploded into full-on screams, his little face turning red; Quinn was rocking and bouncing him, but it wasn't helping, and she couldn't concentrate on anything except what William was saying. "What do you mean *no?* Why not? People die without those, Will!"

"Seriously, Quinn. The baby. Feed him or change him or *something*. Look, I'm a mess, and this has been … I'm going to go and have a bath. Take care of him, please."

He walked away from her, through the bedroom door and then, a second later, she heard the bathroom door close. She stared after him in shock, the baby's cries piercing her ears. He'd just blown her off. Avoided her question entirely. She was afraid she was going to be sick.

And still, the baby cried. His diaper was dry and fastened perfectly. He'd finished eating only a little while ago, but still she sat down on the couch to see if he was hungry again – but that only made him angrier. It was the dance they'd been doing all day.

Finally, she wrapped him snugly in his blanket, scooped him up, and carried him out of the room. Miraculously, by the time they'd gone a few feet down the hall, he quieted. She stopped and looked at him. Immediately, his bottom lip quivered again, and she started walking, quickly. If that was what it was going to take… well, she thought she could probably do with some exercise herself.

Besides, if William wasn't going to give her any answers, she was going to find some for herself.

Bouncing the baby the whole way, she headed toward the family's wing.

She was almost to the common room when she ran into Thomas coming from the other direction. "Hey, Quinn, are you okay? Where's Will?"

"I'm fine, I guess. Will is taking a bath. Where's everyone else?"

Thomas frowned and opened his mouth to answer her when the baby suddenly let out a high-pitched wail. "Whoa," he said instead, "is it really that bad little man?"

Quinn swayed him back and forth, attempting to mimic the motion of walking, but it didn't help. "He's been like this all day. It's why I've been hiding in our room."

"May I?" Thomas asked, holding out his hands.

She passed the baby over willingly.

Thomas unwrapped Samuel and then laid him facedown over his arm, cradling the baby's chin with his hand and patting him gently on the back while he rocked from side to side.

For almost a full minute, she thought it was going to work. The crying quieted to a whimper and the baby's tight fists relaxed a little. Then, Samuel hiccupped, which made him mad all over again and the screaming resumed. Quinn almost felt like joining him. She closed her eyes, needing half a second to compose herself.

"Let me try." Mia's voice came out of nowhere. Quinn opened her eyes, startled. She hadn't heard her approaching – not that she'd have been able to hear footsteps over Samuel's cries, she supposed.

Thomas handed her the baby. She grabbed the blanket from Thomas' shoulder and wrapped Samuel loosely in it. Then she held him, just cradled normally in her arms, gently swaying back and forth. Less than a minute later, he was quiet. Quinn and Thomas both watched in stunned silence as, another minute after that, Samuel's eyelids started growing heavy, his little blinks lasting longer each time.

"Can I have him for a while?" Mia asked.

Quinn tensed, waiting for Samuel to get upset again at the sound of Mia's voice, but he didn't seem bothered in the least. He was almost all the way asleep now.

"I'll bring him back if he gets hungry or if I can't calm him," she said a bit nervously; probably misunderstanding Quinn's hesitation in answering. "It just seems like you could maybe use a little break, milady."

Quinn nodded. "Thank you." She was going to say more, but at the sound of *her* voice, Samuel's eyes fluttered open again, and his tiny lips twitched. She took a step back.

Mia smiled in understanding, and then turned and headed down the hall. At that exact moment, Quinn wasn't even interested in knowing where she was going.

"How did she *do* that?" she asked Thomas, once Mia and Samuel were both safely out of earshot.

"Magic. It's the only explanation. She's going to take him, and he's going to sleep for hours. She'll be able to lay him down in a cradle somewhere and everything. When she brings him back, he'll be happy, and he'll stay that way for the rest of the night. I've seen it a thousand times."

Quinn raised an eyebrow.

"Seriously. How do you think she became my mother's baby nurse at sixteen?"

"I thought it was because her mother had the job first."

"She did. She still does, but Mia was allowed to work part-time as her mother's assistant from the time she was thirteen, and then full-time with the babies and helping the rest of us when she was sixteen. Her mother is magic like that, too. My parents would have probably stopped having children after Alex and Emma if they didn't have those two."

"If they'd have made it past you and Linnea."

"Yeah, that too."

"I'm starting to wonder if I should quit while I'm ahead with this one," Quinn said, chuckling, "or at least while I'm only this far behind."

Thomas rubbed her back. "Two weeks old is hard. He's probably stressed because he can tell you're scared, too. You'll be missing him long before he finishes his nap with her."

She nodded, remembering why she'd come looking for someone else to begin with. "Where is everyone?"

"Um…my father brought Emma back up a little while ago, and I think he's still with her. She's really upset; she thinks it's all her fault, plus she got a few really bad scratches from those thorns. My mother is still down in the clinic with Nathaniel and Alice. Will and Nathaniel ended up putting her out before they treated her bite and her scratches. They didn't want to traumatize her."

"Will said they think the fox had rabies?"

Thomas nodded. "There's almost no chance it didn't. It's so stupid…we haven't had that – we've always called it water disease here – anywhere near the castle for many cycles. The younger children have never even been warned about it. But there have been a few reported incidents lately."

For the first time, she realized how upset Thomas looked; how pale he was, how he wouldn't directly meet her gaze.

It occurred to her, then, that she might have slipped and forgotten about the differences between this world and the one she'd been born in. Her stomach twisted into horrible knots and her voice shook as she asked her next question. "Do you…*not*…have the treatment for it here?" The last part came out in a rush.

He still wasn't making eye contact with her. His avoidance was starting to make her a little nauseous. "Didn't William tell you?"

She shook her head. "The baby was screaming, and … I don't know. It almost felt like he was ignoring me, blowing me off."

Thomas sighed and nodded. "Sounds like Will. The answer to your question is yes and no. Nathaniel has brought the medicine back from your world for … I don't know, as long as he's been traveling there, I guess. They know *how* to make a kind of the medicine here, but it's difficult, and apparently something went wrong with the last batch of the medicine they tried to make. And, apparently they *can't* make the other kind they also use in your world. Jacob's working on it, but in the meantime, we were down to having only one of the medicines in the clinic – in the kingdom, really – and only enough of that kind for one person."

Quinn's arms went limp at her sides, and she felt cold, as if a sudden blast of frozen air had filled the hallway. "And he's giving it to Alice."

"Yes."

It was the same choice Quinn would have made, if she was in the same position, but she knew enough about rabies exposure to know what it meant. The cure, if given in time, was one hundred percent effective, but if not…

"You said Jacob was working on making more?"

"Yes. Nathaniel is going to ride out to him later, once Alice is awake. There's still a chance that at least some of the medicine will be ready in time."

"Okay." She didn't know what else to say.

"I'm sorry, Quinn. I don't think I was supposed to tell you about this."

A million sarcastic responses ran through her head, but she couldn't hold on to any of them. There wasn't an appropriate answer here, and the inappropriate ones were only going to make this harder. Worse, acknowledging this much at all was going to make it feel real. And she wasn't ready for that. So she just nodded. "It's okay, Thomas, I would rather know."

"I know you would."

"Ben and Emma are okay, though?"

"Yes. Scratched up, both of them – Emma's the worst. And if we had enough medicine – if we could get more – Nathaniel would want to treat them both, just in case, but chances are slim they were exposed to anything."

Something wasn't quite right with his voice when he told her that, though, and she frowned. "The truth, please, Thomas."

"Okay. Ben has one scratch that Nathaniel is worried might have come from the fox or gotten exposed to its saliva or something.

Ben doesn't want to tell Linnea though, because it could still be nothing."

Quinn closed her eyes and took a long, deep breath before looking at him again. "A few years ago, my family went camping – well, we stayed in this cabin in the mountains with some friends for a week. It was Zander's family, actually. And my friend Abigail and her brother came up for the weekend, too. Anyway, one night, Abigail and I were asleep in one of the bedrooms, and this *thunk* noise woke me up. I sat up, and immediately I knew there was something in the room. I was freaked out, and I woke Abigail up. We both heard another *thunk*, and we turned on the light. There was a *bat* flying around in the room."

"A what?"

"A bat."

"Is that some kind of bird in your world?" Thomas looked confused.

"No. It's a tiny mammal that can fly. Like a mouse with wings."

"Creepy."

Quinn chuckled in spite of herself. "They're very creepy, especially when you wake up with one in your bedroom in the middle of the night. Abigail and I both screamed our heads off. My dad came running. As soon as he opened the door, the bat flew out, and then it flew around the rest of the cabin. All of these adults were running after it, yelling, trying to catch it or get it to go outside, or something."

Thomas was laughing now. "That must have been hilarious."

"Not at the time. The next day it probably would have been."

"Except what? ... *Oh*, did it bite someone?"

Quinn shook her head. "Not that we know of. My dad was trying to get it to fly out the door, but Zander's dad stopped him, said we needed to catch it, just in case. Abigail's brother finally smacked it with a tennis racket and killed it."

"Well that was good."

"Nope. That turned out to be really bad. Bats have small brains, and Louis had smashed it to pieces. They couldn't test it to see if it had rabies or not."

"But it didn't bite anyone."

"That's what we thought. But Zander's dad was insistent that we call the doctor anyway – Nathaniel, you know."

"Right."

"Yeah, well, Nathaniel flipped his lid. Insisted that they bring me and Abigail to him *right then*. Apparently, bats have really tiny, sharp teeth, and they can bite you without you even feeling it, especially if you're asleep."

"Okay, that's even creepier."

"Yeah. I'm not fond of them. Louis teased us the whole time we were getting ready to go and see Nathaniel, about how we were going to have to get twenty shots with big needles in our stomachs."

Thomas bit his lip, clearly trying not to laugh again.

"Be nice. We believed him. Apparently, it used to be true, when they first invented rabies shots. By the time we got to Nathaniel's office, I was so scared my dad practically had to drag me inside. *Fine, laugh.*"

"I'm sorry. What happened?"

"We did have to get shots. Not twenty, and not in our stomachs, just three."

"So not so terrible?"

"The first two *hurt*, and you know me – at least back then – I'm pretty sure there were tears involved. But Nathaniel promised I'd never have to have those ones again, even if I found another bat in my bedroom. The last one wasn't quite as bad, but we had to come back four more times after that to have more of those."

"Did you ever get back at Abigail's brother?"

"We didn't have to." She chuckled. "Nathaniel was so paranoid about rabies that he said everyone who was in the house had to get the shots. Louis was older and bigger than us, so he had to get more of the ones that hurt than we did."

"He deserved it."

"Yeah." Quinn's lightheartedness over it had disappeared again, though.

"So what you're telling me with your little story is that we can't wash this up for you?"

"No. For once, we're dealing with a situation that I actually know something about." After Nathaniel's extreme reaction to the bat, she'd done her research on rabies. At the time, it had probably been to try and convince her parents that she didn't need the rest of the shots. But what she'd read had changed even her mind. The shots always worked, but without them, rabies was fatal. Always.

She tried to shake that thought out of her mind, but failed. "I know that if we were in my world, he'd be giving those shots to Emma and Ben. Maybe the rest of us, too. Who knows?"

"Don't tell this to Emma, but I'm pretty sure that if Jacob and Nathaniel manage to get more made, that's exactly what will happen." He brushed her hair back from her shoulder. "There's still a chance we'll have some medicine in time. And there's also a chance that Nathaniel treated the wound quickly enough, and got it clean enough that he wouldn't get sick, anyway. He practically did surgery on William's arm down there. It's so clean you could probably eat off of it."

"I don't really need that mental image, Thomas."

"I'm trying here, okay?"

"I know. Thank you. I feel really bad now that I wasn't down there in the clinic with him."

"Hey, Quinn, you were upstairs taking care of his son. You can't do everything. I think he was glad you didn't have to be there when they realized, you know…"

"Yeah." She swallowed. "I should go and see if he's out of the bath now."

Thomas' brow furrowed. "It's William, Quinn. You might want to give him a few minutes. When's the last time you ate?"

She shrugged. "It was before we went outside."

"*Tsk. Tsk.* You can't be doing that anymore. You have to take care of my nephew's mother, you know. Let's go and get some food into you, and then you can come back and deal with Will."

"I'm a queen. You can't boss me around."

"Try that one on someone else, *Your Majesty*," he said, beginning to pull her down the hallway toward the common room. "I don't care what kingdom you're the ruler of; you're still my little sister."

"I'm not your *little* sister. I'm older than you."

"*That* is a technicality. I have thousands of days on you."

"I was born first."

"I see it how I see it."

OWEN'S DREAM

Bristlecone, Colorado

AFTER THE CONVERSATION with his father, Zander knew there was no chance he would be sleeping that night. He wasn't sure he'd ever been angrier or more confused. Had his father been serious? Was this the deal now? It was either major in business and do exactly what his father wanted him to do or…was there even an *or*?

It was because he was still awake at two in the morning, stewing in his room, that he was the first one to hear Owen cry out. He quickly closed the browser windowwhere he'd been looking at military recruitment websites – any way to escape sounded good right now – and dashed across the hall to the guest room where Annie and Owen were sleeping.

"Hey, Owen," he called softly, flicking on a low lamp, and crossing the room to kneel by the bed.

Both children were still asleep, although Owen was thrashing and whimpering, sending the covers everywhere. Zander didn't know how Annie was sleeping through it.

"Owen," he called again, laying his hand on the little boy's back and rubbing gently. "Hey, wake up, buddy. I think you're having a bad dream."

For a second he thought it had worked; Owen's kicking feet grew still, and he turned over, facing him now.

"Have to go," he said. "She needs help."

"No, it's okay, Owen, you were just dreaming."

Owen didn't respond, and that was when Zander realized his eyes were still closed.

He stayed there, perfectly still, watching him. His little body relaxed, and his breathing became deep and even. Maybe the nightmare, or whatever it had been, was over.

Just as he reached for the blanket, to cover both children back up for the night, Owen's eyes opened, and he sat up so quickly that it startled Zander and he jumped back.

Owen looked around for a moment, his eyes wide, like he didn't recognize anything, and he couldn't figure out where he was. Finally, though, his eyes settled on Zander. "I need to go home," he said, "now."

"Owen, honey, it's the middle of the night," Zander's mother called from the doorway. "Nobody is at your house."

The look of panic on Owen's face was gut-wrenching. His whole little body began shaking, and all of the color drained from his face.

Maggie rushed over to him and sat down on the edge of the bed. "It's only for a couple of days, Owen, your mom and dad will be back on Monday. We're going to go stay in a hotel tomorrow night. Won't that be fun?"

Zander was sure Owen couldn't hear her. He was still staring at Zander, his little fists winding over and over again in his pajama shirt. "I need to go home. I need to go home right now."

He looked at his mom. "Maybe I could take him over to his house? He might sleep better if he was in his own bed."

Owen's hands stopped twisting.

"We're leaving in like six hours, Zander."

The hands started going again, and now Owen's body began rocking back and forth. *How was Annie sleeping through this?*

Zander looked at Owen. "Do you want to go to the hotel tomorrow, Owen? And go swimming with Annie and Ashley and Sophia?"

"No." Owen shook his head emphatically. "I need to go home. I don't want to go to Colorado Springs. I need to go home right now."

"Sweetheart, your parents aren't there."

"Zander said he would take me. I need to go home."

His mom looked at him helplessly. Owen had never spent the night here before. Maybe this was why.

"I could watch him, Mom. Tonight, and tomorrow, too. It's not like I have anything else going on."

Owen grew very still now and looked at both of them. "Please, Zander?"

"Can I talk to Zander for a minute, Owen?"

Owen nodded, though his hands were twisting again. "Can I read or something?"

"You don't want to rest?"

"I'm not going to fall asleep, Maggie. I need to go home."

"Okay, we'll be back in a minute, bud," Zander said.

"Are you sure about this, Zander?" his mom asked as they slipped back down the hall toward the kitchen. "It's kind of a big responsibility. I don't even know if it's a good idea."

"I've watched the kids lots of times before, Mom. I've even watched Ashley overnight."

"This is someone else's child, Zander. And it would be for tomorrow night, too. What if he gets upset again?"

"I'll be at his house, like he wants. I can always call Megan and Jeff and ask for help."

"Maybe we should just call them now."

Zander glanced at the clock on the stove. "It's two thirty in the morning. That's what? Four thirty in Atlanta? Do we really need to wake them up for this?"

"They would want to know."

"They want to know he's okay. If I take him home and he's fine, I'll call them first thing in the morning. If I take him home and he's still upset, then I'll call tonight."

"What are you going to do if he's still upset?"

"What would you do?"

"I don't know."

"Why don't his grandparents have him this weekend?"

"They're on vacation."

"Well, then there's really no choice, is there? Megan and Jeff can't just come home from Atlanta in the middle of the night. We know he's going to be upset here. He'll probably be fine if I take him to his house. Anyway, he's a great kid. I can hang out with him until Sunday. We'll be fine."

"We might not be home until late Sunday evening."

Zander shrugged. "Stay until Monday if you want. There's no school that day. I really don't mind."

"Well, Megan and Jeff will be back Sunday night."

"Whatever, Mom. Seriously. Just let me take him."

"All right." She started to nod, but then she frowned. "Why are you still dressed at two thirty in the morning?"

"I just…hadn't gone to bed yet."

"What time did you get home?" she asked suspiciously.

"Don't worry, it was before curfew. You can ask Dad." He couldn't keep the sarcasm out of his voice.

"Uh-oh. Zander, what's wrong?"

He told her everything his father had said earlier.

"Oh, Zander, I'm so sorry. He and I have been arguing about that. I thought I'd talked him into changing his mind, but I guess not."

"Is he serious?"

"I think he thinks he's doing what's best for you, Zander."

"Isn't there something you can do?"

She opened the dishwasher and started stacking the clean plastic cups from the top rack. Zander's chest tightened.

"Isn't it your money, too, Mom?"

She paused, the stack of cups balanced in her hand like a miniature rainbow. "What are you going to major in instead?"

His gaze fell to the floor now. "I don't know for sure," he mumbled.

"Then I don't know what else I can do, Zander. It's really hard to argue that we should just pay for you to go and major in 'not business' at some college you haven't even picked yet."

"You told me the other day that you *want* me to go off to college and be an adult and live my own life."

"And part of *being* an adult is making those decisions. Especially if you're asking someone else to pay for them."

He didn't have an answer for that. He stared at her in silence, trying to wrap his brain around what she was saying, knowing that she was only trying to soften the blow – she agreed with his dad.

It was different than the conversation with his dad had been a couple of hours ago. Although the end result was the same, she wasn't threatening him or trying to force him to make the decision she wanted him to – her expression as she looked at him was full of empathy. He couldn't be angry with her.

A sudden noise from the doorway made both of them turn.

"I'm sorry," Owen said. "I just really need to go home. Can Zander please take me home now?"

"Yeah, buddy. I'm going to take you home in just a few minutes. Can you just go and start getting your things together?"

With a look of overwhelming relief in his eyes, the little boy nodded and disappeared back down the hall.

"Look, Zan," his mom said, "we'll talk more about this. If it was entirely up to me, I would probably let you have a year or two of college to figure out what you want and decide what you're going to do. But I can't keep fighting your father on something when I don't know what I'm fighting for."

He nodded. "I know, Mom. Thanks for trying. I guess it's my fault for not knowing what I want to do with myself, really. I just … learning about business and taking over Dad's office someday – that's not it for me. But I don't know what the right thing is, either."

She stretched up on her toes, and he grinned, leaning down so she could kiss him on the forehead. "Maybe you haven't been able to make a decision because the right thing hasn't presented itself to you yet."

"You think a college major is just going to drop out of the sky?"

"Maybe," she chuckled. "Or maybe it's something you don't know anything about yet."

He raised an eyebrow at her.

"I know. I sound crazy. I just think there's something more for you out there, Zander. I thought maybe you'd find it at college, but I could be wrong about that."

"But you don't think it's doing exactly what Dad did?"

"I love your father, Zander. He's a good man, and he loves all of us, and I'm grateful for his business, for the work that he does, and the way he's always been able to support our family with it. But no, it's not what I imagine for you."

"She's right." Owen's voice startled both of them again. Zander hadn't heard him approaching at all. "You're not supposed to grow up and sell buildings."

"Oh?" Zander held out his hands, forgetting for a moment that Owen didn't usually allow much contact. He remembered before he actually grabbed the little boy, but Owen surprised him and stepped forward, allowing Zander to scoop him up and set him on the counter so that the two of them were at eyelevel. "What am I supposed to do when I grow up, then?"

Owen looked into his eyes with such seriousness that a little shiver zipped down his spine. "I don't know yet, but I think it's important."

He didn't know how he was going to manage something "important" with either no college, or some mountain of debt from student loans, but he wasn't going to say that to Owen. He just smiled. "Well, Owen, all I know is that it's almost three in the morning, and it's *really* important right now to get you home and to bed. I'm going to go and warm up the truck for you."

His mother followed him outside, carrying Owen's backpack. Zander opened the door of the truck, tossed Owen's big pillow and blanket inside, and turned the key, flipping the heater on.

"You're not too upset to drive, are you?" she asked.

"No. Two hours ago, I probably was, but I'm not now."

"It will all work out somehow."

"It's hard to see it that way right now."

"You will, though. I know I don't say this enough, Zander, but I'm proud of you. I always have been, of course, but watching you now...you're becoming a really great young man. Taking Owen tonight – caring for him instead of having a weekend to yourself – not many eighteen-year-old boys would do that. When you do decide what you want to do with your life, I think it will be the right decision the first time."

"Thanks, Mom."

"I love you, Zander. More than anything."

"I love you, too."

"Be safe, okay?"

He nodded and leaned in to her hug, wrapping his arms tightly around her. He didn't know why, but something about this felt...off. Maybe it was just because she was worried about his reaction, but it was like something had changed, and he didn't know what. It was ridiculous, but he couldn't chase away the thought that he wouldn't be hugging her like this again for a long time. He almost couldn't let go.

"I'll go get Owen," she finally whispered against his ear, before kissing him on the cheek, and then turning and heading back into the house.

"You're sure you're okay with this, Owen?" Zander asked when they pulled into the driveway of the Robbins' house. "Nobody is here."

"You're here."

Zander grinned, reaching for Owen's backpack. "That's true. I'm here."

"Thank you for bringing me home," Owen said, as Zander helped him down from the cab. "I know you probably didn't want to baby-sit tonight."

"You're not a baby, bud. You're my friend. All I'm doing is hanging out with my friend."

The shy smile that slid up the corners of Owen's mouth then was enough to make the whole thing worth it to Zander.

"So, what was going on at my house?" he asked as he punched in the numbers for the garage code. "Did you have a nightmare or something?"

Owen was silent as the door went up, and he still didn't say anything as the two of them walked through the garage and then into the kitchen.

Zander was starting to wonder if he'd upset him by asking the question when Owen climbed up onto one of the stools at the island and rested his chin on his hands, looking at Zander with an intense expression in his brown eyes. "It wasn't a nightmare, exactly."

"No? Just a dream that bothered you?"

"I don't know yet. I can't remember enough of it right now. All I can remember is him telling me I needed to be at home, that I should be home."

"Who told you that, Owen?" He was starting to get a little freaked out now.

"Alvin."

Zander's legs suddenly felt like jelly. "Who is Alvin, Owen?" Surely, the little boy had to be talking about someone else – not the strange man he'd met down at the river the other day.

The look Owen gave him then made Zander's stomach flip like it was on a roller coaster. He didn't answer the question, either. After several seconds of studying Zander, he said, "Do you ever think there are things that are just supposed to happen?"

Now Zander paused. "Like things you can't control?"

"Mmm…sort of. But more like there's a certain way things are supposed to be, and that when they're *not* that way, things keep happening to try to get them to be that way."

Zander swallowed, thinking of the conversation with his father earlier. Was it possible that he was going to grow up and take over the business anyway, no matter what he thought he wanted? "Don't we have a choice, Owen?"

"That's not what I mean. You always have a choice. Some people always do the wrong thing, no matter how many chances they have to do something right."

"What if you don't know what the right choice is?"

Owen looked thoughtful. "Nobody *always* knows what the right choice is. Everyone makes a choice sometimes that messes everything up. I guess what I'm talking about right now isn't about right choices or wrong ones. I mean more like … do you think there's something bigger than just what we think we want?"

Zander looked at the clock. Three fifteen. This was so not the time to be dealing with a conversation like this. With an eight year old who was thinking heavier thoughts than Zander ever usually did. "Can I say I don't know right now, Owen? It's really time that you should be in bed."

"Okay."

Getting Owen tucked back into bed was easy. Zander left the door propped open and hung out in the hallway for a little while, listening for any sign of trouble, but within a few minutes the breathing from the little boy's room was slow and steady. He headed back toward the stairs to go get his own stuff.

It was then Zander realized that staying in this house for the weekend might be harder on him than on Owen.

He'd been so preoccupied with taking care of Owen when they arrived, that he hadn't realized it was the first time he'd been at the Robbins' house since the last time he'd come to pick up Quinn – when they were still together.

Now, he was staring at the closed door to her room. Maybe Owen would have called it one of the choices that messes everything up, but he couldn't help himself.

In the next instant, the door was open, and he flipped the switch on the wall, bringing to life the reading lamp on the little table next to her bed.

He looked around the room, the whole time feeling like he'd been kicked in the gut.

Everything was the same. If they'd started packing for their move, they hadn't yet touched Quinn's room. It looked like she'd only just been here. Her desk might have been a bit neater than usual, and the lid was closed neatly over the white wicker hamper, instead of sitting on top of her chest of drawers while the clothes overflowed the basket, the way he remembered it often being, but otherwise…

He half expected her to follow him into the room, to sling her backpack over the back of the wooden desk chair, to flop onto the bed, still neatly made exactly the way she always did it herself. It was all so familiar, he somehow automatically drifted to the cozy reading chair – her prized spot, but where she'd always let him sit, so they could remain a respectable distance from each other in case her mother peeked in through the required crack in the door.

The emotions that overcame him sitting in here surprised him. After all, she hadn't died – she was just living somewhere else right now. But his emotional response was so overwhelming that he'd been sitting there for probably way too long before he realized exactly how strange it was.

Shouldn't she have taken *some* of her stuff with her? The green blanket that was folded on the end of the bed – he knew that was her favorite; she'd slept with it every night since they were little kids. He wasn't sure she was capable of watching a movie on the couch without it. And yet – there it was.

The picture of her and her real father was still on her nightstand, too, and he knew how much that one meant to her. And was that…? *It was.* Her cell phone was there, sitting next to the picture, in the same spot she always left it.

He wasn't even being cautious now. Crossing the room, he picked up the phone, flipping it open and pressing the power button. Nothing. He pulled open the nightstand drawer, where he knew she kept her charger. It was there, too, and he took it out and plugged in her phone. A few seconds later, the battery symbol appeared on the screen, letting him know it was charging. The power button worked now, but it would take a few minutes for it to come all the way on.

He closed the nightstand drawer – there were still journals and papers in there, but looking through those just didn't feel right.

Of course, the next thing he did felt a little intrusive, too –walking to her closet and pulling open the folding doors – but at this point, he had to see. It was still full of clothes. Long sleeves, short sleeves – they were all here. If anything was missing, it wasn't obvious.

He was beginning to feel a little sick to his stomach.

Just as he was closing the closet doors again, her phone started going crazy. It lit up like a Christmas tree and buzzed every second or two for the better part of a minute.

Knowing he was definitely crossing a line, he picked it up and scrolled through the options. There were several dozen new text messages – he could see that most of them were from Abigail, and there were a few from him, too. He knew what those said already.

He was more interested in her sent messages, so he went quickly to those. Once he did, he was even more confused. The very last message she'd sent was sometime in March, to her mother.

I picked up Annie from Maggie's.
Going to spend some time with her, and then I'll bring her home.
I need to talk to you.

He looked at the date using the calendar over Quinn's desk, which was still turnedto March. She'd sent that message on the last day of school before spring break. There was nothing after that.

He remembered that day clearly. It was the day after she'd broken up with him, on the phone.

Scrolling to the outgoing calls, he found it immediately. The twenty-three minute phone call that had broken his heart was nearly the last one she'd made. The only one after that was labeled "Will and Nathaniel – Home". It took him a minute to realize the names must refer to Doctor Rose and William Rose – he'd never heard *anyone*, let alone Quinn, refer to either of them by anything informal. That call had only been three minutes long, made on the first Sunday of spring break – the day he'd seen her having brunch with Megan in the café.

Chained to the wall by the power cord, he sat down on her bed and started looking through all of the calls now. There were several more outgoing calls to the Roses' number, including a few calls mixed in with incoming ones from Zander's own number, labeled as "missed". There weren't any text messages to or from either of them, though.

In fact, the only other text message that was interesting at all was one to Quinn's mom on that same Wednesday she'd broken up with him. It was short, informing Megan that Quinn planned to go to the hospital with William that night to see his brother. She'd sent it during school.

Even in the few sparse words she used in that message, though, he could feel the anger and distance between Quinn and her mom. He knew they'd been fighting then, but he didn't understand all of it.

Megan's response to that message was an equally short,

Fine. We won't plan on staying up for you. Make sure you have your key.

So that's what Quinn had come home to the night she'd called to break up with him.

He didn't understand any of this. It was almost like Quinn had stopped existing after the day he'd last seen her. She didn't have her phone; she didn't have her clothes or her things…

For days, he'd been convincing himself to let this go. But now… There was something just too strange about it. It wasn't right.

He stopped short of listening to her voicemail messages. That was too personal, or at least that's what he told himself. Of course, he also didn't have the password, and he knew that it would be obvious that the messages had been listened to. Anyway, he was almost certain he wouldn't hear anything – it was probably all messages from him and Abigail, maybe some other people from school wondering where she'd gone.

Leaning back against her pillows, he opened the phone's photo album, but he regretted that almost immediately. So many of the pictures were of him and Quinn, laughing and goofy together, clearly happy, and – he'd thought – in love. Maybe that had been a stupid thought to have at eighteen.

There was Quinn standing on the bottom step in her Valentine dress, as Zander put on her corsage, there were pictures at school, pictures of them tubing at the ski resort… At some point, someone – probably Abigail – had even been sneaky and snapped a picture of the two of them kissing at a table at Bruno's Pizza.

There were lots of pictures of her family too, pictures of Annie dressed up in the skirt Quinn had bought her for her birthday, Owen holding up a collection of interesting rocks… His only consolation was that there were no pictures of "Will" or his brother.

Even the pictures seemed strange, though. Zander's phone, too, had once been filled with shots like these ones, but after Quinn had broken up with him, he'd pulled out the memory card and tucked it in a shoebox on a shelf in his closet. He didn't want to *delete* those pictures, but he didn't want them staring at him every time he opened his phone either.

On Quinn's phone, the pictures, like everything else, stopped right at the beginning of spring break. There were quite a few pictures of Annie – far more than Quinn would normally take of a single event – dated the same day she'd sent that text to her mother. It appeared she'd taken Annie out for hot chocolate and then shopping.

And then, there was nothing.

He couldn't slow his pounding heart, or calm the churning in his stomach. If he didn't know better, he would think … there was no way that something really *bad* had happened to Quinn – was there?

THORNS

Rosewood Castle, Eirentheos

THE BABY HAD just finished nursing and was drifting off to sleep in Quinn's arms when William finally returned to their room.

Quinn glanced at the clock over the mantel, and she looked back at him in time to see that was where he'd been looking, too.

"I didn't think you'd still be up," he half-whispered.

She put a finger over her lips and stood up with Samuel. He stirred, but his little eyes didn't open. She carried him into the bedroom and held her breath as she laid him in the little borrowed cradle next to their bed.

For all of her worry, though, he nestled right into the blankets and stayed asleep. Thomas had been right – after three full hours with Mia this afternoon, Samuel's mood had turned around completely. He'd been happy and content for the whole evening, eating well, and napping better than usual. Quinn wouldn't be surprised if he gave her a few hours of peace now.

"Where have you been?" she asked William, once the bedroom door was safely closed. "Did you go out to Mistle Village?"

He nodded. "So you know, then."

She walked over to him, and reached to put her arms around his waist, needing to be next to him, to feel him against her, safe — at least for tonight.

But to her utter shock, he took a step back from her, actually holding his hand out to keep her away from him. The crushing rejection was instant, like the wind had been knocked out of her, and she blinked up at him in hurt confusion.

"I'm sorry," he said. "It's just...the fox for sure had rabies, Quinn. If I have it, I don't want to risk infecting you, or anyone else."

She narrowed her eyes. "By hugging me?"

His hand stayed up. "It's just too dangerous."

"It doesn't happen that fast, William."

"We don't know that."

"Don't be ridiculous. Anyway, you can't get me sick. I've had rabies shots."

"What? When?"

"A few years ago." She told him the same story she'd told Thomas earlier, but when she was finished, he still wouldn't let her get any closer to him.

"The shots don't last that long, Quinn. They're only guaranteed for about two years. After that, they're not always effective unless you have booster doses. We'd have to test you to see if you're even protected at all right now."

"Oh."

"Yeah. That's one of the reasons we don't just give them to everybody — aside from the fact that even in your world they're pretty complicated and expensive to produce. You have no idea how long it took Nathaniel to be able to build up a supply line, or how lucky we are that gold is a lot more valuable in your world than it is in ours."

"*This* is my world too, William. Don't do this. Don't pull away from me now."

"I'm not trying to pull away from you; I just really can't take any chances with you – and especially not with the baby."

She could tell by his expression that he wasn't going to relent on this. It was suddenly hard to breathe. Swallowing hard, she took a step back from him and leaned against the arm of an overstuffed chair. "So what's going on with the vaccine in Mistle Village?"

"I don't know for sure. It's incubating, but I don't know if it will work or not when it's finished. We've never really known exactly what we're doing with it. Studying it in your world only gets us so far, because we can't make it the way it's made in your world. We don't have the technology, or the cell lines to grow the virus on. We don't even have all of the same animals. We have to use other methods. Sometimes what we try seems to work, other times, we mess it up. We won't really know if it's safe or if it will work until we give it to somebody, which we've never done before – at least not to people."

"So you'll be the first?"

He nodded. "The batch we have going in Mistle Village should be ready in a little over a week, hopefully, if nothing goes wrong."

"Is a week soon enough?"

"There's no way to know how long it takes. We have until I start showing symptoms. That could be in about ten days, or it could be a couple moons. This bite," he held up his arm, "is a pretty severe exposure, so I'd say we're probably looking at the lower end of the scale. And, of course, the longer we wait, even if I don't have symptoms yet, the more time the virus has to replicate and spread. The other problem is that even once I have the vaccine, it doesn't protect right away, and we don't have any of the immune globulin at all. We don't even have a way to make it right now."

"But there's still time."

"There might still be time. *If* the vaccine we're making works, and *if* it's effective in time without having the immune globulin. This is bad news, Quinn. I'm not trying to scare you, but, tonight, as I was riding, I decided – you need to know."

"Oh, well, *gee*, William. Thanks so much for *deciding* to include me in your little life-and-death situation here."

"That's not what I meant."

"Yes, it is what you meant. You just didn't mean for me to *catch* that bit."

"I'm trying not to scare you."

"Well, you are scaring me, Will. You're scaring the hell out of me, actually." She pressed her hands together tightly, trying to keep them from shaking, but it didn't work.

His eyes widened a bit, probably at her language, but he only nodded. "I know."

"Is Alice even safe, without the immune-stuff?"

"We hope so. We treated her quickly. As long as the vaccine can work faster than the virus, she'll be okay."

"But possibly *not*?"

"Possibly not. What else do you want me to say? I'm also still worried that Emma could have been exposed, and I'm even more worried about Ben."

She nodded, staring at the floor, and blinking back the moisture that was filling her eyes as quickly as she could force it back. "You've been bitten by an animal before. Why weren't we worried about this then?"

"River boles never carry rabies — or at least we've never found an infected one. I don't know why. Rabies is a lot rarer here than it is in your world — and I don't know why that is, either. Maybe it's the different animals.

"In any case, that bole bite you saw wasn't what we consider a concern. And thank the Maker for that, because if it had been, we would have used up the doses of vaccine we're giving to Alice. It's not like we've been back to your — to Bristlecone — to restock since then."

"If it's so rare, then how does a rabid fox manage to get into the *castle*?"

"I don't know. Does it really matter how?"

"It kind of seems like it does."

"Well, right now it doesn't. The fox did get in, and it *was* rabid, and Alice and I both got bitten by it. That's where we are."

The tears would no longer stay behind her eyelids. She wiped surreptitiously at them with her fingers, trying to hide them from him as she stared down at the floor. As horrible as all of this was, it was still his rejection of her that was cutting her to the quick.

After a long moment, he cleared his throat. "How's Samuel? He seemed really upset earlier. I've never seen him like that before."

She shrugged, trying to make sure her voice would be steady before she answered. "He's fine now. He's asleep."

Will was quiet for another minute before he finally said, "Okay."

"Stay with him for a few minutes. I'm going to get some tea." She couldn't even bring herself to look at him as she walked around him to the door. "I'll be back before you have to do anything crazy like *touch* the baby," she said under her breath as she pulled the door shut behind her.

Once she was out of the room, she realized she didn't even want to get a cup of tea, because that might mean facing someone else in the common room or down in the kitchens. She didn't want to discuss this with anyone else – not while she was so angry with William. That wouldn't be fair, she knew – they'd made that rule together, not to involve anyone else in the heat of an argument.

Instead, she took a short walk out to one of the balconies, needing to get some air on her face. She stayed there for a few minutes, trying to calm herself, trying to get her tears firmly under control. She didn't want to be angry or crying when she talked to him again. Not going to bed angry was another rule.

She wasn't gone long at all but what she found when she got back brought the anger and tears rushing back.

He was already asleep. And he wasn't even in their bed. Instead, he was under a blanket on the small sofa in their bedroom. A half-drunk cup of tea, still warm, was on the wooden arm beside him.

If the electric kettle on their little table hadn't still been filled with hot water, she might have thrown it across the room.

OWEN'S STRANGE REQUEST

Bristlecone, Colorado

IT WAS THE strange feeling that woke him – the feeling of the hair standing up on the back of his neck and behind his ears. The feeling that he was being watched.

Zander opened his eyes slowly, trying to remember where he was, and why he was so uncomfortable.

He *was* being watched, he realized. Owen was perched on the very end of Quinn's bed, by his feet, silently staring at him.

Suddenly, last night's events all came rushing back to him.

He must have fallen asleep here on Quinn's bed, with his neck propped at a strange angle against the headboard. Her phone was still in his right hand, tethered to the wall by the charging cord.

"I'm sorry, Owen," he said, quickly sitting up, and setting the phone on the table. "I shouldn't have come in here."

"Quinn wouldn't mind," Owen said quietly. "She wasn't using her bed. It's nicer than the couch."

"I don't think she'd much like me going through her private things, Owen. She didn't give me permission."

"They're not really Quinn's things anymore. She said that me and Annie could have whatever we want. I don't think it would bother her, but if *you* thought it would bother her then why did you do it?"

He chuckled under his breath. "I don't know why I did. Her room was just here, and…I guess maybe I thought I would find some answers here or something."

"What kind of answers?"

Owen's face was so sincere, his expression so deep and powerful, that for a moment, Zander forgot he was only eight, and that he shouldn't be having this conversation with him. For a moment, he lost sight of all of that, and just spilled his guts. "Like where Quinn *really* is. Why she disappeared without saying anything to anybody. Why she didn't take *any* of her stuff. I'm starting to worry that something really bad happened to her."

As soon as the words were out of his mouth, of course, he regretted them. Owen was just a young boy, and now he was probably scaring him.

But Owen was still just looking at him with those dark, wide eyes, waiting patiently. He was silent for several seconds, looking like he was waiting to be sure Zander had finished. And when he spoke, his words weren't what Zander was expecting at all.

"What if you got answers to your questions, and they changed your life?"

"What do you mean?" His heart sped to a manic pace. "Did something bad happen to her, and everyone is just hiding it?"

Owen slowly shook his head. Too slowly to convince Zander.

"Do you know where she is?"

He nodded.

"Is she in Europe?"

The pause was much longer this time, but finally, Owen shook his head again.

"Do you know why she went so fast and didn't take any of her stuff with her?"

"Yes."

"But you're not supposed to tell me." He knew that, now.

"Nobody told me I couldn't."

He frowned. "Then why won't you tell me the truth?"

Owen blinked several times. "Why do you need to know?"

It was a valid question. He didn't – and yet, he did. "I don't know why I need to know. Honestly, I've tried to forget about it, I've tried to let it go, and just accept what your mom is saying. I've told myself it's none of my business – and I know it's not. But I can't help it, Owen. Something just keeps pulling me into this, and I can't stop wondering. I need to know."

"Okay."

"Okay? That's it? You're going to tell me?"

"Are you sure you want to know?"

"Why wouldn't I want to know? I thought you said nothing bad had happened to her."

Owen sighed – Zander had never seen him do that before. He was obviously struggling with this for some reason. All he knew was that this scared him, all of it. Actually, he also knew that he should just stop now, leave the little boy alone, but he couldn't bring himself to let it go.

"I don't know if I *should* tell you, Zander. But…" For a second, Owen's bottom lip trembled, and Zander's heart leapt into his throat. Then the little boy took a deep breath and his eyes met Zander's again. "But I need help. And I think you're the only one who can help me."

Zander couldn't even identify the mix of emotions that coursed through him then, but at least part of it was pure, unadulterated panic. Something *was* wrong. He knew his voice was shaking as he answered, "Help you *how*?"

Owen took a deep breath. "Alvin told me that it has to be your choice. That I can't bring you into this without warning you."

The encounter with the old man at the river came back in a rush. "You know Alvin?"

"Yes. I've only really seen him once, but he talks to me in my dreams all the time. He said he met you."

"He told you that in your *dream*?"

"Yes."

All right then. He'd somehow managed to meet Owen's *hallucination* down by the river. This was getting better all the time. "What else did he say to you in your dream?"

"That you could help me – you could help *us*, if you wanted to. But only if you were really ready for your life to change forever. Only if you are ready to learn something that you can't unlearn."

Somewhere inside of him, a warning bell sounded. As crazy as all of this was, as little sense as Owen was making at the moment, as much as there was one part of him that wanted to call Megan and Jeff *right now* and demand to know what kind of stories they'd been filling Owen's head with, and another part that was half ready to call the *police*, just in case something truly horrific had happened here – another part of him, one he wasn't so familiar with, told him, unequivocally, that this was for real.

Owen's statement was serious. If Zander didn't drop this immediately, if he pressed it even one step further, he was going to open Pandora's Box. And once he did that, once he let whatever was in there out, he would never, ever, be able to put it back in.

He didn't know how long he sat there considering the unconsiderable. His heart had slowed; everything was silent and still as Zander really and truly weighed the question in front of him.

He thought of the weeks of wondering and agonizing over where Quinn had gone. He thought of his conversations with his parents last night, how they'd pointed so strongly to the fact that he didn't even know where his life here was going anyway.

He even thought about what it would be like to just drop this now. To take everyone's word for it that Quinn was fine, and it was none of his business anyway. This wasn't his problem, and if he got involved, he wouldn't be able to take it back.

In fact, that last option was almost tempting. Right now, right this second, he still had a chance to get his life back — a life that was familiar, and comfortable. One where he knew most of what he was doing, and would somehow be able to figure out the rest. He'd almost landed on this decision when he looked at Owen's face again — really looked at it this time, deep enough to see the worry hidden in the very back of the little boy's eyes. And he suddenly understood that, while walking away from this was probably the *best* choice he could make, it would also be the selfish one. And that, though he didn't know how or why, in the end, leaving this behind was the decision he would regret.

"Okay, Owen, where is Quinn?"

The little boy nodded. He didn't ask any more questions, didn't double-check Zander's thought process. Whatever had just happened, they both knew the decision had been made.

"I can't tell you, Zander. I have to just show you. If you're going to help me, you're going to have to just follow me today, and do what I ask. I can't explain it right now — not until later."

Zander closed his eyes. "Tell me she's okay, Owen. Tell me you're not going to take me to her body somewhere or something."

Owen's eyes grew wide as dinner plates, and this time Zander knew he'd made a mistake. He hadn't dared even articulate that thought yet in his own brain, even though it had been dancing around the edges. It had just slipped out on its own.

"I'm sorry. I didn't mean that … I'm just scared, Owen."

"She's alive, Zander. And she's okay right now. But she needs help. We have to help her. And you can't ask me any more questions, and you can't stop in the middle. If you're going to come with me, you have to promise you'll do *everything* I tell you."

Eight hours later, Zander was well past questioning his sanity. He had also lost any desire to be the one to call the police to report any suspicions he might have about Quinn – mostly because he was now pretty sure that if anyone called the police, he was going to have to do some serious explaining of his own.

After calling Megan and Jeff to let them know that Zander was staying at their house, and calling Zander's parents with the news that Owen had been fine for the rest of the night, and they could relax and enjoy their trip to the Springs, Owen had flitted around the house for hours, gathering up items and putting them in a duffel bag, and writing some kind of note to his mother, which he sealed in an envelope and left on the counter without letting Zander see it.

Zander, who had only gotten a few hours of sleep the night before, had actually dozed off for a while on the couch while Owen was doing his thing.

But around five in the evening, Owen's instructions got a little strange. At first, his request seemed almost innocent. After dragging the surprisingly heavy duffel bag out to Zander's truck, Owen told him there were a couple of things he needed to get from Doctor Rose's house. Apparently, Doctor Rose had signed the deed on the house over to Megan, and Owen had the keys to prove it.

"You promised," Owen said. "Everything I say. Nobody's there, and even if they were, we'd knock, and Nathaniel would let us in. But he's not, and he wouldn't be mad. He needs our help, too."

Although Zander had never been inside the house of Nathaniel and William Rose, and had nothing to compare it to, going in there had given him the same creepy vibe he'd gotten in Quinn's room. It looked like nothing had been touched. All of the furniture was still there; there were jackets hanging on the hooks in the hallway, everything anyone would need to live ordinary life there. There were even still two laptop computers sitting on a long desk at the back of the living room.

"Who's paying the power bill?" Zander wondered aloud, as Owen walked through the house, flipping switches on without a care.

"Um, I think Nathaniel has everything set to come out of his bank account automatically."

"You're eight. How do you even know stuff like that?"

"You're the one who asked me."

"I suppose I did."

Owen shrugged, not looking at Zander as he headed to the wall of floor-to-ceiling bookshelves. "People don't think I'm listening most of the time. Or maybe they think I don't understand."

Zander had no idea how he knew what he was doing, but Owen carefully selected several black binders, and tucked them into a large hiking backpack he'd found somewhere in the house.

When he'd finished carefully arranging the binders at the bottom, he looked back up at Zander. "Nathaniel talks *to* me, though. So does William. Maybe they knew I'd need to know this stuff sometime. William said I could come here and use his microscopes and read his books whenever I wanted. And Nathaniel told me if he doesn't ever come back, that I can keep whatever I want."

Somehow, Zander didn't doubt for one second that Owen was telling him the truth. The little boy was clearly familiar with the house, moving about with ease, and touching whatever he wanted to. Owen wasn't a child who was usually so comfortable in strange places. "Do you come here a lot?"

"Yeah, I like it here. My mom doesn't like it so much, waiting around for me, but now that my dad's home, he'll bring me sometimes after I finish my homework. He likes the books, too."

"What does your dad think about all of this?" Zander wondered, realizing he'd never thought much about Jeff's part in this. He'd still been in Afghanistan when Quinn left.

"He's sad. He misses Quinn, but he's glad she finally knows about Nathaniel and her family. They fought about it a little – he thought my mom should have told her about it a long time ago, and maybe it wouldn't have happened like this. Quinn wrote him a letter. And he wrote one to her, too. He wants to give it to her when he visits her, but I brought it with me."

There was something Owen was still not telling him – well, there was a lot he hadn't told him yet, but there was something very specific Owen was avoiding mentioning right now.

"Why are you bringing the letter, Owen? Why not let your dad do that himself?"

Owen hesitated for far too long.

"Is your dad going to be *able* to see Quinn again, Owen?"

"Maybe."

"*Maybe?*"

"Probably not. At least, not for a very long time."

It was likely at that point that Zander decided just to turn off reality for the rest of … well, however long this was going to take them. But he did have to ask one more question.

"Wherever you're taking me, today, Owen … however it is that we're going to help Quinn – are we going to come home?"

Owen stopped what he was doing and turned to face Zander, a serious look in his eyes. "Would it change your mind about helping me if the answer was no?"

Zander looked around the living room; he thought about the duffel bag in the car, the strange experience of being in Quinn's room, the conversation he'd had with Owen this morning, and finally, he shook his head. "I promised."

"Then the answer is probably. We'll probably come home."

"Okay." *Fabulous. Nothing at all to be concerned about with that, right?*

Owen headed into the kitchen now, turning on the lights in there, and then Zander heard the sound of a door opening. "Come on," Owen said, his voice disappearing down what sounded like stairs.

Zander followed him through the door at the back of the kitchen, down a set of carpeted stairs.

Most basements in Bristlecone weren't finished, but this one was. There was no laundry room or storage down here – the whole thing had been converted into what looked like a very nice laboratory. The white tiled floor was pristine, as were the metal tables and countertops, which reflected the bright overhead lights. Organized neatly along the counters and on built-in shelving, were a number of microscopes and machines Zander couldn't identify.

There was another library down here, though these shelves were contained behind glass doors. Zander had the impression that everything here was sterile.

A large refrigerator dominated a back corner of the room, with separate thermometer readings showing on the front of the doors at the top and the bottom. Owen, after washing his hands thoroughly at the large stainless-steel sink, headed immediately for that refrigerator and pulled open one of the doors.

Zander was staring at the huge glass-doored cabinets that held a wide variety of medical supplies – bandages, gauze, gloves, tubing ... he didn't even know what most of it was. "Does, uh...Doctor Rose bring his work home with him?"

"A little bit, I think. But they mostly used this lab for their other research, and so William could study. And a lot for storage, I think."

"So William could study *what?*" Zander had certainly used a microscope in school, and he'd dissected a few organs and creatures in his biology classes...but there was nothing he'd ever have needed a set-up like *this* for.

"Medicine. William is a doctor, too."

"William wants to be a doctor, too?" Zander clarified.

"No, he already is one. Can you hand me that cooler over there?"

It was time to stop asking questions, Zander thought. He wasn't getting any answers that made sense, and every new thing Owen told him was just making his head spin even more.

He found the cooler Owen was talking about on a metal rack near the sink. It looked like an ordinary picnic cooler with a handle and a blue lid. Like everything else down here, it was absolutely clean.

Zander had no idea whether to be very impressed at the set-up Doctor Rose had down here – or terrified out of his mind. He was beginning to wonder when he was either going to wake up, or discover that he was on the set of a science-fiction movie. He got creeped out again for a minute, thinking how easily this could have been an operating room … when his thoughts drifted to bodies again, he turned them back off.

He carried the cooler over to Owen, who was meticulously examining boxes that looked like they contained some kind of drugs.

"Thanks," Owen said, and he began pulling out boxes and carefully laying them in rows on the bottom of the cooler.

"Whoa, Owen! What are you doing? Those are not ours!"

Owen didn't stop; he didn't even look up from his task, which seemed to be emptying the entire refrigerator. It had been mostly empty, except for a couple of fully stocked shelves. "Everything I say, remember?"

"I didn't think that was going to include *stealing* stuff!"

"I'm not stealing it. If I leave it here, it's just going to expire before anyone can use it."

"This seems like a bad idea."

"Well, if Nathaniel gets mad about it, I'll tell him it was all my idea – that I made you do it."

"I'm supposed to be the responsible one here."

Now Owen looked up, locking his eyes on Zander's. "Do you think he won't believe me?"

No, Zander didn't think that at all.

"Why would Doctor Rose leave all of this stuff here? *Drugs*?"

"This wasn't all here when he left. This shipment came about two weeks ago. My mom had to sign for it."

Zander's jaw dropped. "How did you know what to do with it?"

He shrugged. "The boxes all say what temperature they have to be stored at. I just read them, and looked at some of Nathaniel's notes for how he does things."

"None of that is dangerous, is it? Or illegal?"

"No."

"Do I have to just take your word for that?"

Owen didn't answer; he finished arranging the boxes in the cooler and then took what must have been some kind of cooling pack from the refrigerator and laid it over the top of them before closing the lid. After that, he carried the hiking backpack around the room, opening random cabinets, and pulling things off shelves, filling the backpack as full as he could before closing it.

LINNEA

"WILLIAM! I NEED an explanation for this." Linnea's voice found him even before the main door of the castle clinic hit the wall as it came slamming open.

He set aside the petri dish he'd been working with and came out of the lab in the back, peeling off the gloves he'd been wearing and dropping them in a metal bin.

"What's going on, Linnea?" he asked, when he saw her standing there with Ben.

In answer, she grabbed Ben's wrist and held it out toward him. Ben shrugged apologetically.

William washed his hands at the sink, and then walked over to Ben. The deep scratch that they'd noticed and cleaned three days ago was now swollen and bright red. Ben's whole arm was getting warm. "It looks like it's infected. When did this start?"

"I don't know." Linnea looked up at Ben with a demanding expression on her face. "I just now saw it. I'm suddenly seeing a whole new side to the long sleeves he's been wearing for the last three days."

"Ben?"

"It seemed fine yesterday, a little swollen maybe, but this morning it was hurting a lot more, and it's just gotten worse."

"He came upstairs a little bit ago to get changed, and I find him having trouble getting his shirt off because it hurt so much. Why didn't I know about this?" Linnea was clearly upset.

William could barely touch Ben's arm without making him wince. "I'll clean this out again, and get some antibiotics into you, too, to be safe. I'm going to go and get some supplies, hang on." The last place he wanted to be was in the middle of Linnea and Ben's conflict, though he knew he was going to have to answer to his sister eventually.

"Can I help you?" Ben asked. William could hear the underlying plea for a private conversation, and he nodded, motioning for Ben to follow him. This, of course, nearly caused steam to come out of Linnea's ears.

Once they were inside the small supply room, William closed the door. He started gathering the things he needed while he waited for Ben to talk.

"How much danger am I in?" he asked. "What are the chances that this thing really is infected with water disease?"

"Pretty low," William said. "But it's still possible. With the way that thing is infected, I'm going to bet you were in contact with something from that fox."

"Is your bite infected? It was much worse than mine."

"No, but Nathaniel has cleaned it out every day, and I've had lots of antibiotics, too. You really should have let me know as soon as it started to bother you."

"I'm sorry. I'm a little scared about all of this, and I've been trying not to upset Linnea, but now I'm getting worried. Should I be avoiding touching her, too? I know you're not touching Quinn."

William stopped short. "How do you know that?"

"Um … I don't mean to be impertinent here Your Majesty, but, your wife and mine do consider themselves to be sisters."

"And Quinn has been talking to Linnea."

"Can I be frank here Your…"

"It's William, Ben. Or Will. You're my friend and my brother long before you're my servant. That was meant to be a statement a second ago, not an accusation. You can *always* be frank with me, please."

"Then, yes. Quinn and Linnea have spent a significant amount of time together the last few days. Linnea doesn't tell me everything, I'm sure, but from what I gather, Her Majesty is quite upset."

"I know she is." Truthfully, he'd barely seen Quinn. Most of it was his fault – he'd been spending his days holed up here in the lab with the dead fox's brain, trying to remember the notes he'd made when researching rabies in Bristlecone – notes that were still there, on the other side of the gate. When he wasn't in the lab, he'd been riding out to Mistle Village to see how things were going there.

Even when he did return, though, she'd been distant – taking long baths before bed, or even being in bed and asleep before he came in. Last night, he'd sat and watched from the couch when the baby woke for a middle of the night feeding. Quinn had to have known he was awake, too, but she'd never once looked over at him.

"So is it safe? Am I putting Linnea at risk by touching her?"

"I don't know, Ben. Nathaniel thinks it's perfectly fine. I'm honestly probably being an idiot with Quinn, but when I think about the chance of doing something to the baby… Even if we can get this vaccine made in time and it works – which is a slim enough chance to begin with – there's no way it would be safe enough for someone so tiny. And he's so little and susceptible. Maybe I wouldn't get her sick, but what if I got something on her skin that he got in his mouth?"

"Have you talked to Quinn about it? Told her all of this?"

"I tried to the first night, but I was upset, and I know I did it wrong. I have never seen her hurt like that before – I've never hurt her like that before, for sure, and I don't know how to fix it. I can't tell her what she wants to hear."

"What do you think she wants to hear?"

"That everything's going to be all right."

Ben nodded, pausing thoughtfully before he spoke. "Again, if I'm not overstepping here … I suspect Her Majesty is well aware of what might happen. Do you think it's possible, though, that what she actually wants to hear is that things are okay between the two of you *today*, and that you both can face even the worst case scenario together?"

William raised an eyebrow wryly, nodding toward the front room where Linnea was still waiting for them to return. "Do you ever wonder why something as obvious as that sounds is so much easier to see about someone *else's* relationship?"

Ben chuckled and nodded. "Indeed. I'll go and speak with her now."

"I'll give you a few minutes."

When William finally emerged from the back of the clinic twenty minutes later, things were calm. Linnea's face was streaked with tears, and she gave him a look that let him know he still had her to answer to later for keeping this from her at all, but she was okay. She and Ben were sitting on one of the cots, facing each other and holding hands.

"Is that for me?" Ben asked, a little wide-eyed at the sight of the syringe on the tray William was carrying.

"Yeah. Sorry. I'm going to clean up that scratch again, and put some ointment on it, but then I'm going to give this to you, too."

"If it's all the same to you, I think I'd rather you do that bit first."

William chuckled. "Not a problem. Stand up for me for a minute."

"Am I still going to be able to ride my horse right after this?" Ben asked as William was prepping.

"Sure. I did it the other day. You might want to take some pain reliever and have a nice hot bath afterwards, though. Okay, look at Linnea now and take a deep breath, then let it out slowly."

"Oh, ow. I thought I got out of this part the other day."

"In the other world, there are all of these stories about foxes being sneaky. Those stories always seemed kind of silly to me until now. But that fox found a way to bite just about everyone, even after you killed him."

"I don't know if that was stealth or revenge," Ben said, wincing as William finished. "But if I was the referee in that game, I might have to give the final point to him."

"I'm not giving it to him yet. We still have some moves left. I'm done with the bad part here. Sorry about that. You should be good to go — at least until we have the other medicine."

"Is that medicine going to be done on time?" Linnea asked.

"Maybe. So long as we manage to not destroy this batch and it *works*, then Ben's chances are really good — he probably hasn't been exposed anyway, and *if* he was, the exposure was much more minor than mine and Alice's. He likely has a lot more time before he would be in any real danger."

"But he still could be." Linnea was biting her lip.

"I can't say that he's not, Linnea. Obviously. I'm sorry we didn't tell you immediately, but now that you know, do you really regret the extra three days you had where you weren't sharing in our nightmare?"

Linnea flew off the cot and was in his face so quickly that he knew he'd said exactly the wrong thing. "That is bole splick William! I don't care how many worlds you've lived in — in not one of them do you get to write yourself off like that. This did not become my nightmare an hour ago when I found that scratch on Ben. We have *all* been living with this for three days over *you*."

Tears were streaming down her face again, but she didn't even stop to take a breath. "I know you're scared. We all do. We all know you're down here and out in Mistle Village trying to fix this, and solve it, and pretend like you're in control, but *damn it*, William, this is not just yours. You don't get to protect us from this. If you keep this up and something happens – if, the Maker forbid, you don't make it through this – I will not be able to forgive you for taking this time away from us."

William lost it. His sister's words gutted him completely. When he turned to hide the sudden torrent coming down his own cheeks she grabbed his shoulder and wouldn't let him go, instead wrapping her arms around him despite his protests – even in his anguish he was afraid to get his tears on her – but she didn't care, and wouldn't be convinced otherwise.

When it was all over, Ben handed him a handkerchief and patted him on the back. It should have felt awkward, but it didn't at all. Ben hugged him then, an unspoken understanding passing between them.

William excused himself for a moment to go and wash his face. When he returned, everyone had collected themselves, and it was like nothing had happened, but everything had changed.

"Where are you planning on riding your horse to tonight, anyway?" he asked, as he turned his attention back to cleaning Ben's wound.

"Today is the day the gate would have been opening. Even though it doesn't open anymore, Luke likes to ride around the area, just to check things out. We still wonder how Hector knew about it, and we just … like to make sure it's secure, Your Majesty. My father and I were going to go with him, if that's all right."

"Of course it's fine. Luke has never seen anything, has he?"

"Nothing substantial. A couple of moons ago, he found someone wandering near the bridge alone. He questioned him, but of course, there was no cause to detain him. The gate was still closed. It's all just precautionary."

William nodded. "I would be tempted to join you – if I wasn't quite sure that I very much need to remain here at the castle this evening."

"I have to say I believe that's a good choice, Your Majesty."

THE RIVER

Bristlecone, Colorado

WHEN ZANDER SAW where Owen was leading him, he knew for sure that he was losing his mind.

Outside of Doctor Rose's house, Zander had headed for the truck, but when they reached it, Owen had pulled out the large duffel bag, and motioned for Zander to follow him.

"Leave the truck here; it's better this way."

"How far are we planning on going like this?"

"I can carry the backpack." Owen turned and tried to lift the heavy frame over his tiny shoulders.

"How about you carry the cooler?" Zander picked up the backpack and put it on his own shoulders, clipping the belt around his waist before he reached for the duffel bag.

"Okay," Owen agreed, though even the cooler was going to get heavy for him after a while.

"We're not going to be crossing any state lines like this, right?"

"Not exactly."

"Owen, this is starting to feel like a really bad idea. Where are you taking me?"

"Just follow me."

Zander sighed as Owen took off down the sidewalk. He supposed they'd already gone this far – already broken into Doctor Rose's house and taken all of this stuff. Although he was starting to worry that all of this was some strange fantasy on Owen's part, he figured he might as well humor him for a little while longer. No more than fifteen minutes, though. They wouldn't be able to carry this stuff for more than half an hour, roundtrip.

Less than five minutes later, though, they emerged from one of the hiking trails in a spot that made Zander's head spin – because it was so familiar. He'd been here just a couple of days ago.

There was the tree with the muddy, dug-up hole underneath it. Zander stopped and watched in shock as Owen headed right for it. And all of a sudden his weird theories about bodies came bouncing back.

It wasn't just his head spinning now – the entire ground felt wobbly underneath him.

"Come on, Zander. I need that bag."

Terrifying thoughts raced through Zander's mind as Owen unzipped the bag, put his hand inside, and withdrew...*a rock*? That's what had been making the bag so unusually heavy and lopsided? Owen was kneeling on the ground, perched over the hole, holding a huge, jagged chunk of shiny dark gray rock.

"What are you doing, Owen?" He was calming a little – he'd already investigated that hole, after all, and it was much too small for a body.

Owen looked up at him, a very serious expression in his eyes. "I suppose I should tell you now that I'm not one hundred percent sure this will work."

"You're not sure *what* will work?"

"Putting this back. I had to break it a little to get it out of here, and I don't know if I damaged it enough to make it not work."

"And what will happen if it doesn't 'work'?"

"We'll have to go and put all of this stuff back and go home."

Zander sighed in relief, finally seeing a light at the end of what had been turning into a very dark tunnel. Maybe Owen had just needed this – needed Zander to play along, to follow his little story. Now he'd done it, and they could just take this stuff back, *un*-steal it, and go home. Put all of this behind them, and go back to normal.

He still wouldn't have any real answers about Quinn, but at that moment, it seemed like something he could work on letting go.

He was actually relaxed as he let Owen carry out the rest of whatever he was doing. He picked up the duffel bag and zipped it up – it was much lighter without that rock. He'd be able to carry it *and* the cooler back the few minutes to Doctor Rose's house. Holding on to them both, he followed Owen.

The sun was beginning to dip below the horizon. Hopefully they'd at least make it back to his truck before it got dark.

"Okay," Owen said. "Let's try it."

"After you."

Owen walked away from the tree and over to the river, stopping right next to the broken-off bridge. Zander watched as he knelt down, picked up a rock – a smaller one, fortunately, than the one he'd put in the ground – and lobbed it into the air.

This gesture, at least, felt normal. Throwing rocks into the river was something Zander liked to do when he was upset or frustrated, too. He waited for the satisfying splash of the rock landing in the water.

Hmmm... He must have missed it. Maybe the rock hadn't been big enough to be noticeable in the current? That didn't seem quite right.

Zander walked closer as Owen picked up another rock – this one was definitely big enough to see – and he threw it.

It didn't land.

Owen turned around, grinning now.

What in the…

Owen grabbed the duffel bag and another rock and scrambled up the steps of the broken bridge. Zander had no idea what he was doing.

Once he was on the little platform at the top of the stairs, Owen stopped, looking over the water. Then, very deliberately, he tossed the rock forward. Again, there was no resulting splash in the water below.

It wasn't until Owen had the duffel bag all the way in front of him that Zander realized what it was about to do.

"Owen, don't do…" But he already had. He'd tossed the duffel bag forward.

But the bag didn't fall into the water, either. It was just…gone.

"Give me the cooler," Owen said, reaching his hand back.

"Owen, there's probably hundreds of dollars of drugs in here…"

"Thousands," Owen answered. "Maybe more."

"Yeah, well, I'm not going to let you throw them into a river."

"I wasn't going to throw the cooler. There's glass in there. I was going to carry it. But if you want to, that's fine."

"I'll hang onto it."

Owen shrugged, and, before Zander could stop him, the little boy stepped forward, off the platform over the river.

Zander panicked. He didn't know what to do. He looked around frantically, but Owen wasn't anywhere. No little boy fell from the bridge or into the water. Like the duffel bag, Owen was *gone*.

After several seconds of worrying his heart was literally going to explode, he heard Owen's voice. "Come *on*, Zander. We don't have much time. Follow me."

He looked up at the top of the bridge and saw Owen's *head.* Just his head, no body underneath it.

And then it disappeared.

Without even thinking about what he was doing, Zander dashed up the stairs and reached for the spot where he'd seen Owen. One second, he was staring out over the rushing water below the bridge, and an instant later, his feet were on solid ground, and Owen was standing there, several feet ahead of him.

"Come on," Owen cajoled, taking a few more steps backwards.

Zander was too stunned to do anything but follow. Somehow, the bridge was no longer broken. The stone continued in a smooth arc all the way across the river. It didn't even look like the same bridge.

Come to think of it – it didn't look like the same river. The water here wasn't rushing below them; it flowed lazily in the semi-darkness. It didn't sound right, either.

He spun around.

Nothing was familiar in that direction, either. The same bridge, whole and complete, stretched to the other side of the river and then down, into a vast forest of trees that looked nothing like the ones he'd just been looking at.

And the mountains were missing.

He turned back to Owen. The boy was walking now, almost to the bottom of the steps at the end of the bridge.

"Owen! Where are you going?"

"Come on, Zander. It's getting dark and we still have a long way to walk."

A long way to walk? He chased the boy down the steps, onto some kind of dirt path that definitely should not have been there. "Owen, I'm not going anywhere. Where *are* we?"

"Eirentheos."

"Excuse me?"

"We're in Eirentheos."

"Well, I don't know what that means, but I think I've reached my limit here, Owen. Let's go put this stuff back and go home."

"Come on Zander!" Now Owen took off running and Zander had no choice but to follow him. He ran for several minutes; when he finally slowed to a walk again, Zander could no longer see the bridge.

"Owen Robbins!"

"What?"

"I'm not kidding, Owen. I've changed my mind. I want to go home."

Owen stared at him for several seconds, and then glanced behind him, up toward the sky. "We can't go home."

"What do you mean, we can't go home? This isn't funny anymore Owen."

Owen frowned. "Was this funny before?"

He didn't have an answer for that. Of course none of this had ever been funny. It had been scary and strange since the very beginning. But not *this* strange. This was too much. "I'm not kidding. Let's go."

He reached for the boy's hand, intending to drag him back down the road and up the bridge if he had to, but a sudden noise stopped him. *What was that?* It sounded like…

Horses.

What the…?

He looked behind him in time to see three horses coming down the path.

Each horse carried a rider – three men who were dressed in clothing he'd never seen before. Two wore green tunics with a gold circle emblazoned on the chest, while the third wore one in purple with a different symbol in silver.

All three of them carried swords. And all of them stopped short, just a few yards in front of Zander and Owen. One of them, the one wearing purple, dismounted.

Zander got the distinct impression they were some kind of soldiers.

Without hesitating, he scooped Owen into his arms, though his hands were already slippery with sweat. His heart pounded as the man approached.

"Sorry to bother you," the man said. The words were kind, but Zander could hear a suspicious undertone in his voice. "We just thought we'd stop and see if the two of you needed any assistance."

The hidden question in his words was clear. *"What are you doing here?"*

Zander's arms tightened defensively around Owen. "We're all right. Thanks."

But at that moment, Owen, who had been straining to look around and see what was happening, wriggled loose, dropped to the ground, and ran – not in the direction Zander so desperately wanted him to, but *toward* the horses.

"Owen!" Zander yelled.

"Ben!" Owen shouted.

The man who had been questioning Zander suddenly turned his attention to the little boy and followed him.

Zander was sure he was having a heart attack as he took off after Owen again. As soon as Owen got close to the other men, one of them climbed down and approached him, bending down so he could get a better look at him.

"Prince Owen?" Zander heard the man ask incredulously as he reached them.

"Yes, Ben. It's me. What are you doing here?"

"I could ask you the same question," the man said, chuckling as he straightened. Zander could see now that he barely qualified as a man – he couldn't have been more than a year or two older than Zander was.

The third man had now dismounted his horse. "It's really you, Owen?"

"Yes. Hello Marcus."

"Hello." Marcus smiled. He was quite a bit older than the one Owen had called Ben – though they kind of looked alike. "I don't know how you got here, but I know Her Majesty will be well pleased to see you."

"Is she the queen now?"

"Indeed."

"Is she here, then? In Eirentheos? Is that why you and Ben have new uniforms?"

Zander still had no idea what was going on, or what they were talking about, but he gathered that he'd been right – these were soldiers. Possibly from two different armies. It was not a comforting thought.

"Yes, she is, and yes, that's why."

"Who's your friend?" Ben asked. "Did he come here with you?" Being looked at with suspicion by three soldiers was not going on Zander's list of experiences he wanted to repeat. He squared his shoulders and met the man's gaze.

"Yes. This is Zander."

"Does he know?" Ben asked, dropping his voice. "About the..." he tilted his head down the road to the place they'd just come from.

"Not really," Owen answered. "I just made him follow me. I couldn't carry all of this stuff by myself."

Zander didn't understand what was going on here at all, but he didn't like it. Talking to soldiers in some weird world, who kept referring to "Her Majesty"... He'd seen Alice in Wonderland. Even if he was dreaming, he didn't like playing this game where he was the only one who didn't know the rules.

"How did you get through?" Marcus asked. "We haven't been able to..."

"Father," Ben said in a low voice. "Should we really discuss this out here?"

"No, we shouldn't," the third one said. He was looking around warily, Zander noticed, and not just at him and Owen. "We need to get back to the castle and let King Stephen deal with it."

Oh, so there was a *His* Majesty here, too. Even better. Owen had somehow managed to drag the two of them into a strange world where they'd been found by soldiers who wanted to take them to be *dealt* with by a king. He'd officially transitioned from worrying he was losing his mind to hoping he was going to wake up soon. This was the last time he was going to stay up past four in the morning.

"Hold up," Zander said. "I'm not going anywhere with you. I want to go home. Owen, let's go *now*."

All three soldiers looked at Owen. "Is the gate still…*open?*" Ben asked, still so quietly that Zander had to strain to hear him.

Owen shook his head. Whatever he said to Ben in response was entirely too quiet for Zander to hear.

The one whose name he didn't know— the lone one dressed in purple – was still looking around like he'd seen or heard something unusual, but he didn't say anything. Something else was going on here aside from the arrival of him and Owen, but Zander wasn't sure what.

Owen looked at him. "Anyway, even if it was open, I'm not going home. I want to go to the castle."

Zander's fists clenched in frustration. Here he was trying to keep the two of them from a situation they might not be able to go out of, and Owen was trying to lead them into it. "No, Owen. It's not a good idea."

"I'm sorry, Zander. This is not your decision." Owen turned back to Ben and Marcus. "Take me to the castle, please."

"Owen, I'm *serious*. This is dangerous. Let's go home."

The little boy nearly growled in his frustration. He walked over to Zander, took his hand, and began pulling him back down the road. He didn't even stop to pick up the cooler or the duffel bag that they'd set down, but at this point, Zander didn't care.

The soldiers followed him, two on horse and one on foot, as he allowed Owen to take him the whole way back down the road, and march him up the steps of the bridge, back to the spot they'd come from. But when they passed it, and walked all the way to the other end of the bridge, then turned around and came back, reality began to sink in.

Standing there, at the end of the bridge, still staring into the eyes of the three strange soldiers, Zander realized that wherever they were, they were stuck.

"Let's go," Owen said, walking toward the road.

"I've got your things, Owen," Ben said, holding up the cooler and the bags. Zander hadn't even seen him pick them up. "Would you like to ride on my horse? I can lead him and walk with Zander. I'm sure your friend would rather walk than be stuck sharing a saddle with one of us."

Yes, Zander thought, *Owen's friend* would much rather that, thank you very much.

Owen's eyes lit up like it was Christmas. "Are you sure you don't want to ride?"

"No, I could use the walk, actually." Zander noticed that Ben was absentmindedly rubbing his hip with his free hand.

"Do I get a choice here?" Zander asked, in a last desperate plea.

The purple one looked him up and down. "The fact that you came here the way you did is probably enough to justify at least bringing you in for questioning – by force if I had to."

"And Owen, too?"

"I'm only a guard. Prince Owen's status in our kingdom ranks him far above me. He's clearly expressed his desire to be taken to the castle, and I'll get him there safely – even if I have to defend him against you."

Whoa. What?

"Now," the man continued, "I'd prefer for you to just come along voluntarily, because I don't sincerely believe you're a threat to our kingdom. I would also like you to consider exactly where you're planning on staying if you *don't* come with us."

He didn't have an answer to that. This was entirely too weird to be real. Perhaps he was living in one of *Owen's* dreams.

By this point, he was in too much shock to do much of anything but watch as their things – even the heavy backpack he'd been wearing – were loaded onto the horses, and Ben lifted Owen up onto the back of the tall chestnut stallion.

Then, suddenly he was walking down the dirt path next to Ben. Owen was up on the horse next to them, while the purple one led them, and Marcus followed behind.

"Where are we going?" he asked Ben after a few minutes.

"To the castle."

For real. A castle. "What is going to happen to us there?"

Ben frowned. "Happen to you? What do you mean?"

"Are we going to be thrown in prison or something?"

"For what? Have you done something I'm not aware of?"

"I don't even know how we got here. You found us about two minutes after we arrived."

"You don't know how you got here? I thought Prince Owen brought you."

"He did. But I don't know how. One minute we were someplace … *normal* … and the next minute we were here. Do you know how we got here?"

"It's not my place to discuss such things. I'm sorry. You'll have to speak with Prince Owen or the queen or the king about it."

COINS

Rosewood Castle, Eirentheos

WILLIAM STOOD OUTSIDE the door to the suite he shared with Quinn for several minutes, mentally sorting out how to do this right. He thought about waiting, about taking care of the other thing he needed to do first, but he knew that would be wrong.

Even if he couldn't have a full conversation with her right now, he couldn't let things stand this way between them for any longer – he couldn't let her be in there, alone and hurting. He reached into his pocket and pulled out a small gold coin, etched with a dandelion on one side, and the thorn of a rose on the other. It was a symbol – a reminder, that as painful as it might be to deal with the problem, it would be far worse to let it continue to grow.

He shouldn't have forgotten that.

Taking a deep breath, he turned the doorknob.

She looked up immediately from her place on the couch, but as soon as she saw it was him, her eyes dropped back to the baby, who was contentedly nursing. *Oh, that sliced right through his heart.*

Blinking several times, and taking another deep breath, he closed the door behind him, set down his medical bag, and turned to face her. "Hey."

She glanced up for a fraction of a second, not even long enough for him to make eye contact with her. "Hi."

"Can I talk to you?" he asked quietly, rubbing the coin again for strength.

Now she looked at him. "You don't have somewhere else you *need* to be right now?"

Oh Quinn. He crossed the room and sat down on the table right in front of her. "I *do*, actually, but I couldn't … I had to come and see you first."

"I'll be here later, William. Or tomorrow, or next week, or whatever."The tone in her voice crushed him even more. He'd hurt her so badly she was pulling away from him. Her bottom lip trembled as she said it, though, and the fingers on her free hand twisted nervously around something … moisture pooled in his eyes when he realized she was fidgeting with her coin, too.

He reached out and took her hand in his, pressing her coin between both their fingers. Then he held out his other hand, palm up, showing her his coin. "I'm sorry, Quinn."

Her whole body went limp as she let out a breath – one he knew, instinctively, that she'd been holding for the last three days – the same breath that was curled tight at the bottom of his chest.

"You're touching me now?" she whispered.

That was the thorn, piercing deep inside of him. The pain in her voice was so real, so visceral; suddenly he could *feel* what that would be like – if, for some reason, *she* had refused to touch him when he needed her. "I'm sorry, love. I still *need* to be careful, but… I can't … I know … I'm just so sorry."

"Me too," she said, blinking back her tears. She withdrew her hand from his, and used it to shift the sleeping baby off her lap and onto the couch cushion beside her.

Then she slid off the couch, onto her knees in front of him, reaching for him. He knelt down on the floor with her and pulled her into his arms, holding her as he rocked her.

"I'm so scared, Will."

"I know, love. Me too," he said, stroking her hair now. Then, cradling her head with his hand, he pulled her to his shoulder. Warm drops fell on the back of his shirt, but he only held her tighter.

He didn't realize he was crying too until she finally pulled her head up, and reached to wipe his cheeks with her thumbs.

"Don't," he said, taking her hands in his again and pulling them down. "It's not that I don't want you to, but … I'm just so worried about you – about him." He nodded toward the baby. "I don't want to hurt you here anymore," he laid one hand over her heart, "but I need you to help me. Deal with my overreacting, please. Help me feel like I'm keeping you safe."

Her tears were still flowing, but she nodded. "I'll try."

"Me too."

After several minutes they were both finally starting to get themselves under control again when the baby stirred on the couch, opened his eyes, and began to fuss.

"Always," Quinn chuckled, standing and picking him up. "Have to make sure you're in the middle of the action too, don't you?" she cooed.

William leaned in close. His heart ached to hold the baby, to feel the solid, tiny weight of his son in his arms, but he still couldn't bring himself to dare. He did take hold of his little foot, securely protected by socks and a blanket, and rubbed it with his thumb.

"So what is it you need to go and do?" Quinn asked him after a few minutes.

"Hmm?… Oh, nothing fun. It'll only take me a few minutes, though, and then maybe we could eat dinner together?"

She nodded, but frowned. "What is it?"

"I have to give Alice the next dose of the medicine."

"Oh."

"Yeah."

"Of all the days Nathaniel could have chosen to go to Cloud Valley, huh?"

He shrugged. "He might as well. Nothing is happening here on the medicine front. We're in the middle of a really awful waiting game."

She bit her lip, making him regret saying that, but then she looked up at him. "Can I come with you?"

"To do this with Alice? It'll be okay. I'm going to try not to make a big deal out of it, you know. She was asleep for the first dose."

She nodded. "I wasn't asking to be there for Alice, Will. She's tough. I know how much you hate it, though. I want to come."

"I'm not tough?"

She raised an eyebrow, and he chuckled. "I'll be fine. You have Samuel."

"I could ask Mia to watch him for a little while."

"Mia? You'd let her?"

"She's the only reason I've bathed in the last few days. I don't know what I'm going to do when we go back to Philotheum."

"We have to find a baby nurse. You're the queen. I'm a healer and the king. We'll have to have someone to tend to him so we can do the things we need to do."

"I never even thought about that. How do you find a baby nurse? Oh my gosh."

"Well, if we don't, I'm afraid Sophia will."

Her breath hitched as she considered that possibility.

"We'll think of something, love. I'll ask my mother for help, okay?"

She nodded. "All right. For now, let's go take Samuel to Mia, and then I'll hold your hand while you take care of Alice ... and then maybe we could have a few minutes alone to talk."

"That would be really nice."

Fifteen minutes later, Quinn was standing with William just inside the playroom, watching all of the children play. She felt better than she had in days, though she was still far from one hundred percent. Of course, with a very real threat of William dying hanging over their heads, she supposed that was too much to ask for.

She did need some time to just be with him tonight, though, and was grateful Mia had been happy to take Samuel for a while.

"Hey, Alice," William called lightly.

Alice had been intently focused on a card game with Alex, but at the sound of William's voice, she popped up and ran across the room as fast as she could. "Will!" she screeched, throwing herself into his arms.

"Hi, baby girl," he said, picking her up. Quinn noticed he wasn't quite as careful about touching her – but then, Alice was the one person he probably didn't have to worry about. She'd been exposed as much as he had – and she was getting the medicine. "How are you?"

"Good."

"How is your arm?"

"It still hurts a little. Nathaniel put a new bandage on it yesterday." She held it up to show him. "How is your arm?"

"About the same," he said, smiling at her. "Nathaniel gave me a new bandage yesterday too."

"You didn't come see me, and you weren't in your room."

Quinn was grateful that William had finally come upstairs, and she knew how much it meant for him to make the effort he was making. They'd get through this – but she wondered if he was ever going to realize what it was like for everyone else, what it had been like for her to have Alice knocking on their door, looking for him, and for Quinn to have to tell her no, and that she didn't know when he'd be back.

"I know, sweetheart. I'm sorry. I came to see you tonight, though. Do you want to come with me for a minute?"

"Sure."

Quinn followed him as he carried her across the hall to the common room where Charlotte was waiting for them. William walked with her all the way to the high counter, and then he set her up there. Quinn set the medical bag she'd been carrying beside him.

"Will you let me check your arm today?"

Alice nodded, holding still as William checked the bandage, feeling around her wound, and then making sure everything was still clean and tight – or at least that's what he told his little sister.

Finally, he looked up at her. "I need to give you some medicine, sweetheart."

"Is it so I don't get sick from the fox?"

"Yes."

Alice shook her head, making Charlotte, who'd been watching from nearby, move closer to her. "I don't want it," she said.

"Why, honey?"

Quinn thought that was a stupid question; Alice was five, and the medicine was a shot. But the little girl surprised – and devastated – her with her answer. "If I take the medicine, there won't be enough for you."

Charlotte gasped, and Quinn saw William's jaw tighten. "Who told you that?"

"Nobody told me. I just heard it. It's true, isn't it? There's not enough medicine for both of us, and if I take it, then you could die."

Quinn had to bite her lip again, and she felt Charlotte's hand on her shoulder. She reached for Charlotte's hand with her own and held on tight.

Alice's little voice was steady, though, and she was looking at William with a determined gaze.

"We're making some more medicine for me, Alice."

"I'll take that kind then, and you can have some now. We can share it."

William's Adam's apple moved fiercely up and down, but his voice was still utterly gentle with his little sister. "Baby girl, the kind we're making is for grown-ups. You're too little for it. I need to give you this kind."

"I won't take it, Will. I won't swallow it. I want you to have some."

Now William's hand started shaking. Quinn grabbed it and squeezed it tight. He closed his eyes for several seconds, taking deep breaths before he opened them again.

"Come here, Alice," he said, dropping Quinn's hand and reaching for her.

She went willingly into his arms.

"Give me a minute," he said to both Quinn and Charlotte. He took his medical bag with him as he carried Alice over to a far corner of the common room, and curled up in a chair with her, facing away from everyone.

Charlotte wrapped her arms around Quinn; she felt the tears building up inside of her again, but they didn't fall. She'd cried too much, and couldn't do it anymore. There was no choice but to get through this.

"You okay?" Charlotte whispered.

"Are you?"

Charlotte just sighed and held her tighter.

William and Alice were over in the corner for what felt like a very long time. When he finally carried her back, his eyes were a little puffy and Alice had a couple of tear stains on her cheeks and a small bandage on her upper arm – one of the coveted decorated ones Will had brought from the other world and reserved for special circumstances. Her little hand was curled around several pieces of candy, too.

Will smiled as he handed her over to Charlotte. "She's good. Hungry for some dinner, I think, and then she deserves some of those treats."

Charlotte kissed Alice's forehead, and then reached toward William. "And you?"

He took his mother's hand for a moment. "I'm hungry, too."

"All right. I could take care of having some food sent up to your room for you two, if you'd like."

They were almost to the door, William's fingers twined with Quinn's, when Thomas appeared in the doorway, looking disheveled and breathing hard. "Quinn!"

"What's wrong?"

"You have to come. Right now!"

SURPRISE

Rosewood Castle, Eirentheos

"WHAT'S GOING ON, Thomas?" Quinn shouted as she and William followed him down the hall, nearly at a run. "What's wrong?" she could hear the fear in her own voice.

Thomas stopped long enough to turn and look at her. "Nothing is *wrong*, settle down, just *come*."

"Settle down?" William muttered, taking her hand. "He's the one racing down the hallway."

Quinn giggled, though she was trying to keep her mind from racing to unwelcome possibilities. Thomas had said there was nothing wrong, but his behavior wasn't exactly convincing.

They'd just turned the last corner before they would reach Stephen's private office when Quinn stopped in her tracks. There, in the middle of the hallway was a small figure. It wasn't possible – it didn't make any sense that she would see him here, but she'd have recognized him anywhere.

"Owen!" She didn't care that she'd screamed, or that anyone was watching. She took the remaining distance at a flat-out run, scooping the little boy into her arms while she was still moving, continuing to run with him several more steps, pulling him tight to her chest.

If she'd been convinced a few minutes ago that she didn't have any tears left in her, she'd been wrong. Oh, but these were different. She buried her face in his neck, holding him, rocking him, smelling his sweet scent.

"What are you *doing* here?" she screeched, when she could finally speak.

"I came to see you."

"But how? The gate's closed."

"I opened it."

There were so many problems with that statement, but she couldn't think about them right now. She didn't even care how he'd gotten here, or why. She just held him closer.

"Who brought you?" she asked, after several more hugs and kisses. "Is Mom…?"

"No, Quinn. Don't. Mom and Dad and Annie are not here. I'm sorry. Just don't get excited about it."

"Okay." She took a deep breath. "Did you come here all by yourself?"

"No he didn't, Quinn. You need to come here," Thomas said, from the doorway of Stephen's office.

If Zander had thought this whole thing was surreal when Owen first disappeared on top of that broken bridge, it was nothing compared to arriving at an honest-to-goodness medieval castle.

Worse, he'd managed to convince himself that he really wasn't dreaming.

Owen, sitting excitedly atop the soldier's horse on the way here, had given him no helpful information at all. And Ben, while he seemed like someone Zander might like in different circumstances, wouldn't answer any of his questions, telling him several times that he needed to wait and speak to the king or the queen when he arrived.

Finally deciding that it probably wasn't a great idea to annoy a big guy with a real sword, Zander had just been quiet for the rest of the walk.

All … *something* … had broken loose when they'd arrived at the castle gates.

The one in purple – Zander had finally figured out that his name was Luke – had ridden ahead and talked to the soldiers at the guardhouse. He noticed quickly that all of the soldiers near the castle were wearing the purple uniforms, and he wondered what that was about – why only Marcus and Ben were in green.

As soon as the rest of them neared the castle, there was a wild flurry of activity; the horses were led away, and they were ushered quickly inside.

Just inside the entrance they were led through, they ran into three young men – all of them were younger than Zander. These weren't soldiers, or guards, or whatever. They just looked like boys, coming back from some activity. All of them were sweating.

"Thomas!" Ben called, as soon as they saw the boys.

One of them, the oldest, stopped and looked at them. Zander had no idea why, but he looked vaguely familiar – even though he couldn't have possibly met him before. This Thomas seemed to know Owen, though. His eyes flicked to the little boy immediately.

"Whoa! Ben! Owen! What is going on?"

"I need Her Majesty. And your father."

"I'll be right back," Thomas said. "Are you taking them to my father's chambers?"

"Yes."

And then Thomas had disappeared.

Owen was waltzing around the castle like he owned the place. Zander didn't think the kid was usually this comfortable in his own house.

Ben, Marcus, and Luke led them through several hallways, finally stopping in front of a massive set of wooden double doors.

Luke opened one of the doors and held out his hand, gesturing for them to step inside.

Zander did, but Owen didn't follow. "I want to wait for her out here," he said.

Nobody objected to the little boy at all, but the three soldiers followed Zander into the room. And here he'd thought he wasn't being detained.

He'd had some time to think about things while they were walking down the strange dirt road, and into the weird city, and an idea was starting to dawn on him that he wasn't quite ready to accept – mostly because none of the details made sense together.

He didn't have much more time to think about it in here – this room that so very much belonged inside a castle with its rich wood paneling, marble floors, massive wooden desk, and plush couches and chairs.

Just as Ben was offering him one of those armchairs, though, another man walked into the room.

All three guards immediately stood at attention as the man entered, though none of them seemed intimidated by him. Really, the man wasn't intimidating at all – he looked … friendly, Zander decided, maybe because the man smiled at him right away, his dark gray eyes sweeping up and down over Zander's features.

The three guards remained close to him, keeping themselves between him and Zander. He had to wonder what kind of threat they thought he might be to the man. They were the ones with swords.

"So, I hear you've accompanied our dear friend Owen here on his journey to us."

"Uh…I guess so."

"Zander, is it?"

He nodded.

"Well, Zander, I'm Stephen. Welcome to my home."

His home … did that make him …?

He didn't get an answer to the question he was forming, nor even a chance to respond to the man, because at that moment there was a huge commotion in the hallway just outside the room. First, there was the sound of several people running along the stone floors, and then he heard a shout – only a single word – "Owen!" – but he would have recognized the voice anywhere. He froze in place.

At the sound of her voice, the two guards in green both disappeared through the door, in a synchronized motion Zander couldn't quite understand. Luke, however, moved closer to Stephen, coming to stand right at his side, the lone guard protecting him.

"Am I correct in assuming you know Quinn, Zander?"

He nodded, unable to make himself speak. She was here. That was her voice in the hallway with Owen. What was she doing here? How did these people know her?

It was the piece he hadn't been able to wrap his head around. Owen had told them they were going to "help" Quinn. If she was trapped in a castle in Wonderland, she certainly would need help – but ever since the soldiers had found them, Owen hadn't exactly been behaving like they were somewhere anyone needed *rescued* from.

The boy they'd met in the hallway a few minutes ago – Thomas – appeared in the doorway. With a little more context now, Zander was starting to vaguely remember where he'd seen him before. If his memory was right, this boy had once been in the hallway at Bristlecone High School, hugging…

"No he didn't, Quinn," Thomas was saying. "You need to come here."

Zander's whole body tensed as Thomas moved out of the way for someone to come through the door. But it wasn't Quinn who came through first. It was Marcus again, though this time when he came through, his hand hovered much closer to his sword, and he was scrutinizing Zander much more closely.

Right behind Marcus, though … it was her. Owen was in her arms, his legs wrapped around the top of her long skirt as he hugged her close.

Zander had to remind himself to breathe as she entered. *How was this even possible?* She was followed by another person he recognized instantly. *William Rose.* Given the way William walked right at her shoulder, his hand resting on the small of her back, Zander was suddenly very sure that he was not her cousin.

Behind the whole little group was Ben, and when they were all inside, just a few feet from where Zander was standing, the two guards flanked them so closely that they nearly blocked his view. For a few short seconds, Zander tried to reconcile this behavior with the scenario he'd been building in is head – that Quinn was being held here as some kind of prisoner and needed rescued – but it just didn't fit. She didn't look scared of the soldiers; if anything, she appreciated their presence.

At first, she looked around in a confused kind of way, but he saw the exact second she recognized him. Her eyes widened in disbelief, and her grip on Owen loosened – so much so that the little boy decided then to climb out of her arms.

William recognized him at almost the same time Quinn did. He could see it. As soon as Owen was safely on the floor, William took hold of her hand in a gesture that was impossible to misunderstand.

"Zander! What are you doing here?"

"I could ask you the same question. What *is* this place, Quinn?"

"It's …" She frowned. "*Seriously,* Zander how did you even get here?"

"I don't know. I just … one minute I was following Owen, who said we had to get this stuff to you," he nodded toward their things that someone had brought in and set over close to the door, "and the next, I'm on some weird bridge and we're being captured by soldiers."

"Captured?" Quinn raised an eyebrow, and looked over at Marcus.

"Prince Owen asked to be brought to the castle, Your Majesty. We brought his companion along."

Your Majesty? What in the...

"We did briefly consider honoring his request and leaving him there at the bridge," Ben said, "but the sun had already set, and it didn't seem like the best idea."

Zander was looking back and forth between all of them, unable to comprehend any of what was going on. William had disappeared from Quinn's side, and he was over by the door, kneeling down to see the things Zander and Owen had brought. Maybe he'd recognized the cooler and the backpack from his house in Bristlecone.

"No," Stephen said, from the other side of the room. "You were right in bringing him here. Where else would he have gone? We can't have him loose in the kingdom."

Zander didn't like being talked about like he wasn't even here. "So are you going to keep me here then?" he demanded. "Am I under arrest or something? Because I want to go home."

"Well, you can't go home," Quinn said. "The gate's closed. You're not under arrest, but, really, Zander, there's nowhere else for you to go."

"What gate? And what do you mean that it's closed? Owen said he opened it. He needs to just open it again."

Quinn looked at Owen. "Will the gate open again?"

Owen nodded. "Probably. I put the magnet back where it goes. It worked like it was supposed to."

"Then, how do we open it?" Zander asked him. "I did what you wanted, Owen. I brought you here so we could help Quinn. Now, can we just take her and get going home?"

"Excuse me?" Quinn's voice had turned icy. "*Take* me somewhere? What in the world do you think you're doing here,

Zander?" She looked at Owen. "Did you tell him you were coming here to get me or something?"

"No." Owen shook his head. "I told him you needed help."

"What do you mean, buddy?" She knelt down next to him. "What kind of help? Why did you open that gate? You know it's dangerous, right? I thought that's why you closed it, because you knew how bad it was. What's going on?"

That was exactly what Zander wanted to know.

"I know how dangerous it is," Owen said quietly. "I didn't know if I should do it, but then I had a dream about William, and I had to try…Quinn, I just had to try."

"Try what?"

"To bring you the medicine."

All of the color went out of Quinn's face – Zander literally watched it flow downward from her temples, all the way down, until she was pale white from the collar of her blouse up. He almost took a step toward her, to hold out his hand and steady her so she wouldn't fall, but Ben was too fast; he had his hands under her arms in an instant, keeping her firmly on her feet.

"What medicine?" she whispered.

"The rabies medicine," Owen answered, frowning as he looked over to where the cooler was.

Or had been, anyway.

"Where did it go?" Owen asked. Sometime in the last couple of minutes, the cooler and the backpack had disappeared. The duffel bag was still there, though.

"Was it a backpack?" Thomas asked. Zander had forgotten he was still standing there.

"It was a cooler," Owen answered.

"Oh, William said something about needing to get something put in the refrigerator right away. He grabbed all that stuff and left."

"I'm going to go find him," Quinn said.

"What about…" Thomas tilted his head toward Zander.

"Right..." Quinn rubbed at her temples with her fingers. She was obviously distressed, but Zander couldn't figure out why. Was this her reaction to his coming here? She looked at him.

"Look, Zander ... I don't know how you got here, and I don't know why or ... I can't think straight right now. Thomas, Stephen, can I impose on you...?"

"Of course, Quinn," Thomas said. "Just go."

"Can I come?" Owen asked, already following her to the door.

"No, buddy." Thomas reached for Owen's arm. "Why don't you hang out with me for a little while, and let your sister deal with William, okay?" He picked Owen up and whispered something to him, to which the little boy nodded.

The fact that Owen was so comfortable with these people — allowing them to touch him and hold him — spoke volumes to Zander. He wasn't sure what to make of it, but he didn't think he liked it much. Could Megan Robbins possibly know about all of this?

He also noticed that Ben and Marcus didn't follow Quinn — solidifying his growing belief that the two guards weren't restraining her at all. In some bizarre way, they were serving her.

The mood in the room had changed completely, in a way Zander didn't quite understand. Quinn's reaction had been the most extreme, but everyone had responded when Owen had told them he'd brought the medicine. Ben and Marcus were exchanging odd looks with each other, and Thomas seemed edgy now, too.

Until that moment, Zander hadn't known that what they'd brought was rabies medicine — that was serious stuff.

Stephen cleared his throat, bringing Zander's attention back to him. Even his demeanor had changed.

"You'll have to forgive us," he said. "It's been a very challenging few days for everyone around here. Ordinarily we wouldn't welcome a guest in such an awkward fashion. Although, I must admit, your arrival here is a very unexpected event. We were under the impression that the gate was sealed shut."

"It was," Owen said, rather solemnly, still perched in Thomas' arms.

"So I gathered from what you told Quinn. But you were able to open it again?"

He nodded.

"How did you know how to do it? Was it you who closed it in the first place?"

"Yes."

"Why?"

Owen closed his eyes for several seconds. "I had a dream…a man with a beard was coming through the gate."

"Yes, his name was Hector."

"I didn't know his name. I didn't know why it was bad; I just knew – after the dream – why Alvin had told me where to find the magnet."

"It could have been very bad indeed, Owen. You did exactly the right thing. We were all searching, here on this side, for a way to close it, but we couldn't find one."

"You can't do it from this side, I don't think. Only on my side."

"Can you close it again once you go home?"

"Yes. I have to, don't I?"

"We're afraid it's still really dangerous, Owen. For us, here, and if the wrong people use the gate, it could be dangerous for you on your side, too."

Owen nodded, looking extremely serious for an eight-year-old boy.

"Look, this is all very interesting," and it was – or at least it would have been, if Zander had the first clue as to what they were talking about, "but all I really want to know is how you get the gate open *now* so we can go home."

"*That* I have no control over. If the gate is operating normally right now, it will be open again in ten days, and you'll be able to go home again then."

It was suddenly very difficult to breathe. "Are you telling me I can't go home for ten days?"

Stephen's eyes were sympathetic as he nodded, but his expression also told Zander that this was far from his biggest concern right now. "Yes. The gate is closed, and it won't open for ten days."

While Zander was still standing there open-mouthed, Stephen looked back at Owen. "Did you say you brought the rabies medicine here with you?"

"Yes. I brought everything that was in the refrigerator at Nathaniel's house. Most of it came in a shipment a couple of weeks ago."

Zander cringed at the confession that they'd broken into Doctor Rose's house, but Stephen didn't seem bothered – quite the opposite, actually. He leaned against the massive wooden desk in what looked like relief.

"You and your mother have been taking care of things there?"

"Yes."

Stephen nodded. "She doesn't know you're here, though, does she?"

"No. She was out of town when I had the dream. That's why I asked Zander to help me."

Stephen's eyes flicked to Zander's and then back to Owen. "But you didn't tell him what he was getting into, did you?"

"I kind of tried. I warned him that he might regret it."

Zander supposed that was true. Owen had offered him several warnings, and he'd ignored all of them. Still – how could he have anticipated something like *this*?

"Was he right, Zander? Are you regretting this yet?"

"So far, I haven't actually managed to convince myself that this is real."

Stephen chuckled and so did Thomas. The guards somehow managed to remain stoic.

"You know Quinn well, I take it?"

"You could say that."

"If Zander is who I think he is," Thomas interrupted, "then he and Quinn were courting before she came here the first time."

"Ah," Stephen raised an eyebrow. "Is that true, Zander?"

"I don't know what you mean by courting, but she was my girlfriend."

Stephen smiled at him. "Well that complicates things, doesn't it?"

"I don't know. Does it?"

"I have seven sons, Zander – four of whom have entered the treacherous world of girls. It's always complicated."

Seven sons? Was he kidding?

"Are you hungry?" Stephen asked.

"Excuse me?"

"You and Owen must have had a long walk and I'd imagine discovering all of this would be a little taxing. You're probably hungry."

"Food isn't the biggest thing on my mind right now."

Stephen didn't even seem to acknowledge him. "What about you, Owen?"

"I'm hungry."

Stephen smiled. "We've got plenty of time to sort out some of this other stuff, Zander. If you'll excuse me, though, I have a lot of other business I need to attend to this evening. Thomas, would you please take these two upstairs and find some help in getting them settled?"

"So you're just going to keep me here, like a prisoner."

Stephen met his gaze levelly. "I'm sorry if it looks that way to you, Zander. The truth is that there is nowhere else for you to go, and while it is not usually my policy to detain anyone against their will when they haven't committed a crime, the fact remains that if I allowed you out of the castle, you would pose a very serious security risk to my kingdom. Aside from which, I do feel a duty of care for you, given that you are a friend of Quinn's and Owen's. I'm not going to allow you to starve in the forest for ten days."

"Is that why Quinn is being kept here, too? Because she's a *security risk* to your kingdom?"

Stephen sighed. "No. Quinn is not being held here in any way. While I think we'll all be better off to leave some discussions between you and her, I will tell you that she and I are on equal footing here, and – outside of what I believe to be reciprocal love and concern between us – I have no authority over her."

"Aren't you the king or something?"

"You're very astute, Zander. It's a quality that will serve you well, I should think. Yes. I am King Stephen of the kingdom of Eirentheos. Welcome to my home. I hope your stay is more pleasant than you're worried it will be. Now, if you'll excuse me, I really do have some things I need to attend to. Please allow my son Thomas to escort you upstairs.

"Thomas," he continued, "you should discuss this with your mother and the staff, but I'm thinking Owen might enjoy Quinn's old room – and that Zander would be comfortable in one of the empty suites close to Ben's and Marcus'.""

He wasn't a prisoner – they were just going to keep him in between the guards. Fantastic.

"I'll take care of it, Father."

"Thank you."

Stephen stopped near the door to speak quietly to all three guards, and then they followed him out of the room, leaving Zander with Thomas and Owen.

"Hi," Thomas said, grinning. "I don't think we've had a chance to be properly introduced. I'm Thomas." He extended his hand.

THE CLINIC

Rosewood Castle, Eirentheos

QUINN WASN'T ENTIRELY sure where William had gone, but Thomas had said he was going to put the medicine in the refrigerator, so she headed first to the clinic, relieved when she could see the lights on inside the little building once she was halfway up the path.

The fact that Owen and Zander – *Zander!* – were here was both astounding and overwhelming, but right now, her only thoughts were of William and the medicine.

"Will?" she called as she opened the door of the clinic.

"I'm back here," he answered, and she followed the sound of his voice to the lab where they kept the refrigerator. He was in the very back, behind everything. She could just see the back of his head as he stood at one of the long counters.

"Is it true? Did they really bring the rabies medicine?" She hadn't allowed herself to believe it yet.

"Yeah." He didn't even turn around as he spoke. "All of it – a whole huge shipment that Nathaniel ordered a while ago. Both kinds even, the vaccine and the immune globulin."

"Oh, wow."

"I know."

When she finally reached him, she grabbed his shoulder and turned him to the side, pulling him into her arms. He shuddered and then reciprocated, holding her tight, running his fingers through her hair, the relief pouring off both of them.

"This is in time, isn't it? It's only been three days."

"This is in time." He nodded. "I know I was overreacting – I do know that. But it just…"

"I know. I'm sorry, too. I know I need to be patient with you sometimes, Will. I know that's what you do when you get scared, and I know you didn't mean it the way I took it … but …"

"But we both freaked out at the same time."

"Yeah."

"There's a reason we have a rule against that, you know." He ran his fingers down the side of her cheek.

"Yeah, well, rules kind of fly out the window when you try to contract a deadly disease on me two weeks after I have a baby."

"I'll try to time it better the next time."

"There better never *be* a next time … what are you doing?" she asked, looking for the first time at the counter where he'd been working. He had several syringes and vials laid out on a metal tray, along with a stack of cotton squares and a little brown bottle with its lid off; the smell of the antiseptic inside it made her nose twitch.

"Nathaniel's in Cloud Valley. Even if we send him a message tonight, he wouldn't be able to get here until at least tomorrow afternoon. A message tonight would get there late enough to disturb him anyway. I don't want to do that, and I can't wait for him to get back. I need to do this as soon as possible."

"Were you planning on doing this to *yourself?*" she asked, aghast.

He shrugged, his eyes not meeting hers all the way.

"William! We could get Jacob, you know."

"Not until tomorrow, either. It's late. They have a baby, too. I'm not going to haul him on an almost four-hour round trip to do this at night, but every second I wait scares me to death, Quinn. Doesn't it scare you?"

It scared her more than she could bring herself to talk about, but still … "Someone closer, then? There are healers right here in the city."

"Every last one of whom knows we're out of the medicine and we're waiting on that batch in Mistle Village. They don't even know where we were getting it in the first place. They think we've already been making it somehow. Whenever they get a case of water disease, they call me or Nathaniel or Jacob for the treatment. How in the world would I explain where this came from?"

"I didn't even think about that."

"Yeah. So … it's me. I want to do Ben tonight, too, and Emma. And give the immune globulin to Alice – she's still in the window where I can do that, and then I'll know she's safe."

"You really think you're going to be able to give this stuff to yourself?"

He glanced over at the needles and grimaced. "Yeah, I can. I've done it before."

"You've done it before?"

He nodded. "How do you think I got good at it?"

"Um, I didn't think you practiced on yourself."

"Well, I did. Just with saline, though, not with medicine. Saline doesn't hurt – and once I knew what I was doing, the needle didn't hurt, either."

She knew she was staring at him like he'd grown another head. He shrugged and smiled at her sheepishly.

"Well, those don't have just saline in them, Will. I've had that immune stuff…"

"No, they have something that's going to save my life. I can get over it."

"Can you even reach everywhere you need to in order to do it right?"

He shrugged again.

"Good grief." She glanced at the counter again. "I'll do it."

"You're just as scared of needles as I am," he said skeptically.

She shook her head. "I was. That was before the tattoo and the whole natural childbirth thing. Besides, you being scared of needles never stopped you from sticking them in me. It has to be my turn sometime, doesn't it?"

"No. It doesn't actually."

"Just tell me what to do, William."

"Okay, you see this one?" He tapped one of the larger syringes.

"Yeah."

"You have to get as much of that stuff intothe bite as possible."

She stared at him. "That's not how Nathaniel did it when I had them."

"You didn't actually have a bite he could identify. When you get bitten, it's different."

"You're serious."

"Be grateful you'll never have to have this part again. If I'd have thought there was a real chance I'd be bitten by a rabid animal, I'd have let Nathaniel give me rabies shots while we were in Bristlecone."

"I thought you said they don't last long enough to make it worth it."

"They don't last long enough to keep you protected from rabies – but they do protect you from needing the immune globulin shots. If you were exposed to rabies now – or ten cycles from now, you'd still need to be treated, but you'd only need two shots of vaccine – not this stuff." His voice was steady, but a little bit of green seeped around the edges of his face.

"Stupid fox," she said.

"It wasn't his fault."

"I don't care. I'm still pissed at him."

"Such language, my queen."

"Oh, you haven't heard what's been going through my head for the last three days." Although she'd nearly *said* some of it, a couple of the times he'd been in the room with her. Maybe it would have been better if she had.

He was chuckling. "Mine, too," he admitted. "And I think there's going to be a lot more of it in the next few minutes."

She laughed, too, although it was only partly funny. "Yeah. All right, show me what I'm doing. Let's get it over with."

"So … Zander Cunningham…" William said, as they carried the trays out to one of the cots in the main room. "How did *that* happen?"

"I wish I knew." Although at the moment she was still more freaked out by it than she was curious. She had a feeling that it wasn't going to go well – she'd seen the way Zander had looked at her when William took her hand. What was he going to think when he found out they were married – and had a baby?

"Do you care what he thinks?" William asked, with the uncanny ability he sometimes had of knowing what she was thinking.

Looking up, she considered that for a moment, but then she stepped over to him and tapped him on the shoulder until he turned to face her. "Are you jealous of him?"

He took half a step back – until he was all the way up against the cot. "What?"

"Are you jealous of Zander?"

He rubbed the back of his neck with his hand. "I don't know. I never even – I didn't think I was ever going to see him again."

"Well, I'm married to you, William," she said, reaching up for that hand and pulling it down to her. "You don't have to be jealous of him. I chose you. But yes, I do kind of care what he thinks. We used to be friends. I don't like the idea of hurting him more than I already did."

He sat down on the cot, holding her hand in his and playing with her fingers, twisting her wedding band around in a circle. "I was jealous of him before, you know. When we were still in Bristlecone, even before everything happened."

"You never told me that."

"I didn't realize it at the time – that jealousy felt that way. It wasn't until you were here, and we were courting, that I looked back at it and understood."

"I feel bad. I should have broken up with him sooner – as soon as I started lying to him … for sure after I kissed you."

"I thought *I* kissed you."

She giggled and leaned down closer to him, bringing her lips to his … but he held up his hand. "Not yet. Once I've had the medicine in me for twenty-four hours."

Deflated, she took a step back. "You are being ridiculous. Nathaniel told me the only documented cases of rabies transmission from human to human were from *organ transplants*."

"There were a couple of questionable ones where there might have been kissing or biting."

"In third world countries."

"In case you haven't noticed, love, we live in a third world country."

"I talked to Nathaniel, William. I really did. He said those exposures were never confirmed, and that, in any case, you would have to be contagious first. After only three days, there is no way you're contagious."

"If it was the other way around, Quinn, and you had that animal's saliva all over you – inside you – and I asked you to touch me or Samuel…"

She took a deep breath through her nose and let it out through her teeth. "Give me the needle."

STUCK

Rosewood Castle, Eirentheos

ZANDER RAISED AN eyebrow, but accepted Thomas'
handshake. "I'm Zander," he said. "Though it seems like you
already knew that."

"Yeah, well, when you randomly pop into our kingdom from
another world – word gets around."

"Another *world* – that's really what this is?"

"Yes," Owen said.

Thomas only shrugged. "As far as we can tell, anyway. Is this
all you have – this bag here?" he asked, reaching for the strap of the
duffel bag.

"That's all we have, and Owen brought that. I don't even
know what's in there. He didn't tell me I needed to pack for a long
trip. I suppose I'm going to be wearing these clothes for ten days."

"Oh, we can take care of that. I have three older brothers. I'm
sure between them we can keep you in clean clothes until we can
get some new things made for you."

153

Zander didn't really want to wear someone else's clothes – especially … "William's your brother, right? Or was that a lie too?"

"Will's my brother."

"And he and Quinn … how long have they…?"

"I am not getting involved in that one, Zander." Thomas started walking, leading them out into the hallway.

"So that's what the issue was? She was cheating on me with a *prince* from another world? You and William are princes, right, if your father is the king?"

"I'm a prince. William is no longer a prince, at least that's not his official title. And, really – I enjoy gossip as much as anyone, but as far as I'm getting into this with you is to tell you that, no – Quinn was not cheating on you with William. She was here for a while before the two of them started courting, and it was after she broke up with you."

"She *told* you she broke up with me?"

"Quinn and I are friends. We were friends while you were still courting her."

Courting was such a weird word for it. "Well, she never told me about you."

"Yes, she did. I know she did. She just didn't tell you that she'd met me *here*. I'll bet you can guess why."

"She's been here before this time?"

"Yes. A couple of times."

Zander didn't understand how that was possible – he didn't remember Quinn ever going anywhere for ten days – but at the moment, he was still preoccupied with the interaction he'd seen between Quinn and William Rose in that office. "She only broke up with me a month and a half ago. What I just saw of the two of them in there looked like it had been going on for a lot longer than that, Thomas."

They were at the bottom of a staircase now, and Thomas stopped and turned to look at him.

"That's the other part you don't know, Zander. Although I'm a bit surprised you're not freaking out more about being stuck here for ten days than you are – the first time Quinn came here and realized she was stuck for ten days, she was definitely not as calm about it as you are."

"Maybe I'm just not ready to think about the fact that when I get home, I'm probably going to be *arrested* for kidnapping Owen."

"No you won't," Owen said. "I left a note for my mom."

"As nice as that is, I don't think a *note* is going to cover you disappearing for ten days, buddy."

"We're only going to be gone from home for one day."

"What do you mean? I thought everyone just said the gate can't open for ten days."

"Ten days in this world," Owen said. "One day in ours."

"*Excuse me?*"

"Time doesn't work the same in our two worlds. In ten days, when the gate opens again, and you and Owen are able to go home, only one day will have passed in your world. It will be the evening after you left."

"That's not possible."

"Possible or not, it's true."

He quickly did the math in his head. Ten times… "So, if Quinn has been here this whole time, then – in your time she's been here for…?"

"Over eleven moons, now. Roughly equivalent to your months."

"A *year?*" Zander was startled when Owen's took his hand in one of his little ones, rubbing the back of it with his other hand – possibly to try and calm him.

"If our time were measured the same as yours, it would be about that long, I think, yes." Thomas' explanation of this was absentminded – a topic he'd grown bored with.

Zander didn't get to go any further in his questioning of *that* insane revelation, though, because at that moment, they heard footsteps, and he looked up in time to see a girl coming down the stairs.

"Thomas! What is going on? I heard … *Owen!*" As soon as she saw the little boy she ran the rest of the way down and grabbed him, scooping him into her arms.

Owen hugged her back. "Hi Linnea!"

She was very pretty, with long, dark curls that reached to the middle of her back, and the same gray eyes as Thomas. Her features were fine and delicate, her eyelashes so long and dark that she'd never need mascara – did they have makeup in this world? Realizing he was staring, he looked back at Owen.

"Ben just told me I would want to get down here to see this, but I didn't expect you!" she said to Owen. "What are you doing here?"

"It's a long story," Owen said.

Thomas patted Owen on the back. "He's told it a lot tonight, Nay. I'll fill you in on the details later."

"And who are you?" the girl asked, looking at Zander.

"This is Zander," Thomas said, patting him on the back. Zander stepped to the side, just out of his reach. These people were awfully touchy-feely.

"*Zander? That* Zander?" Linnea asked, eyes wide.

"That would be the one." Thomas chuckled. "Zander, this is my twin sister, Linnea. Also, Ben's wife," he added pointedly. *Touchy-feely and telepathic. Great.* It wasn't like he'd been thinking about asking her out.

She didn't look old enough to be married. Every time he thought this day couldn't get any stranger, it turned out he was wrong.

"It's, er, nice to meet you," he said to her.

"It's interesting, anyway," Linnea said, holding out her hand. "Does Quinn know about this?"

"Yes. She went to go find William. Zander and Owen brought back the rabies medicine."

Linnea's reaction to that statement was a lot like Quinn's had been. She went slightly gray, and her eyes got very wide. "For real?" she demanded of Zander.

He shrugged. "Apparently. I didn't know what Owen was putting in that cooler until just a few minutes ago. Why? Is somebody dying of rabies or something?"

"Not yet," Thomas said quietly, "but we were cutting it close there for a few days. A rabid fox got into the castle yard and bit both William and my little sister, Alice."

"Oh. I'm sorry." He wasn't quite sure what else to say. "But don't you have the vaccine here? Isn't Doctor Rose here?"

"You mean Nathaniel?" Thomas asked.

"Yeah."

"Yes, he is – well, he's not in the castle tonight, but yes, he's here in our world. But no, we didn't have any more of the vaccine here. Our world is a little … less developed than yours is, Zander. We don't have everything here that you have, and enough vaccine to deal with this issue right now was more than we had."

Zander looked at Owen. "Is this what you meant when you said Quinn needed help?"

He nodded.

"But Quinn's okay?" Zander asked suddenly, looking back at Thomas and Linnea. "I mean – she's had rabies vaccine before."

"Quinn is healthy. It's been a very upsetting few days for her, but physically, she's well."

Zander nodded, staring down at the marble floor. This was all too much information for him. He needed to sit down, to have a few minutes to process all of this.

"Let's get Zander upstairs," Linnea said. "I'm guessing he could maybe use a few minutes, and he could stand to get some food into him."

He looked over at her gratefully, but despite her considerate words, her expression was still wary and suspicious. He wondered exactly what these people had heard about him.

By the time he followed them up the stairs, he had to watch his feet carefully on the steps, just to make sure he wasn't going to miss one and trip over himself.

He didn't even pay attention to where they were taking him, but somehow he ended up sitting on a couch in the very back in what seemed like some kind of really large family room with a kitchen in it. There were a lot of people in and out – mostly kids and teenagers, and some lady with a baby left after he'd been there for a few minutes.

Owen was more excited than he'd ever seen him; all of the kids shrieked when they saw him, and they fawned over him, pulling him in and out of the room. After a while, Zander mostly gave up trying to keep track of him.

Linnea had disappeared as soon as they got upstairs, but Thomas only left for a few minutes, and when he returned, he was carrying a silver tray with a lid, which he set on the table in front of Zander before uncovering it to reveal a plate full of food.

"Owen's probably hungry, too," Zander said.

Thomas held the plate out toward him. "He's eating already."

"I don't even need to take care of him here, do I?"

"Not really. My brothers and sisters are all excited to see him, and my parents will be more than happy to see to all of his needs."

Zander nodded. He was sort of hungry, but nothing on the plate looked familiar to him. There was some sort of meat covered in creamy gravy, and mixed vegetables – but he could only recognize carrots in there. He did find himself picking at the meat a little. It wasn't terrible. The vegetables scared him, though.

"So you have six brothers?" Never had he imagined William Rose with siblings – let alone that many of them.

"Yes."

"And how many sisters?" He wondered if it was just the one.

"Six."

He nearly choked on the bite he'd taken. "*Thirteen?*"

"That always surprises people. It is a lot, I suppose – even for my world."

"Are these them?" he asked, gesturing at a couple of the children who'd just run back into the room to retrieve something.

"Some of them, yes. That's Emma, there, who just ran out the door."

"I won't remember that." He took another bite of the meat.

And then, there she was again. Quinn had just appeared in the doorway. Again, she was with William. He had his hand in hers, and he appeared to be looking for something – *someone?* in the room, but he didn't seem to find whatever it was. Zander found himself unable to look away as William bent down and kissed Quinn – not on the lips, he noticed, but on the cheek, and then he left.

Zander sat up straight as Quinn headed right for the corner where they were sitting. He felt awkward as Thomas stood to greet her. They stayed close enough that Zander could hear everything they were saying. He concentrated on his food.

"You okay?" Thomas asked.

"Yeah. Will's going to track down Alice, and then Emma and Ben."

Thomas nodded. "Are you hungry?"

"Starving."

"I'll go and get you a plate – unless you want me to stay." He glanced at Zander.

She shook her head. "That's okay. Mia hasn't come looking for me, has she?"

"No. I just talked to her a few minutes ago actually. Everything is fine. You've got a little more time, I think."

"Okay, good. Thank you."

Zander set his plate back down on the tray as Quinn sank into an armchair across from him. He didn't think he was going to be able to eat any more right then.

Quinn, on the other hand, was eyeing his dinner. "You didn't even touch those," she said, looking at the vegetables.

"I barely eat vegetables I can identify at home. I'm not quite brave enough for those. You want them?"

"If they're going to go to waste anyway…" she said, and she reached to grab the little bowl and one of the extra forks off Zander's tray.

"Help yourself," he muttered.

"Where are my parents?" she asked. "How do you have Owen?"

"Your parents are in Atlanta for the weekend, looking for a house there. Owen was staying with us."

"So Jeff did take that job."

"Yes. Have you not been in contact with them at all, Quinn?"

"Yeah, I Skype them every weekend." She held up her hand, gesturing around the room, at a wood-burning stove behind a long counter, and the fireplace at the other end. "Really, we barely have enough electricity here to keep the lights on. And most parts of this world don't even have that much. Where I live, we don't have electricity at all."

"Where you live? I thought you lived here."

"I don't. We're just visiting – for Ben and Linnea's wedding, actually – did you meet Linnea?"

"Yes. For a few minutes."

"Good – I guess. Anyway, it's turned into kind of a longer trip than we expected, but it's still just a visit."

He was silent for several seconds – not wanting to ask the question he had now. But eventually, he had to know the answer. It couldn't be any worse than what he was thinking, anyway.

"When you say *we're* just visiting, you mean…"

"I mean me and William." She paused, letting that sink in, and he dared the glance at her left hand he'd been avoiding. Although it wasn't as flashy as he would have expected to see inside a flipping *castle*, it was there. Two silver-and-gold braided bands on *that* finger.

"There are some other people who came with us," she was saying, "Ben and Marcus, namely – but that wasn't what you were asking, was it?"

His head felt like it was disconnected from his body as he moved it from side to side.

"You're married. You married *William Rose*."

"Yes."

"You *married* him."

"Yes, Zander. I married him. He's my husband."

"You're *sixteen*. That's not even old enough to get married."

"I'm seventeen. I had a birthday."

He knew that. He'd remembered the day, even – by shoving the heart necklace he'd bought for her into the back of his closet along with the memory card. Now, he noticed the sparkling gold of a new chain peeking out from the collar of her blouse. Probably a necklace from *William*.

"Seventeen is still not old enough."

"It is here. Sixteen is, actually."

Of course it was. Here in this weird world, why wouldn't it be? Heck, if one day in his world equaled ten here, that made seventeen like a hundred and seventy. Old enough to be married. Why not? "Does your mom know?"

"Yes. She was at my wedding."

"What about your dad?"

"Jeff wasn't here, no, but I assume my mom told him. She said she was going to."

"And Owen? Annie?" He was getting desperate.

"They were here, Zander. But even if they weren't – what does it matter? This isn't something you can argue me out of. It's done. I married him. A while ago, now, in this world's time."

Right. The time thing again. Quinn was a hundred and seventy, and she was married. He stood up, trying to take a deep breath, but it wasn't working – the air couldn't get past his throat.

Quinn was just looking at him; she was calm as could be, still eating the vegetables and waiting to see what his reaction was, he supposed. And this was too much.

Without even thinking about what he was doing, he stood and walked out of the room.

HISTORY

Rosewood Castle, Eirentheos

OF COURSE, THE second time he turned a corner, Zander realized his mistake. He was in a castle. An unfamiliar castle. And he was starting down a long, wood-paneled hallway he didn't recognize at all. He didn't know where he was, or what he was doing, and now he was lost.

Sighing, he slumped backward against a wall, though he had to be wary even in that gesture so he wouldn't bump into one of the little shelves inset in the paneling every few feet. The shelves each held a little oil-filled lamp – Quinn must have been serious about the lights.

He didn't understand this. None of this could be real – it wasn't even possible. Quinn married? To William Rose, who turned out to be not just a weird, reclusive kid, but a prince who came from a castle in an imaginary world? Just thinking about it was making him dizzy. He slid down to the floor, pulling his knees up to his chest and dropping his head into his hands, trying to breathe.

He wasn't sure how long he'd been there when he was startled by the sound of footsteps on the marble floor. Scrambling to his feet, he tried to make sure he was composed before looking to see who was coming – probably it was going to be a guard with a sword, coming to arrest him for trespassing where he didn't belong.

He was half correct. The figure was unfamiliar at first, because he was wearing black pants and anun-tucked white button-down shirt instead of the green tunic that made him recognizable, but after a few seconds, Zander realized who it was.

Ben came to a stop right in front of him. "Is everything all right?"

No. That was such an absurd question that he ignored it. "Did they send you here looking for me?"

"No. My wife and I were almost to the common room when I saw you leave and go in this direction. It looked like you might need a few minutes, so I took the long way around in following you."

That was … *nice.* Weird, but nice. Weren't guards supposed to chase down people who went where they didn't belong immediately? "Am I in trouble?"

"For what? Getting upset and needing a breather? If they beheaded people for that in this castle, we'd all be dead."

"I meant for taking off and coming somewhere I'm not supposed to be."

"King Stephen has declared you a guest, Sir Zander. He's not one for imposing undue restrictions on the activities of his guests."

"So, what? I can just go anywhere I want in the castle?"

Ben frowned. "His Majesty is rather protective of his family – the children in particular. I wouldn't go into their private quarters uninvited. And you will run into guards near the areas where he conducts his business. But," he glanced around them, "you're welcome to use the hallways in the guest areas however you need."

"Is that what this is? A guest area?"

"Indeed. Although these rooms are empty at the moment. The occupied guest rooms are in the next hall. I believe they're just about finished opening and preparing a room for you there."

"I thought they were putting me under guard – near you."

"They're putting you in one of the empty guest suites that happen to be near the ones my father and I are using at the moment, yes."

"Are you a *guest* here?"

Ben raised an eyebrow. "Yes, I suppose I am. I grew up in this castle – though I lived in a much different area, one reserved for the families of King Stephen's personal guards – but now, yes, I'm a guest here."

"Marrying the king's daughter upgraded you to guest?"

"No," Ben answered, frowning. "My new position as personal guard to the Queen moved me out of this castle. I'm a guest now because I don't live here anymore."

Zander's head was spinning again. He shouldn't have asked. "The king and queen live in different places?" He wondered how they'd managed to have so many children.

But Ben looked very confused. He stared at Zander for several seconds before his expression shifted into one of understanding. "Oh," he said, "you don't know."

"There is, apparently, an entire *world* of stuff I don't know tonight, Ben. Which thing do I not know at this moment?"

"I'm sorry. It isn't my place to get involved in these matters."

"Well, then, don't. I don't want you to get beheaded by your queen or something on my account."

Ben's stoic façade slipped for just a second, and Zander saw the corner of his lip twitch. "I'm in no danger of that. Her Majesty has yet to order anyone beheaded, not even the one man I'd personally like to stand over while his head is on the block."

He swallowed. He'd only met Ben this evening, but the idea of him wanting to behead someone surprised – and frightened – him.

"Well, whatever your 'Majesty' would do to you, don't let it be on my account."

Unexpectedly, Ben cracked a grin. "I doubt she'd even be upset at me, to be honest. I know her well enough to know she'd probably appreciate my taking the burden of explaining things off her shoulders – she's had enough to deal with tonight and recently. It's merely that I rather thought Prince Owen would have told you about this one."

"Yeah, well, *Prince* Owen didn't even tell me where we were coming, so…"

"And yet you came with him."

"He said Quinn was in trouble."

"Yes." Ben was studying him intently. "You care about her."

His shoulders stiffened. "What's it to you?"

"I care about her, too – not in the way that you think you still do – I don't have romantic feelings for her, but I care very much for Quinn as my friend, my sister…and as my *queen*."

"Excuse me?"

"You heard me correctly, Zander. We both know that. I serve as personal guard to Her Majesty, Quinn Katriel Rose, Queen of Philotheum."

Zander was glad he was still standing close enough to the wall to lean against it for support. The name didn't sound right, but it was obvious enough what Ben was trying to tell him. "Quinn is the Queen? *My* Quinn?"

Ben's eyebrow went up again. "The only Quinn here."

"Is the *queen* of this … wherever we are?"

"No. Not of this kingdom. She is the queen of Philotheum. It's a different kingdom than the one we're in right now."

"Is that why she married William? So she could be a queen?"

The look Ben gave him then made him want to crawl into a hole. "I'm going to remember that you're upset and disoriented, so I'll ignore your tone – this once. And then I will ask you to remember you are speaking of my queen and my king, both of whom I love and respect."

Zander swallowed and nodded.

"The answer to your real question is no. King William was a fourth-born prince and as such, is only king by virtue of his marriage – not the other way around. And while we're at it – no – he married her because he loves her. Queen Quinn's real father was from our world, he was the first-born son of King Jonathan, and the true heir to the throne of Philotheum. When Her Majesty discovered this world, she also learned the truth about herself – that when her father died, she became the new heir. It wasn't easy for her, for many reasons, but eventually she chose to accept her place and her throne."

"This is for real."

"Yes, it's very real. I'm sure you must have trouble understanding it."

"Trouble – yeah. That's one word for it, I suppose." His voice was starting to sound faraway and small, even to him.

Ben cast him a sympathetic glance, which felt even stranger. "I would think you've had enough new information for one evening. I could escort you to your room if you'd like."

"Why are you being so nice to me?" Zander wondered as he followed Ben through the twists and turns of the hallways. They didn't need to worry about guarding him – there was no way he'd be able to navigate this place by himself.

"Why shouldn't I be kind to you? I don't know what issues you may have had with Her Majesty in the past, but here, to me, you're the man who saved my king's life, and possibly mine."

A *man* – nobody had ever called Zander that before – not in a meaningful way as Ben just had.

"Was William really exposed to rabies?"

"Yes. Quite severely. You can't imagine what he and the queen – and the rest of us – have been through in the last few days. His little sister – Princess Alice – was bitten by the rabid fox as well, but we had enough of the medicine left for one person."

Ouch. "Who had to decide *that*?"

"There wasn't really a discussion about it. It all happened quite quickly. We knew William and Alice had both been bitten badly, but they were treating the little girl first. Nathaniel and William gave her some medicine to put her to sleep so they wouldn't hurt her. Then … I don't even know if I realized when William disappeared for a few minutes, but by the time the rest of us understood that there was only enough medicine for one person, William had already given her the first dose."

"He knew."

"Yes, he knew exactly what he was doing. He and Nathaniel and another healer here have been working frantically to make a batch of medicine, and they've been optimistic about it, but it's still possible the medicine they've been making either won't work, or won't be safe, or won't be ready on time."

"Wait. How did William know how to give it to her?"

Ben looked confused again. "Because he's a healer."

"Pardon?"

"You say doctor in your world, I'm sorry. The term is becoming more widely used here as well – because of Nathaniel and William."

Zander rubbed at his temples with his fingers. "I suppose in this world he's old enough to be a real healer or whatever, right?"

"Yes, although only just. However, William has always been so talented at healing that he's been working at it for much longer than is typical. I think he was still really a child when Nathaniel began allowing him to assist with real duties in the clinic."

Fantastic. William Rose was a king and a *doctor*, and the kind of guy who would sacrifice his own life for his little sister. He probably rode around the kingdom on a talking unicorn that pooped rainbows, too. So much for any fantasies Zander might have been entertaining about showing Quinn that he was a better guy than William and that she'd made the wrong choice.

"What do you mean I possibly saved *your* life?" he asked, ready to change the subject.

Ben took a few more steps down the hall and then stopped and turned around, pushing up one of his loose sleeves to reveal a large, thick piece of gauze taped to the side of his forearm. "I got a scratch on my arm when I killed the fox – we were never sure that it actually came from the fox, but William and Nathaniel both say they consider it an exposure. Will just gave me a ridiculous amount of the medicine you brought."

Somewhere in the conversation, the guard's formal speech had disappeared completely – "His Majesty" had been replaced by an affectionate nickname. This man was clearly more than just a guard to William and Quinn. "I'm sorry. I've had that stuff before; it's not very fun."

"One moon ago, I was lucky enough to marry the most amazing, beautiful woman in the entire world. I never thought I'd be so lucky. I'd smile and accept a hundred shots if it meant not being ripped away from her. I think it's a reasonable trade."

Zander swallowed hard.

Rather than continuing down the hall, Ben opened the nearest door. "We are all forever in your debt," he said, before stepping inside.

"I didn't really do anything," Zander said, following Ben into the room. "It was all Owen."

Ben turned around and looked at him. "Would Owen have been able to come here tonight without your help?"

"No – but I'm sure his mother would have brought him here if he'd told her what was going on. She'll be home in two days."

"Two days in your world – twenty days in ours. Too late for us."

Right. He would never understand – or even believe, probably – that time thing.

"Anyway, thank you for being willing to listen to Prince Owen and help him, even though you couldn't have understood where he was taking you. Not many people would have done that."

"I think I might have done it for selfish reasons," Zander admitted.

"My father has always said that the reason you do something is not as important as what you actually do – if you do the right thing, it's still the right thing, no matter why you did it, and doing wrong is wrong, even if you believe your reason is good. Tonight, you trusted a little boy who deserved your trust, and you helped him when he needed to be helped. That was the right thing. In the process, you likely saved at least one life. *Why* you did it doesn't really matter."

"I'm certainly paying the consequences for it, regardless," he answered, looking around at what appeared to be a well-appointed living room, replete with overstuffed couches, dark wood tables, and heavy brocaded curtains.

"You'd have paid some consequences either way. Perhaps there's a reason you were there to answer Owen's need today."

Zander was reminded again of his conversation with the old man at the river, and he shuddered. "I don't need to think about that right now, do I?"

"No." Ben was smiling again.

Zander wasn't sure if he was actually starting to calm down, or just go into shock from the events of the evening, but he was a lot more comfortable with Ben than he been all evening. At least he wasn't worried that the guard was going to start yelling at him – or touching him.

"This is your room – there's a bedroom through there," Ben pointed at a partially open door, "and a washroom in there as well. It should be stocked with everything you need for the night. It looks like someone has brought up some clothes as well."

There was a wicker basket on one of the low tables, filled to the top with clothing – it was all unfamiliar, but Zander guessed there was probably something in there that would fit well enough. A taller table near the window held a metal pitcher and two glasses, along with a bowl of what he assumed was fruit – it looked like there were apples in there, anyway, even if their bright pink color was a bit surprising.

"If you'd like some privacy, I can let the staff know that you'd prefer not to be disturbed again tonight."

He nodded.

Ben already had the door halfway open when Zander turned to him again. "Hey Ben?"

"Yes?"

"Even though you probably don't feel like it, I would suggest moving around as much as possible before you go to bed."

"Excuse me?"

"When I was fourteen and I had those shots, my dad wouldn't even let me relax for a minute after we got home. He made me lift weights in the basement and then go for a run with him. I was so mad at first – but he was right. A couple days later, when we had to get our next shots, Quinn and her friend Abigail were still sore, but I'd never had any problems."

Ben nodded. "Did you tell Quinn – at the time?"

"Yeah, actually. I talked her into going on a walk down by the river after that second one; we spent an hour throwing the heaviest rocks we could find into it, and then I think we went wading or something. Neither one of us got sore after that. After the third one, we went bowling." He found himself smiling at the memory.

"Bowling?"

"Yeah. It's a sport in my world – throwing heavy balls at pins and trying to knock them down."

"We have something similar here, if it's what I'm picturing. Did the other girl go with you?"

Zander chuckled, shaking his head. "If you'd met Abigail, you wouldn't need to ask that question."

Ben's laugh surprised him – it was deep and rich, betraying an entirely different side to the serious guard. "We have girls like that here, too."

"I'd bet they exist everywhere."

"Probably. Are you all right?"

"Uh, I suppose I'm as good as I'm going to get right now."

"Okay, then. I'm sure I'll talk to you again in the morning."

Once Ben was gone, Zander knew he'd been lying; he wasn't even close to all right. Here he was stuck in this strange world where Quinn was a queen, and married to William Rose, and now he had these memories flooding back.

He wondered if Quinn remembered all of it. Probably not; until just a few minutes ago, Zander had forgotten nearly all of the details himself. It was all there now, though – his family and Quinn's packing into Dr. Rose's office for the second round of shots. Their siblings had been so little then – two babies and two preschoolers, one with autism. Owen had suffered an epic meltdown before they even got inside. Back in those days, Owen hadn't even been verbal, he remembered. There was no real explaining to him that the second time wouldn't be nearly as bad as the first.

Zander's sister, Ashley, who was a year younger than Owen, had made it to the waiting room before she was a lost cause.

He and Quinn had been on their own when Doctor Rose offered to take them back first. He didn't remember where Abigail was – her parents must have taken her in at a different time. They'd been – inexplicably – angry about their children being exposed to rabies while staying at the cabin with the rest of them. It wasn't like someone had let the bat in on purpose.

Quinn had been terrified. Zander hadn't been giving her advice when he'd told her about the exercise thing; he'd been trying to calm her down, to get some color back into her chalk-white cheeks. He'd talked to her the whole time she was getting the shot, actually, and it had worked – she'd barely flinched when it happened. After it was over, they'd escaped the rest of the craziness and gone down to the river. It had been nice.

Even though she had to know by then it wasn't a big deal, the crazy girl had still been scared for the third dose. That time, she'd let him hold her hand while distracting her with outrageous ideas about where they would go afterwards. The outcome — bowling — might not have been outrageous, but it had been a whole lot of fun. She'd beaten him rather soundly. He'd teased her about letting her win — but that wasn't entirely true. He'd promised her a rematch a week later, when they had to get their fourth shots.

Except that had never happened. That was the memory clouding his heart now.

Sometime that week, Adam had called him, so excited Zander was afraid he might wet himself. They'd both been invited to a pool party at Damian Dirkshaw's house. Damian was a senior and the quarterback of the football team at the high school. There would be upperclassmen there. And cheerleaders. It had seemed like a big deal at the time. In the world of a fourteen-year-old boy about to enter high school, it *had* been a big deal.

He couldn't take an eighth-grade girl. Or at least that's what he'd told himself.

He could have told her, though. Sometime before they were walking into the clinic.

But he hadn't.

When he'd finally told her, she'd shrugged, and she'd teased him that he just didn't want to lose to her in bowling again.

But she'd walked to that back room with Doctor Rose alone and closed the door behind her.

And when he showed up for the final shot a week later, he learned that she'd already been there earlier in the day.

A few days after that, high school had started. For the first time since kindergarten, Quinn hadn't even been in the same building with him. She was back at Bristlecone K-8, and he had a whole new life – new classes, new friends, parties on the weekend, and football. It had taken him three and a half years and completely forgetting about the whole incident to ask her to that dance.

On second thought, maybe she did remember it. Maybe this time she'd gotten out before Zander could treat her like that again. At least she'd been fair and talked to him – he hadn't been left waiting for her when she'd decided to run off to a new life.

He didn't know much about William Rose, but something told him William would have chosen a scared friend over a party with cheerleaders.

BLOOM

Rosewood Castle, Eirentheos

"THAT WENT WELL." Quinn turned to see Thomas standing there, holding the promised tray of food.

"Yeah," she chuckled. "You and I might define that word somewhat differently."

He set the tray on the table in front of her, and handed her the plate. "There was no yelling and no tears. I call that a win."

"I think there was almost yelling – I'm pretty sure there would have been some if he hadn't stormed out."

"We might have to be happy with what we can get at this point."

"Yeah." She smiled. "What would I do without you Thomas?"

"You seem to have been managing just fine without me in Philotheum."

She studied him for a minute; he was grinning, but… "That's really hard on you, isn't it?"

"It was a joke, Quinn."

"No, it wasn't. Not underneath, anyway."

The grin faded – not all the way, but he was more serious now. "You did take yourself and my brother five days away from me, and now you're back for my twin."

"We miss you too, you know."

"You have your lives there – you and Will have each other, and now the baby. Linnea has Ben…"

"And you think you're losing Mia."

He raised an eyebrow. "Have you been talking to Linnea?"

"No. I don't know what Linnea knows – we'll talk about our own issues, but if you think your sister would gossip about you, you're wrong. I've seen it, Thomas. The distance between the two of you. I can't figure out what's causing it, but…"

"But it's obvious enough that everyone sees it, not just me."

"I don't know about that. I've seen Mia more than most the last few days – and you less than I would have expected when she's spending so much time with the baby."

"It's not about that, Quinn. I don't begrudge her – or you – that time."

"I know that. It's not about the time at all, is it?"

He shook his head.

"Do you think it's because she knows that your heart isn't really here in Eirentheos, anymore?"

Thomas frowned – almost convincingly. "This is my home. Where else would my heart be?"

Now it was her turn to raise an eyebrow.

"I'm still underage. Even if I did want to be somewhere else, I'm not old enough. And I'm needed here. My parents are already sending two of their children to Philotheum."

"I was underage in my world – I'd *still* be underage there. My parents weren't ready to lose me. Neither were Annie and Owen – but it wasn't about them."

"That's different. You were the heir. You left to assume your throne. If I entertain thoughts sometimes about going to Philotheum to be with you and William – it's only that, *thoughts*. I'm sure it's the same thing Linnea felt for all of the cycles I was allowed to go with Will sometimes to your world and to travel around Eirentheos with him and Nathaniel. I'm just jealous of your adventures without me."

"Technically underage or no, Thomas – you're not a child anymore. It's not the same."

Thomas was silent for several seconds – in other circumstances she might have teased him about it being a first.

"I just think it's something worth discussing with your parents," she said, "and it's definitely a topic you need to bring up with Mia."

"Speaking of whom," Thomas said, looking over Quinn's shoulder.

She turned to see Mia standing in the doorway across the room, holding Samuel. The baby wasn't crying, but even from where she was, Quinn could see his hands and head moving as he searched for his next meal. She smiled and stood.

"We're not finished with this conversation, Thomas."

"I didn't imagine we were," he said wryly.

"I'm going to take him back to my room. Could you please bring Owen to me in a few minutes – just Owen?"

"Sure."

She knew she'd asked for a few minutes, and that Thomas was probably intentionally giving her time to get Samuel fed, changed, and comfortable, but Quinn was starting to get impatient waiting for him to bring Owen. She was so excited now that she was pacing back and forth in the sitting room, cradling the baby to her chest.

Owen was going to get to meet Samuel. It had broken her heart to worry that it would never happen – that her son would never get to meet his beloved uncle, that she'd never be able to share this tiny miracle with anyone from her family.

She had to blink back a few tears at the thought that her mom wasn't here, or Annie, or Jeff. But at least Owen was. Owen would get to see and hold Samuel – she was definitely going to need a handkerchief. She stepped into the bedroom to retrieve one, all the while wishing she had a camera.

Her hand was in the drawer, reaching for a handkerchief, when the knock came. It startled her so badly she accidentally pulled the drawer out too far, and then had to catch it, nearly hitting the baby's foot in the process. Heart pounding, she pushed it shut, very narrowly missing closing her finger inside.

"Quinn?" Thomas called. "Are you ready?"

"Yeah, come in."

She made it back into the sitting room at almost the same second Thomas led Owen inside – with no handkerchief to use on the tears that welled up the second Owen's mouth fell open.

"Hey buddy," she said, noting that her voice didn't sound as shaky as it felt. "I have someone here I'd like you to meet."

The door clicked quietly shut as Thomas disappeared, leaving the two – the three – of them alone in the room.

"Is this…" Owen breathed.

Quinn carried the baby over to the couch and sat down with him, patting the cushion beside her. Owen climbed up.

"Yes, Owen. This is my little boy. Your nephew. You're an uncle."

"Wow."

She scooted closer to Owen and tucked him under her arm, snuggling with him and the baby at the same time, leaning down to bury her nose in her little brother's hair and kiss the top of his head.

Owen's grin took up nearly his whole face as he leaned in closer, holding his hand hesitantly over the baby.

"You can touch him. It's fine."

Ever so gently, he ran the back of his finger over the infant's hair and down the side of one cheek. Samuel stirred and opened his eyes.

Quinn held her breath, but the baby didn't fuss. Instead, he blinked and – she swore – looked right at Owen. For a long time, the two of them just stared at each other, each checking the other one out.

"He likes you," she said.

"I love him."

"Would you like to hold him?"

Owen nodded vigorously, but he wiggled away from her, sliding down to the floor. "Wait a second." He opened one of the pockets on his cargo pants and pulled out a little black zippered case.

Quinn frowned, not understanding, but a second later she gasped as Owen unzipped the case and withdrew a small digital camera.

"Where did you get that?"

"Dad bought it for me as a present when he came home. I had to bring it – I just knew there would be something I wanted to take pictures of."

Quinn's throat suddenly felt very thick. She didn't have any pictures of the baby. An artist had already been commissioned to do a painting of him – and one of the three of them, the new royal family, when they returned to Philotheum – and a few of the more artistically inclined members of William's family, including William himself, had made some very nice sketches, but there were no photographs of him.

"You'll be able to show Mom and Dad."

Owen nodded. "I have a little photo printer, too, and some paper for it. It has a rechargeable battery. I didn't know if you'd be here in Eirentheos or not, but I brought it just in case. I thought William or Nathaniel could maybe help me find a way to plug it in here at the castle so I could give you some pictures. I brought some pictures I already printed at home, of me and Annie and Mom and Dad."

She was really wishing she'd managed to bring a handkerchief out here now – she had to settle for the extra diaper she was using as a burp cloth.

The bright flash made her flinch again – it was surprisingly powerful for such a tiny camera, but again, Samuel wasn't fazed. He was still watching everything Owen did as if he was interested in him.

After Owen had snapped half a dozen photos of both Samuel and Quinn, he was finally ready to sit down and hold the baby. He settled himself carefully against the pillows, putting his legs out and positioning his arms precisely the way Quinn told him to as she set the baby gently into them.

"He's so beautiful," Owen said, clearly in awe.

"I think he looks a little like you."

Owen smiled, leaning over to plant the softest kiss on Samuel's forehead before resuming staring into his eyes.

After a moment, though, his expression clouded.

"You don't think he'll *be* like me do you – if he looks like me?"

Her heart jumped into her throat and her eyes felt hot and prickly. "Owen..."

"Actually, we hope he's very much like you." Quinn jumped at William's voice from behind them.

"I'm sorry love," William said, walking around the couch and putting his hand on her shoulder. "I came in quietly, in case the baby was asleep, and then … I didn't want to interrupt, but…" He turned to Owen, kneeling by the couch so the two of them were eye level. "We love you so much, Owen – you're exactly who you're supposed to be. And if Samuel grows up to be even half as loving and smart and wonderful as you, we will be as proud of him as we are of you."

"William is right, Owen," she said, wrapping her arm around his shoulders again. "There's nothing about you I wish was different – *nothing.*"

"What about when I'm upset and you can't calm me down?"

"It makes me sad when you're scared or you're hurting and you don't know how to tell me and I don't know how to help, Owen, but it doesn't make me not love you or wish you weren't who you are. And it will be the same with Samuel, whoever he grows up to be. Okay?"

"Okay."

They were all quiet for a moment, watching Owen and the baby look at each other.

"Is that his name, Samuel?" Owen asked.

"He hasn't officially had his Naming Ceremony yet, so we can't just call him by his name in front of everyone, but yes, his name is going to be Samuel."

"Like your real father?"

"Yes."

"He's going to be a king someday."

"He is. And do you know what his middle name will be?"

"What?"

"Owen."

The little boy's eyes widened as he looked back and forth between William and Quinn.

"Yeah, buddy. We really do love you that much. We really do want him to be just like you." Quinn kissed his head again. "Do you want to show William what you brought?"

Owen and Will were both so excited about the camera that the discussion was forgotten quickly. They probably snapped a hundred pictures – some of them of just Samuel, but plenty of Owen holding Samuel and Quinn holding him, too.

William still didn't want to touch the baby for another twenty-four hours, and although she didn't agree with him, she was able to let that go. He was meeting her halfway and was touching her, at least. Maybe someday she'd find a way to convince Owen he wasn't the only one who needed special care sometimes.

Yesterday, she'd almost been convinced that she was never going to be this happy again. And now, William was going to be okay, and Owen was here, meeting Samuel, taking pictures they'd get to keep and share – there were very few ways it could get better than this, and she was deliberately choosing not to think of them.

Nearly an hour later, there was a knock at the door, and William opened it to reveal both Thomas and Linnea.

They, too, were fascinated with the camera. Linnea had never seen anything like it, and she had to spend several minutes trying it out, taking pictures of everyone, but especially of Samuel, fast asleep in Owen's arms. Once the novelty finally wore off, Thomas turned to Owen.

"Did you pack any pajamas in that magic bag of yours, or just fancy toys?"

"I didn't bring pajamas – or clothes," the little boy admitted, as Quinn took the baby from him.

Linnea laughed. "I wonder if any of the clothes you wore last time even still fit you. I think you've grown four inches."

"Well, I am an uncle now." Owen was so proud, Quinn thought her heart might burst from seeing the joy on his face.

"And a mighty fine one, from the looks of it," Thomas said, smiling at the sleeping infant. "He's lucky to have you."

Owen beamed.

"But I think we should let him sleep, and let William and your sister get some rest, too." Thomas put his hand on Owen's shoulder. "Let's go look and see if we can find you some pajamas and things for the night okay?"

"Okay."

William gave him a hug, and Quinn, whose arms were full of baby, kissed him on the top of his head, then whispered "I love you" in his ear. Even knowing she'd see him in the morning, and that he'd be here for the next ten days, it was hard to watch him walk out the door with Linnea and Thomas.

Once the door was closed behind them, William put his arm on her shoulder and squeezed it gently. "Are you all right, love?"

"Yeah," she whispered. The baby stirred a little, and she hurried to carry him into the bedroom and set him ever-so-carefully into the cradle. His little head moved back and forth, and his eyelids fluttered, but after a tense, silent moment, they stayed closed, and he sighed, deep in whatever kind of dreams babies had.

"That was close," William whispered as they left the bedroom, closing the door behind them as softly as possible.

"We'll be lucky if we get fifteen minutes, but…"

"But I get a little bit of time alone with you." He moved behind her and pulled at the clip in her hair, letting the tresses fall around her face. She hadn't even seen him get the brush, but he had it, and he started brushing, gently tugging the tangles out.

"That feels so good," she said, relaxing into his touch, relishing peace for the first time in days.

"I'm sorry I haven't been here to do it the last couple of nights." Setting the brush down, he swept her hair over her shoulder and then lightly massaged her neck for a minute before resting his chin on her shoulder and wrapping his arms around her waist.

She put her hands over his, though she was careful to avoid the spot where his shirt hid the bandaged-over bite. "How are you feeling?"

"I'm all right. That bite is on fire, and I'm sore everywhere else you stuck me, but it'll be fine."

She rubbed his unbitten lower arm gently – he hadn't had any shots there, at least. "How are Ben and the girls?"

"Ben's fine. Relieved. Emma hates me. She wants to trade me in for a different brother."

Quinn chuckled. "I'd have felt the same way when I was eight."

"Me too. You're lucky I don't know what I would do without you, or I might feel the same way *now*. Alice was awfully sweet, though. I felt so bad going to her with a needle for the second time in one night – but she spent half the time reassuring me, and then she gave me a big hug afterwards. We need to go to the next market day – I'm out of candy."

She giggled. "Did you see what else Owen had in his pockets tonight?" she asked, pointing to the coffee table.

He gasped when he saw it – a small package of Skittles candy from the other world; those had always been his favorite.

"He didn't say anything, he just set it there, but I know what it's for." She brought his fingers to her lips and kissed them.

"I love that kid so much it hurts my heart."

"I love that you do. I just want to hold him right now and never let him go home. I won't do that, but…"

"But it sure would be nice if he never had to leave." He squeezed her hand. "How does he *know*?"

"I don't know. I don't think we'll ever know. I think we're probably not supposed to. It just…*is*."

He nodded, nestling his head next to hers, holding her for a long time before he spoke again. "Are we okay, Quinn? I'm so sorry. I love you – I never meant to hurt you like that. I don't know what got into me…"

She turned around in his arms so she could see him, look into his eyes. "Yes, we're okay. I know what got into you. You're my Will. It's who you are and how you handle things sometimes. *I'm* sorry for taking it so personally, and for letting you get away with it for so long, instead of coming and knocking some sense into you."

He laughed, and it sounded so wonderful; the deep rumbling in his chest reverberated through hers, calming and filling the empty places inside of her. "We'll get better at this, won't we?" he asked.

"We've got a lifetime to practice – now that neither one of us is going anywhere."

Just as he was kissing her forehead, a loud cry came from the other side of the bedroom door.

"We'll get better at *that* one too," he chuckled, following her in to retrieve the baby.

"You are on diaper duty for the next week after that medication kicks in," she said, as she picked up Samuel and smelled what had wakened him.

"For the next *moon*," he agreed. "And I'll take him after the first morning feeding so you can go back to sleep for two hours if you want."

"As soon as he goes longer than twenty minutes after that feeding to be hungry again, that might work."

BEN

Rosewood Castle, Eirentheos

ZANDER HAD BEEN certain he would never be able to sleep in this strange room in a castle in another world. But he'd been wrong. For a long time after Ben left, he'd wandered around the guest suite, examining the intricate wood of the furnishings, opening and closing empty cabinets, digging through the basket of clothes, searching for something that seemed familiar, and finally getting hungry enough to sample the fruit. The apples had tasted like apples, thank goodness.

Eventually, he'd tried the bathtub, rather surprised to discover that there was hot running water. He wondered how they pulled that off, when Quinn had told him they didn't even have electricity in most of this world.

He could see she wasn't kidding. Although there had been electric lights in the room where he'd talked to her, the "guest suite" he was staying in was lit with some kind of gas lamps he'd had to extinguish before going to bed. Apparently some parts of the castle had been retrofitted for electricity, but others hadn't.

He'd thought about it the whole time he was taking a bath, actually, finally shaking his head at himself when he realized he was entirely too interested in a topic that didn't concern him at all. Who cared how they got hot water up here, as long as he was able to take a bath in it?

At home, he didn't always wear pajamas, but he thought it was probably a good idea to adopt the practice while he was here – someone might just decide to come in through the unlocked door at any time. In the basket, he found two pairs of pajamas that were startlingly like something he might have been able to buy at home – if he'd been into conservative two-piece pajama sets.

Finally, once he was clean and dressed, there'd been nothing left to do besides check out the large four-poster bed.

It had been unbelievably soft and comfortable – all down comforters and soft sheets, and cozy pillows. The lack of sleep from the night before combined with the most stressful day of his life and the soft bed … he didn't remember anything after settling under the blankets.

He had no idea what time it was when he awoke, but it wasn't early. Pulling open the heavy curtains revealed a bright, sunny morning. If waking up in a room in a castle wasn't enough of a reminder of yesterday's strange events, the view from his window would have done it.

His window faced what must have been the back of the castle; it looked out over an expansive garden with rows and rows of vegetables and beyond that an orchard. The trees confused him though; their leaves were reds and browns, and most had fallen to the ground below. Were seasons different here, too? At home, it was mid-spring.

He looked closer. The bushes that lined the wall on the outskirts of the vegetable patches were familiar-looking – yes, they were rose bushes. His mother had several of those at home. The ones in his front yard were beginning to leaf, and in the last week, he'd even seen a few buds.

These ones were growing fallow. What few flowers were left had turned brown and crunchy; there were dried petals all over the ground underneath them. Most of them had actually been pruned all the way down, and now there were only rose canes, ready to survive a winter before coming to life again in the spring.

It was late fall – or this world's version of it, anyway.

In the distance, beyond the gardens, a high stone wall surrounded the castle, and just beyond that he saw the pointed roof of what he assumed was some kind of guard tower.

No, there was no chance he was escaping this place.

Not that he would have tried. A full night of sleep had brought him some clarity. If the gate was really closed for ten days – and he didn't have any reason to mistrust Owen or Quinn on that point – then trying to escape a *castle* and then survive on his own in a strange world for ten days was akin to suicide.

Besides, he didn't know exactly when the gate opened again, or even how to find it. As much as it pained him, he was just going to have to trust these people until then.

The morning had brought him some clarity about Quinn, too. Now that he knew a little more about it, it was hard to be quite as mad about the way things had gone between them in Bristlecone.

He was still pretty edgy about the fact that she was married to William Rose – there was just no way he could have prepared for that kind of news – but he understood the lying a little bit more. There was nothing she could have told him about where she'd gone that would have worked out well. Either he wouldn't have believed her, or – perhaps worse – if he had…

At any rate, some things made a lot more sense now. That weird injury on her arm, when she'd showed up one day with stitches, and then three days later it was mostly healed – she must have come to this world twice in that time.

He wondered when she'd found out about her real father. All of this explained why she'd been acting so weird, and why her mother had, too.

He didn't really want to think about what it would be like for him when he went home. There was nobody there he could explain this to. At least he probably wasn't going to be charged with kidnapping Owen. If they really did get back after just one night, anyway.

After dressing in the strange clothes – he wondered if the loose shirt with a drawstring neck might be one of Ben's, it was very similar to the one the guard had been wearing last night – Zander wasn't entirely sure what to do with himself. He wanted to talk to Quinn again, but he had no idea where to find her. Should he stay in the room and wait for someone to find him?

That idea wasn't very appealing. Ben had told him he was free to wander the guest areas of the castle. Now that he had resigned himself to staying here for ten days, the idea of being in a real castle was actually intriguing. He realized he wouldn't mind knowing more about the place.

Grabbing another apple from the bowl on the table, he decided to go exploring.

He'd only just opened the door when he heard voices in the hallway. The shock nearly made him slam the door closed again, but he didn't. He took a breath and then braved it, stepping outside of his room.

"Zander, you're awake."

He hadn't expected to find Quinn so easily, but there she was, standing in the hallway, only a few feet away from him, chatting with Ben, Thomas, that girl Linnea, Owen, and William.

"We were just debating if we should knock," William said.

But Zander didn't really comprehend anything, because he was staring at Quinn's arms.

That was a *baby*. The bundle of green blankets cradled in her arms was wiggling. There was definitely a baby in there.

Why was Quinn holding a baby?

There wasn't any way … it couldn't possibly…

But as he watched, the baby fussed, and Quinn shifted it up onto her shoulder, making shushing noises in its ear and kissing its thick tuft of black hair – the same color as William's.

"Zander!" Owen called. "Did you know I'm an uncle now?" The little boy laid his hand on the bundle, beaming with pride.

William hovered protectively over the little group, his back straight, his eyes scrutinizing Zander closely, waiting for his reaction.

"You have a *baby?*" He was sure he wasn't disappointing those who were waiting for the show, but he didn't care. Finding out that Quinn lived in an alternate world was bad enough … learning that she'd *married* William Rose at seventeen was … but a *baby?* It hadn't even been two months since she'd broken up with him.

"Yes, Zander," Quinn said quietly. "This is our son. Mine and William's." As she spoke, William's arm curled all the way around her waist.

"Is *that* why you married him?"

The words were barely out of his mouth when he knew he'd made a mistake. Nobody said a word. William closed his eyes, and Zander could see his chest rising and falling as he kissed the top of Quinn's head, the arm around her waist pulling her tightly to him.

Ben, however, separated himself from the group and moved to his side so fluidly and silently that Zander almost didn't see it happen.

"Let's take a walk," the guard said.

There was nothing threatening about Ben's tone, but Zander didn't for one second consider ignoring him.

He almost had to run to keep up as Ben led him through a maze of hallways, down three flights of stairs, and through more hallways. Finally, they went through a doorway that led into an odd sort of outdoor hallway. There were stone walls and a stone ceiling, but none of the numerous windows had glass. When they exited this hallway, they were in some kind of walled-in yard. The ground here was packed dirt.

They were alone.

Zander's heart thudded when Ben turned to him. He was dressed in casual clothes, and he wasn't carrying his sword, but Zander suspected he was probably still somehow armed. And even if he wasn't … no amount of playing running back could have equipped him to take on Ben.

His fear only grew when Ben didn't speak for almost a full minute.

By the time he did, Zander's hands were so slippery he was having a hard time holding on to the apple he was still carrying.

"That was the second time."

The apple hit the ground with a *thud.*

"I don't know what things are like in your world, Zander. Her Majesty has tried to tell me about some of the differences, and I understand you live somewhere where there are no kings and queens. But here, insulting my queen – implying what you just did against her character – that's very serious."

"I didn't mean…"

"I hope you didn't. The prince is the legitimate child of King William and Queen Quinn, conceived after their marriage. He is the much-anticipated heir to the throne of Philotheum, and the proof of the strength of our alliance with Eirentheos."

"I'm sorry." He didn't understand half of what Ben was saying, but he got the message.

Ben stared at him for another long moment before finally nodding. "Come."

Zander was perplexed – and still nervous – as he followed the guard across the dirt yard and through a set of double doors that led into a very large room. The floor here was still tightly packed dirt, but they were inside. He wondered what the guard was going to do to him in here.

At first, he couldn't understand the purpose of the room. There were bales of hay stacked all along one wall, and wooden crates full of various – odd – things stacked on shelves along another. He saw a crate full of strange metal balls, another with what looked like dull swords – were those knives in a third?

It wasn't until he looked into the corner and saw an enormous box filled with leather balls that it began to dawn on him that this was some kind of gym.

Ben was already pulling out a wooden crate and carrying it to some kind of platform in the middle of the floor on one side of the room. The why-are-you-just-standing-there look that Ben shot him sent Zander jogging over to join him.

The crate was filled with what looked like long metal cylinders in varying sizes. Zander had no idea what any of it was for, or how it worked. Ben didn't explain anything to him; he worked without speaking to set up the cylinders on the platform.

The platform was about two feet off the ground. Ben stood two of the longest cylinders up on either end of it. These cylinders each had a piece of metal protruding out to the side, turned toward the center, and a second later, Zander saw why. Ben balanced a square-shaped bar on those protrusions, making an H shape.

Then, he took the smaller cylinders – five of them in all – and arranged them in a pattern, one in the center, and the other four flaring out to the side, like a triangle missing one side.

"What are you doing?" Zander finally asked.

"I thought maybe we'd play a game. Our version of what you were telling me about last night."

A game? All of this and now they were going to play a game? What had he told Ben about last night? "Bowling?" he asked, remembering.

Ben shrugged.

"This doesn't look *anything* like bowling." Maybe the arrangement of the cylinders, but not really.

"Well, it's not your world. Maybe it's not anything like your sport. This is what we call bar drop."

That was … *original*, Zander thought, thinking he could see the object of the game. "How do you play?"

Ben walked to the other side of the gym and came back with two leather balls. They were small – bigger than softballs, but not by much. Just large enough that they'd be really awkward to throw with one hand.

Ben handed one to him. It was surprisingly heavy for such a small ball.

"Now we throw it at the…"

"Pegs." Ben nodded. "But carefully. You get five points for every peg you knock to the ground, but zero if you drop the bar that's hanging there."

He frowned. "If it drops at all?"

"No, only if it drops to the ground. If it drops and stays on the platform you lose ten points."

It sounded easy enough, but it wasn't. They had to stand behind a line several feet back from the platform. The balls were just large and heavy enough to be too awkward to throw with one hand, and throwing with two made it difficult to aim only for the pegs. On his first throw, Zander hit the bar hard enough to knock the two sides of it down, and sent the whole thing crashing to the ground.

"So what were you hoping to accomplish with that remark to Quinn, anyway?" Ben asked as he reset the pegs.

It wasn't "Her Majesty" now – it was Quinn. He almost commented on it, but quickly decided not to. "I don't know if I was trying to *accomplish* anything. I was shocked."

"You were angry."

Zander watched as Ben carried the ball back behind the line and drew it back to his chest with both hands, and then threw it in a perfectly straight line, sending it right under the bar, knocking all of the pegs to the ground without disrupting the frame. Twenty-five points.

"All right. Yes, I was angry." This time, he went to reset the pegs himself. "Wouldn't you be angry if a girl broke up with you, and then two months later you found out she had a baby with someone else?" The bar wouldn't stay balanced on the top of the frame for him. He knocked down the whole thing twice before he stepped back and allowed Ben to do it.

The bar didn't move an inch when Ben placed it. He made it look effortless.

"I courted a girl a couple of cycles ago, Mila. She was – is – the daughter of one of the other castle guards. We were friends for a long time and then… Anyway, I could see all of it, asking her to marry me, a wedding, all of it was there in my head. I was getting close to speaking to her father about it."

While he talked, he demonstrated for Zander the correct way to hold the ball before throwing it. This time, when Zander tried, he knocked down a couple of the pegs on the side. The bar still fell, but not to the ground.

"And then one day, she came to me. She told me that she still cared about me, but that she didn't want the kind of life she'd grown up with – didn't want a husband who was on duty all the time or who had to travel for weeks at a time with the king. And she didn't want to live in the castle."

"Ouch."

"At the time, yes. I hadn't even proposed to her yet, but there I found myself, telling her that we could always get a little house in the city – that I could ask for a transfer into a regular regiment, instead of guarding the king or his family."

"Wouldn't that have been a demotion?"

Ben nodded as they worked together to set the pegs again. This time, when Zander set the bar on the frame it wobbled, but stayed. "At that time, I didn't think I cared. It would have been worth it not to lose the girl I thought I loved. But it didn't matter. She didn't want to be married to a soldier at all – the idea of never knowing whether I'd come home at night or not was too much for her. She talked about it like it was all hypothetical, but … she married one of Queen Charlotte's nephews eight moons later."

"And you're telling me you weren't angry?"

"The day we heard the announcement of her betrothal, yes, I was. I thought about going and finding her – confronting her and asking her if she'd lied to me, if she had broken things off between us because of him. Fortunately, my father was around to stop me from doing that."

Ben's second turn resulted in another perfect score.

"Why fortunately?" Zander had to know. "Don't you think you deserved to know whether she left you for that other guy or not?"

"No."

"No?" This time, Zander got the bar to stay on the rack with almost no trouble.

"No. My father pointed out – correctly – that Mila didn't owe me anything. She ended it with me. What else was she supposed to do? Ask my permission for every relationship she wanted to have for the rest of her life?"

Ben wasn't talking about his ex-girlfriend now. They both knew that.

"She just barely broke up with me, Ben."

"Even if time worked the same in both of our worlds – and it isn't Quinn's fault that it doesn't – so what? How does her relationship with William – her *marriage* – have anything to do with you?"

"Well if she cheated on me…"

"Then what? Then she's obligated to walk away from him and marry you instead?"

"Obviously not."

"So, then it just means you get a free pass to hurt her? To wound her as deeply as you possibly can with your words or your actions? Now you can undermine her relationship with William, insult her, question the legitimacy of her child?"

Zander was silent.

"Because how you treat her is not about her. It's not about whatever you think she did to you. How you treat her is about *you.*

And I don't know exactly how old you are, but you look old enough to start being a man rather than a boy."

Zander launched the ball at the pegs again, this time, missing completely and hitting the platform. The pegs fell and rolled, and the bar dropped in *front* of the platform.

Ben chuckled, and went to go start picking up the pegs. "I did go and see Mila eventually. I congratulated her, and brought her a gift. My father and I attended her wedding. Linnea and I invited her to ours. She didn't come; apparently she's just had her second child."

"Maybe you're just a better person than me," Zander said.

"I doubt it. Whoever you are, you were friends with Quinn. You were someone she thought it worthwhile to try and have a relationship with. Just because it didn't turn out to be the right one doesn't mean you're not the person she thought you were. And it doesn't mean you won't find the right relationship with someone else."

"You managed to find a princess, right?"

"No." The withering look Ben gave him made his insides all wobbly.

"I'm sorry."

"Thank you. I managed to find a girl who loves me, and is willing to make the sacrifices that she has to make to follow me in my work. A girl who shares my values and wants the same things I want – and who understands and accepts the potential sacrifice my calling entails. The right girl, in other words. She also happens to be a princess. Which is not somehow magically easier, by the way. For her to follow me to Philotheum and be the wife of a guard means giving up a lot more than if she'd been someone more ordinary, like Mila."

"Sounds like you were very lucky."

"I *am* lucky, very much so, but I believe there's more to it than just that. If I *had* married Mila, I wouldn't have been the person I'm supposed to be. And she wouldn't be as happy as I know she is, either."

"So, what, like, fate or something?"

Ben shrugged, just before throwing the ball again. This time, the last peg on the right side didn't fall right away. It fell a few seconds after the others, and nearly bumped the frame when it hit the platform, but the bar stayed up.

"Not fate, really. Over time, as I've had the chance to look back at it, I see it more as Mila being brave enough to make a decision that had to be hard on her – and braver still to do the right thing and tell me about it. I would probably have given up everything I cared about for her if she hadn't had the courage to do that."

"You don't think it's worth giving things up for someone you care about?"

"That's not it at all. You *always* have to give something up to make a relationship really work. That's in the definition, I think. But they have to be the right things, and you have to be able to be happy with those choices outside of the other person. Eventually, I wouldn't have been happy taking that kind of demotion, or with not being able to take the job I have now – this is who I am. Sometime down the road, I wouldn't have been able to keep her happy, because I would have been pretending to be something I'm not actually, and it would have shown."

"And you think Quinn was courageous, too?"

"I'm not saying she's perfect, Zander. I don't know everything that happened between the two of you – and it's none of my business, really. But I am saying she made her choice, and she told you about it, which is all she owed you. And she married William – committed to him for the rest of her life. She had to give up a *lot* – the entire world she grew up in, her family, just about everything."

"She didn't *have* to give all that up. If she would have stayed with me, she wouldn't have given up any of it."

"And that's exactly what makes you the wrong man for her."

Zander had almost managed to make the bar stay on the stands again, but it fell at Ben's words. "And William's the *right* one because she had to give up all of those things for him?"

"She didn't give up any of those things for him, Zander. She gave them up for herself. She gave them up to free her hands to take hold of the things that really matter to her, to her birth family, to an entire kingdom. William is the man who didn't *make* her give up anything in either world. He's the man who sacrificed the things in his own hands so that they would be free to put under hers, to support her and work with her. More importantly, he's the right one because he's the one she chose."

"And you think I need to just get over it."

Ben was silent for several moments as Zander threw the ball again. This time, he managed not to drop the bar, but he didn't drop any pegs, either. The ball went right through the space in the middle.

Ben nodded and went to retrieve the ball. "Here's what I think, Zander. I'm just going to say it. I think you're probably a good guy. Like I said before, at one point, Quinn was willing to vouch for you. I don't care if you get over her or not in your own mind. But you absolutely need to stop, right now, thinking you have some right to hurt her. It won't be allowed."

He threw the ball, landing another clean, perfect score. The frame didn't even twitch.

If anyone else had talked like this to Zander, he would have probably gotten angry, he might have lashed out and argued, but somehow Ben – this strange guard he'd met only yesterday – had the opposite effect on him. Right now, he felt small and ashamed.

This time, Ben didn't go immediately to reset the frame. He stood in front of Zander, making eye contact with him. "I also think that you really care about Quinn, and you would find yourself able to still have a friendship and be at peace with her if you decided to accept her decision with grace. There's not any reason it has to be like this between you. You have ten days here. You can either spend them being angry and thinking this is all about you and whining about how hurt you are, or you can experience something new."

The words stung – mostly because he knew how true they were. "There's a reason Quinn trusts you, isn't there?"

"I hope so."

QUINN

Rosewood Castle, Eirentheos

ZANDER AND BEN were kneeling on the ground, stacking the pegs back into the wooden crate when Ben suddenly looked up, over toward the entrance to the gym. Zander followed his gaze.

Quinn and William were both standing there, just inside the door.

"Excuse me, Zander," Ben said, standing and walking toward them.

Zander's insides slithered down toward the pit of his stomach.

The door was too far away to hear what the three of them were saying to each other, but he could see them chatting and nodding, and then, making his insides drop further, this time to his feet, Quinn started walking toward him, alone.

He silently counted to ten, wiling himself to be calm, to not say anything to her – anything *else* to her – that he was going to regret.

"Hey," she said, when she finally reached him.

"Hey."

"We didn't know you guys were out here. It took us a while to find you."

He shrugged, not knowing what to say to that. It surprised him they'd been looking – he was grateful they hadn't found him before he finished his conversation with Ben.

"Look, Quinn. I'm sorry for what I said to you earlier … upstairs. I didn't mean it like that."

"Yes you did." She didn't look as angry as he expected her to.

He chuckled under his breath. "Yeah, I guess right at that moment, I kind of did. That was a pretty big shock. I am sorry, though. It was a mean thing to say."

"It wasn't as bad as what I imagined I'd hear if you or anyone else from school found out I had a baby."

"Abigail would lose her…"

"Yeah, I know," she said, rolling her eyes.

"Where is the little squish, anyway? You have a nanny and everything, too?"

"I don't. Apparently I have to find one. I am a queen, I need help. I've been 'borrowing' one of the baby nurses who works for William's parents for the last couple of days. She's a friend of mine, too, and she's amazing. Wish I could take her back with me."

"Maybe you should ask. Offer her a raise. I'm sure she's dying to leave here and go live somewhere without electricity."

She laughed. "It's not quite as simple as that, Zander." Her expression told him she was thinking about it, despite her words.

"People can't change jobs here?"

"Yes, they can. She's not a slave or anything."

"Well…you'll never know if you don't ask."

"Maybe."

"Does the baby have a name? How old is he, anyway?" He'd looked tiny, not much more than a newborn. Now that he wasn't in quite as much shock and he was looking, he could see the small changes in Quinn's body, too. He didn't know how he'd missed it yesterday, actually – though her clothes were different today, too. Her long skirt and dressy blouse had been replaced by much more normal-looking clothes today – soft gray cotton pants and what he could only describe as a t-shirt. She looked like she belonged here in the gym.

"He's two weeks old, and he doesn't officially have a name yet. It works differently in our world. We'll have a crazy huge celebration and ceremony where he'll officially be named."

"Seriously?"

She nodded. "There will be parades. Hundreds of people. Thousands maybe. There might be more than there were for my coronation, which was … it was something. If we were home, it would have happened already, but his arrival sort of put a kink in our traveling plans. Everyone is so paranoid about his health and safety that I've been forbidden to travel with him until he's a full moon old."

"I don't suppose I can get you to talk with normal words to me, can I?"

"Sorry. I know it's weird, but I've gotten used to it already. At this point, I think it would be strange to go back to Bristlecone. I'd slip and say the wrong thing there."

"Well, you'd have to live without a bodyguard." He glanced over at Ben and William. They'd moved inside the gym, but they stayed over by the wall where all of the equipment was, and they were talking, clearly trying to give him and Quinn some privacy.

"That part I think I could manage. I love Ben and Marcus, but…"

He laughed. "I'm actually surprised they're all the way over there. I mean, what if I slipped and said something rude to you?"

"Like *that*?" she snickered, raising an eyebrow.

"See? And they didn't even hear it to come running."

"Out of the three of us, I'm the only one who's killed somebody," she said. "I can take care of myself."

His head snapped around. "What? Please tell me you're joking."

"I'm not joking."

"Holy sh… What do you mean, you killed somebody?"

"It's a long story. I should not have started it that way. But the man who murdered my father was pointing a gun at me. So I threw my dagger at him. Marcus threw his, too – I can't say for sure that mine was the one that killed him. But yeah. I can defend myself if I have to. Although," she patted her lower leg, "I'm not currently packing my dagger – don't tell them. If they knew that, they might hover."

Zander had no idea what to say to that. She was looking at him like she'd just said something completely normal. "I suppose that kind of thing isn't illegal here?"

"I'm the law."

He couldn't help it. He started laughing. This was entirely too absurd not to be funny.

Quinn must have agreed, because the next thing he knew, they were both laughing so hysterically that he found it hard to breathe, and tears were running down her cheeks.

It was like that for several minutes. He saw both Ben and William turn at different times to watch them, but neither of them intervened.

Finally, Quinn calmed herself for long enough to pull out a handkerchief – from where, he didn't know – and dry her eyes. "I hate fighting with you, Zander."

"Me too," he sighed. "I never…" he looked around. " You realize how ridiculous all of this is, don't you?"

"Yeah. I'm sorry. It was crazy enough discovering this place the first time I came through the gate. I can't imagine what it would have been like if I'd come through and found you here, married to someone and with a baby."

He almost started laughing again.

"I never meant to hurt you, you know. I didn't know all of this was going to happen. I broke up with you because I didn't want to lie to you anymore. I couldn't explain any of this, and I couldn't walk away from it anymore. This is where I'm supposed to be."

"So it really wasn't because you were cheating on me with William."

She looked down, playing with the hem of her shirt. "I'd kissed him. I know everyone here is probably defending me, and telling you that we weren't courting before I broke up with you – and that's true, we weren't. But I hate lying and hiding things, and I don't want to do it even in a small way when I don't have to. I didn't break up with you because I was already with him, but we had kissed, the last time I was here, and I didn't know what it meant. I didn't know anything. I was confused, and scared, and I was lying to you … it wasn't fair to put you in the middle of that anymore. I'm sorry."

And somehow, seeing her like this, so vulnerable and honest … he couldn't do it. He couldn't be angry with her anymore. Ben was right. What Quinn had done really didn't have anything to do with him, even if she had kissed another guy. But …

"*William Rose*, Quinn? Really?"

"Yes. Really."

"He's so…"

"So… what, Zander? You've been in the same class with him since third grade, and I dare you to tell me one thing about him."

"He reads a lot."

She closed her eyes and sighed. "*I* read a lot."

"He's crazy smart – he was always doing work that was like three grades higher than the rest of us. And he never talked, to anybody, unless you count when the teachers called on him. Otherwise, I really don't remember him saying anything."

"His life was never there. What was he supposed to say? *Hi, I'm William. I'm a prince from an alternate universe. Will you play with me at recess?*"

He snickered, which made her laugh again. "You might have a little bit of a point."

"Anyway, you might feel different about him if you did get to know him."

He rolled his eyes. "All right, then, are you going to introduce me to him for real, or what? If he's this fantastic guy, and I'm going to be stuck here for ten days…"

Giving Zander an appraising look, she shrugged, and then called across the gym, "Will!"

The *"Will"* bit got to him. Like Quinn had said, he'd been in the same classes as William Rose since third grade. In all of that time, nobody had ever shortened his name. Most of the time, nobody even called him just William. It was always William Rose.

But here he was, *Will*, jogging across the gym to them. "You okay?" he asked, when he reached Quinn.

Zander had to force himself not to roll his eyes at that. *Yes*, she was okay. Jeez.

"Yeah, I'm fine. Zander and I were just talking, and he was saying how he'd never really been properly introduced to you, and that he'd like to get to know you better."

"Oh, okay."

Zander had to hand it to the guy, really. He could see it – the way William's fingers twitched, how he wanted to put his arms around Quinn, maybe kiss her head again or something to mark his territory – but he didn't do it.

Instead, he smiled – had he *ever* seen William Rose smile before? – and he held out his hand. "I know it seems strange, Zander. You know my name, and I know we've spent a lot of time in the same rooms, but, I guess this sort of is our first real conversation. Welcome to my world."

Zander accepted the handshake.

"I'm sure it must be difficult for you to come to terms with landing here and seeing all of this. I can only imagine how overwhelming it all is. But I want you to know how grateful we are – how grateful *I* am – that you were willing to help Owen and bring him here. It would take a special kind of person to put that kind of trust in a little boy. Because you did, you saved my life. There isn't any way I could ever repay you for that, but I will start with my sincere thank you."

Whatever he'd thought William would say to him first, that wasn't it. "You're welcome." That sounded weird, but what else was he supposed to say?

"Were you comfortable last night? Did you have everything you needed?"

"I was fine, thank you."

Suddenly, William frowned. "You haven't had breakfast yet, have you?"

He shook his head. Even the apple he'd grabbed was probably still lying on the ground in that yard.

"I could get you some eggs and toast if you'd like, with butter and strawberry jam – those all taste about the same here as they do in your world, and I'm thinking you might prefer something familiar right about now."

It wasn't fair. After all of this, William was going to turn out to be someone he *liked?* He was going to have to ask about the unicorn.

He nodded. "That sounds really good, actually. Thanks."

"No problem. I'll be back in a minute."

Once William was gone, Zander turned to Quinn again. "Does it really taste the same as home?"

"Yes. I think the bread's actually better here – don't tell my mom."

He chuckled. Quinn's mom had always baked her own bread. "I'll keep it quiet. Although, I do think I'll be having quite the conversation with your mom after I get back."

"Yeah, wish I could be there for that."

"You could come, you know. If the gate's open, or whatever, you're not stuck here."

She shook her head. "I made the decision to stay here when I didn't even know it was possible to close the gate, Zander. I'm not here because of that."

"Are you really happy here, Quinn?"

She looked him straight in the eyes and nodded. "Yes, I am. Not every second of every day, obviously, but nobody's that happy anywhere. I wish for things like cell phones and television – and tomatoes – please tell me you brought a tomato with seeds in it…"

He turned the pockets of his pants inside out, which made her giggle again. "Uh, no."

"Dang it. This world is severely lacking in pizza and spaghetti."

"And you *live* here?"

She chuckled. "Seriously, though, Zander. I know there's probably no way you could understand this, but this world is my home now. As much as I would like to be able to go back sometimes, and as hard as it is to be separated from my mom and Jeff and Annie and Owen … I *couldn't* go back there to live. It's not even who I am anymore. I don't think it was ever who I was supposed to be."

He studied her for a long moment. "It isn't just about William, is it?"

"No, it's not. It's not *about* him at all. It's about me. I mean, I love him, Zander. More than I ever imagined loving someone. I'm so grateful that he could even exist – that there could actually be someone who's so willing to accept exactly who I am, and what I have to do, and who understands both parts of my life, because he's shared them with me. He is my best friend and my partner in every way. And I just spent the past few days thinking I might lose him."

He could see it so clearly now – how she'd changed. Not just physically, but in other, more subtle ways, too. She carried herself differently – she was more confident, wiser. She'd been through things he would probably never be able to understand.

"And I thought about it – what it would be like if I did lose him. How my heart would be broken forever, knowing this part of me that *is* his wife would die, too, but … it wouldn't have changed my mind about what I have to do – to go back home to Philotheum, rule my kingdom, raise my child as the next heir to the throne."

He looked down at his hands. This was not what he had expected. Seeing her like this, so honest and vulnerable, and yet, so … he couldn't even define it … it just made his earlier anger and irritation seem so trivial.

"Zander, I have you to thank for the fact that I'm probably not going to lose him right now, and … I know this is hard for you. I know the last thing you probably want to be hearing is my gushing over someone else, but for the rest of my life, you're going to be the man who brought that medicine for him."

"I didn't do anything, Quinn. I didn't even know what Owen had in that cooler."

"It doesn't matter. He couldn't have done it on his own. You were there for him when he needed you, and for us."

"He's a pretty irresistible kid," he said, smiling.

She chuckled, but then her expression grew serious again. "I know you'd never admit it – the real reason why Owen was able to talk you into it. And I'm so sorry about the shock it must have been to come here and find things this way. I wish it hadn't happened like that – that there had been a better way for you to find out."

He looked down at the ground again.

"It makes me wish I'd never said yes to dating you. Not because I didn't want to – I did. I cared about you that way.If I was really the girl I thought I was, it wouldn't have been a mistake. I just wish I'd found all of this out before I put you through that, because I feel like it's cost me something I valued even more – your friendship. I never wanted to lose that."

He sighed. "You're making it awfully hard for me to stay mad at you and hate William, you know."

"I'm sorry. I could be horrible and snotty about it if it would be easier on you to be mad."

"Evil plans don't work as well if you tell people about them in advance, you know."

"I know." She stretched her hand tentatively toward him – an offering. He knew he didn't have to take it, but he did, squeezing her fingers gently.

"I'm sorry I was such a jerk," he said.

"I deserved it."

"No you didn't. I might have had a right to be angry about the lying…"

"You did. I never wanted to lie to you."

"I know that now. I'm going to find myself lying when I get home."

She shrugged. "It's not like you can just tell people the truth."

"No. But either way, Quinn, yes, you lied, but you were never as awful to me as I've been to you about the whole thing. I really am sorry."

She looked up then, over his shoulder. "William's back. Is it okay if he comes back over?"

Zander glanced behind him. William was standing there with a covered silver tray, just far enough that he couldn't overhear their conversation. He looked more like a servant than a king, and far too much like someone it would be impossible to hate. Sighing, he waved William over.

The toast and eggs were delicious – just like home, only Quinn was right, the bread was better. The thick sausage links on a plate of their own were somewhat different than the ones at home, but Zander thought he could get used to them quickly.

A small glass bowl of really weird-looking green berries was also on the tray. Just the sight of them made him wary – there was no way he was ready for something like that – but William handed the bowl to Quinn, along with a second glass of milk.

"There is someone around to insist on taking care of me twenty-four hours a day," Quinn grumbled, rolling her eyes, but the way she looked at William as he sat down next to her told Zander that her annoyance was feigned.

"You do have a newborn prince to take care of," Zander said around a mouthful of eggs, earning him a scowl.

William chuckled.

"I wouldn't mind actually meeting him." It sort of surprised him that this was true. If he was going to have to deal with the fact that Quinn had a son, it would be nice to see him up close.

"Well," William said, "either Mia or my sister is supposed to be bringing him down in a few minutes. It's another nice day. We were thinking about a crumple match."

"A what?"

Quinn grinned. "It's a lot more fun than bar drop."

"But I'll probably suck at it just as badly as I do at that game."

"Maybe," William said. "But your football skills might come in handy."

CRUMPLE

TWENTY MINUTES LATER, Quinn climbed up into the bleachers at the crumple field, cradling the baby, who was still making quiet fussing noises.

He'd been screaming when Linnea carried him outside.

"I swear, he hates me," Linnea said, sitting down on the cushion beside her, watching as he pushed his face against Quinn's shirt, hungry again.

"He's a baby," Owen said, climbing onto the bench one row down from them. "He can't hate anyone. He just likes his mom best."

"Sometimes," Quinn said, laying the baby on a pillow Linnea set on her lap and getting him settled in to nurse. "Other times, I think he likes Mia better than me."

"He doesn't like her better. He's just trying to help you know you're supposed to ask her to go back to Philotheum with you to be his nanny."

Linnea's mouth fell open, and Quinn very nearly dropped the baby. He fussed at the interruption to his meal.

"What, Owen?"

"Mia is supposed to be his nanny. She knows that, and she wants to, but she's afraid to ask anyone. She thinks Queen Charlotte will be mad at her for wanting to leave, and she's really afraid she'll ask you and you'll say no, and then Charlotte will be mad and she won't have a job, and Thomas will be mad because she really loves him, but she thinks this is the job she's supposed to do."

Linnea stared at him. "Owen, you haven't even *talked* to Mia since you've been here."

Owen frowned, blinking several times before his eyebrows knitted together in confusion. "Was it a dream?"

Quinn's eyes met Linnea's, and she knew that they both wore the same expression of shock. Linnea's hands were trembling; Quinn looked down to make sure her own hands weren't shaking the baby.

"Yes, Owen. I think it must have been a dream," she said, trying to hold her voice steady.

"Oh." He shrugged, unperturbed, turning back around to watch as everyone else trickled onto the field and bleachers for the game.

Simon's wife, Evelyn, and William's sister Rebecca had just arrived together, both of them with their sons. They sat together in the bottom row, chatting animatedly with each other and the infants. Charlotte would probably come out to join them, to let little Hannah be with her nephews.

Linnea was watching them too. "That will be us in Philotheum soon," she said. "You with Samuel, and me with someone a tiny bit smaller."

Quinn raised an eyebrow.

"Not yet," Linnea said. "At least, as far as I know."

"Well, I hope it's soon," she said, sighing. "It's hard to know that I'll be raising Samuel so far away from his cousins and his family."

"You're stuck with me. I'm excited, actually, about going. I'll miss it here, but … I'm ready for a new adventure in a different kingdom."

"Yeah?"

"Yeah. Even if I hadn't married Ben, I think I would have tried to find a way to go with you guys. I love Rebecca, but you've become my sister just as much as she is – and she has Evelyn now. I missed you and William when you were gone more than I think I'll miss everyone here."

"What about Thomas?"

A shadow passed over Linnea's face, but then she nodded toward Owen. "It sounds like *that* problem might find a way to solve itself."

"Maybe so." Quinn had no idea what to make of it.

"If he's right, *I* can find a way to make it happen," Linnea whispered.

"*If* he's right?" Quinn was speaking under her breath, though Owen didn't seem to be paying any attention to them at all. "He was right when he dreamed that William needed that medicine. He brought it."

"Well, then, he's probably right, and we'll all be together in Philotheum, and you won't have to worry about dealing with a baby nurse hand-picked by Sophia. Which she is busily trying to do, you know."

"What?"

"Oh, yeah. William got a message last week from Ruth about how Sophia was driving her nuts, making people come in and practice putting sheets on the cradle and listing out their daily baby care schedules to the minute."

Quinn had to take a deep breath in through her nose and let it out slowly. Ruth was the head of housekeeping at the castle in Philotheum – and Quinn's biggest ally in the daily struggle for control she had with Sophia.

"There's a reason William didn't tell you about the message. He wants to try to get it sorted out before you have to deal with it, but I think you should know how serious it is, if there's any chance we could come up with a much happier solution."

"How long am I required to allow the old queen to stay in the castle? Forever, since she's my grandmother?"

"My parents built a really nice estate by the sea for my grandmother less than a cycle after my grandfather died and my father was crowned. And I don't think she was as bad as Sophia is."

"She wants to take over my child."

"Yes, she does. She wants to have a say in every detail of everything you ever do with him. What she really wants is to raise him herself."

"Well, that is not going to happen. Whether she's my grandmother or not. I'm tired of hearing people say 'but she means well' – I don't think she does. I think what she says is exactly what she means. She's the woman who raised Tolliver."

"I know. But relax, Quinn. You've got a couple more weeks here in Eirentheos with him, and then I'll be going back with you."

"Thank the Maker for that, Nay. Really. I've missed you so much."

"I've missed you too, Quinn," Linnea said, putting an arm around her and squeezing her shoulder. "I love you – even if your baby hates me."

Quinn shrugged. "Nobody can hate you forever, Nay. You won't let them."

"That's true." She bent down and kissed the top of the baby's head. "You're not going to have a choice but to *love* your Auntie Linnea, little man. You're stuck with me, too."

"Zander!" Owen called from the bench below them. "Up here!"

Zander, Ben, William, Mia, and Thomas had all just arrived at the field, after going upstairs and getting changed for the game.

It was still just so weird to see Zander here; she wondered whether their tenuous peace would hold.

He was smiling as he climbed up into the bleachers to sit by Owen, though, which was a good sign. She had meant what she'd said earlier – there was no part of her that wanted to fight with him. She'd always cared about him, even when she'd broken up with him, and now that he had saved William's life, and brought Owen to her – she would hate it if he was miserable and angry the whole time he was here.

"What do you think?" Zander asked, holding his arms out to display one of Ben's green-and-white-striped crumple shirts. "Do I look like I belong here yet?"

"Next thing you know, you'll be eating our vegetables – and liking them," Linnea teased.

He rolled his eyes, turning his attention to Linnea. "I wouldn't go that far. Are you playing too?" he asked her, sounding a little surprised.

She was just finishing pulling her long, dark brown hair into a ponytail. Her eyes narrowed at his tone. "Just because I'm a girl doesn't mean I can't knock you into the ground at crumple."

"Oh?" Zander's eyes twinkled at the challenge. "It's hardly fair when you have a husband who would slice open my throat if I touched you."

Linnea shrugged as she stood. "I never said I'd play fair."

"Girls," Zander said, shaking his head.

"I know, right? Always one step ahead of us, no matter how hard we try." Thomas had his hand on Mia's shoulder as he spoke. It made Quinn happy to see that. Maybe things were looking up between the two of them. She wondered if they'd talked.

A moment later, though, one of the babies started crying, and Mia ducked away from him to see if she could help. It was a normal enough thing, but the look on Thomas' face as he watched her go told Quinn that no, they hadn't talked, and that things weren't going so well.

And considering what Owen had just told her about Mia…this was getting complicated.

"Are you going to play, too, Quinn?" Zander asked, taking Linnea's place on one side of her as Linnea climbed down toward the field to help Ben and her other brothers finish setting up the goals. William took the seat on the other side of her.

"Hopefully I'll get to take a few turns as an alternate, if this little guy will let me."

"You're playing, right, William?" Zander asked.

"I wish I was. My ordeal with this isn't over yet, though," he said, tapping gingerly on the bandage wrapped around his arm. "This is killing me today; I don't think I could throw a ball if I tried. And I have to be careful with it anyway. There's at least one of the bite marks that needs stitches when Nathaniel gets back. If I get tackled, I'm going to make it bleed everywhere."

"Where is Doctor Rose, anyway?" Zander asked.

"He went to stay for a couple of nights at a clinic in a village a few hours from here," William answered. "He's getting married in a couple of moons and his fiancée lives in the village. He's been helping her get her farm ready to sell. He was going to come back later today, but I sent him a message last night about you bringing the medicine, and now he's going to take another day or two."

"Doctor Rose ... finally getting married. That would shock some people at home."

"Not nearly as much as they'd be shocked to find out about me and William." Quinn said.

"That's true." Zander actually chuckled.

The baby had finished, and she lifted him up to her shoulder to burp him.

"So this is him," Zander said. "Your ... son."

"This is him." She turned him so that he was facing Zander.

"He really doesn't have a name yet?"

"Not officially. We're going to name him after my father, though – my real father, who died when I was little. Samuel."

"Samuel Owen!" Owen piped up. The look of pride on his face sent shivers through Quinn's body, and she had to blink a few times.

"Wow. I never… Wow, Quinn. He's beautiful."

"Thank you. I kind of think so."

At that moment, the baby let out an enormous belch.

"And a real prince already, I see," Zander teased, as they all laughed.

"I'm going to go and find Alice, okay?" Owen asked. Stephen and Charlotte had just arrived with the rest of the younger children.

"Of course," Quinn answered.

They all watched Owen run down the bleachers to join them. Although, in theory, they were preparing for a game of crumple, everyone was kind of milling around, chatting more than anything. Two large tables had been set up along the side of the field, and they were covered with food – bread and toppings for sandwiches, many different kinds of fruit, and fixings for salad.

"Is this what you usually do in a castle?" Zander wondered.

"Sort of," Quinn said. "Today is Sixth Day – the first day of what we would think of as the weekend, so it's a bit more relaxed. Almost all of the servants are off either today or tomorrow, or both, so there's not a lot of hot food. The family usually tries to spend more time together. And the weather's really nice. We've had a lot of days where there's either been rain or snow, or the ground's been too wet to play, so we've kind of missed crumple. Or they have. I don't think I've played since before I got pregnant."

William put his hand on her knee. "You really want to play, don't you?"

"Yeah, I kind of do."

"You're sure you're up for it?"

"I had a baby, Will, not a traumatic injury."

"Sorry, I was just asking."

She put her hand over his. "You do take good care of me. Sorry if I'm ungrateful about it sometimes."

Zander coughed and stared intently down at the field. "They look like they might finally be getting ready to start."

Quinn followed his gaze. William's two oldest brothers, Maxwell and Simon were standing on the sidelines, trying to gather up teams.

"I have no idea what I'm doing," Zander said. "But I'm going to go figure it out."

"Let me hold Samuel," William said, as Quinn watched Zander walk away.

She looked at him in surprise. "It hasn't been twenty-four hours yet."

"I know, but it's been more than half that, and I figure it's time for me to compromise a little, too. Besides, I miss him. I need some father-son time. If I don't stop being an idiot, he's going to forget how much he likes to snuggle with me, and then he'll cry like he does when Linnea holds him."

"Thank you," she said, laying the baby in the crook of his good arm.

William's whole body relaxed a little – just enough for Quinn to be able to see it – when the baby twisted contentedly, searching for the most comfortable position, and the sight flooded her with warmth, with love for this man and the child they shared.

"This feels good," William said, taking hold of her hand as he looked down at Samuel. "I've missed it so much."

She smiled. "Yell down to me if he gets hungry."

"We'll be fine, love." He didn't let go of her hand like she expected him to, instead he pulled her toward him. "Come here for a second."

She raised an eyebrow, confused until she realized what he was trying to do. The kiss was tender and sweet, and very hard to pull away from. When she finally managed it, she gave him a wry look. "That wasn't because you're jealous of him, was it?"

He shook his head, looking sincere enough that she believed him. "I was avoiding doing that while he was watching, actually. I know you're mine, I don't need to rub his face in it. I needed that for me."

Smiling, she kissed him on the forehead. "I needed it too."

"Wish I could play today – I'd kind of like to be down there when Zander experiences his first taste of sports in our world."

She giggled. "I'll fill you in on any funny things he says later."

"Thanks." He rubbed the back of her hand with his thumb. "Things seem to be going pretty well with him right now. I'd suggest playing on the *same* team as him if you want to make sure to keep it that way."

"I love you," she said, squeezing his hand.

"I love you, too. Now go have fun."

"That game is exhausting," Zander said to Quinn when the game finally broke for halftime.

"We're winning, though."

"Yeah, no thanks to me."

Quinn shrugged, taking a plate from the long table and beginning to fill it. "Linnea's an intense goalkeeper." She was being nice. Quinn hadn't had any difficulty scoring four goals against her. Even Queen Charlotte had managed a goal when she'd traded in and out with Quinn for short breaks.

"I never pegged you for such a sports girl," he said. "You never played any in Bristlecone."

"I never did a lot of things in Bristlecone."

"I suppose that's true." He chuckled, looking up into the bleachers to watch William, who was carefully climbing down with the baby in his arms.

"Are you doing all right with all of this?" she asked him.

"I don't know. I think I've decided to just ignore reality for the next ten days. Pretend I'm on some sort of weird, unexpected vacation or something."

Truthfully, he'd been enjoying himself today. Crumple was fun, and he was really enjoying William's older brothers; they were so different than anyone he had imagined being related to William Rose – or at least the version of William that had existed in Bristlecone. Here, he was discovering an entirely new side of him.

He'd been playing so hard that even the strange spreads for the sandwiches set out along the table looked almost appealing. He was even sort of tempted by some of the bowls of fresh fruit – although he was definitely still intimidated by the green berries Quinn was scooping into her bowl.

"What *are* those?" he asked her.

"They're called glasberries, and they're amazing."

"That's kind of a weird name." Although, for some reason, the name was ringing a bell, which was impossible – where would he have heard it before? "What do they taste like?"

"Um…they taste like glasberries."

"You're very helpful."

"I don't know Zander. They're kind of sweet. What does an apple taste like? If you want to know what a glasberry tastes like, you should eat one."

"They're green."

"Blueberries are green on the inside, and you eat those. Apples can be green, so can pears. What's wrong with green?"

He rolled his eyes, but held out his hand. She dug in her bowl for one of the berries, and gave it to him.

"Well?" she asked, watching him as he chewed.

"It's good. I don't know if I'd call it *amazing*, but they're definitely not as scary as I thought."

"They're my favorite food here. I'll be sad when it's the middle of the winter and we can't find any."

And suddenly, he remembered *exactly* where he'd heard the word before. "Quinn, do you know someone named Alvin?"

Her reaction to the name was immediate, her whole expression changed as she looked around the field and the bleachers, just as William reached them. "Yes, I do. Why, is he here?"

"Is who here?" William asked.

"He just asked me if I know Alvin," Quinn answered.

William started looking around, too.

Zander frowned. "Wouldn't you have seen me if I was talking to him *here?*"

"With Alvin, you never know," William said, "but if it wasn't here, how do you know about him? Did you see him somewhere last night or this morning?"

"No. I saw him in Bristlecone."

"In *Bristlecone?*" Quinn looked shocked. "Like when you and Owen were crossing the bridge?"

"It was before – I wasn't with Owen. It was a few days ago – in Bristlecone time, I guess."

Quinn's shock had turned to alarm as she looked at William. "You don't think the gate has been open for longer, do you?"

"I don't think so," Zander interrupted her. "I don't know exactly how all of it works, but Owen was carrying around this big chunk of rock that he put in this weird hole in the ground before we went through the gate. If I'm right, I don't think it opened until he did that."

She nodded. "It's a magnet. I don't know how it works either, but we know there's somehow a magnet on each side. We tried to find the one here, but we never could. Alvin told Owen where the one on the other side was, though. We never knew for sure if he was the one who closed it, but that was our guess."

"Well, now you know."

"Where did you see Alvin?" William asked.

"It was actually close to the gate. I was walking down by the river, and he just came up to me and started talking to me. He introduced himself ... and he mentioned you." He didn't like saying that last part, because he was afraid it was going to open up all sorts of other questions about why he'd been down at the river in the first place. He didn't want to admit to how much he'd been thinking about Quinn back in Bristlecone.

But nobody commented about him. "Do you think there could be another way to open it?" Quinn asked. "Or another gate?"

"Anything is possible, but … it's Alvin. I don't know if he needs a gate."

"I suppose that's true," Quinn said, setting her half-filled plate down so she could reach for the baby, who was beginning to fuss. Her eyes were still scanning the field as if she expected him to be here.

"Wait … what?" Zander spluttered. "How could he not need a gate?"

"Do you want me to finish making your plate?" William asked Quinn, seemingly unperturbed by the whole idea. "You don't have a sandwich yet."

"Yeah, he's hungry again, I think. I'm going to go sit down and feed him. Can you get me a drink, too?"

"Of course. I'll come find you in a second."

Quinn carried the baby back toward the bleachers, leaving Zander in open-mouthed shock. Was this kind of conversation just *normal* for them?

When his thoughts were finally halfway coherent again, he turned back to William. "Are you having a greenhouse built wherever you live so Quinn can have those berries all year?"

"Yes," William answered. "Although it's supposed to be a surprise. Who told you?" He frowned. "Linnea wouldn't have told you."

"No. It was that guy. Alvin. I had no idea what he was talking about. He called you the king of Phila-whatever."

"Philotheum."

"Whatever."

William chuckled, which sort of angered Zander even more. "Is it just not a big deal to you that there's some crazy old guy popping back and forth between here and Bristlecone when the gate's closed – just coming up and starting random conversations with people? It's not like I mentioned Quinn to him first."

"It's Alvin," William said, like that was some kind of explanation.

"And who is Alvin?"

"He's … Alvin."

Zander narrowed his eyes.

"I'm sorry, I know that isn't a real answer."

"It's not an answer at all."

"I know. But that's kind of how Alvin is. I don't know *who* he is exactly. He's always been around; he's always looked the same. He shows up when he wants to, and leaves just as easily. He married Quinn and me – both times."

"Both times?"

"Yes. We had a small ceremony here with just our families – when Quinn's mother was here – and he appeared for that, and then we had a very large, elaborate public ceremony in Philotheum when we returned there."

Zander supposed that made sense, but hearing the details like that just made things way too real again. He shook his head, as if that would somehow clear it. "And you think he could just travel between the worlds, even if the gate was closed?"

"The guards don't see him when he enters the castle – not here, and not in Philotheum. Nobody's ever watched him leave, either. I don't *know* if he can travel between the worlds, but he's said things in the past that lead me to believe he's probably able to."

"So he's like … magic or something?"

"I don't know if I would call it magic. Most people here believe that Alvin is sort of a prophet or a messenger from the Maker."

"The Maker? Like God?"

"Yes."

This was definitely getting too weird for Zander. "Maybe I'm wrong. Maybe it wasn't him."

"What did he look like?"

"Old guy … sort of, anyway. I don't think he would have looked old if it wasn't for the white hair and eyebrows. He was wearing a fly-fishing outfit."

"Was he fly fishing?"

Zander shrugged. "I think so. He was wet, and it sounded like he had a fish in his creel."

"And he mentioned Quinn, and he told you that I'm building a greenhouse for her in Philotheum?"

Zander swallowed hard. "Yes."

"And you think you'd be *less* creeped out if it were someone else?"

"Okay, yeah, probably not."

William chuckled.

"But why would he come and talk to me in Bristlecone?"

"I don't know. I can rarely explain anything he does. I've never seen him in Bristlecone, and I don't think Nathaniel ever has – at least he's never told me anything about it. But Quinn … she's had dreams about Alvin ever since she was a child."

"*What?*"

"Yeah. She never realized it – not even the first few times she met him here. But then, when Owen saw him at our wedding, he recognized him. Knew exactly who he was. Apparently Owen has always had dreams about him as well."

Zander looked over at Owen. He was sitting on the bottom bench of the bleachers, all the way over to one side, chatting with a little girl who had to be one of William's sisters. She looked just like William, straight dark hair and glasses. She even had her arm bandaged the way William's was – though it looked much worse on her tiny arm. It must be the sister he'd given the medicine to.

The two of them had a large notebook open between their laps, and they were looking at it, taking turns drawing in it, and neither one of them was paying attention to anything else around them. He wasn't sure he'd ever seen Owen look so peaceful and content in spending time with anyone – except maybe Quinn.

"Is that how Owen knew to get that medicine? He dreamed about it?" Now that he thought about it, he remembered Owen talking about his dreams – at the time, he guessed he'd just been too preoccupied and freaked out to pay much attention.

"Yes." William nodded. "Owen still dreams about Alvin, and even about Quinn. Quinn dreams about him, too. The night before the baby was born, she had a dream that she was talking to Owen and he knew about the baby – it's almost like they communicate to each other that way, and Alvin's somehow a part of it, too."

"Is he real?"

"In dreams and in Bristlecone – I don't know. I think so. Here, in our world, he's real. We never know where he's going to show up, but everyone can see him and talk to him when he does. He was just here recently. When the baby was three days old, Thomas found Alvin in the hallway outside our room. He'd come to meet the prince, he said."

"And you don't think that's weird?"

"If I were you, I would probably think it is. He still sort of scares Quinn sometimes, although she sees him quite often. It's very rare for him to miss an important event for the royal family. If you were going to be with us for the baby's Naming Ceremony, I could guarantee you a chance to speak with him."

"At this point, I'm not sure I want to."

"Fair enough," William said, smiling.

"Do you want some help carrying that?" Zander asked, noticing that William was having some trouble figuring out how to balance two plates and a glass when he was so obviously trying to avoid using his injured arm any more than he had to.

For a second, William looked like he was about to refuse, but then he nodded. "Sure, I'd appreciate it. Thanks."

Before they made it back to Quinn, Zander risked one more question. "Why do you think Alvin came and talked to me?"

William stopped walking. "I don't know, Zander. Alvin is not something I'm an expert on. I would guess that it means something, though. Quinn now believes that Alvin has appeared in her dreams all these years for a reason – that he was leading her back here where she belonged. I don't know why he appears to Owen, though, and I have no idea why he would show up in the daytime, in person, to you. Maybe it was just to prepare you to face something weird."

"Well, it was weird," Zander said. "But I can't say that it prepared me for this."

HORSES

Eirentheos

THE THIRD MORNING he was in the castle was the first time Zander was brave enough to scoop some of the hot grain cereal from the serving dish into his bowl. If every person in the castle ate it nearly every morning for breakfast, he figured it couldn't be that terrible.

He almost didn't actually try it, though. His courage dissipated as he stirred the strange-looking mush, waiting for it to cool. He set the bowl off to the side, at the top of his plate, hoping nobody would notice, but he looked up to see Linnea smirking at him.

Grabbing the bowl again, he shoved a big spoonful in his mouth.

That was a mistake. The cereal was still hot enough to burn his tongue, and he blinked several times, trying to hide the fact that his eyes were watering. The little he could taste of the cereal was bland and slightly bitter, and he had to force himself to chew the bite and swallow.

Linnea was giggling quietly now as she reached for a small ceramic pitcher in the center of the table and made a show of pouring what looked like honey from the pitcher onto the cereal in her bowl. Then she added milk from her glass and some dried berries from a bowl, stirring the whole thing before taking a bite.

Zander glared at her, and then, very deliberately, put his bowl as far in front of his plate as he could reach.

He didn't know when Ben had started watching the whole thing, but Zander saw him roll his eyes at Linnea. She only smiled and stretched up to kiss him on the cheek.

Ben shook his head and whispered something to her – whatever it was didn't change her amused expression at all – before looking back at Zander.

Ben cleared his throat. "Linnea, Thomas, and I were thinking about going on a horseback ride after breakfast. Would you like to join us?"

The idea sounded so much more interesting than hanging around inside while Quinn and William took care of the baby and soaked up their time with Owen, that Zander agreed immediately, forgetting – at least until they reached the stables – that he didn't know much about riding horses.

The problem came into sharp focus when Ben came back from the stables leading a large, chestnut-brown horse and stopped in front of Zander.

Linnea, of course, noticed the hesitation he was trying to hide. "Have you ever ridden a horse before?"

Zander narrowed his eyes. "Yes."

She raised an eyebrow.

"A few times," he mumbled under his breath. Of course, those "few times" had been once on a guided trail ride with a mellow horse. Quinn had talked about teaching him to really ride this summer – but that obviously wasn't going to happen now.

Ben was giving him an incredulous look – the kind of look Zander supposed he would have given one of the senior guys at school if they'd said they didn't know how to drive. "Horses aren't really a thing in my world," he said. "But I know enough." *Sort of.*

"Are you sure you want to go?" Thomas asked.

Now it felt like a challenge – and besides, he was *not* going to go back upstairs and tell Quinn and William he was back because he couldn't ride a horse.

"I'm sure. I'll be fine – it will be fun."

"Good." Thomas smiled, and turned back to what he was doing.

"Quinn probably has her own horse and everything, doesn't she?" he asked, watching the other three tend to horses that were very obviously *theirs*. Linnea's chalky-white horse almost looked like it was hugging her, nestling its nose into her neck as she stroked it and fed it an apple.

The brown horse had no interest in Zander.

"Yes. My parents gifted Dusk to her on her first visit here – before we even knew who she was," Thomas answered. "Now, of course, she owns an entire stable of them, but Dusk will always be special to her, I think."

"I wonder how Dusk is doing, actually," Linnea said. "This is the first time she's been separated from Quinn for this long since after the first time Quinn came here. I know Quinn misses her."

Zander frowned.

"Dusk and Skittles – William's horse – are back in Philotheum. Quinn was very pregnant when they traveled here, and they weren't planning on being here this long."

Skittles. It wasn't quite a rainbow-pooping unicorn, but close enough, Zander chuckled to himself.

"Yeah, she told me about that – not about the horses, though." He didn't know anything about missing a horse, but he guessed it would be even worse than the way he really would have liked to see his truck right about now. "What's your horse's name?" he asked Linnea.

"This is Snow," she said, rubbing the horse's neck. "That's Storm," she pointed to Thomas' horse, "and Scruffin is Ben's. The one you'll be riding is Chestnut. He's pretty old and gentle. If you've ridden before, you should be able to manage him."

Linnea's optimism made him think he was hiding his apprehension better than he thought he was.

Thomas and Ben finished loading things into the saddle bags and onto the saddles. Ben, Zander noticed, was especially heavily armed. He wasn't in full uniform, but he wore a shirt with the crest of Philotheum embroidered on the sleeve, and he carried both his sword and a concealed dagger on his body. Attached to holders on the saddle were more weapons, most notably a crossbow and a sheath of arrows.

He hoped Ben was just paranoid.

So far as Zander knew, the biggest security risk in the kingdom right now was *him*. He was under strict instructions not to tell anyone where he was from, aside from the few members of the immediate family and three guards who knew. Actually, for the most part, he was kept so far away from people that he wouldn't have had a chance to tell anyone.

While he sort of understood everyone's concern about keeping the bridge to the other world a secret, it also confused him. Obviously, William and Nathaniel had been using the gate on a regular basis for many years – didn't anyone know where they'd been going?

And while he obviously had no way of knowing for sure, the few stories he'd heard about Quinn's first visits here suggested that she hadn't been under nearly the same level of restrictions he had been.

Now that he'd been here for three days, and he'd calmed down a bit, and mostly come to a place of understanding with Quinn and William, he was starting to become a bit fascinated with the whole thing. He was staying in a *castle* – a real, honest-to-goodness castle in an alternate universe. He had to admit that was kind of cool. Especially as he looked around at the elaborate yards and stables. Quinn lived in a place like this all the time?

"Do you need help getting on?" Linnea's voice jolted him back from his reverie.

He glared at her. As if a tiny little thing like Linnea would have been able to help him get on a horse in the first place? "No, I think I can manage, thanks."

She shrugged and jumped on Snow so lightly that he almost didn't see how she did it. Once she was in the saddle she turned to watch Zander, her gray eyes full of amusement.

It couldn't be that hard.

Deliberately avoiding looking at Linnea – or checking to see if either of the guys were watching, he placed his foot in the stirrup and climbed up. He hit his leg on the back of the saddle as he swung it over, and he landed a little too hard as he sat, causing Chestnut to make a slightly disgruntled sound, but he was on – without help.

Ben shot Linnea a warning look when she giggled, but Thomas looked like he was biting his lip to keep from joining her.

This might be a long day.

Much to Zander's surprise, after a few false starts, and having to have Linnea and Thomas demonstrate for him how to get Chestnut to walk and stop, by the time they passed the guard at the gatehouse and were on a dirt road outside the castle grounds, he was actually starting to feel a little more confident.

"Where are we going?" he asked Thomas, as they followed Ben and Linnea into a wooded area.

"Nowhere in particular. Just thought we'd get the horses out for a bit, have lunch outside. Are you doing all right?"

"Yeah, I'm fine." He could almost get used to this, he thought – riding a horse on a path through the woods.

Most of the trees were bare, or close to it, with a few brown crunchy leaves clinging tenaciously to the spindly branches. It would have been almost eerie, but for the view through them. When the path veered to the left, Zander could turn enough to see the majestic outline of the castle against the pale blue sky.

Past the castle, in the distance, he got an occasional glimpse of what he supposed was the capital city of Eirentheos – the low stone buildings and houses he caught sight of were so different from what he thought of as a city.

Nobody was talking; everyone seemed to be just enjoying the ride and the fresh air. Ahead of him, Ben and Linnea were riding so close together their feet were nearly touching in the stirrups. She kept her horse perfectly in line with his, and more than once Zander saw one reach over to touch the other in affection.

Suddenly, from seemingly out of nowhere, an enormous black and gray bird swooped right in front of Linnea's horse.

Zander pulled Chestnut to a stop so quickly that the horse tapped his front foot in protest, making him wobble in the saddle.

Thomas, ahead of him now, turned around and frowned.

Linnea didn't even seem startled. The horse kept moving, although she dropped the reins and held out her elbow; the bird landed lightly there for a second, accepting a quick pat on the head before fluttering back away into the trees.

Once he was sure he was breathing again, Zander nudged Chestnut to catch back up to Thomas and Storm. "Does that kind of thing happen often?" he asked.

"What?"

"Birds just dropping out of the sky to say hello." Just when he was starting to feel like this world was mostly normal, even if he did have to cross a magic bridge at midnight to get here, something happened to make him feel like he'd stepped into a fairytale again.

Thomas chuckled. "That's Zylia. She's Linnea's."

He put his hand under his chin to make sure his mouth wasn't hanging open. "And Linnea can just let her land on her like that? Even with those talons?"

"Zylia's gentle. Unlike *some* seekers," he said, letting out a long, low whistle.

Zander watched, amazed, as a different bird swept out of the trees – where could it have been hiding? This one had the same long gray wings with black tips, but its head was lighter, and there were white spots on its chest. It landed on the ground near them, but took off almost immediately again when Thomas didn't stop. It circled a few feet over their heads for a moment, and then disappeared again.

"Meet Sirian."

"Wow. Does *everyone* have a bird like that here?"

"No. All of the people in my family who are old enough do. Some guards raise them. There are only a few genetic lines of the birds who will allow it, though. They're kind of rare."

"Does Quinn?"

"Oh yes. Her Raeyan is the offspring of Sirian and William's bird Aelwyn – and that little bird has more personality than the rest of them put together. He rescued her once, when she'd been kidnapped."

"When she'd been *what*?"

"It's a long story."

"Would now be the time to ask you exactly what's going on here? I mean, I sort of get that Quinn is the queen of another kingdom, but I don't understand how anything else works. Her real father was from here?"

"Yes. You want the short version?"

"Whatever version you have. I think we have time."

Thomas chuckled. "So, yes, Samuel, Quinn's father, was from here."

"Okay, but that doesn't make any sense. Why would a king or whatever from this world go to my world and have a child?"

"Well, he was never the king. He was supposed to be, but before he was old enough to take the throne, his father died, and his mother got married again to a man named Hector – a man who wanted nothing more than to steal his throne, or actually to put his own son there – a man who was willing to kill Quinn's father to accomplish that."

"I thought Quinn's dad was killed in a car accident in our world."

"He was – or at least that's what we always thought. When Samuel was still a teenager, he realized that his stepfather intended to have him killed. He managed to escape Philotheum and come here, to Eirentheos. He lived with my grandparents for a while, but when they learned how to use the gate to the other world, he went to go live there. It's more complicated than that, of course, but that's the basic story.

"Nathaniel, who was also aware of his stepfather's intentions also left Philotheum and ended up going there too, when they saw the advances your world had – the electricity, the medicine. He believed his life to be in danger as well, and I don't think he was wrong."

"So why did Quinn tell me that she killed the man who killed her father? A car accident isn't murder."

"Unless it was – somehow. For all of these cycles, ever since Samuel died, that's what everyone believed – he was accidentally killed in your world when he was hit by a car. Nobody ever really questioned it, I guess. After all, there was nobody in your world who would have wanted him harmed, and everyone was certain the gate was a well-kept secret here."

"Except it wasn't. Was it?" Zander shifted in the saddle, wondering how the rest of them still seemed so comfortable after riding for so long.

"Apparently not. About ten moons ago, shortly after William and Quinn's wedding and after her family had returned to your world, Quinn began having some very vivid dreams about the gate. Dreams that convinced her the gate needed to be permanently sealed before something terrible happened."

"What would be so terrible?"

"Look around you, Zander. Our world is behind yours in so many ways. In power, in communication, in medicine, and – perhaps most significantly – in weapons."

A little thrill of fear slithered down Zander's throat and settled in his stomach. "You don't have guns here."

"We don't have many of the weapons I'm told exist in your world, but yes, guns are one of our greatest fears. If someone brought your world's weapons into ours, especially in any quantity, it would change everything. An imbalance of power in the hands of a few would easily disrupt hundreds of cycles of peace."

"So why don't you bring the weapons first?"

"Even if my father wanted to rule that way – by force and by fear – and he doesn't, there are bigger issues with the gate. Having it open and using it was always risky. What do you think would happen if the wrong people from your world found out about the gate? Do you know how many untapped resources we have here? Gold. Silver. Probably a thousand other things that aren't nearly as valuable to us as they are to people in your world. What could happen if the wrong people found out about the world on this side of the gate?"

He shuddered, not wanting to imagine that.

Thomas nodded at his reaction. "Exactly. That possibility alone was enough to make Quinn decide that we needed to close the gate – permanently, if we could. She made that decision even knowing that it meant it was likely she would never see her family again."

He didn't really want to imagine *that*, either. How could she have ever brought herself to do it? Her loyalty to this world was stronger than he could really comprehend. "But I thought Owen closed the gate."

"Yes. We tried, here on this end. We searched the banks of the river for days, digging up every rock we could find, but we never found the magnet. William and Nathaniel think maybe it's buried in the bedrock under the river itself. It doesn't matter; the point is we weren't able to do it. The search went on, right until dusk, right when the gate should have opened, and that's when he showed up – Hector.

"He *knew* about it?"

"Apparently he'd known about it for a long time. I don't know how, we never got a chance to find out. But that's when he confessed to Quinn that he'd killed her father. That still doesn't make sense, but that's what he said. He had a gun, somehow, and he told Quinn he was going to kill her, too. He tried to shoot my brother and missed, and he tried to escape through the gate, but it didn't work. The gate wasn't open, even though, timing-wise, it should have been."

"Because Owen closed it."

"We always suspected he had. But we never knew for sure until he came back here with you and told us. William and Quinn were standing with him when Alvin described the location of the magnet on the other side."

"But how did he know to close it?"

"I don't know. Dreams again, I think. Whatever it was, it was the right thing to do. I'm obviously grateful that Owen opened it to bring that medicine – that he saved William, and possibly Ben and Emma too, but it scares me. I'm worried about what the consequences of opening it will be. You have to promise me, Zander, when the two of you go back home, you'll help Owen close it again, and you'll make sure it stays closed. Break the magnet into a thousand pieces if you have to."

Zander swallowed hard as images from the last few days played in his head – of Quinn and Owen curled together on a couch, whispering secrets – of the way Owen looked at his tiny nephew.

"But if Hector is dead…"

"Hector might not have been the only danger. If he knew about the gate, chances are he wasn't the only one. His son is still alive."

"Where is he?"

"Tolliver is in prison – sent there for kidnapping Linnea and putting a knife to her throat."

"Jeez. What happened with that?"

Thomas smiled – though probably only at Zander's choice of words – the memory didn't seem like a happy one. "During the rescue attempt, Ben slipped her a knife and she stabbed Tolliver in the leg. Severed an artery – he could have died. I don't know what it says about me that I wish he had."

"I think it says you're protective of your sister."

"Protective." Thomas shrugged. "Angry." He was rubbing the leather of Storm's reins between his fingers. "Before that, he'd once had me kidnapped by one of his – I don't know, followers? Minions? It was me that nearly died that time. When I was in the hospital in your world – when you were angry with Quinn for coming to visit me – I was having surgery to repair the damage done to my leg. If I hadn't had the option of traveling to your world then – well, I wouldn't be riding horses now. Maybe not ever."

Zander let out a deep sigh. "And there was me – mad at Quinn." He thought back, remembering that day. "That was the night she broke up with me."

Thomas nodded. "That was the day she realized how unfair she was being to you – that she understood how wrapped up in this world she had become – even though we still didn't know the truth about her inheritance – and she knew she was never going to be able to give back to you what you were trying to give to her. She'd never be able to share all of herself with you."

Zander suddenly felt ... *old? young? lost?* He couldn't define it. Here he'd been obsessing over the end of the school year and nursing hurt feelings over his girlfriend breaking up with him and Quinn had been dealing with this? And here was Thomas, younger than him, and yet so much wiser.

He didn't know what to say now, not to any of it, but Thomas seemed to understand. They rode in silence for a long time until they came to a clearing near a river, and Ben and Linnea – who'd gotten quite a bit ahead of them – brought their horses to a stop and dismounted.

When Zander tried to climb down from Chestnut, he realized he had a problem. He could not get his right leg to move up and over the saddle. It would barely budge. He tried the left, but the result was even worse. After that attempt, he couldn't even get his left foot to cooperate and go back into the stirrup.

Down on the ground below him, Thomas coughed.

Heat seeped from Zander's forehead all the way to his neck.

"Do you need some help?" Thomas asked. Zander had to give him credit – there was almost no hint of laughter in his voice.

There was no way out of this, he might as well make the best of it. "I don't know. I think if I manage to get down, I'm going to be stuck in this clearing for a week. I don't think I'll be getting back on."

Now Thomas laughed. "There's three of us. We'll lift you back up somehow. We've got some rope somewhere, if we need it." He held his hand up to Zander. "You'll feel better if you spend some time down and walking around."

Although he was grateful that he was able to get down with only Thomas' help, the sensation he felt once both feet were on the ground was far from relief. His legs were so stiff and sore that it took several minutes before he dared take even one step forward. When he finally did, the first few steps were painful enough to make him wish he'd never agreed to come on this ride, but by the time he made it all the way down to the edge of the water, he knew Thomas was right. Walking around was helping.

"I take it this gets easier?" he asked when Thomas came to stand by him after he brought both Storm and Chestnut down to the water.

"I guess you'll find out." Thomas grinned. "You have to get back somehow."

"People from my world must seem kind of silly to you. Can't even ride a horse for an hour without limping afterwards. Can't swing a sword, or hit a target with an arrow."

"Quinn managed all right from the beginning," Thomas said.

"Of course she did."

"Well, on the horse, anyway. She's still better with daggers than swords or arrows."

"She's probably better than me on either."

"Yes, but she's been here longer, practiced more. I can't drive a car, or figure out your video games. And I can think of a few things I'd be willing to give up in exchange for television."

"Really? You'd trade your world in for television?"

Thomas looked around, over at the horses drinking from the river, over at where Ben and Linnea had found themselves a more secluded spot in a strand of trees and were curled together, talking where nobody could hear them, and then he shook his head.

"No. To be honest, I wouldn't give this up even to have a car – or a hospital here where my leg could have been repaired the way it was in your world – but it would be nice to have both sometimes." Thomas picked up a rock from the riverbank and threw it, making it skip on the water's surface three times before it clunked into the shallow bed. The river wasn't much more than a stream here – it wouldn't have come up any further than the middle of Zander's calf if he'd waded in, but it was wide enough to skip rocks on.

Zander smiled and started to reach for a stone of his own, but – nope – his legs weren't ready to let him bend that way yet. "What are you going to do when you're an adult, Thomas? Or do you have to do anything, since you're a prince?"

Thomas threw his head back and laughed. "Do you think being a prince means I get to sit around in a castle all day and order servants around?"

Zander's cheeks grew warm, but he held his composure. "I honestly don't know anything about princes and castles besides what I've read in storybooks in my world. They don't exist in the place where I live."

"Fair enough. And it was a reasonable question, too, because I don't really know the answer. I grew up helping William and Nathaniel when they were here, traveling around the kingdom and helping them with setting up medical clinics. I didn't do the medical stuff – that is *not* my gift – but I did a lot of the other work. Helping transport supplies, building rooms and cots in clinics, and – maybe the biggest challenge – talking people into accepting some of their new ideas about treating certain things, without giving away where they were learning it.

"I can see where you might be good at that."

Thomas smiled again. "William's gift is healing, but mine is charm. I am pretty good at getting people to accept things."

"Why don't you keep doing it, then?"

"It's different now. William is a king, Nathaniel is back at the castle in Philotheum. I've still been working with the clinics here in Eirentheos a lot, but it isn't the same without them."

"So go with them. To Philotheum or wherever it is."

"That's the first time you've said it right."

"I know I must seem like an idiot with the way I don't know how to do most of the things you can do, and the fact that I can barely get myself from Point A to Point B, but I am capable of learning."

"Yes, but are you capable of trying our food without gagging or making faces?"

"I'm working on it!" Zander said, laughing. "But you have some strange food here. Weird vegetables, strange fruit…"

"Maybe it's the food in your world that's weird," Thomas said. "You should have seen the look on Will's face the first time he tried to describe a tomato to me."

"He doesn't like them?"

"No. He hates all the food in your world that even has tomato sauce on it."

"I knew there had to be at least one legitimate reason not to like him." Zander chuckled.

"He's crazy, right? Nathaniel ordered me a pizza once when I went there to visit them, and after that, he had to order one every time I went."

Thomas scooped up another handful of rocks, handing a couple of them to Zander. They took turns skipping the rocks across the water – here, at last, was something he could do as well as Thomas.

His fifth skip was impressive, the rock skipped seven times before landing – not in the water – but on the opposite bank, making a loud *plunk* and scattering some of the rocks and gravel on the other side.

He was about to turn to Thomas with his grin when he noticed a motion in the trees over there – the sound had startled something. He held his breath as a large animal came out from behind the thick brush – it was a deer, he thought, though her silky black fur was unlike anything he'd ever seen at home. She sniffed at the air, investigating, perhaps trying to determine the origin of the sound, but she clearly hadn't seen them yet.

He looked over at Thomas – but Thomas wasn't there. When he spun around to look for him, he saw him – already halfway to where Linnea and Ben were still sitting on the ground together, his footsteps as light as he could make them on the forest floor.

As Zander watched, Thomas said something quiet to Ben, and Ben rose immediately, his own footsteps silent as he hurried to where Scruffin was standing, and reached up to retrieve something off Scruffin's back – the crossbow.

Oh. Zander didn't think he wanted to watch this. He'd been hunting with his dad before – with rifles and not arrows – and it had never bothered him. Those hunting trips had always been something he looked forward to, even. Hunting and going to the shooting range were second nature to him; guns, he understood – but something about this was different.

There was no time to do anything else, though – not even to say something. Ben pulled the bow down and shot it in a motion so fluid it bordered on magic. Zander didn't even see the arrow fly, he only saw it hit the doe right in the neck; he was both fascinated and horrified when the doe crumpled immediately to the ground.

"Ugh," he heard Linnea say as she walked up behind him. "I hate this."

"You don't like hunting?" he asked her.

"I wouldn't put hunting on my list of favorite activities, no – but this isn't hunting. Not in the normal way, anyway."

"What do you mean?" He looked over at Thomas and Ben, but they weren't listening. Thomas had opened Storm's saddle bag, and was pulling out some kind of map, unfolding it in front of him. "This isn't going to be our dinner at the castle tonight?"

"No. If they test the deer and it's safe to eat, the meat will be preserved and distributed to anyone in the area who normally relies on hunting as a source of food – not that there are really any people in this particular area. We should be almost at the edge of the clear zone."

"The what zone? Why wouldn't the deer be safe to eat?"

"They have to check to make sure it's not carrying rabies. The clear zone ... it's..." Linnea sighed. "It's because we've had an unusually high number of rabies cases, both near the capital city, and in another place called Cloud Valley. My father declared a clear zone in a perimeter around each place – any animal capable of contracting rabies has to either be tightly controlled and observed during the entire clearing period ... or killed and tested."

Wow. "I guess you can't control and observe a deer," Zander said, trying to wrap his head around what she was telling him.

"No. That's mostly for pets and horses – any animals that people own, if they can keep them locked completely inside when they're not outside watching them."

"That seems ... a little extreme. I thought rabies was rare here."

"It is rare, and it is extreme. But the other option is one where people – and the animals they really care about and *need* – die. The wild animal populations will replace themselves over time – more animals will migrate in from outside the zone."

"How long is the clearing period?"

"For thirty days from the last positive case they find – human or animal. Right now it's been six days since that fox at the castle. We need to hope that deer's test comes back clean."

"Okay, Nay," Ben said, coming up behind her holding a small, leather-bound notebook, "this is our location. Can you and Thomas get a message back to the castle so some men can come pick up that deer?"

She nodded. "What are you going to do?"

"I'm going to go and take a look around, make sure there aren't any other animals in the area. I'm not sure this spot has been searched yet. We're really close to the edge of the perimeter here."

"By yourself?"

"I can't have you wandering around in a place where the animals haven't been cleared. It's too dangerous. What if we startle the wrong animal in a bush?"

Linnea rolled her eyes. "What are the chances?"

"Slim, but not zero, Nay. Not zero is too much for my comfort, okay?"

"Owen and I brought back a *lot* of that medicine. Isn't there enough if something did happen?" Zander wondered.

"No," Thomas said. "Not really. There's enough to cover a few more emergencies, but not enough to go inviting them. It's not the vaccine that's as big a concern as the immune globulin. Now that we have more vaccine sample and more time, Nathaniel, William, and Jacob are pretty certain they will be able to make and test a safe enough version of the vaccine. But we don't have a way of making the immune globulin. In order to make it, you need blood from a large number of people who have had the vaccine – or from horses that have. But we don't have those numbers. So we need to be extremely cautious of anyone who hasn't had the vaccine and would need it if they were exposed."

"Besides," Ben said, "someone needs to stay with the horses and keep an eye on them. We can't risk their safety either. I should have checked to make sure this area had been cleared before we came out here."

"I just don't like the idea of you in the woods alone, Ben." Linnea had taken hold of his hand.

"I'll go with him," Zander said. "I know I'm not all that useful, but I can at least keep him company and be an extra set of eyes."

Thomas shook his head. "We try to send our visitors home in the same condition they arrived in."

"You sent Quinn h – back once with stitches and bruises all down her arm." He didn't know when it had happened, but he couldn't really think of Bristlecone as Quinn's home anymore.

"That's because she didn't listen to us."

"Well, I'm not going to listen to you either. I've had the vaccine before, so I'm not at risk of needing immune globulin. I'm safe. You don't want Ben to go alone, so…"

"Just come on, then," Ben said, tucking the map into a leather pouch and slinging it over his shoulder. "Carry this." He held out a long-handled knife in a leather sheath that was attached to a belt.

"I'm probably more dangerous *with* this thing than without it, you know," Zander said, though he accepted it and began buckling the belt around his waist.

"I don't know about that," Ben said. "You were starting to do pretty well with the knives in the gym yesterday afternoon. I'd still appreciate a warning to stand clear if you need to take it out, but I think I'd rather you had it."

Linnea chuckled, but for once it didn't irritate Zander. Instead, he felt a strange warmth in his chest – Ben had said he was doing well at something here. Maybe he wasn't entirely useless.

Of course, some of his pride faded a bit when he took a few steps away so that Linnea could kiss Ben good-bye, and he realized how sore and wobbly his legs were – a vivid reminder of how far he still had to go.

"Don't leave yet," Thomas said, again letting out the low whistle Zander had heard earlier. The giant bird swooped immediately into the clearing, landing only a few feet in front of Thomas.

"Oh, good idea," Linnea said, and a second later, she, too, whistled, bringing her bird down from the trees.

"Do they follow you everywhere?" Zander asked, stunned.

"Yes. Unless we send them somewhere – with a message, or to find someone." Thomas walked to Storm and pulled something small out of the saddle bag before returning, and holding the little item toward Zander.

It was a pouch, he realized, made of some kind of thick cloth – oilcloth, maybe? It felt waterproof. Frowning, he opened it. There was dried meat inside.

"Feed him a piece," Thomas said, nodding toward the bird, which was – to Zander's discomfort – strutting closer. Linnea's bird was looking at him, her black liquid eyes blinking in interest.

He raised his eyebrows. "*Feed* him?" The bird's beak looked razor-sharp and he wasn't even considering the…

"Don't worry. He won't use those talons on you if you're giving him a treat. He has better manners than that. So does Zylia. Go ahead. Take out a piece of meat, and then kneel down and hold it out toward him."

He couldn't believe his hands were actually trembling as he reached into the pouch for some of the meat, though he was grateful when crouching down to the ground wasn't as hard as he'd feared it would be – his legs were beginning to recover.

The bird wasn't nearly as shy as he was expecting – *hoping?* – it to be. As soon as he extended his hand with the treat in it, Sirian headed straight for him, snatching the meat away from him. He didn't even have time to pull his hand back before Zylia startled him by knocking her head on the underside of his hand, obviously looking for hers.

Linnea chuckled. "You'd better hurry."

"Or she'll what?" he asked, suddenly nervous.

But Zylia answered the question for him. A second later, she closed her beak on the pouch itself, pulling it right out of his other hand and carried it several feet away.

They all laughed as both birds descended on the pouch, managing somehow to get all of the meat out and eat it without even damaging the leather.

Linnea clicked her tongue at them. "And after we just praised your manners to Zander," she chided them. "You ought to tell Zander thank you now that you've enjoyed your snack."

For a moment, he thought Linnea was only being facetious – the birds couldn't have understood her – but then both Sirian and Zylia strutted toward him, and, one at a time, rubbed their heads against his hand very gently, in a gesture that seemed like supplication.

Zander nearly fell over backwards.

"Do they really understand you?"

"Yes. And now they know who you are, so we can send them searching for you if we need to."

"That is amazing," he breathed. Though he was awestruck by the birds, he was nearly as impressed when he was able to stand back up on his feet without help.

"All right," Thomas said, as the birds took off into the sky again. "Here are some sandwiches. You two have an hour to do your exploring before we send the birds after you for real."

THE TENT

Carperos Forest, Eirentheos

LESS THAN FIVE minutes into his walk in the forest with Ben, Zander knew that he was worse than useless; he was counter-productive. Even armed with a heavy sword and the crossbow, Ben's steps were silent, undetectable – a feat Zander wouldn't have been able to manage even unarmed and on a day where he wasn't walking bow-legged and sore from sitting in an unfamiliar saddle.

Every twig that Zander snapped, every leaf that crunched under his heavy steps had to have been grinding on Ben's last nerve, but if that was the case, he didn't show it. He walked slower than necessary, matching Zander's pace, moving overhead branches out of the way for both of them. Several times he stopped and pointed atan interesting bird in the air or a hearty plant that was still growing at the base of one of the massive trees.

After a while, Ben even gave up the pretense of silence, chuckling and pointing up again. "Zylia has decided to just go ahead and be protective of us."

Sure enough, the enormous bird was perched in one of the trees just behind them, her watchful eyes seeing everything. When they continued moving, she waited only a moment before taking to the air, landing again where they would have to walk directly under her.

"She should be protective. If she's half as smart as she appears to be, she's got to be worried I'll get you killed out here."

Ben snickered. "I'm not worried about you getting us killed. You are probably scaring away anything big that might be out here, I'll admit."

"Sorry."

"Don't be. If I see any tracks or signs of anything, we can sweep the area again when help comes to haul away that deer … and at least you'll scare away any bears, too."

"What? Are there bears in this area?" Zander suddenly wished Ben had given him a few more lessons with knives before he'd said yes to the horseback ride.

"Well, not with the noise you're making. But, yes, sometimes we've heard reports of them in this area."

Somehow, thinking about the possibility of running into whatever this world's version of a *bear* was improved Zander's stealth considerably. Over the next several minutes, he paid attention to the careful way Ben was placing his feet, and soon, he understood how Ben either avoided the twigs and leaves, or managed to muffle the sounds they made when he had to step on them.

But even though they were now silent and probably not scaring anything away, twenty more minutes of searching the area turned up nothing bigger than a chipmunk. Ben shook his head when Zander pointed out the tiny creature nibbling away at something right next to a rotting log.

"We don't have to worry about anything that small," he said, barely even glancing at it as he continued scanning the area.

"I thought any mammal could get rabies."

"I think any mammal probably *could* – if it could survive the bite that would cause it."

Okay then.

"Let's just finish searching this spot – I'm going to go down and take a look along the riverbank – and then we can head back."

"Okay," Zander said, nodding as he headed for a stand of trees.

The long, unfruitful search had caused him to drop his guard much too soon – a fact he didn't realize until he walked confidently into the grove and stepped on something that squirmed underneath him.

His yelp was much louder than the creature's.

Ben was beside him before he even had a chance to fully catch his breath. "What's wrong?"

"What…is…*that?*" he asked, pointing to the animal that he'd now taken several steps back from.

It was like nothing he had ever seen in his world. About the size of a terrier, its long fur was mottled brown and gray, except for the black stripe that extended from its forehead all the way down its back and the black rings circling the length of its incredibly long tail. He assumed it had eyes, though they were impossible to see underneath the thick mass of fur on its face.

It was shaking and making odd *humph* noises every few seconds – though Zander didn't know if that was due to the fact that it had just been stepped on, or if it was because the thing was trapped. A rope was secured just under its front legs, tied tightly enough to reveal just how much of what appeared to be the animal's mass was really only its excessive fur, and the other end was secured to the nearest tree.

"*That* is a capiya," Ben said, sighing. "You should step away if you don't want to watch." He pulled out his sword.

Zander didn't want to watch, but he couldn't look away, either. Ben's technique was so clean that the animal didn't suffer at all; only seconds later, the capiya was completely still.

"Let me guess. Those things can get rabies."

Ben looked up from where he was cleaning his sword. "Capiyas are one of the biggest carriers of rabies. Do you not have them in your world?"

"No."

"You're lucky. They're kind of cute, but they're vicious. They'll eat anything. Sometimes, three or four of them will work together and take down a sheep."

"I was sad about you killing it right up until you said that."

Ben stood, tucking his sword back in the scabbard. "The real question is where did this trap come from? Someone was trying to catch something out here." He started looking around, and Zander followed.

At first, there was nothing — the same nothing they'd been seeing their entire search. But then he saw it — a patch of gray between the trees that didn't quite match the surrounding landscape. "Ben!"

Ben looked where Zander was pointing. "What?"

"Down there, close to the river. Is that a tent?"

Ben froze, putting one hand on the hilt of his sword, and using the other to push Zander behind a large tree, whistling as he did so.

Almost instantly, a bird flew out of the trees — not Sirian or Zylia; this one was pure alabaster, except for her black hood and the undersides of her wings. "Cielian," he whispered to Zander, by way of introduction.

When the bird landed, Ben knelt next to her, reaching to open a small metal cylinder attached to her leg that Zander hadn't noticed. From inside, he retrieved a rolled-up piece of paper and some kind of pencil.

"Are you sending a note to Thomas and Linnea?"

"No. To the castle. I need more armed guards than they're sending to pick up that doe — someone who won't have a wagon so they can ride faster."

Once the bird was gone, Zander and Ben stood there in the trees for a long time, staring down at the structure. Whether it was actually a tent or not, Zander wasn't sure, but it was most definitely a shelter of some kind. Someone had built it there. Perhaps the same person daring enough to set a trap for capiyas.

After about ten minutes had passed with no movement from the shelter, though, Zander looked over at Ben.

"I know we were trying to be quiet and all of that, but … don't you think that whoever is down there has probably already heard us?"

"If they're even *there*," Ben said, nodding. "It's possible someone is just using it as a hunting shelter."

"I thought there weren't many people living out in this direction."

"There aren't."

"I think we should go and check it out."

Ben raised an eyebrow, though it was obvious from the look in his eyes that he'd been considering the same thing for several minutes.

"Our hour is almost up. We can't wait here, or Thomas and Linnea are going to come looking for us, and then it might really get dangerous. And if we go back to them and wait for soldiers, someone might sneak out of there and we'd miss it."

"That sounds like a safer option."

"Okay," Zander said, turning his body back toward where Thomas and Linnea were waiting and taking a step.

"Come on," Ben sighed.

Slowly, silently, the two of them crept toward the shelter. As they sloped downward toward the river, more of the structure came into view. It was much larger than he'd thought at first – an enormous canvas tent. They were facing the side of it, but when they curved their path to avoid a large felled tree, he could see the sides of the unsecured entrance flapping in the breeze.

They were only about ten feet from the tent when the wind suddenly shifted, and Zander nearly fainted.

Ben buried his face in his elbow.

Zander's eyes were watering as he looked around, desperately searching for the source of the stench.

"Something's dead," Ben said. "In that tent, or the smell wouldn't be so concentrated." He had his hand clenched tightly on the hilt of his sword.

Zander turned his head to the side as far as he could to try to suck a breath of clean air through his mouth. He wasn't sure if the rolling in his stomach was only from the appalling odor, or if the thought that there might be a dead body only a few feet away from them was contributing. "There can't be anybody *alive* in there. The smell alone would kill them."

Nodding, Ben reached into the leather pouch he wore on his belt and pulled out something white – some sort of cloth. Zander realized there were two pieces of the cloth when Ben separated them and held one out to him. A handkerchief – or something like one, anyway, although they were quite a bit larger than normal handkerchiefs.

"Tie it around your face," Ben said, demonstrating with his own.

It was a little easier to breathe with the cloth covering his nose and mouth – but only a little. The closer they got to the tent, the more tempted Zander was to turn and run away. "Maybe we should wait for the other soldiers; you've already asked them to come."

"If this is too much for you I understand. You can wait for me back up the hill away from the smell."

Yes, sure, he could go wait back up the hill like a coward and let Ben do this alone. Pulling the cloth as tight as he could, he matched his steps to Ben's.

When they reached the entrance, Ben pulled out his sword and stepped in front of Zander, motioning him back with his free hand. "Stay out here for a minute."

Although he was expecting it, and he'd made sure to inhale as much upwind air as he could first, the wall of fumes that escaped when Ben pulled the flap all the way open nearly knocked Zander over. He tried to hold it together, but finally he couldn't, and he managed to rip the handkerchief away from his mouth only a fraction of a second before he vomited on the ground, right there on the side of the tent. Ben was already inside.

"Zander!" At the sound of the alarm in Ben's voice, Zander's nausea was instantly replaced by a jolt of adrenaline. He barely managed to get the handkerchief tied back over his face as he ran into the tent.

He had almost forgotten about the knife he was carrying, but he remembered just as he slipped through the opening in the canvas, and he grabbed it, wrapping his fingers tightly around the handle.

The scene inside the tent nearly made him drop it, though. The source of the smell was obvious almost immediately. Just inside the entrance of the tent, off to the side, there were two animals – a gray thing that looked like a fox, and another capiya – lying on the floor under two wood-and-wire crates. Aside from the smell, they weren't a danger to anyone, although they appeared to be a boon to the thousands upon thousands of flies buzzing around them.

But the animals weren't what had made Ben cry out.

Next to the back wall of the tent, there was a cot – the folding wooden kind that reminded Zander of military movies, in the same way the tent itself did. And on the cot, there was a man.

He didn't know how the man could possibly be alive; even in the dim light in the tent, it was obvious how ill he was, but his chest was rising and falling in shallow breaths, and as Zander approached, his eyelids fluttered, though they didn't open for long. Zander suspected that even the action of blinking required a level of effort the man was no longer capable of exerting.

"Hello?" he said, but the man didn't respond at all.

Ben had re-sheathed his sword, but he seemed unable to make any other moves; he was frozen in the middle of the tent. "It's water disease," he whispered. "Be careful."

"Water disease? Rabies?"

"Yes."

He didn't know if that was true, though he had no reason to doubt Ben. The man was barely alive. "We need Thomas and Linnea now."

Ben nodded woodenly – he wasn't handling this well. Zander didn't know if it was the shock or the smell. Either one would have been enough. He was actually surprised that he hadn't passed out on the dirt floor of the tent himself, leaving Ben to deal with this alone.

"We need to get the tent down," he said to Ben. They needed the light to see what was going on – and the *air*. They needed fresh air. He felt like they should be helping the man more than this somehow, but right now the most important thing was to get everyone away from the fumes. "Should we get them out of here?" he nodded toward the man and then to the animals. Not that he had any idea how to go about it. He was going to need more air sooner than that if he was going to avoid getting sick again.

The concrete suggestion of action seemed to unfreeze Ben, and he pulled out his sword.

Abject terror washed over Zander when Ben walked toward the back of the tent – toward the sick man, with his sword raised. He was too stunned to move.

But Ben walked around the cot and plunged his sword right into the back wall of the tent, slicing open as wide a strip as he could before sheathing the sword again and pulling out the shorter knife. He used that to rip the opening larger, making an enormous hole all the way to the bottom of the tent, shoving the material he removed onto the ground outside.

The sudden burst of cool, fresh air made Zander almost weak with relief. The smell in the tent was so overpowering, he hadn't even noticed how stiflingly warm it was.

"Okay, help me," he said to Zander, putting away the knife and moving to the head of the cot.

Zander went to the foot of the little bed and bent down to help lift it. He closed his mouth – while much of the smell was coming from the rotting animal carcasses in the other corner, they weren't responsible for all of it. He wondered how long the man had been there.

It didn't take much effort for the two of them to get the cot outside; the man didn't weigh as much as a full-grown man should, although he probably once had.

The motion and the outside air did seem to revive the man a little. His eyes opened all the way, and a low-pitched sound came from his mouth –almost a moan, but not quite. When the man saw Zander and Ben, he looked terrified.

"It's all right," Ben said. "We're going to try and help you."

It almost looked like the man was shaking his head. His eyes were wide with panic.

"Do you need anything? Would you like something to drink?" He'd seen what looked like a metal water bottle on the ground by the cot – not that he had any desire to go back into the tent.

But at Zander's words, the man's whole body began convulsing, and the low moaning sounds became choked gasps. He watched in horror, afraid that the man was going to die right there in front of him. Eventually, though, the convulsions subsided, and the man's body relaxed – as much as it could, Zander supposed, and his eyes fell closed again.

"That's why we call it water disease," Ben said, low next to Zander's ear. "At the end, even just thinking about drinking…"

Back at the time of the bat incident, although Zander hadn't been terribly bothered by the shots – except maybe for the ones on the first day – he had thought Doctor Rose was overreacting when he'd insisted on everyone getting them. Now he prayed that he was still protected by them.

"We need to burn this tent," Ben said. "There's nothing about this that's possibly safe."

"What about those animals?"

"They don't need to be tested. They're dead of rabies. They have to be. I don't know what he was *doing* with them in there. I don't understand what's going on here."

"Do you think he was hunting and just got really unlucky?"

"I don't know. Normal people don't hunt capiyas. Or foxes, usually."

"He had other animals in there, too."

"What?"

"Yeah. Not now, but there were other crates stacked along the far wall."

Ben frowned, and began walking around the outside of the tent, his sword drawn again. When he reached the corner where they'd seen the animals, he slashed at the fabric, revealing them – and letting another cloud of the putrid air escape. Zander gagged, but this time held on to whatever was left of his sandwich as he squinted and tried to see what was under there.

Now that light was pouring in from three sides of the tent, it was easier to see. "He had more than just capiyas and foxes in here," Zander said. "Those droppings over there by those crates are different."

Ben slashed away even more of the tent, opening as much of it as he could before walking over to where Zander was pointing and kneeling down to investigate. "You're right. What was he doing?"

"I don't know." Zander was still overwhelmed by the stench, but he was curious now. Pulling the cloth tighter around his face and taking a deep breath from the open flap in the tent, he knelt down between the two cages. "The fox has been dead much longer than this thing." Another day or two, and it wouldn't have been recognizable. The capiya, though, seemed to have died much more recently – possibly in the last day. The horrible smell wasn't as strong by its cage, and there weren't nearly as many flies surrounding it.

"It was bitten," Ben said, nodding at the capiya's leg.

It was worse than just a bite. The capiya's entire front right leg had been mauled and torn. Its fur was clean, though, and the edges of the wound had begun to heal before it died. It had survived the attack.

"I don't think this thing died of rabies, Ben." He looked around more, noting two empty metal bowls in the corner of the cage, and the animal's sunken ribs. "Or at least, I think it needs to be tested. I think maybe both of them do."

He stood and walked back out of the tent, scanning the whole area. The relief he felt when he finally got far away enough from the odor to remove the cloth on his face was overshadowed by the sense that something was really wrong here, though he couldn't put his finger on what.

"I could really stand to wash up," Ben said, coming to stand beside him.

Zander nodded. "Let's clean up in the river, and then go and find Thomas and Linnea while we wait for the soldiers to come and find us."

Putting his face into the cool, clear stream was going to stick in his mind as one of the best sensations he'd ever felt in his life. His cheeks actually ached from grimacing against the smell for so long. He didn't even think to ask Ben whether the water was safe to drink or not before opening his mouth and drawing in long sips straight from the surface, replacing the sour taste with the sweet fresh water.

When the question of safety finally crossed his mind after several minutes, he looked over at Ben and was relieved to see the guard doing exactly the same thing. Smiling, he turned back to the water and took several more gulps.

CHARLOTTE

Rosewood Castle, Eirentheos

THE SITTING ROOM was empty and the door to the bedroom was almost all the way closed when William entered the suite he shared with Quinn.

Quietly, so he wouldn't disturb any conversation that might be going on in there, he crept to the door to take a peek.

The scene inside made him smile. Quinn was at the top of the large bed, propped up with lots of pillows, Samuel cradled in her arms. Owen was right next to her, curled into her side, his head resting on her arm, his hand wrapped protectively around the baby's legs.

They were all asleep.

It had been a long few days for everyone, especially Owen and Quinn who were trying to make the most of every second they had together. Last night, William had finally walked Owen to his own bed after what should have been the first feeding Samuel usually woke them up for – only they'd all still been up talking.

He was enjoying watching them so much that he accidentally leaned too hard against the door, pushing it all the way open, and making it creak a little. *Oops.* He'd have to remember to ask for some oil.

The noise didn't disturb Quinn or Owen, but Samuel's eyes flashed open, and he started to stir.

As silently as he could, William hurried over to the bed. He held his breath as he moved Owen's arm a couple of inches away from the baby, and then he carefully lifted Samuel into his arms and rushed him out of the room just as he opened his mouth to fuss. Whether it should have been possible or not, the baby was looking wistfully toward the bedroom.

"I know," he said, kissing Samuel on the forehead after he closed the door. "You want your Uncle Owen. But can you settle for your father for a few minutes while your mama and your uncle get some rest?"

At the sound of his voice, the baby actually did stop fussing and looked up at him. "See, I'm not so bad," William cooed at him, rocking him back and forth in his arms. "I took a bath this morning and everything."

Samuel only blinked.

William chuckled. "You, on the other hand, need cleaned up a bit, I think."

He hummed softly as he carried Samuel over to the couch, retrieving a clean diaper and outfit from a basket of fresh laundry as he went. The baby seemed to like the sound, and lay there contentedly as William took his time, securing the new diaper just-so, and changing him out of the old, spit-stained outfit.

"Good as new," he said when he was finished, smiling when Samuel wrapped his tiny little fingers around his thumb. "You're pretty awesome, little love."

Owen's camera was still sitting on the table by the couch. It had been a constant fixture for the last three days. William had never been terribly interested in any of the technology in the other world that wasn't medical in nature – but he was sure he would miss being able to snap the everyday images of his son's infancy once Owen took it back.

Samuel's current peaceful mood allowed him to take a few more nice shots.

"Want to go for a walk?" he asked, once he'd scooped the baby back into his arms.

Interpreting his son's relaxed silence as consent, he scribbled a quick note for Quinn, and carried Samuel into the hallway.

"William!" He heard his mother's voice as soon as he turned the corner that led to the common room. "I was just going to head to your room to ask if you'd returned and to see if Quinn was going to remember to eat lunch."

"I'm keeping my wife fed, Mother, don't worry."

"It's my job to look after you when you're here. You'll be leaving again soon enough, and then I won't be able to annoy you with my concern."

He smiled, looking – *down* – at her. When had that happened? She'd once been the tallest woman in the world, the perfect height for him to hide in her skirts when things got overwhelming.

"You just wanted an excuse to see the baby."

"Can you blame me? Look at him."

Grinning, he held the little bundle out toward her. A happy little thrill ran down his spine at the look on her face as she kissed his son, cradling him close.

"You never get tired of it, do you, Mother?"

"Of babies? Of my children and grandchildren? No." She reached to squeeze his hand in hers before taking her hand back and using one finger to sweep the tiny delicate strands of black hair away from Samuel's forehead. "I am truly blessed. Thirteen beautiful and loving children, one of them already a king, another who will be one someday … and two grandsons who will grow to be kings as well." She moved her finger and kissed Samuel's forehead.

"No mother could deserve that honor more than you do."

She looked at him, warmth and love in her eyes. "It would have been as much an honor to be your mother, William even if you'd grown and chosen to stay in the other world with Quinn."

"Thank you, Mother. I think I'm the honored one."

"When I thought I was going to lose you…"

"I know. I'm sorry to have worried you all so much."

She squeezed his hand again. "Where is Quinn, anyway?"

"I found her and Owen asleep. I thought I'd take this one for a little while and make sure she gets a nice nap."

"I suppose I did raise you well. How are things in Mistle Village today?"

"Good." He nodded. "Jacob and Essie send you their regards, and they promise to bring little Patrick to see you soon. He's smiling and babbling already."

"And the vaccine?"

"Should be ready in the next several days. The challenge now is finding someone to test it on. It's good news, of course, that we don't *need* it for anyone. Jacob actually wants to test it on himself, to see if he develops enough antibodies, and Nathaniel is considering testing whether it will work as a booster dose on himself."

"Do you think it will be safe for them?"

"Now I do. Not perfect, maybe, but not dangerous. The notes and articles Owen brought back for us were more helpful than we could have dreamed. It's so fortunate that he brought them."

"He's a very special child."

"Yes."Special in so many ways.

"Well, since I have you to myself for a few minutes, without Quinn, could you spare me a word?"

He frowned. Weren't they talking already? "Of course."

"In my room?"

"Is everything all right?" he asked as he closed the door to his parents' sitting room.

"Yes, everything is fine. I just thought this conversation called for a bit more privacy than the hallway." She sat down on one of the overstuffed couches, still cradling Samuel.

"Well, it can't be all that wonderful if you need to talk to me without Quinn."

She smiled. "I suppose it does look that way, but it isn't anything I mean to keep from her – just something I thought I'd talk to you about first."

"Okay. So what is it, Mother?"

"I've been getting some very ... *interesting* messages from Sophia."

He took a deep breath. "I'm not surprised. I've gotten a few of them myself."

"She's going to make Quinn's life miserable."

"She's very good at what she does."

"Yes."

"I don't know how to handle her, Mother. She's the former queen – she knows every inch of the castle and all of the servants ... and she's Quinn's grandmother. Quinn has so little family – anywhere, really, but here in this world especially. I don't want to get between her and her family."

"I know, son, but Sophia is overstepping her bounds. Her most recent message was asking about how to choose between her final three candidates for a baby nurse. I finally got irritated and wrote back that she needed to hold off on the whole thing until you all return and allow Quinn to pick. I haven't heard from her since."

William let out a deep sigh. "That would explain the message I just received about how I was really asking too much of my family to have you all travel to Philotheum at this time of the cycle for the Naming Ceremony. Apparently, I don't have enough regard for the safety of the children."

His mother threw her head back and laughed. "I don't suspect she also suggested waiting until the new cycle to travel back to her with *your* child."

"Of course not. There's some rationale, you know, about our only going one way and not a round trip, but…"

"Exactly. I know, William." She chuckled. The baby stirred in her arms, but she shifted him, quickly and expertly to her shoulder, patting his back. He let out a big belch, making them both laugh.

"I should have checked that. I think he might have fallen asleep while Quinn was feeding him."

"He's my grandson. He can burp on me as much as he wants to." She kissed the top of his head. "Anyway, what I wanted to speak to you about is Mia."

"What about her?"

She sighed. "The reason I'm talking to you first and not to Quinn is that I don't want to overstep my bounds with her, either. I don't want her to feel as if I'm trying to control her choices."

"I don't think she feels that way about you at all."

"Perhaps because I choose to be careful. It's a skill I've really had to practice with Evelyn, who will someday rule this castle beside Simon, and who is already trying to raise her child here. I'm sure there are some days she probably feels the way about me that Quinn does about Sophia."

"You underestimate Sophia."

"Maybe. Anyway, I don't want Quinn – or you – to feel obligated by what I'm about to suggest to you. Your family … your castle … how you handle things is your choice."

"Understood, Mother. Thank you. Now what about Mia?"

"I've been watching her lately. I've seen her interact with Quinn and Samuel, and I know she's very close with both of you."

"Yes, we care for Mia very much, and are very thankful for the help she's been with him."

"I think she would be interested in the job of baby nurse at the castle in Philotheum."

"You would be open to something like that? You've trained her here – *raised* her here, really. The girls are still little…"

"Your father and I are extremely grateful for the service that Mia and her entire family have provided to us for many cycles. She grew up here as a wonderful help – one of the best natural baby nurses I've ever seen. It's been a pleasure to train her and watch her grow. But we don't own her. And she still works under her mother here. It would be a tremendous honor for her to be offered a job as the head nurse in Philotheum. An honor I think she is deserving of and prepared for. Although that, of course, would be Quinn's decision and yours."

"I think we'd be hard pressed to do better."

"I agree."

"It's actually something we've thought about. Owen even said something the other day … he had a dream. He told Quinn and Linnea that Samuel himself was trying to convince us that Mia was supposed to be his baby nurse."

She chortled. "I think he might be right. Your father had quite a similar dream the other night."

"We just didn't know what you might think about it. We didn't even know how to approach you with the idea."

"That's why your father and I decided that I should be the one to bring it up to you."

"I don't even know if *Mia* would be open to the idea, though. That's asking a lot of her. To leave her family, and her home for such a far-away job."

"Well, of course you'll have to discuss it with her, but I suspect she's more open to it than you'd think. She's so … there was such an immediate difference in her when you and Quinn returned, William. And when Samuel was born. She's been asking subtle questions for weeks now that have led both your father and I to suspect that leaving us is on her mind. I think there's been a lot of everyone thinking the same thing, but everyone being afraid to come right out and ask."

William nodded, considering that. "She's afraid to lose the job she has, probably."

"That. And afraid of sounding impertinent by coming out and asking about the job in Philotheum."

"And Thomas…" William frowned. "That would crush Thomas. We can't do that to him."

"Your father and I talked about that as well – both in the context of Mia possibly going, and even if she doesn't. What do you think about Thomas going to Philotheum with you?"

"To stay?"

"Yes. To live."

"He's underage."

"That's hardly a fair standard to hold him to, William. He's earned far more than that. Your father and I have no intention of withholding the recognition he very much deserves."

"You're talking about losing three of your children to Philotheum."

"Four, counting Quinn – and we do count her. But we don't consider it a loss. It's difficult on us, of course, having you so far away, but you weren't ours to begin with, not really. You all have your own lives, your own choices and destinies. We have to share you all with the rest of the world sometime. I'll just be grateful that the Maker saw fit to bless us with enough children to keep our hands and our minds occupied here for many more cycles."

"You'd really let Thomas go – if he wanted to."

"Yes. It's hard, but it's also hard not to see that if we keep Thomas here when this isn't where he wants to be, we would still lose him. He's already been struggling all these moons without you and Quinn … and to keep him here while Linnea goes … and then if Mia decided to … I can't do that to him, William. If you and Quinn would agree to it, it would feel so much better knowing he's happy there. And from what I can see, you all could use a little more support there."

"We could, Mother. There's no question of whether Quinn and I would agree to it. Even discussing the idea feels like a celebration. Quinn's getting our sister. I need my brother."

The conversation with his mother left William smiling to himself as he carried Samuel back down the hall. "Should we go see if *your* mother is awake?" he asked the baby. "I want to talk to her."

In response, the baby pulled his fist to his mouth and began sucking on it.

"You want her even more than I do, don't you, little one?" he said, chuckling. "Even if she is still asleep, you're going to demand that she wakes. You're a little monarch already." His words were far from criticism; he snuggled little Samuel close and pulled one of the tiny hands to his lips.

He opened the door of the suite quietly, but Quinn was already awake, standing by the little table, holding the note he'd written to her.

"Hey," he said, coming to stand next to her.

"Hi." Turning around, she stretched up to kiss him.

"Did you have a nice nap?"

"Mmm-hmm. I'm surprised I fell asleep like that."

He smiled. "Is Owen still asleep?"

She nodded.

Samuel began to fuss. William chuckled and began rocking and bouncing him. "You're an impatient little bug. Let your mama get settled and get a drink first."

"Good luck with that, Daddy," Quinn teased.

William smiled – the term "daddy" was foreign to him – he'd only heard it in passing in Bristlecone. But he sort of liked it when she used it in reference to him. He offered his finger to Samuel, who accepted it, quieting down as he clamped his little gums onto it and sucked. "You were saying?"

"That our son lucked out in the father department." She rested her head against his shoulder and wrapped her arm around his waist.

"I didn't think I could love you any more than I did on the day you proposed to me, Will, but you just keep surprising me."

"I think Samuel and I are the lucky ones."

Quinn was just getting settled on the couch, and William was in the process of handing her the baby when there was a knock at the door.

She frowned.

"One minute!" William called. He finished nestling Samuel into her arms and kissed her on the head before answering it.

"I'm sorry to interrupt, Your Majesties," Marcus said when William opened the door.

"You're never a bother, Marcus," Quinn said. "Come on in. Is everything all right?"

"Yes and no. We've had a bit of an interesting afternoon."

"What do you mean?" A little twinge of fear twisted in William's stomach.

"Don't get worried. Everyone is all right. But Ben sent a bird earlier about a very strange situation they encountered on their ride. Luke took two groups of men out to retrieve three potentially rabid animals – and one man who sounds to be in grave condition."

"Well that sounds like something to be worried about, Marcus." Samuel fussed at the agitation in her voice.

"Yes, it is very troubling. I'm very concerned about the man, of course."

"And three more animals with rabies?" William knew his own voice was strained. Three animals at the same time could indicate a much larger outbreak than they were prepared to deal with. "That's a very big deal. Were they inside the clear zone?"

"Near the border, I think, just inside Carperos Forest. An area I'm afraid hadn't been cleared as well as it could have been."

"Maybe we didn't make the zone large enough. Have you told Nathaniel?"

"Yes. They should all be beginning to arrive here in the next twenty minutes or so. Nathaniel is down in the clinic now preparing to receive the man and the animals. He's also sent a bird to Jacob. We're going to need as much help as possible with this, I think."

He looked apologetically at Quinn. "I'll head down there now."

She nodded; her expression held only understanding and concern.

"Hold on. There's something else."

They both looked at him.

"Her Majesty has just had a visit from Prince Jonathan's bird." Marcus opened the flap of the leather pouch he carried on his shoulder and reached inside, withdrawing a small, rolled-up slip of paper. Quinn's name was on the side of the roll, written in the elegant script of her uncle.

William took it from him, breaking the seal and unrolling the letter so that Quinn wouldn't have to do it one-handed as she fed the baby. He didn't look at it before he passed it over to her.

The letter was short. Quinn's eyebrows knitted together as she scanned it quickly and then looked back up at them. "He's coming here. He'll be arriving this evening."

"This evening?" William was surprised. Philotheum was a long journey away. Even a single rider pressing his horse would need close to three days. "When did the message come?"

"Just a little while ago. And the bird flew away immediately. Returning directly to him, I presume. I don't know why he didn't give us more warning."

"I guess he'll tell us when he gets here," Quinn said, sighing.

It shouldn't have been concerning news — both he and Quinn liked and trusted Jonathan — at least mostly — but something about this felt off.

"All right, Marcus," Quinn said, making eye contact with him. "I think it's time now for you to fill me in on all of the little concerns you've been keeping from me the last few weeks. I know some of it, but I don't want to be off-guard when Jonathan arrives."

Marcus smiled sheepishly. "I was only trying to give you a bit of time to relax, Your Majesty."

"I know, Marcus. That's why I didn't say anything before. I have appreciated it, truly. But reality seems to have come creeping back in on its own. Have any other messages gone missing, do you think?"

"All of our messages have been answered recently, milady. The few that we're worried about didn't contain any sensitive information."

She sighed. "Meaning it's likely that whoever may have intercepted them determined that we don't know whatever it is they don't want us to know about, and it's just not worth the risk of us catching their spies."

"That's a strong possibility, yes." Marcus nodded.

"And the hostilities in the border towns?"

"Quiet in the last two weeks, actually. Ever since we sent the troops to Milderan things have gotten better, but there's just something I'm not quite comfortable with. Charles doesn't like it either. I have some messages from him for you to read."

"All right. Let me finish here, and get Owen over to play with the other children and see if Mia can take care of the baby for a while, and then you can brief me."

"Let me take them," William said. "Nathaniel can hold his own in the clinic for a few minutes."

EXPOSED

Rosewood Castle, Eirentheos

AT FIRST, WHEN Ben had asked Zander to ride with one of the wagons rather than on Chestnut to go back to the castle, he'd thought it would be a much easier option. Anything had to be easier than the prospect of putting his sore legs back on a saddle.

An hour on the wooden seat of a utility wagon quickly convinced him otherwise. It didn't help matters even a little that this wagon carried the carcasses of the animals they'd discovered in the tent, along with the black deer and the remnants of the strange discovery Zander and Ben had made along the riverbank.

They had covered the animals with canvas cloth, and at first he'd thought that it was going to work, but fifteen minutes into the journey, he found himself wishing for a world where large sheets of plastic actually existed.

Twice, he'd had to bury his nose in his hands, taking deep breaths through his mouth and thinking about something else – anything else – to keep himself from getting sick again.

One of those times, the driver, a young-looking guard named Tobias, actually had gotten sick. He hadn't stopped, though, he'd merely leaned over the side of the wagon while it was still moving, done what he needed to do, and then pulled a cloth over his own face when he was finished.

For obvious reasons they were riding behind everyone else, and so when they pulled up in front of the clinic behind the castle, everyone was already busy, attending to the man in the other wagon as Ben and Nathaniel worked to get him inside.

He could see Thomas and Linnea riding toward the stables, away from the clinic. Ben had been very adamant about keeping them away from everything. Even the other guards who'd been assisting them had been forced to take precautions – handling the animals only with shovels and making no direct contact with the man, but Ben had made Thomas and Linnea stay on their horses, at least ten feet away from everything at all times.

Thomas had been a bit chagrined about the arrangement, but Linnea, for once, had complied without complaint – though Zander was certain it was only because Ben was the one asking.

William came running up to him as he climbed down from the wagon, though he stopped short a few feet away. "Oh, whoa," he said, fanning his hand in front of his face. "What *is* that?" He peered into the wagon.

"The animals." Zander knew the information had gotten back to the castle before them. "The fox has been dead for too long, and it and the capiya were closed inside a tent for days, probably. You don't want to lift that cloth if you don't have to."

"I'm sure I'll have to eventually, but I'll hold off." He took a few more steps back from the wagon and Zander followed him, grateful to get as far as he could away from the stench. "Ben was just telling me something about bones, too?"

"Yeah. That's when it got really creepy. The tent was bad enough, but then when Ben and I were down by the river washing up, we found these little areas that had been dug up recently."

"And there were animal bones in there?"

"Some of them had more than that. One was still a pretty intact raccoon. Ben is certain it died of rabies – and someone buried it. Maybe that guy. There were raccoon droppings inside the tent."

William's jaw dropped. "I don't like the sound of that."

"No. I don't think it's good at all."

William raised an eyebrow. "Do you have a theory, Zander?"

He swallowed. "I don't think I know enough about your world to be coming up with theories."Especially not ones this macabre.

"Sometimes, not knowing the lay of the land gives someone an advantage in situations like this. You see the issue without the preconceived notions we have about what things should be like."

"All right then. I don't know who that guy is, but if I had to guess, I would say it looks like he was somehow intentionally infecting those animals with rabies. Trapping them, infecting them, and then burying them when they died."

"Yes, that's what it sounds like to me, too."

"But that doesn't make any sense. Who would do a crazy thing like that and then get himself bitten and not get help?"

"People in our world don't understand rabies very well. Honestly, most of them don't even know that we have any means of treating it. If he's from a village far from the capital, he may not have ever heard of someone receiving the treatment here at the castle or in the three other clinics where we've used it."

"I guess you don't advertise it when you bring back drugs from an alternate world."

William looked around, but there was nobody standing near them – Zander had already checked. Everyone was either in the clinic or quite a distance from them and busy. "No, we don't advertise it at all. The few people we have treated believe that we came up with the treatments ourselves."

"So, maybe he's a scientist? A doctor or something? Trying to figure it out himself?"

"It's possible." William shook his head. "He'd also have to be insane. Intentionally infecting an animal … keeping it in his living space, and *handling* it after it died … even in your world, people have developed rabies without an actual known bite. Living in close proximity to that much of the virus is asking for trouble. And with animals that could attack or escape at any time…"

"You're right, insane … there's one more thing."

William raised an eyebrow.

"Once we pulled down that tent and really got to look around at what was there…. It was a lot of stuff, William. Materials for traps, a stockpile of food, several cages with bite marks from different teeth, droppings inside the tent and another area outside where it looked like he'd been cleaning up after them and dumping the waste…"

Although Ben had listened to Zander's train of thought when they'd discovered all of those things, he hadn't wanted to quite believe it – he had a lot of other theories. William's expression, though, told Zander that his gut-level reaction was the same as his own. "And the bones?"

"Unless there are a lot buried somewhere else, there were nowhere near enough to explain that amount of stuff."

William closed his eyes for a long moment, then finally nodded. "Did you touch that man or any of the animals?"

"Yeah. Someone had to. We had to get them packed up and out of there, we had to carry that guy out of the tent and get him onto the wagon. Ben and I were the only ones who'd ever been vaccinated, and we didn't want anyone else touching anything."

"Nobody else touched anything?"

Zander knew who he meant by "nobody else." "I'm willing to bet that even in this world, there aren't a lot of guards as good as Ben."

"Okay, let's get you into the clinic. I want to check you out."

"I didn't get bitten," Zander said, as he followed William up the wooden steps and into the building that he called the clinic. He sucked in a breath as he looked around. Being in the castle for the last few days was surreal enough; this clinic was truly a space from another world – or at least another time.

He could see where William and Doctor Rose had worked to make the clinic as much like a doctor's office or hospital in his world as they could – but they just weren't working with the same materials and technology.

Like the castle, it was wired for electricity, but, like the hallways and bedrooms in the castle, there were also gas lamps and candles in strategic locations for the inevitable times when the unreliable power failed them.

The cots along the walls were covered with crisp white sheets and blankets, but the frames were wood – they couldn't be adjusted and rolled away in an emergency.

There was a room in the back where they'd taken the sick man. Through the open door, Zander could see the clean tiled floor and the metal-topped table they'd laid him on – this world's version of an operating room, he guessed. Ben was in there, along with a figure who was very familiar to him – though he hadn't yet seen or talked to him in this world – Doctor Nathaniel Rose.

"Have a seat," William said, pointing at one of the cots as he washed his hands in an iron sink.

Zander thought it was unnecessary, but he could see that William was serious, so he sat.

"Can I take a look at your hands and arms?"

He held them out and waited as William looked over every inch, even prodding gently at a tiny scab on Zander's forearm that he hadn't even realized was there. "Really, William, I didn't get bitten, or anything close. Ben and I were as careful as we could possibly be. We knew how dangerous it was."

At that moment, Doctor Rose walked out of the back room and over to them, smiling. "I'd heard you were here, Zander. I apologize for not making the time to come and seek you out before this."

"Quinn and William said that you were away, and that you only came back to the castle last night."

"That's true. I did mean to come and say hello sometime today, before all of this happened. Circumstances aside, it's nice to see you."

Zander had almost forgotten how much he'd always liked Doctor Rose.

"It's nice to see you too, Doctor Rose."

"If you'd prefer, you can call me Nathaniel."

"I think that might take more getting used to than I have time for before I have to go home."

"Fair enough," Doctor Rose said, chuckling.

"How is that man?" Zander asked.

"He's dying. I think you and Ben probably knew that. He has rabies and he's very far gone. There's no cure, and there's nothing I can do for him except try to keep him out of pain until it happens. I've given him a lot of medicine and he's asleep now. It's very unfortunate – not only for his sake, but because I very much wish we could question him and find out exactly what was going on here, but I'm not sure he'll wake up again, and even if he did, I'm doubtful that he'd be able to speak."

Zander nodded, subdued. The news wasn't unexpected but it was still such an awful thing to hear. He found himself glancing at his own hands, wondering if something could have gotten in through one of the cracks in his cuticles.

"I don't really need you down here, Will," Doctor Rose said. "You don't need to watch that man die. And I don't want you helping with those animals until I have the brains isolated and we can do the testing with gloves and aprons – let's not risk taking any of this upstairs near that baby. But I will give you and Ben the next dose of vaccine while you're here, and then you can take care of Emma." He looked over at Zander. "And let's just be safe and start the booster series for Zander."

William nodded. "That's what I was thinking, too."

Zander shook his head. "You don't have enough of that vaccine to be wasting it on me. I've had the shots. It can't be that much of an emergency."

William looked behind them at the room where the man was. "I'm not sending you home to have that happen to you."

"Well, what about the other vaccine? The one you're making here? Don't you need someone to test that on?"

"It won't be ready until probably at least the day after tomorrow."

"So?" He looked at Doctor Rose. "When you gave me the vaccine before, I remember you telling me that now I could go exploring in bat caves without worrying if there was a hospital nearby."

"You still need to have the booster doses after an exposure."

"Yes, but not today, right? I can wait for the other kind. You don't have to use the good stuff on me. There are *kids* here who might need it." The idea of Owen, or one of the little girls always running around the castle … he couldn't be responsible for using medicine one of them might need.

"We don't know if it will work for sure." Doctor Rose shifted his weight from one foot to the other.

"So test me. Test me today to see what my antibody levels are, and then test me again before I leave."

William raised an eyebrow.

"What? I might not be as smart as you are, but I paid attention in class. And I've been listening to you talk about this stuff for three days. I'm not so stupid I don't understand you."

"I don't think you're stupid, Zander. I don't think people don't *understand* what I'm talking about, I just usually think they'd rather I shut up and talk about something interesting."

William's words surprised him. He'd always known William was smart and into reading and studying more than most people, but he'd never guessed that he was self-conscious about it. It was sort of an odd thought.

He realized that he'd always sort of assumed that William thought he was better than the rest of them when he had his nose buried in books while they played, but maybe that wasn't true at all. Maybe William had really always believed they wouldn't like him or be interested in the things he was.

"Well, maybe I'm stranger than I thought I was, because I actually think most of it is interesting."

That got a smile. "There's a critical flaw in your plan, though."

"What's that?"

"If it doesn't work, and your levels are too low, there's no way I'm going to be able to tell you that once you're in Bristlecone."

"Oh." It was true. He hadn't thought about that.

"I'll go start getting the doses ready," Doctor Rose said, disappearing from the room before Zander could think of a better answer.

"We're going to be cutting it close as it is," William said. "When you do the boosters, it's supposed to be two doses a week apart, and we'll be just at that, if I give you one right now. You'll be going home with a bandage on your arm. That's the other thing, too. There's not time to give you both the doses of the other vaccine that you'd need, since it's not ready yet."

"I'm not worried about that. I'm worried that someone here in this world is going to die because I took two doses that I didn't need."

"Well, we don't want even a slim chance of you dying. We have a pretty strict policy about not killing our guests. We wouldn't have had that medicine without you in the first place. I'd say you're entitled to two doses of it."

Zander sighed, resigning himself. He still didn't like it. He'd overheard William lamenting that *he* was using up the safe stuff. It wasn't right. Zander understood now exactly how over-privileged he was, just by virtue of the world he came from. He'd never had to make decisions like the ones William was making. It wasn't right for him to take from what little they had here.

Then, another idea came to him. "What if I didn't need to know what those numbers were before I went home?"

"What do you mean?"

"I mean, if I go home, and I drive down to the emergency room in Pine Spar, and I tell them that I woke up with a bat in my bedroom, but it escaped, they'll give me the booster doses. It won't matter if the vaccine here worked or not. You could still test me, of course. You need a guinea pig."

"How are you going to explain that to your parents?"

"I'm eighteen. I don't have to explain anything."

"The vaccine we're making here is also not as safe, Zander. It will probably be more uncomfortable than the shots from your world, and the chance of side effects is higher."

It didn't matter to him. He knew he could afford the chances more than anyone here, but he decided to let William say his piece. "What kind of side effects?"

"Headaches, sore muscles, fever, nausea, I don't really know."

"Then I'm definitely not stealing even one dose that might go to a kid, William. Seriously. It's not going to happen."

"You'd take that chance? Why?"

He sighed. "I don't know, William. It just feels like the right thing to do. You need to not waste the good vaccine – especially if that guy was infecting animals on purpose and there are more of them around somewhere. You need someone to test your new vaccine on, and I'm a good candidate for that. If it hurts more, or it makes me a little sick – I can handle that. Worst case, I go home and check myself into a hospital that has a *lot* more resources than you have here. I just think I should."

William nodded halfway – he was hesitant, but Zander could tell he was considering it now. "It's ridiculously expensive in your world, especially if you wouldn't be using your parents' insurance. You'd have to let us give you the money for it."

Relief started to wash through him – not because of the money. He didn't care about that, but because William was relenting.

"That part is not optional," Nathaniel said, setting a tray of supplies down on the cot. Zander hadn't even seen him return. "I'm willing to allow that, if you're sure. But I'll give you enough money, and the name of a good hospital to go to, so I know you're taken care of. And you'd have to promise me that you would do it right away. No taking chances. Within twenty-four hours of the minute you step through that gate."

"Agreed. I'll drop Owen off and drive to the hospital."

And just like that, it was settled. Nathaniel nodded at William, and Zander felt a million times better.

"Okay, then I guess it's just you and Ben for this stuff, Will. Take your arm out of your sleeve for me."

He saw William go just a little pale around his temples and cheekbones as he shrugged out of one sleeve of his knitted sweater. He chuckled to himself – apparently Quinn had managed to find a guy who didn't like needles either. Whether he liked it or not, he had to admit they were kind of a matching pair.

"Quinn's better at this than I am now," William said – maybe Zander's chuckle hadn't been quite as silent as he'd thought.

"Whoa," he said, as William's chest came into view. "If you don't like needles, that is one heck of a wicked tattoo."

"It's a symbol," William said. "Actually two. It's the emblem of Eirentheos together with the emblem of Philotheum." He ran his finger over first one of the circles in the design and then the other. "It represents the joining of our kingdoms as two parts of a whole – something we were fighting for before Quinn took the throne and our marriage made it permanent. And you're right, it hurt like … well, you can guess. I hated every second of it."

"Did you have that before you got together with Quinn?"

"No. She and I both got the tattoos at the same time, the day we joined the resistance that was fighting to restore the throne to its proper occupant."

"Quinn has a tattoo." Surely at some point they were going to run out of ways to surprise him. She'd only been here the equivalent of a year. How much more history could she possibly have?

"Yes. As I said, she's braver than me. Having it done was enough to get her over her fear of needles. I still don't like them much." He sighed and looked away as Nathaniel cleaned his upper arm with a cotton ball.

"You're a doctor."

He shrugged. "Nobody's perfect."

"Well, those ones aren't that bad," he said, trying to sound sympathetic.

"I know."

Doctor Rose was fast. A few seconds later, William's shirt was back on; he was rubbing his shoulder, but otherwise no worse for the wear.

"All right," Doctor Rose said. "I'll do Ben's, and then I think the three of you should go on upstairs." William nodded, and Doctor Rose turned to Zander and smiled. "It is really nice to see you again. I'm sure it's been a very unexpected and challenging experience for you, and I know you'll be happy to get back home as quickly as you can, but I'm glad to see you're doing well."

It occurred to him that this was the first time today that the thought of going home had even crossed his mind. Weird. Two days ago, it was all he could think about. "It's good to see you too, Doctor Rose."

"I apologize for being so tied up at the moment. I would love to talk more, and hear how your parents and sisters are doing."

"I understand," Zander said, glancing at the back room. "They're good."

"You might be able to catch up more at dinner," William said, with a strange sound in his voice. "I meant to tell you that Quinn just heard from Jonathan. He's coming here.

"*Tonight?*"

"Apparently. Marcus was going to let my parents know to make plans."

"Why? What's going on?"

"That's all I know."

"Well, then I guess I'd better get things settled here. Jacob is on his way to help as well. He should be here within the hour."

William nodded, beginning to dig in the drawers of the supply cart as Nathaniel headed back to the other room. "So, you don't have a problem with needles?"

"No, not especially."

"Good, because I'm going to get some blood from you so we can see where your antibody levels are now. We won't have the results for days, though."

Zander held out his arm. "You know, if we were in my world, I might be pretty freaked out to have a guy my age doing this," he said, as William tied a tourniquet above his elbow.

"If we were in your world, I'd never let someone our age near me with a needle," William agreed, chuckling.

"Did you always know you wanted to be a doctor?"

"Yes. I started following Nathaniel around and trying to do the stuff he did when I was about two. For my fourth birthday, he brought me a real stethoscope from your world as a gift. Looking back, I feel bad for Thomas and Linnea. They were my captive practice patients."

"You didn't draw blood did you?"

William laughed. "Oh, definitely not."

"Then I doubt Thomas minded."

"That's probably true. Thomas would let me do anything. He has more patience with me than anyone, except maybe Quinn. I don't know how they put up with me sometimes."

"They're crazy," Zander teased. He didn't know how it had happened, but he really did like William. Not as much as he liked Ben and Thomas maybe, but still ... he wasn't nearly as difficult to deal with as he made himself out to be.

"Certifiable, probably. But I love them anyway," William said, grinning.

"I sort of envy you that."

"What? Having a crazy family?"

"Well, that, yes, but also knowing what you want to do. Growing up just training for it and walking right into it."

"Walking right *away* from it, more like. All those cycles of training, and now I spend more than half my time on my duties as a king, which I in no way prepared for."

"Still, though, you never had to be undecided. And you still get to practice medicine, obviously."

"I do. And you're right. I've always thought that part of living in your world must be hard – all those choices, and all that time you spend waiting to be allowed to be useful."

Zander had *never* thought about it that way. He'd done a lot of things, had a lot of opportunities, and a lot of fun … but William was right. None of the things he'd done were actually *useful*.

"Are you *finished?*" Zander asked, startled as William taped a piece of cotton to his arm.

William held up three glass tubes of blood. "All done."

"I didn't even feel you do anything."

"I'm good."

"And modest, too."

William's shoulders shook with laughter.

"It's not bragging if you really are the best at something." They both turned at the sound of Ben's voice. He was smiling. "Are you feeling better, Zander?"

"I'm fine, now that I'm away from that smell. You?"

"Much better, too. Although I could use five or six showers."

"Well, we'll all need to get cleaned up before dinner," William said. "Jonathan is on his way here."

Ben's reaction was much like Nathaniel's had been. Zander was beginning to feel really out of the loop. "Okay, who is this Jonathan everyone's all up in arms about? Should I be worried?"

"There's no reason for *you* to be worried about anything," William said.

Zander wasn't sure why that bothered him. William was right, of course, nothing that happened here really affected him, but still having it pointed out somehow rubbed him the wrong way. "So who is he?"

"He's Quinn's uncle. Nathaniel's youngest brother. And we're not worried about him coming here, exactly. It's more that it's surprising that he's coming."

"So it's *Prince* Jonathan, then."

"Yes."

"Maybe he just wants to meet the baby."

"That would be a likely explanation – it would just be less disconcerting if he'd sent the message that he was coming a couple of *days* ago when he had to have started traveling, instead of only hours ago."

"Oh." Zander frowned. "Any chance he wanted to surprise you?"

William sighed. "Actually, I wouldn't put that past Jonathan. He can be a little ... unexpected at times. Come on, let's go and take those showers. If we have a visitor coming, it'll be a semi-formal dinner in the castle tonight."

Zander stared at him. "That doesn't sound like something I would be invited to."

"Oh, why not? You're here, in a castle in another world for seven more days. You might as well get the full experience while you're here. You're not going to get a lot more chances."

"Or any," Zander said, laughing.

"Exactly."

"But I thought you were keeping me hidden."

"I think we can trust you to keep quiet about your origins, can't we?" Ben asked. "It's not like someone's going to ask you if you're from a different world."

DINNER

Rosewood Castle, Eirentheos

AND SO, THREE hours later, Zander found himself standing in the hallway with Thomas waiting for William, Quinn, Ben, and Linnea.

He'd taken a very long bath. The warm, soapy water had felt ridiculously good on his aching legs and backside. Relaxing had felt so good, in fact, that he'd gone almost straight from the tub to his bed and fallen asleep.

Sleeping had felt even better. He could have stayed there all night if Ben hadn't knocked on his door. When he did, Zander limped over to answer it, bleary eyed. His legs did *not* feel better after the nap – he was paying the full price of his time in the saddle and on the wooden seat of the wagon. "I think I'll skip the dinner tonight."

"Oh, no, not a chance," Ben said, holding out two hangers full of clothes. "You've been invited by the king himself."

Zander groaned. It was not entirely amusing that William was a king.

"Besides, you'll need to stretch and move some more tonight or you'll be *really* sorry tomorrow."

Now here he was, decked out in black dress pants and a nice, white button-down shirt that was only a little too big for him, standing next to a prince.

"Where's your girlfriend tonight?" he asked Thomas.

"She's tending the baby upstairs during the meal, so that Quinn can do the whole queen thing."

"So you have to go it alone?"

Thomas shrugged. "It's her job. It's an honor, you know, to care for the heir to the throne. Not too many people will even have the privilege of *meeting* him while he's still so young."

"You don't mind?"

"No. She has to put up with me attending boring functions or traveling around the kingdom or any number of things, really."

And then, there they were. William and Ben were dressed similarly to Zander and Thomas. Slacks and nice shirts. Both William and Thomas were wearing some kind of silver chains around their necks, with silver pendants hanging from them. They looked a little dressy, he supposed, but mostly they looked pretty normal.

But the girls… For a moment, Zander felt like he was in a movie again. He'd been assured that the dinner was only "semi-formal", and wasn't a particularly fancy occasion, but the dresses Quinn and Linnea wore would have put anything at prom in his world to shame.

Linnea was in a long, flowing purple dress that gathered just at her waist. Her long, dark curls fell down her back, framing her pale face, and those gray eyes … well, it would be better for everyone if he just avoided looking at Ben's wife altogether.

And Quinn – he'd never seen her look anything close to this. Someone had done her hair, sweeping the auburn curls up off her neck, but leaving perfectly formed ringlets framing her face. She wore a necklace much like William's and Thomas', only hers was gold.

She came down the hall with William, smiling as she approached.

It hurt to watch – hurt to even think about – but as the two of them came closer, he could *really* see it.

They walked with their hands linked, his steps keeping perfect time with hers, even in her heels. Had she stumbled, he would have caught her before she even knew she'd lost her balance. But of course she didn't stumble. Somehow, in the short time since she'd been in Bristlecone, she'd transformed. Whatever her physical age, she wasn't a young girl anymore.

For the first time, he almost believed she was a queen.

When they came to a stop, she let go of William, but his hand slipped around to rest at the small of her back.

He wasn't showing off for Zander. The two of them were so comfortable together that the motion was automatic; no thought went into it at all. When she talked, his whole body responded, turning toward her just a little, giving his full attention to her, and when he talked, hers did the same.

Despite Quinn's smile and her relaxed conversation with everyone, something was off.

She wasn't wearing makeup, so it would have been impossible to hide the paleness in her face. Her hands moved too much when she spoke – far more than they usually did, even in an animated discussion. Enough so, that when William caught Zander watching her, he took one of her hands in his, holding it close to him, rubbing the back of her hand with his thumb.

The gesture made her look up at him, and she nodded after some sort of wordless communication between the two of them.

She turned to Zander then. "So who talked you into attending the excitement that is dinner with the king and queen?"

"That would be your husband. And your … uh … bodyguard."

She giggled.

William grinned and held up his free hand. "I figured why not. It'll be a fun story he can … well, never tell anyone."

"Yeah. Everybody needs at least ten of those," she said, rolling her eyes.

"I suppose I can always talk to Owen. He might just be my new best friend after all of this."

"Well, at least he'll make a good one," William said. The affection in his voice was obvious, and it pained Zander again to realize how very far Owen would be from these people who loved him so much once this little adventure was over.

"Where is he, anyway? I thought he'd be glued to your side right now."

"He's glued to Alice's right now, I think," Quinn said. "The children are going down to dinner together, and Owen's going to hang with them for a while."

"She's so much littler than him," Zander said. "I'd think he'd spend more time with Emma and Alex." He was impressed with himself that he was finally starting to get at least some of William's siblings straight.

"He plays with them a lot," William said. "He's been sleeping in Alex's room instead of his own, but he and Alice are just … they're each other's speed, I think. Her arm is still bothering her quite a bit, and he's protective."

"Right." Owen always kind of had been that way – he took care of his own sisters like that, too – even Quinn who was so much older than him. "How's *your* arm?" It was an awkward change of subject, but thinking about taking Owen away from here was suddenly just too hard.

"It's healing. It would be better if I learned to keep it out of the path of the baby's feet, and I will definitely have some scars, but I'll be fine, because of you. Thanks for asking."

"Uh, sure." He was glad that it looked like they were getting ready to head downstairs.

Dinner wasn't as awful as Zander had imagined it would be. Maybe a "formal" one would have been worse than semi-formal.

There were all kinds of weird formalities in the beginning – he and Thomas, Linnea, and Ben were escorted into the dining room by a servant before Quinn and William and then King Stephen and Queen Charlotte were announced – yes, *announced*, at *dinner* in their own home – and then seated.

Zander sat next to Thomas, across from Linnea and Ben, and close to a couple of William's younger brothers – Josh and Daniel – and he actually enjoyed the conversation. Linnea was still clearly unsure how she felt about him, but she was friendlier tonight than she had been, and Thomas and Ben both made an effort to include him and ask him questions. There was a lot of talking about crumple and horses, and he was surprised when he actually had some things to contribute.

He was getting braver about the food in this world, as well, and that bravery was rewarded with an extraordinary meal of some kind of succulent, juicy meat with gravy and roasted vegetables that he was surprised to discover were delicious. Maybe it was only because he was starving after the exertion of the day, but he actually took a second helping of the vegetables.

The honored guest, Quinn's uncle, wasn't sitting close enough for Zander to really hear, but from what he could see, he wasn't sure what the fuss had been about. The man seemed friendly and funny – and considerate, too. More than once, he refilled someone's glass before a servant could get to it, and he was especially attentive to Quinn and Queen Charlotte.

After the meal was finished, the atmosphere was much more relaxed.

The dishes were cleared, and the servants pulled away all of the smaller tables that had been pushed together to make one very long one. Zander was close enough to overhear Jonathan.

"I didn't come all this way to have to still wait to meet the prince, milady."

Mia was summoned immediately and she brought in the baby. It was clear the introduction to Jonathan had actually been planned –

the infant was dressed in a long green gown, embroidered with a gold design that looked sort of like William's tattoo.

Once Quinn had taken him in her arms, Jonathan actually knelt down in front of them, bowing his head in respect.

The baby, for his grand entrance, remained soundly asleep.

After that, the atmosphere grew much more relaxed. Everyone wandered around talking and chatting. Joshua and Maxwell invited Zander to join them in a card game at one of the new, smaller tables. It was interesting for a while, and he actually won a hand, but then he had to get up and walk around – too much sitting was not going well for him.

Thinking that the chocolate cake he'd just seen someone eating looked too good to pass up, he headed over to the buffet table that had been set out with desserts and drinks.

Once he got there, he was a little stymied by the choices. The table was beautiful, draped in a dark purple cloth, everything on silver dishes surrounded by glowing candles. It was every bit as fancy as the dinner table itself had been. And the desserts… cookies and pies and several kinds of cake, as well as some other foods he didn't recognize, but looked like they might be worth the risk.

"Just take one of everything," a voice beside him said.

He turned to face Quinn a little too quickly – his sore legs were not getting better as the evening progressed – and he winced.

Quinn giggled. "Monkey butt?"

"Excuse me?"

"You know, spending a couple of hours in the saddle when you're not at all used to it? Makes your butt look like a baboon's?"

He stared at her. "I haven't actually looked, but considering how it *feels* right now…" and then he couldn't help but start laughing. His laughter made her laugh – hysterically – and neither one of them could stop until tears were rolling down her cheeks, and his stomach hurt. "If we keep this up, I'm barely going to be able to make it back up the stairs," he finally choked out.

"William could give you something to help, you know."

He snorted. "Yeah, Quinn, I'm going to ask your husband for something to put on my sore butt."

"Your choice."

"Where is he, anyway?"

She pointed to the other side of the room. William was holding the baby, and surrounded by several members of his family, many of whom were carrying other babies.

"How come you're not over there with them?"

"There's glasberry pie." She nodded toward the table as she picked up a shiny silver plate.

He rolled his eyes. "There aren't ten people falling all over themselves to get it for you, Queen Quinn?"

She shot him a dirty look. "There probably would be, if I'd *asked* anyone. However, I think I'm still capable of dishing myself up a slice of pie." With that, she unceremoniously scooped up a piece of the pie and dumped it on her plate – upside down – the green filling oozing everywhere.

"You were saying?"

"I like it this way."

Maybe the friendship thing wouldn't be so hard if they could still laugh. "It gets to you, doesn't it?" he asked, finally deciding on the chocolate cake he'd come over for in the first place, and grabbing his own plate. "The whole servants and guards and 'Your Majesty' and all of that."

"Sometimes," she agreed. "I'm honored, of course, and extremely grateful for most of the people I do have. But it makes me feel … I don't know … like why should someone else have to stop their conversation or get up from what they're doing to get me something I can get for myself?"

"I don't know," he said. "From what I can see, they like doing it – I think it makes some of them feel uncomfortable, like they're not doing their job if you have to do it."

"Now you sound like William."

He shrugged. "Nobody can be wrong all the time."

"You're managing it all right."

"Hey, now! What did I do to deserve that?"

She grinned. "Nothing. Sorry, that was mean of me. You've gotten plenty right lately – starting with saving my husband's life. I don't know how to repay you for that."

"You're a queen. Maybe you should make me a knight or something."

She giggled. "We have guards here. You could be Sir Zander, honorary guard of Philotheum, if you'd like."

He grinned. "Is that a real title?"

"I don't know." She shrugged. "I'm the queen. I suppose if I say it is, it is." She stuck her fork in the pie and ate the bite with a flourish that made him smile.

"Is it weird that actually sounds better than, "Zander Cunningham, college dropout?"

"No. Most things sound better than 'dropout.' What are you talking about?"

He swallowed hard. Saying that had been a mistake. He didn't want to talk about that right now. Not here, not with her. He took a bite of cake to buy himself a little time. "Wow," he said, even with half the bite still in his mouth, "this is amazing. What's in this? Fairy dust?"

"I've never convinced anyone to tell me, but yeah, there's nothing like that on Earth, is there?"

"I'd say it almost makes up for the lack of tomatoes."

"Almost." She was concentrating on her pie now, chasing a small glasberry around with her fork – and *not* pursuing the question she'd asked him. He knew her well enough to know that she never just dropped something that made her curious. She was distracted.

"What's going on, Quinn?"

She looked up at him – but she didn't meet his eyes all the way. "What do you mean?"

294

"You're upset about something. Is everything all right?"

"Do you mean aside from the fact that there's a man dying of rabies out there in the clinic right now, and you and William both suspect that he might have been infecting animals on purpose?"

It was a good point – that was enough to upset anyone. He watched her as she talked, though – noticed when she had to stop and re-balance her plate twice before she sent glasberry filling dribbling down to the floor. Finally, she set it on the table. "Yeah. I do mean besides that. There's something else. Is it that guy – your uncle?"

He glanced across the room to Jonathan, who was now engaged in an enthusiastic discussion with Doctor Rose. For the first time, he noticed that Doctor Rose had a companion with him – a nice-looking woman with very light brown hair pulled into an intricate braid; she was also dressed up for the occasion. He wondered if this was Doctor Rose's fiancée.

"You don't need to be so observant right now, Zander. It's a very complicated situation, and you don't need to worry about it."

"Is he – safe?"

"Jonathan? Yes. He's not the problem. He brought some news that's pretty concerning, but … let's just enjoy the evening, okay? You can go home in a few days and forget any of this ever happened."

She was shutting him down – she'd actually picked up her plate and taken two steps back from him, and that would have been the end of it – if Thomas hadn't chosen that moment to approach her.

He came up fast; he was determined, on a mission. He didn't even appear to see Zander standing right there. And the look on his face told Zander that whatever was going on was much more serious than Quinn was trying to make it sound.

"Is it true?" he asked, speaking low, through his teeth.

"Probably."

"Come here." Motioning for Quinn to follow him, Thomas took off across the floor, heading toward a door at the back corner.

Zander didn't even think about following.

But he did look around the room to see if anyone had reacted to that little scene.

Ben had. He was standing near one of the tables, his eyes flicking over toward that door in the corner every few seconds, even as his hand rested on Linnea's arm, and the two of them chatted amiably with another couple he'd seen before — one of William's siblings, perhaps.

Marcus, too, was keeping an eye on things from his position near Nathaniel and Jonathan.

William, however, hadn't seen anything, but he was looking around in a sort of confused way. He wasn't holding the baby now — someone else must have asked for a turn. When William's spotted Zander, he walked over to him.

"Where did Quinn go? I thought she was talking with you."

"What is she so upset about?"

"What happened, Zander? Where is she?"

"Nothing happened. Your brother came and got her and ran off with her. He's just as upset as she is. What's going on? Is she okay?"

William sighed. "None of us is doing particularly well right now. We've had some very upsetting news today, and I think Thomas just now caught wind of it."

"What was the news?"

Maybe it was the long day, maybe his guard was down, maybe William just needed someone to talk to who was outside the situation, but whatever the reason, he didn't push Zander away the way Quinn and Thomas had — the way Zander had been bracing himself for.

Instead, he stepped away from the dessert table, into an empty space far from everyone, and allowed Zander to follow him. "You remember the other day when I was telling you about Tolliver?" he asked.

"Is that the guy that tried to kill Linnea?"

William nodded. "He held her at knifepoint, anyway. He also kidnapped Thomas, and tried to assault Quinn the first time she was here."

"He *what?*"

"Yeah, the temperature of my blood tends to raise about a hundred degrees whenever I hear his name. Trust me."

Zander had to work at prying his jaws open far enough to get words out. "What about him?"

"Jonathan just traveled here to tell us that Tolliver has escaped from prison."

About that blood temperature thing… "What do you mean he's escaped? How is that even possible?"

"I don't know. It's something that's being investigated. Jonathan traveled all this way to tell us in person to avoid the risk of sending that kind of message that far with a bird. But that, of course, leaves us not knowing what's happened in Philotheum since he left."

"If you don't have prisons that people can't escape from here, you should have just killed him."

"Don't think I haven't thought about that, Zander. It's more complicated than that. He's not just a random criminal. He's Quinn's half-uncle, and the son of the man who was prince regent for many cycles. There are a number of people in Philotheum who supported his bid for the throne before they knew about Quinn. Some of them haven't let go of that, and don't yet trust Quinn. Having him executed could have set off problems we weren't prepared to deal with."

"Well, are you prepared to deal with this, William? If he has supporters, how do you know he's not running off to them, planning some kind of attack against Quinn?"

"My guess is that's exactly what he's doing."

"So what are we going to do?"

"We, Zander? *You* are going to take Owen home in a few days where both of you will be safe and out of this mess. You are going to make absolutely sure that Owen closes that gate in a way that it stays closed, because the last thing we need is for someone like Tolliver to be able to travel between the worlds."

THE LETTER

Rosewood Castle, Eirentheos

THE BABY'S SOFT fussing noises woke Quinn. William was already holding him, waiting for her as she struggled to sit up, glancing toward the curtains as she did.

"Yes, it's morning already," he said, as she saw the tell-tale line of light reflected on the wall under the curtains. "Did you sleep at all?"

"Just now for a little while I did, I think." Most of the night had been plagued by restlessness, frightening dreams, and a wakeful baby. "I don't think I'm dealing very well with this news." She looked at him again, suddenly noticing that he was already dressed. "How long have you been up?"

"An hour or so. I took him out of here for a while when I thought you might actually be asleep. But he's hungry now." He scooted close to her, helping her get the baby settled in, and then wrapping his arm around her back. "I don't think there's a way to deal well with the news. I have half a mind to go out and hunt for Tolliver myself."

She looked at him in alarm.

"I won't, Quinn. Of course I won't. We'll stay here and wait for more news from the scouts."

Hours of meeting with Jonathan, Marcus, and Stephen last night hadn't yielded much of a plan. They simply didn't know enough. Today, Stephen was going to be gathering soldiers to head to Philotheum and get as much information as they could find. Jonathan had probably already left to go and seek out some of his contacts.

"We need to get back to Philotheum as soon as we can," Quinn said. "There's too much I can't do from here. Too many people it's not safe to send messages to. I want to know who's responsible for this happening."

He nodded. "We can speak to my family about leaving a few days earlier than planned – right after we get Owen home safely."

Breakfast felt almost normal, although Quinn could see in Stephen's face that he was as tired as she was.

Nathaniel, too, looked exhausted, and she saw him glance at William and give a shake of his head. The strange, rabid man was gone.

At least the conflict with Zander had reached some resolve. He no longer seemed edgy and angry. He sat at the table across from them, pouring honey and cream on his cereal as if it was a normal thing for him to do, chatting politely with everyone and keeping to the unspoken agreement not to talk about the disturbing revelations of the day before.

Although Ben and Marcus were in a hurry to finish the meal and run off to busy themselves with tasks that would make them feel like they were doing something to help, and Linnea wanted to be with them, Thomas and Joshua invited Zander to go with them down to the gym to practice with swords again. Everyone was needing to feel prepared.

"You should give him a horseback riding lesson," she said to Thomas as they got ready to leave.

She'd meant it as a joke, but nobody took it that way. Not even Zander, who nodded somberly, even though he was probably more sore today than he'd been yesterday. He was really going to get on a horse again. She didn't know why or what to think about that.

In the end, she turned to Owen. "Want to come upstairs and hang out with me and William for a while? The other kids have their lessons this morning."

"Yeah. But I want to get something first."

"Okay."

She and William watched as Owen scampered off. Almost immediately, Samuel, who was in William's arms, began to fuss.

"I really think he knows," William said incredulously, lifting the baby to his shoulder and trying to calm him.

"I feel the same way when I watch him walk away from me," she said, leaning up against William's arm as they started heading toward the stairs.

By the time they arrived at their suite, though, Owen was already back. Samuel grew completely calm at the sound of his uncle's voice, remaining that way even as William carried him over to one of the couches and began changing his diaper.

"What's that you have there?" Quinn asked, as she settled in to the middle of the largest couch, patting the cushion beside her so that Owen would climb up.

Owen was holding a bag – a nice big one, heavy cloth in a pretty floral pattern, with a large strap and several compartments. He had to have brought it from home, though Quinn had never seen it before.

"I meant to give this to you when I first came," he said, hefting it onto the couch as he climbed up next to it. It looked heavy – full.

"But I forgot, and it ended up under the bed somehow. Mia found it under there and got it out for me this morning."

Quinn smiled. As smart as Owen was about so very many things, organization was not his strong suit. "That's okay." She kissed him on the forehead. "They're kind of tall beds, aren't they?" Poor Mia was probably spending lots of her time digging stuff out of there for Owen. "But what is it?"

He looked down at his pant legs, rubbing at something that was probably visible only to him. "Mom bought the bag for you one day when we went shopping, after we got back to Bristlecone. She said it looked like something you would like."

"Oh. It is nice," she said quietly, around the little lump forming in her throat.

"She's been filling it up with things she wants to give you when we come and visit after the school year is over."

Quinn closed her eyes for several seconds. "You didn't tell her that you closed the gate, did you?"

He shook his head. "I'm *going* to tell her – when it's summer."

She didn't know if it was better or worse that her mom wasn't aware of the gulf that separated them. Better, maybe, because surely she wouldn't be sitting here looking at a present from her if she'd known how unlikely it was that Quinn would ever receive it.

William had finished changing the baby and wrapping him back up in his blanket, and he carried him over. Samuel was beginning to fuss quietly again, and Owen held his arms up.

"I think he might be hungry, buddy."

"He's not eating his hands. Let me try."

William chuckled and knelt down to place Samuel in Owen's outstretched arms. Owen cuddled him close, and the fussing immediately quieted. Quinn had to use the edge of a burp cloth on her eyes again as William sat down on the other side of her, putting an arm around her shoulders and kissing her temple. He also pulled a handkerchief out of his pocket and laid it in her lap – he was always so much more prepared with those than she was. "So what's in the bag?" he asked.

Curious as she was, unzipping the bag was *hard*, as if she were really reaching across universes to touch her mother. The first item she pulled out didn't help. It was a tiny pair of shoes – though a bit big for Samuel yet – still bearing the tags from a boutique in Bristlecone. They were nestled inside a little green-and-white baseball cap. It was very soft.

She looked at Owen in shock. "Does she know?"

"I don't think so," he said, shaking his head.

William squeezed her shoulder. "She may just know it's been long enough in our world, that by the time she was planning on visiting…"

"Yeah." Owen held Samuel a little more upright so she could put the hat on his head – it fit perfectly. The baby didn't even fuss; he seemed to like it.

"What if we'd had a girl?"

From where he was sitting, William could see into a different part of the bag than she could. Stretching across her, he reached inside and pulled out another pair of shoes – this time little white, patent-leather Mary Janes. A pair of lacy socks was tucked inside one, and a soft little green headband with a bow was inside the other.

"We'll save these," he said.

She nodded, reaching in again, this time her hand landing on something that was soft in a very familiar way.

"How?" she gasped, as she pulled out the tiny knitted blanket. It was familiar, not because she remembered it from her world, but because, right there next to her on the couch, her son was wrapped in one that was almost identical – though Samuel's was much newer than the one in her hand.

William lifted the corner of it, revealing three perfectly stitched words: Quinn Katriel Rose. "My mother will finish Samuel's like that after the Naming Ceremony," he said quietly. "She must have made that one for you."

The bag didn't get any easier. There was a whole pocket of small trinkets from Quinn's room – things that had been important to her, a little photo album of her friends she'd been keeping for several cyc – years.

The hardest part of looking through everything wasn't that it was full of nostalgia, though – it was the fact that there was so little of it.

Every item in that bag had been selected carefully – she could almost imagine her mother packing, then unpacking, then re-packing as she chose things Quinn would enjoy or appreciate having, but that wouldn't undermine her choice to stay here. Megan had accepted it, and although it had to have been next to impossible for her, she was doing her best to support Quinn's new life.

There was Quinn's favorite rain jacket – nothing like that waterproof material existed here in Deusterros – and the book of fairy tales that had been her most beloved as a child. She'd start reading that to Samuel tonight.

In one of the pockets, she even found a whole stack of packets of seeds – tomatoes and cantaloupe – oh, how she missed cantaloupe. She looked up at William in disbelief. "Will these grow here?"

"I don't know why they wouldn't. We can try as soon as we get them home."

She smiled.

"Don't think that means you're going to get me to eat tomatoes, though."

"I wouldn't presume." She'd reached the bottom of the bag now, and pulled out a small cardboard box decorated with tiny gold hearts, the kind you'd keep pictures or mementos in. It was old – the edges were worn a bit, and the top was more faded than the sides, but she'd never seen it before. She was a little hesitant as she pulled off the lid.

The things inside were definitely old. A baby book – Quinn hadn't even known that her mother had made one for her – a little baggie with the trimmings of very fine auburn hair inside, and a stack of pictures. The picture on top was of a much-younger Nathaniel holding a bundle in a green blanket, sitting on a couch that these days resided in the basement at Quinn's mom's house.

She wasn't ready to look through the rest of the pictures yet.

At the bottom, underneath all of the baby memories Quinn would have to sort through later, there was a thick envelope, yellowing slightly with age. On the front, written in elegant script that she didn't recognize, was the word "Quinn."

She didn't know why her hands were shaking slightly as she picked it up and turned it over. William pulled her just a little closer.

It was still sealed with green wax – the same way she now sealed official messages in Philotheum – though it was missing the stamp with the emblem of her kingdom. The person who had written it – and she was almost sure she knew, now, who the handwriting belonged to – probably hadn't had access to the stamp while he'd been in her world. Instead, he'd etched a tiny rose into the wax.

The paper inside was heavy and thick – of good enough quality that age hadn't much affected it. The script on it matched the handwriting on the envelope. Her hands shook even more when she read the date at the top. The letter had been written only the day before her father had died.

Sweet Princess Quinn,

I hope there never comes a time when you're reading this letter. If you ever do have to read it, please know that I am sorry. There are so many, many things I wanted to tell you myself, rather than have you read them in a letter or hear them from your mother or Nathaniel.

As I write this, you and your mother are asleep, stretched out on the bed together at the cabin in the mountains we rented for the summer, enjoying an afternoon nap after playing in the lake all morning. You caught two fish today with the little pole Nathaniel brought up last week. You even helped me clean them. Your smile was so big when I told you we would eat them for dinner tonight. Although I'm hoping to have time while you rest to finish this letter, I can hardly wait until you wake and we can begin our adventures again.

If you are reading this letter, it's because we never got to have all of the adventures I'd hoped to have together, and writing this only makes me more anxious to not miss a single one we have left.

This evening, once you are asleep for real, I will show this to your mother. She won't be happy with me when I ask her to hold onto it, to give it to you only after you know the truth about me — the truth about yourself — and when the day comes you might need to know what's inside.

Maybe you understand, now that you're reading it. Now that you know who you are, the true Queen of Philotheum. Maybe you're still angry with me for hiding it from you. Please be angry with me, sweetheart, and not with your mother.

She has always done her best to trust me and to do what I ask in a very difficult situation. If you need any more proof of that, you need look no further than the fact that this letter is in your hands, and the seal was unbroken. It breaks my heart to write something as important as this and not share it with her. I only hope that someday you are able to find a companion as worthy of your trust and affection as your mother is of mine.

If you have this letter, it means you've not only discovered who you really are, but that you have also chosen to return to our world to attempt to assume your rightful place. When I dreamed that day might come, the dream always included my standing beside you — you returning as a real princess, and not the affectionate nickname I use in this world — and myself as the king. But clearly that wasn't to be.

The reason I'm writing this letter now is because some things have happened recently to make me fear that our safety has been compromised.

I wonder if you think I'm a coward for leaving my kingdom and coming and hiding in this world. It's all right if you do; I wonder the same thing myself. I don't know what you've been told of the events that led up to my decision, but there are parts I never told anyone.

I'm sure that at this point, you have been told of Dalphius' prophecies. I wish I could tell you that I was never young and vulnerable to such nonsense, but I was. The day Dalphius predicted that my son would never live to sit on the throne, I allowed fear to dictate my decisions. My childhood had already been torn apart, my siblings and I lived in fear, and I wanted none of that for my child.

Imagine my surprise, though, when I discovered Dalphius' prediction was correct. My son will never sit on the throne. Instead, by the grace of the Maker, it will be my beautiful, strong daughter who lays all of this to rest.

I should never have given myself to fear. It is a vicious, soul-destroying weed. Had I told others of the prophecy, instead of fearing it, I wouldn't be writing this letter now. You wouldn't be the first to know.

My stepfather, Hector, is a frightening and determined man, who is capable of great damage. His greatest asset, however, is a man named Rahas. Rahas is, unofficially, Hector's most valued guard. The title is unofficial, however, because most people don't even know he exists. Rahas has always moved like a shadow at my stepfather's side, obeying his every command, carrying out deeds that Hector either takes credit for, or ones he wishes to have no association with.

It is Rahas who killed my father, and who, after my father's other guards failed, was tasked with murdering me.

And he's here in our world.

Earlier this week, when I went back down to Bristlecone for a couple of days to check on the store, I saw him. It was early evening by the time I got there. I was driving, down near the bridge like I always do, there's just a part of me that has to check every time, and there he was. I've only ever actually seen him twice in my life, but I would recognize his midnight-black hair in any world.

The next thing I did was the worst decision I've ever made in my life, but I didn't stop to think about it, Quinn. I drove straight to the store and got the gun we keep under the counter, and I drove back over there and confronted him.

At first, he was much more worried about the car I drove up there in than anything. Once he was between me and the car, though, he laughed, and wouldn't answer my questions. That was when I pulled out the gun and shot an unlucky rabbit that was foraging nearby. I think that in the end, though, the rabbit may get off easier than I will for that choice.

I got most of the answers I was looking for. I still don't know how Hector knew about the gate, but he hasn't known for long. He only suspected I might be here, but he didn't know for sure — oh what a mistake it was for me to confront Rahas and reveal my position. He'd been here for five days without learning anything. He still doesn't know about Nathaniel, and most importantly, he has no idea about you.

Using the gun, I was able to convince him to leave and go home, but I'm afraid the damage has been done. While I never saw Rahas return in the three days I spent in Bristlecone, this morning, my store manager, Felipe, called to tell me that someone broke into the store overnight. The only things missing are the gun and the spare keys to our delivery truck.

I asked Felipe not to call the police. There are too many things that would be difficult to explain if they were involved. This may, of course, prove to be another of my many mistakes.

My most important task now is to make sure Rahas stays out of our world, and that he never finds out about you.

I need to also protect Nathaniel if I can. He is expected to return to this world in just two days. I can't allow him to be discovered here. Tomorrow, after I have spent every possible second I can with you and your mother, I am going to leave the two of you here go back to Bristlecone and return to Deusterros.

I don't know what the result of my trip will be. My most fervent hope is that I will reach Nathaniel in time and seek help from Stephen and from Marcus whom I trust with my life. But if you are reading this letter, you already know that, for whatever reason, I didn't succeed. Maybe you know why, but it's possible you don't. Hector and Rahas are both dangerous and stealthy. And if Rahas has my gun ...

Whatever happened, I'm sorry. I'm sorry I didn't make better decisions. I'm sorry I ran from a ridiculous prophecy. I'm sorry I didn't seek help sooner. And most of all, I'm sorry I left you. You are the child of my heart, Quinn. The thing I wanted most in my life. I wanted to be there, to watch you grow, to teach you to ride, to tell you about the strong princess you truly are, to provide you with a pack of siblings and a home full of love.

If your mother remarried, please let her know that she has my absolute blessing. I never wanted her to be anything but happy. I hope she was able to give you those brothers and sisters — at least one of each. If she didn't, tell her it's time now.

I wish I could help you more, tell you what to do, and more than anything I wish I could protect you. All I can say is trust Nathaniel, Stephen, and Marcus. Seek help when you need it, but don't rush into things, especially not a confrontation with Hector or any of those who serve him. If I had taken any of that advice, my story would have ended with my burning this letter and eventually telling you all of these things myself.

More important than any move you make, though, sweetheart, take the time to cherish those you love. Spend *every moment you can with them. Hug them and kiss them, dance and play. It's the one thing I know I did right with you and your mother, and I will carry that with me forever, wherever I go.*

I hear you stirring in there now, so I will end this, because the most important thing on my mind at this moment is a tiny princess who needs a very sound tickling.

Love Always,
Your Father

Quinn's vision was blurry as the letter fell from her hand onto her lap. She couldn't speak, couldn't even wrap her thoughts around what she'd just read.

After several moments of silence, William stretched his hand toward the sheets of paper. "May I, love?"

She must have actually managed to nod, because he reached for it, though she still couldn't move the whole time he was reading it.

On the other side of her, Owen continued to quietly rock the baby, snuggling him close. Samuel was content – as he always was in Owen's arms – his blinks growing heavier by the second.

"Wow," William finally breathed.

She looked at him now, dabbing at her eyes with her sleeves. Both of them were too stunned to bother digging out a handkerchief.

"Are you all right, love?"

"I don't know."

He took her hand and squeezed it gently. "We need to show this to Nathaniel."

"We do," she said, "but not right now. Right now I just want to snuggle with you and Owen and Samuel."

Wrapping his arm around her, he leaned in and kissed her on the temple, taking a long time to hold his face against hers.

A TRIP

Mistle Village, Eirentheos

ZANDER WAS SURPRISED when there was a knock on his door shortly after he'd returned from eating breakfast. As far as he knew, everyone was busy. The last three days in the castle had been strained with all of its occupants preoccupied with the news brought by Quinn's uncle.

Ben and Thomas had both been considerate about carving out time for him – enough so that he'd started avoiding them. As much as he was enjoying the sword fighting and horseback riding lessons, not to mention how much he was really liking getting to know both of them – he knew they had more important things to do right now than entertain him.

If the knock had surprised him, it was nothing compared to the shock of opening the door and seeing Doctor Rose standing there.

"Hello, Zander."

"Hi."

"I apologize for not getting that chance to catch up with you that we talked about a couple of evenings ago."

"I know you've been busy." Zander mostly felt useless. He *wanted* to do something to help, to find some answers, but he didn't know what to do.

"Yes, busy is one word for it. Today, though, I was going to go out to Mistle Village where we've been making the other vaccine. My friend there, Jacob, sent me a message this morning; he thinks it might be ready."

"That's good news."

"Yes. Good news is something we could use more of, but I'm happy to take what I can get right now. Anyway, I was wondering if you'd like to come along with me on the trip."

"Me?"

"Yes. I thought it might be nice for you to get out of the castle for a while, and also, then we could go ahead and give you the vaccine there without worrying about transporting it and delaying it even further. I know I told you we have time, but it makes me nervous."

Zander nodded. He'd had some really wicked dreams about rabies the last couple of nights. "You don't know the results of that antibody test do you?"

"No, not yet. It takes several days to complete. That's why I want to do this as soon as we can. I was going to take a wagon out with me so I could bring some supplies along. You could sit on a pillow in the back if you're not up to riding that far again."

A wobbly, ashamed feeling rose in Zander's chest and his arms; he fervently hoped it wouldn't show in his face. He hated feeling incompetent the way he did here. "How far is it?"

"About two hours one way."

He frowned; he was feeling much better, especially after William had stopped by his room that first night with some salve – and no judgment. He'd never expected that he'd have so much respect for William Rose, but it was creeping up on him.

Yesterday, he'd been able to ride around the paddock – albeit slowly – with Thomas for close to an hour without issue.

Four hours of riding in a single day, though … that might be a little beyond him. "I don't think I need a pillow," he finally said.

"Dress warm," Nathaniel said, "and I'll have someone bring you a coat. Our spell of Indian Summer seems to have come to an end."

"You call it Indian Summer here?"

"No. We call it Eternolis Interlude – we get a lot of spells of it in our fall season – sometimes for a moon or more at a time, and even quite a few of them in our winter but you wouldn't have known what I meant."

"We must be at a different latitude in this world than Bristlecone is in ours."

"That's a good observation, Zander. Yes, Eirentheos is closer to our equator and lower in elevation, too. We're also closer to an ocean. The weather here is more mild than what you're used to at home. It does still get quite cold, though, and we do get snow. I wouldn't be surprised if we saw some of that later this week."

"I hope I'm back home before that happens. We just finished winter in Bristlecone."

Doctor Rose chuckled. "I'll see what I can do."

He was a little surprised when they reached the little yard in front of the castle clinic and Thomas was there, loading supplies into the wagon.

"Are you coming, too?" Zander asked.

"Yes. I'm coming and William and Marcus are as well."

"I guess the king must have guards wherever he goes?"

Thomas tilted his head to the side. "Well, yes, although Marcus is only sort of a guard these days. I know he's been acting like one, with Quinn here. But that's more habit and needing to keep himself busy than anything. I think he feels better knowing he and Ben are the ones in charge of the guards when they're away from their castle. He's actually Quinn's advisor now. Although today, with Quinn and the baby safe, and no new information coming in, I think he just wants to spend time with Nathaniel. They've been good friends for a long time."

Zander could see them now – William was headed toward them with more crates, while Marcus and Nathaniel – he surprised himself by thinking of Doctor Rose by that name – busied themselves with the horses.

"Oh, good," William said when he reached them. "Nathaniel talked you into coming."

"Yeah, how can I help?"

"You don't have to…" Thomas started to say, but William shook his head at his brother.

"There are a couple more crates stacked up there on the porch. Want to help me grab them?"

"I would have thought you'd be staying here with Quinn and Owen," Zander said, as they carried the wooden crates down the steps.

"She could use a day with him without me, too."

"You just didn't want to miss an opportunity to watch me be a medical experiment." He set his crate on the tailgate of the wagon, and then climbed up beside it so he could organize the crates snugly along the sides.

"Well, there's that, too," William said, chuckling. "You're getting close to your last chance to back out on being a guinea pig."

"Nah, I'm interested in the whole thing now. I may never get another chance to sacrifice my immune system for science."

"You could always go to medical school."

"I've been tempted before, but I don't know. After watching that guy the other day … I'm not sure I could handle seeing that kind of thing on a regular basis."

"That might make you better at it." Thomas had joined them again now, and he jumped up in the wagon beside him. "It's the people who enjoy seeing those things that you have to worry about."

"Yeah, I still think I'd rather watch from the sidelines. Maybe build things that would help people instead of actually interacting with them."

"We could use more people like that here," William said, pushing the gate closed. "Especially someone who was educated on Earth and knows what some of the differences are and how things work there."

"As tempting as that is," Zander said, glancing up at the gray sky and pulling his hood up against the sudden breeze, "I think I'm going to have to run, not walk, back to the world where a twenty-mile trip would take me half an hour in a heated car in this kind of weather."

"I don't blame you." William was laughing again. "I wasn't exactly inviting my wife's ex-boyfriend to stick around, anyway."

It didn't even sting any more to hear William refer to Quinn as his wife.

Somewhere in the past week, all of the animosity between Zander and William had disappeared. Maybe it was because he was in such a strange world, and *everything* was so different that he could barely even think about Quinn in that way anymore. Perhaps it was because it felt like he'd been here so much longer than just a week – as if time had stopped and he'd had an entirely different life here. The Quinn he was getting to know here was not the same girl he'd known at home.

Thomas was looking at him funny, though. "Did Nathaniel tell you how far we were going?"

"Um ... he said it was about a two-hour trip one way. Horses go ... what? Maybe ten miles an hour or less?"

"Less, usually, it's not quite twenty miles from here," William said. "But you got it pretty close."

William and Thomas were driving the wagon while Nathaniel and Marcus rode. Zander huddled in his coat in the middle of the stacks of crates, watching first the capital city and then the rolling hills go by. Riding in the wagon was easier than it had been several days ago. He was learning how to hold himself steady, to not be slammed against the saddle with every bounce and jostle.

Or perhaps his muscles were getting stronger, enabling him to do more.

"Did I hear right that they found more rabid animals?" he asked after a while.

"Yes," William answered, turning around to face him. "I don't know how unexpected that is after what you and Ben found. They've been sweeping that area and the surrounding forests for the past few days, and have turned up another deer and several capiyas. My father expanded the clear zone quite a bit yesterday. Then, this morning, a family in Mistle Village reported finding bite marks on their dog from something that it must have fought with in the night."

"Despite warnings all over the kingdom to keep pets indoors at night," Thomas added, sighing.

"Yes. Despite that. Anyway, that's another reason we're all going out there now – to determine if we'll have to kill the dog, and to vaccinate anyone who may have been in contact with it after it was bitten."

"Would you really have to kill the dog?" Zander asked, aghast. "You don't even know if the animal that bit it was sick. Can't you watch it or something?"

"In your world, that's what we would do," William said. "Cage it and observe it for a few weeks. But there are no safe ways or safe places to do that there. Where would we keep it here?"

"You have cages here. I've seen them."

"Yes, but most pet dogs in our world have some outdoor freedom and hunt for themselves. Dogs aren't ever in cages. It's already been a strain on most dog-owning families in the clear zones. Nathaniel's fiancée and her children have a dog and it got out one night a week or two ago in the clear zone where they live – it was a very stressful situation."

"Wow."

"Exactly. And escaping is the other thing. We'd either have to take the dog from the family – and I don't know where we'd keep it or who would be responsible for it without traumatizing the dog and turning it completely wild – or we'd have to trust a family with small children to keep an unhappy dog locked up for weeks on end."

"Risking killing people and spreading rabies across the whole kingdom if they couldn't do it." Zander could see the problem now.

"Right. Now, Mistle Village is just outside the perimeter of the clear zone. We haven't had any reports of rabies near there, so we haven't made a final decision about what will be done with the dog. We might be able to take the risk, depending on what the dog was attacked by. Jacob hadn't gone to take a look at it before he sent the message to us, and I guess the family didn't know. If it just got into a fight with another dog, we might be okay if they can just try and keep it quarantined for the next moon or so. There haven't been any reports of problems with dogs in the area."

Zander nodded. "If it was a capiya or something, though, it's probably toast."

"Probably."

He understood it – why they would handle the situation this way. He'd watched that guy with the rabies, had helped Ben and Nathaniel carry his body out of the clinic the other day and load it into a wagon so it could be taken out of the city and cremated away from where anyone might come into contact with it. A dog wasn't worth that.

Still, it was someone's pet. There was a whole family who was likely to be traumatized if it had to be put down. A family that would also lose its protector against the wild animals that roamed in the night.

The thought preoccupied him so much that he lost track of time, and he was surprised when the wagon slowed and Marcus and Nathaniel fell back to come alongside them. He looked around for a moment, wondering if they were simply stopping to water the horses and let them rest, but then he saw it – the little building with a sign hanging from the covered porch. *Mistle Village Clinic; Jacob and Essie White, Healers.*

"Is it new?" he asked William as they rode into the yard. Everything about the place, from the richly stained wood of the porch to the freshly painted fences around the paddock behind looked as if it had been recently built.

"Yes. It was only finished a couple of moons ago, after the old clinic burned to the ground."

It didn't seem like a story William was very interested in discussing, and there wasn't time, anyway. A young man, maybe around Ben's age, had stepped out onto the porch and was waving at them in welcome.

As soon as Zander stepped down off the wagon, he was there to greet them.

"Zander, this is my cousin Jacob. Jacob, this is Zander."

Jacob didn't ask any questions about who Zander was or how William knew him – which led Zander to wonder if someone had already told him, but he figured it was better to not ask and to just ignore it, so he just smiled and shook Jacob's proffered hand.

The clinic was large and cheery. Jacob walked them around the covered porch to a door at the back of the building. It was large enough that Zander was beginning to wonder if maybe there wasn't a place here where they could keep a caged dog to observe it – right until they walked in the door and he realized they were in a home – complete with a wooden cradle tucked in the corner next to the couch. Zander's heart sank. There was nowhere here to observe a potentially rabid dog, either.

He didn't know why it was so important to him, but it was. The thought of the dog being killed bothered him. He wondered if it bothered any of the rest of them, or if they were used to things being this way here in Eirentheos. Maybe people didn't get as attached to their dogs here as people did in Zander's world.

William introduced him to Jacob's wife, Essie, and then he followed William and Thomas into the kitchen.

There were people seated around the table – a young couple and two young children; a boy who was maybe eight or so, and a little girl who was probably four. The mother was visibly pregnant, but she and her husband both stood when William and Thomas entered the room.

Although he seemed content as he ate a sandwich at the table, the little boy's eyes were a bit puffy and red. Zander was sure he knew why, and he felt even worse about the dog.

"This is Carrie and Raymond Ragland," Essie said, "and their children, Bryce and Clare."

"King William," Raymond said, bowing his head, "it's truly an honor. And Prince Thomas, as well."

For a moment, Zander wondered if that was how he was supposed to be reacting every time he saw William – *King William* – but after shaking the man's hand, William smiled and said, "I'm not going to be able to be very helpful today if you're treating me like a king, so for now, I'm just William – or Doctor Rose if you really must. All right?"

The couple didn't look too sure, but they relaxed a little. Thomas stepped behind Carrie's chair and held it for her until she sat back down. Raymond waited until William pulled out a chair for himself, but then he sat, too.

"So tell me what happened with your dog this morning," William said.

The little boy's lip started trembling again. Zander took a seat on the other side of him and smiled at him. "Is your lunch good?"

Bryce nodded, calming a bit and taking another bite.

Raymond sighed. "After breakfast, Bryce went out to feed Digger our leftovers and fill up his water bucket."

"He's our dog," little Clare said.

"Yes. It's Bryce's job to feed him."

"He doesn't hunt for himself?" Zander asked, frowning, then suddenly feeling bad for interrupting.

"No," Raymond smiled, though his expression was sad. "He catches rabbits and other small things every once in a while if they wander into the yard, but otherwise, I'm afraid he's spoiled. Three meals of leftovers every day, and whatever else the kids happen to drop on the floor."

This was only getting worse.

"We have a fenced in yard around the house that he never leaves. We have been keeping him inside at night, but he knows how to open the latch on the back door, and we forgot to tie it down last night so he couldn't."

"Did he get out?" William asked.

"I don't think so. All of the gates were secure, and there aren't any problems with the fence. But almost as soon as Bryce went out there this morning, we heard him scream. By the time we got to him, his hands were all covered in blood from a bite on Digger's front leg. I don't know what got him, but we knew that there'd been some cases of water disease in the kingdom. We made Bryce wash up outside and brought him right here."

"Where is Digger now?"

"Still in the yard, I guess – I hope. I set a fresh bucket of water out on the porch before we left, and he's got the food Bryce took out there."

"Nobody else touched him?"

"No. We haven't even touched Bryce. I gave him a washcloth and water outside before we brought him here. It was awful, but we knew… Jacob finished cleaning him up when we got here."

Zander could see it now – a few spatters of watered-down blood on the edge of Bryce's shirt – how his mother had also been crying at some point. The only one who seemed unaffected by it all was Clare.

"All right." William's voice was calm as he turned and smiled at Bryce. "Pretty scary morning, huh?"

"Is my dog going to be all right?"

"I don't know, Bryce. I don't know what happened to him. In a little while, we're going to go out to your house and have a look at him and see what we can do. Or, Prince Thomas and Sir Marcus are going to, for sure. I might stay here with you and make sure you're okay."

"I'm fine." Bryce finished drinking the last bit of milk in his glass just as Essie came over to collect his dishes.

"I know. Will you let me take you into the clinic and check you out, though?"

"Should we come?" Raymond asked.

William held his hand toward the door, but Bryce was shaking his head. "I'm okay, Father," Bryce said. "Right, William?"

Zander followed William and the little boy through a door that led to the other side of the building where he discovered a clinic area much like the one in the castle, only it was new.

Nathaniel and Marcus were already in there – Zander hadn't even noticed them disappear. It looked like Nathaniel was doing something with all of the supplies they'd brought.

"Just one dose, I think," William said to him. "Nobody else was anywhere near the dog."

Nathaniel nodded. "That's what Jacob said. I have it ready for you, and the other dose for Zander as well. I was just getting ready to give one to Marcus."

Zander looked at Marcus in surprise. "Are you testing it for them, too?"

"Someone has to," Marcus said. "It might as well be an old guy."

"I haven't seen any of those around here."

Marcus smiled. "Then I guess it will just have to be me."

"Marcus, Jacob, and I are all testing it," Nathaniel said. "Marcus and Jacob have never had any of the vaccine, so we'll get a chance to see how it works for building an initial immune response, while you and I are the test cases for booster doses – so long as you're sure you're willing to do it."

"Yeah, I'm game." He definitely wasn't going to back out on it now. He might not have what it took to compete with any of them on the bravery front, but he wasn't going to be a coward in comparison.

"All right. Can you take this over to William for me?" Nathaniel asked, holding out a small wooden box with a lid, along with a brown bottle filled with some kind of liquid.

William was already as far from them as he could get, helping Bryce up onto a cot on the other side of the room.

"You can tell me the truth," Bryce was saying as Zander approached them. "Now that my parents aren't listening. Digger's going to die and now that I touched him, so will I."

The little boy didn't start crying again, but Zander had to swallow back a lump in his throat as he set the supplies on the bed.

"No," William said firmly. "You are not going to die. You're going to be fine. I will be completely honest with you and tell you that I don't know about Digger. I hope he'll be okay, but yes, he might die."

Now Bryce's lower lip grew wobbly again.

"Nothing bad is going to happen to you. I have a special medicine I'm going to give you that will make sure you're safe."

"What kind of medicine?" The boy frowned, but his expression was one of curiosity.

"It's just a little shot," Zander said. "If it hurts, it will only be for a second."

Bryce's eyes grew very wide, and the look William directed at him made him want to crawl under the bed. Trying to insert himself into situations where he wasn't needed was *not* always a good habit.

"Why would it hurt?" the boy asked. "What are you going to do to me, William?"

"It's *not* going to hurt," Zander said, trying to redeem himself. "It's really easy. William is actually going to give me one, too. I got too close to an animal that had water disease, too."

"Did it die?"

"Yes. But it wasn't anyone's pet. It was a capiya."

"Oh, I hate those."

"Me too."

"And now you have to have the medicine, too?"

"Yes. And it isn't my first time. It's not a very big deal. Do you want to watch William do it to me, first?"

William shot him another look, but it was too late, Bryce was nodding vigorously.

"Have a seat." William ordered, pointing at the cot across from where Bryce was sitting. He was annoyed, but Zander wasn't exactly sure why. It seemed like he'd solved the problem he created.

"My arm?" Zander asked.

William nodded, so he rolled up his sleeve.

"Keep eye contact with the child, please," William said, close to Zander's ear as he cleaned his upper arm with the harsh-smelling liquid from the brown bottle.

So Zander did. He looked right at Bryce and smiled. "See? He's only touching my arm."

"I'm cleaning it," William said, though he didn't turn around. "It probably feels a little cold." He was using his body to block everything he was doing. Zander started to see his technique now, and he realized that even his solution was probably interfering with William's much better plan.

"Now, Zander might feel a pinch on his arm."

Yes, Zander did. He kept his smile as he looked at Bryce, though. "It's really easy, buddy."

Except it wasn't exactly. He'd forgotten that William had told him this might be worse than the shots in his world, and it was. The medicine stung all the way down his arm and up into his shoulder.

He used his free hand to grip the edge of the mattress tightly and breathed through his teeth, working to keep the smile on his face.

William was finished and had turned back around to take care of Bryce when Thomas came out. Zander still had his grip on the mattress.

"Is everything all right, Bryce?" Thomas asked. "Your mother and father wanted to come and see you."

The little boy nodded. "You can tell them I'm going to be okay."

"How about you go tell them yourself? I'm all done," William said.

"That didn't hurt," the boy said.

"Good. It wasn't supposed to. Go talk to them." He helped the little boy jump down from the bed. "Thomas, will you see if Essie can get him a bath and find some clean clothes for him?"

Once they were gone, William turned back to Zander. "Are you okay?"

He nodded.

"Kind of rough?"

"Kind of. I'm glad you gave Bryce the good stuff. You don't think he could tell, do you?"

"No. You hid it well. I'm pretty impressed, actually. I wouldn't have known if I hadn't had my hand around your arm when your pulse shot up."

"You didn't do that on purpose, did you?"

William chuckled. "You really think highly of me, don't you?"

"I mostly think I probably deserved it. Sorry for opening my big mouth."

"It's all right. I'm kind of a control freak about certain things. It's not really your fault. Besides, you did your best to fix it and it turned out okay. And *no*. I wouldn't hurt anyone on purpose – not even you. Is it feeling better now?"

"Not really, no. I think it might be getting worse."

"You are going to run away from this world as fast as you can, aren't you?"

Zander started to shrug – that was a mistake – "I don't know. I might miss the horses. I'm actually starting to learn how to ride them."

William laughed out loud; his annoyance was gone. "Well, do you want to go riding again now? I think Thomas and Marcus are going to go out to the Raglands' place and see about the dog."

"Digger. The dog's name is Digger."

William nodded, looking right in his eyes. "Don't go if you can't let Marcus do what he needs to do, Zander."

"*If* he needs to."

"*If* he needs to, it's going to be hard enough without you causing a problem over it. Do not go with them if you can't handle that."

"I'll handle it."

Zander really was getting better at horses. Even though his arm was killing him, and he was on a different horse – a black mare named Chancey – he had no problem riding the fifteen minutes to the Raglands' home. His legs weren't even wobbly when he dismounted just outside the wooden picket fence.

Marcus rubbed his arm one last time before pulling his sword out of its sheath.

He'd told William he could handle this, and he was *going* to, but the sight of Marcus' sword made bile rise in Zander's throat. Thomas, too, had his hand at his hilt.

"The dog isn't rabid yet, even if it was bitten," he said. "It's not dangerous. Let me go."

Marcus was clearly unsure, but Thomas nodded at him, and he held his hand out toward the fence. "At the first sign of trouble, Zander…"

"I know."

Before he was even to the gate, he found the dog – or, rather, it found him. Digger came running up to the fence, wagging his tail excitedly as he waited for Zander to open the gate.

"What good are you, Digger?" he asked, letting himself in and kneeling down beside the dog. "They have to feed you, and you obviously don't guard them against anyone." Digger was smaller than he'd expected, maybe the size of a cocker spaniel, though he didn't recognize the breed. He was dark gray all over, with short hair that curled to his sides.

And the fur on his left front leg was all matted together with blood. Another thick, sticky mess stretched across his muzzle.

"Can I see?" he asked, reaching for Digger's leg.

The dog whined, but allowed him to take his paw. Zander looked at it as best he could, but he couldn't see anything around the dried blood.

"You are going to be devastated if you get attached to that dog." Thomas' voice was suddenly beside him as he lifted Digger into his arms.

"I can't help it. You should stay away, though, Thomas."

"He's not contagious. Besides, I'm going to ask William or Nathaniel to try out their new concoction on me, too."

"Good luck with that." He spotted what he was looking for – the bucket of water on the porch – and carried the dog up to it, setting him down and then coaxing him to let him dip the injured leg into the water. Washing out the cuts really made Digger whimper, but he didn't pull away or get aggressive with Zander. He wouldn't let Zander near the blood on his face, though – and Zander decided it wasn't worth the fight that close to the dog's teeth.

Thomas – apparently disregarding caution – gently patted the animal's back while Zander carefully scrubbed out the blood with his fingers until Digger's leg was clean and he could get a look at the wound.

His heart sank a little lower when he saw that it definitely was a bite; he hadn't realized just how much he'd been hoping that Bryce had been wrong about that and that Digger had injured himself in a different way.

The wounds were small, though, whatever had bitten him had been smaller than him — the teeth marks were close together and formed the impression of a small jaw — the puncture wounds spoke to little teeth. There was so much blood only because Digger had been bitten multiple times. "What do you think did this?" he asked Thomas. "It's too small to be a fox or a capiya."

"Could be a raccoon," Thomas said. "Or maybe something even smaller." Washing the wounds had made them start bleeding again. Thomas pulled a handkerchief out of his back pocket and handed it to Zander.

As carefully as he could, Zander tied the white cloth snugly around the dog's leg. Digger let out a single whimper, but again was patient.

When Zander stood to look around, though, Digger began whining in earnest, pushing his head against Zander's leg.

"It's still bad news, Zander," Thomas said. "This is getting harder every second. Marcus will make it quick and painless."

He knew. He knew what the possible consequences were, how bad it was, how important it was to stop every single case of rabies they possibly could, but still…

"What if it was one of the animals that's too small to get rabies?"

"Those teeth marks weren't *that* small, Zander. And look around. Do you see any dead squirrels? Digger might be tame, but he wouldn't let something do *that* to him without inflicting some serious damage of his own." Zander heard it — the way Thomas' voice changed when he actually said the dog's name.

"I'm going to look around."

Three times around the house, though, revealed nothing. No small dead animals or even injured ones. Just a missing piece in one

of the pickets large enough for something to squeeze through —
probably where the culprit had made its entrance and subsequent
exit.

Sighing, trying to resign himself to the awful inevitable, he made
one last loop around the house.

And that was when he spotted it. A tiny tuft of black, up under
the edge of the wooden porch at the back of the house. A tuft of fur
matted in blood.

"Thomas!" he called as he approached the porch, kneeling down
next to the steps and looking at the little bit of fur, then shifting his
gaze underneath it. He could barely make it out through the small
open spaces between the stairs, but there was something moving
under there.

He heard Thomas' footsteps behind him, and then his voice —
"I wouldn't do that if I were you" — as he stuck his hand back there,
trying to reach whatever it was.

The animal hissed only a fraction of a second before its teeth
clamped into Zander's wrist and wouldn't let go.

"It's a cat!"

A chorus of soft mewling sounds corrected him immediately.
"It's cats. A mama cat and her kittens, I think." He had to put his
other hand down there to finally wrestle the cat's jaw off his wrist,
succeeding in loosening its teeth, but also in getting long scratches
down both his forearms.

"Kittens? At this time of the cycle? That's not normal."

"Well, I don't know if it's normal or not, Thomas, but they're
here." Blood was dripping down his arm now. He used the bottom
of his shirt to wipe some of it off. "I think they're feral."

"The family said they don't have any pets besides Digger. The
only other animals they have are their horses."

"Well, this is what got Digger," he said, examining the bite
marks on his wrist. "I'll bet the blood on his nose is from a scratch."
He held up his arms, showing off his own injuries.

"Are you stupid, Zander? Sticking your hand in there like that? Why would you do that?"

"I don't know. I just wanted to know what was under there."

"That dog is not worth your *life*, Zander."

"Well, I doubt that cat is rabid. I think Digger just messed with the wrong mama cat."

"You might be right, but honestly, having had the rabies vaccine is not license to disregard your own safety here. Now we have to get you back to the clinic to get that bite looked at. And we need to get that cat and her kittens so we can decide what to do and see if *they're* sick. I don't know if you just solved a problem here or created five more."

Zander didn't care. All he heard was Thomas saying he might be right. All he could think about was keeping Digger safe, on the porch on the other side of the house.

MIA

ALTHOUGH QUINN HAD been waiting all morning for Mia to stop by her room and see if she needed anything, she was nervous when she finally heard the quiet knock on the door.

Owen hopped up from the game of choice they'd been playing and went to answer it. "Come in, Mia," he said.

She wasn't even all the way inside the room yet when Owen turned to Quinn. "I'm going to go and see if Alex and Emma are done with their lessons, okay?" He disappeared without even waiting for a response, demonstrating yet again that he somehow knew something he shouldn't have – that Quinn needed to talk to Mia privately.

"Where's the baby, milady?" Mia asked.

"He's in the cradle. He just fell asleep about fifteen minutes ago."

"I'm sorry. I could come back at a better time – unless there was anything else you needed."

"Actually, I do need to have a word with you. Would you have a seat, please?" She almost regretted saying it when she saw the terrified look on Mia's face. It was still hard – this part of learning to have people under her and command them. Although she was getting better at it, it was especially difficult when she was dealing with someone like Mia, whom she considered to be a friend.

"Is everything all right, milady? Have I done something to displease you?" Mia was fiddling nervously with the edge of her skirt, picking off an invisible piece of lint.

"No, Mia. Of course you haven't. In fact, quite the opposite. I asked you in here to tell you how grateful I am for all of the help you've been lately with the baby. You've made a challenging time much easier for me."

"It isn't a problem, Your Majesty. It's my job."

"No, actually it isn't, and yet you've taken on the extra duties without complaint. I do appreciate it, thank you."

"You're very welcome. I'm happy to do anything I can to help."

"There is one thing you could do, Mia."

"Yes, Your Majesty?"

"You could stop calling me that. Particularly when it's just the two of us and we're talking."

Mia blushed – it wasn't the first time Quinn had asked her that. "I'm sorry, m… Quinn."

"That's better. Nothing changed when I had the baby, you know. We're still friends, please?"

"All right, *Quinn*, I'm sorry."

Quinn smiled. "Anyway, my real reason for wanting to talk to you … I'm sure you're aware that when we return to Philotheum with the baby, we will need a nurse for him."

She might have teased Mia about her deer-in-the-headlights look, if there were headlights in this world. She hadn't learned an equivalent phrase here. And anyway, it was time to quit scaring her. "William and I were wondering if you might consider taking the position."

"*Me?*"

"Yes."

"In Philotheum?"

"Yes. It's a big question, I know. It would require your moving to Philotheum with us."

Mia swallowed, smoothing her skirt yet another time. The pink that had been starting to fade from her blush a moment ago flared now to a furious red. "Would it be impertinent of me to ask who I would be working under – who you would be hiring as Head Nurse?"

"For the time being, Mia," Quinn said, smiling, "there will only be one child in the castle. I'm only in need of one nurse. I'm offering you the position of Head Nurse."

"Head Nurse? I'm only seventeen, Your – Quinn. I'm barely an apprentice."

"You're more than that Mia. And regardless, it's what I'm offering."

"You're actually offering it, to *me.*"

"Yes."

"Head Nurse?"

"Yes. That would be your official title; any future hires would report to you, although you would be the only nurse for now. You'd still have the same amount of time off, of course. With probably some help from Linnea, William and I would be able to cover your off days."

"I don't use most of the time I have off now, Your Majesty." Mia was clearly flustered, saying whatever came to her mind.

Quinn reached across the table and put her hand on Mia's knee. "I know. But it's something you need to consider. In all honesty, you would have fewer duties in Philotheum, with only one child. But we'd also be taking you away from your family and your friends here – you wouldn't have the same options on your days off as you have now."

"Yes, I've thought about that."

"You've thought about it a lot, haven't you?"

Now Mia's face was flaming red. "It's crossed my mind. I wanted to speak to you about it, but then I kept talking myself out of it. I never imagined you would think I was qualified for it, though. I only thought perhaps if you needed an assistant, then maybe… And I have no idea what Queen Charlotte and King Stephen's reaction would be."

"What did you think would happen if you never asked?"

She didn't look up as she answered. "Then at least I wouldn't anger them."

"Well, I've spoken to them, Mia. In fact, Charlotte was the one who brought up the idea with William. He and I agreed that you would be the best candidate we could hope for. But I think we've – all of us – been failing to communicate with one another about the big thoughts and ideas that are floating around here. I think it's caused strain in more than one relationship." She did her best to give Mia a pointed look.

"Thomas."

"Yes, Mia. Have you talked to him at all about any of this? About what you might be wanting for your life?"

"I didn't know how. I didn't think he would understand my maybe wanting to move to another kingdom … and then if it was all only a silly dream anyway…"

"Then what? It would all solve itself? You'd be happy to stay with Thomas and never talk to him about this thing that became important to you?"

Mia bit her lip, not answering.

"Well now it's happening … this is real. I'm offering you the job. You're obviously not obligated to take it, and I don't want an answer today. But because we've all been putting this off and not talking to one another and none of us – including me – has been saying what we're thinking – time is short. We head to Philotheum a week from today. I know you were planning on traveling with Charlotte and Stephen there for the Naming Ceremony. William and

I will be needing someone to begin full-time when Stephen and Charlotte return to Eirentheos."

"I have to pack." Mia said, standing and starting to pace in her anxiousness.

"I told you I don't want an answer today."

"What would my answer be besides yes, milady? Another opportunity like this will never present itself to me. Head baby nurse at seventeen. The chance to stay with you and King William, and your son who I've grown attached to already. Perhaps even to be there to assist Linnea when she and Ben have a child… Of course I'll accept."

"It would be all of those things, Mia. But it isn't all simple. The castle in Philotheum is a different place. There aren't as many people there, especially close to our age, there's Lady Sophia, the political issues…"

"If I might be so presumptuous – those are all more reasons for you to have a nurse who has grown up in a castle and has worked for a queen."

"I'll need you to be more presumptuous – and more assertive. I'll need a lot of help, and I'll really need you to be able to take over with the baby, even if my grandmother makes it challenging – which she probably will."

"What is the situation with Lady Sophia? After you and William were first married and Tolliver was arrested – she seemed so supportive. Has that changed?"

"Yes … no … I don't know. When we first went to live in Philotheum, I thought it was going to be fine. She'd arranged the whole wedding, the whole coronation, everything. I didn't mind most of that. I certainly didn't know how to do it, and I wanted it to be right – for the first impressions my people had of me to be good ones. The only specific thing I asked of her was that the coronation, especially, include all of the elements it traditionally would, if it were a king being crowned as ruler."

"Both ceremonies were very beautiful." There was a catch in Mia's voice, though, and Quinn knew that she understood at least part of what she was saying.

"Yes. They were."

"But not quite what you asked for."

"The changes were very subtle – just enough for everyone to notice, but not enough for me to really be able to say anything."

"Like having you sitting for the entire ceremony."

"See, you noticed."

"You were pregnant, though."

"Despite the fact that our families and close servants like you knew that, it was not public knowledge in Philotheum until – probably that very moment."

"Oh." Mia's expression was becoming more and more understanding.

"Besides that, I was pregnant. Not ill or injured. Not incapable of standing up in front of my kingdom and saying my oath. Alvin, fortunately, pulled me up from the throne like the whole thing was planned that way, but still – it was obvious."

"And I'm guessing you really couldn't say anything to her about it without sounding like you didn't care about the baby."

"Or really complain about it to anyone, without them thinking I was just overreacting – or emotional about it because I was pregnant."

"Even William?"

Quinn loved that Mia had finally dropped the formalities and was talking with her the way they'd done so many times – as a friend who, because of her unique position, sometimes understood more about the inner workings of life in a castle than even the princes and princesses.

"It isn't that William didn't believe me or didn't support me. He did – at least to the extent that he understood it. But he was in a weird position. He *was* worried about me, and his biggest concern was making sure that I was comfortable and that both the baby and I were safe and healthy. I was fine with that about *him* – that was his place."

"Not hers."

"Exactly." She'd been holding all of this inside for so long, that the relief of being able to talk about it with someone who understood made it just come pouring out. "And Will hates it so much that I don't have family here – he wanted me to have a good relationship with Sophia, for her to be a grandmother to me. So, while he does listen, and he's sincere, I think he *wanted* it to be true that I was just emotional, or taking things too seriously."

"He didn't *say* that to you, did he?"

Quinn chuckled at the shock in Mia's voice. "No. Not in those words, anyway. He didn't know most of it. She – deliberately, I started to think – waited to do a lot of it when he wasn't even there. One time we had this dinner with the head councilmen of some villages near the border – one of the places I've had the hardest time gaining full support – and William was busy talking with someone while I chatted with one of them, and she came up – right in the middle of our conversation and asked if I was keeping the dinner down all right, or if I needed someone to bring me something for my stomach."

"Had you been sick?"

"Not for weeks. I was about four moons along then. That was the time I felt the best of my entire pregnancy – it wasn't even affecting me at all. William and I had chosen that time specifically to arrange for meetings with some important people we needed to get to know."

Mia rolled her eyes. "And of course – how do you complain about her doing that?"

"Right? Sure, let's go whine to my husband that my grandmother is asking after my health? What am I even supposed to say to that? It's not a crime."

"Except that it completely undermines you, and makes you look weak in front of someone who needs to see you as a competent ruler."

Quinn's relief came out in a huge sigh. "I'm not crazy."

"I don't think so. It sounds deliberate."

"I wanted to be. Wanted it to be true that I was just emotional, or hormonal from being pregnant, but there were just more and more incidents like that. If I wanted to follow tradition, then she found some way to make it just a little bit different. And then the one time I wanted to break tradition…"

Mia raised an eyebrow.

"The Cradle Reveal."

"You didn't want to have one?"

"Of course I did. I wouldn't have taken that away from people. The gifts our guests filled it with are probably going to last us through *all* of our children, but the party was wonderful. What I didn't want, though, was to have an entirely new cradle designed for him. I wanted to have the one that was used for my father refurbished."

"And she fought you on that?"

"I maybe could have lived with her having a problem with it. My father was her son, maybe she didn't want me taking that, or maybe … who knows. But several days after I mentioned the idea, a cradle just *appeared* in our room."

"She *commissioned* it? You didn't even get to help design it?"

"Nope. It was just there. And apparently I'm supposed to just be grateful. William was upset about that one, too. He'd wanted to help – we only get to do the Reveal with the first one, the heir."

"Wow."

"Yeah. Those were the big ones, but even more than that is just how constant it's been. Sometimes I feel like I'm just paranoid – like she really is just concerned about me and the baby, and I'm being too hard on her. But other times…"

"You think she's undermining you on purpose."

"Yes. And I don't know why, or how far she plans on taking it, but I'm almost certain that it's not going to stop just because the baby is here. I have a feeling it's going to get worse."

"You need me, Quinn. I know you said you don't want my answer today, but I'm giving it to you. I've given it enough thought; I know it's what I want."

Quinn nodded. It was what she wanted, too. There was still a big unanswered question hanging there, though – she took a moment to compose herself before asking it.

"And what about Thomas, Mia?"

Mia's gaze dropped immediately to the floor. "I'll have to tell him."

She hesitated for a second, debating whether to tell Mia the other bit of information she'd been withholding. Perhaps it would have been more fair to tell her – but something stopped her from doing it. Instead she asked, "You're willing to leave him for this job?"

Mia was back to fidgeting with her skirt, still staring at the floor. "I love Thomas, I do … but yes, I would take this job even if it means losing him. I can't explain why. It's just that I know I would regret it if I turned the opportunity down, if I gave up what I really wanted, just to stay here and be with him." Her green eyes finally flicked up to meet Quinn's. "I hope that doesn't make you think less of me. I know how much Thomas means to both you and William."

"Of course it doesn't, Mia. I know how much you care for Thomas – maybe it's just not more than you care about making the right decision for yourself. I don't think there's anything wrong with that. I think it's probably best if you talk to Thomas sooner rather than later, though."

"Hi Mia … Uh, Mia?"

Mia turned around to see Ben standing there in the hallway. "Oh, hi."

For a second there, I thought maybe you were going to ignore me completely," he said, smiling. "I was worried I'd done something to deserve it."

"No, of course not."She accepted the hug he was offering. "What are you doing down here?"

"Linnea is spending some time with Rebecca and Evelyn. I thought I'd patrol for a while – but mostly I came to see if there was anyone around here I could bug for a bit." He nodded around them. "But nobody's here. I was just in the common room, and it's empty."

"Well, it is still kind of the middle of the day."

"There is that."

"Do you miss it?" she asked. "Living here?"

"Yeah, a little. This hallway will always be my first home. I miss being chased by you when you were little – and bringing you Cassie's cookies from the kitchen. You're the closest thing I had to a little sister, Mia. I miss you."

"Imagine what it's been like for me. Nine moons with no big brother to boss me around." She punched him playfully on the shoulder.

"Not quite the freedom you expected?"

"I was never trying to get rid of you, Ben. It is different here without you and your father. Fifth Day dinners are not the same without your stories."

He laughed. "But I'll bet you get to keep a lot more of your money when you're playing choice."

"All of it, actually. Of course, I mostly play with Thomas and the others these days – and he doesn't believe me that it can be a gambling game."

"Neither did Linnea," he said, smirking, "but I taught her otherwise after the wedding."

"Don't even *think* about telling me what the stakes are," she said, punching him again.

"You know I wouldn't."

"Good."

"So … when are you going to tell me what's wrong?"

"Nothing's wrong."

"Oh no. You might be able to get away with that nonsense with other people, Amelia Grace, but don't try it with me."

She narrowed her eyes, but he only raised an eyebrow.

"That's not going to work. I just took a plate of cookies into the common room. Nobody's there. Let's go." He marched her into the room at the end of the hall.

The common room in the hallway for the guards' families was much like the one upstairs the royal family used, just as large, and kept up just as well. King Stephen and Queen Charlotte were adamant about providing the best accommodations they could to the families of their staff and servants. Actually, the furniture in here stayed nicer, since there were fewer children with sticky hands wandering in and out.

Grabbing two plates and two cookies from the counter, Ben led her to one of the couches in the back of the room near the fireplace.

"All right, little bird," he said once they were sitting down, "drop your worm. What's going on?"

"Queen Quinn has offered me the position of Head Nurse in the baby's nursery."

His face lit up like candles at the harvest festival. "Really, Mia? That's wonderful! Congratulations! What an honor."

"Thank you." She started to beam a little at his words.

"Are you going to accept?"

"Yes. I've already told her I will. She already spoke with Queen Charlotte and King Stephen and it sounds as if they're fine with it. And I've just finished talking to my parents. Apparently, my mother has anticipated for a while that it might happen, but nobody wanted to get my hopes up."

"That must have been a difficult conversation. My father was coming with me – I really can't imagine having to tell him I was leaving otherwise."

"It was hard. But my parents are proud and willing to come visit. And they'll be traveling with us to go to Philotheum for the ceremony, so the good-bye won't be immediate. My mother's going to help me pack tonight after the children are asleep – but I think I might start a little before then."

"We do leave in just over a week's time. *We* – that sounds very good, Mia. The castle in Philotheum is nice, but somewhat more mellow than here. It'll be good to have more company to spice it up. Perhaps we can even show them our version of choice."

"So long as it's not *your* version."

He laughed – a deep, long, genuine laugh that made her feel at home for a while before his expression turned serious again. "And then there's Thomas."

"Yes."

"What is going on between the two of you lately, anyway? Something seems off – it's not like it was before we went to Philotheum."

She shook her head. "It hasn't been, and I don't know what to do, Ben. He's been so different since you left. I know it's hard for him, how much he misses Quinn and William … but he won't talk to me about it. He just wants to pretend it doesn't bother him, I think. But then, as it's gotten closer and closer to time for Linnea to leave, he's really pulled away from everyone."

"Have you tried confronting him about it?"

"I half have … but I don't know how to do it without hurting him. And then, to be honest, ever since I realized that Quinn and William would be raising a baby in a castle where they wouldn't have had a baby nurse in many cycles…"

"You've been dreaming about that job."

"Yes."

"Without telling him."

She nodded, picking at the cookie on her plate. It was in crumbles, though she hadn't managed to take a single bite. "It's not like I didn't want to tell him, but it just seems like every time we do talk lately, we end up arguing, and I hate that. So then I just stay away from him, because I'm afraid he doesn't want to hear what I need to say."

"Hmm… Is that making things better?"

"Is that a rhetorical question?"

"So it sounds like you're not talking to him, he's not talking to you … and nobody's happy."

"I love him, Ben. More than anything. How do I tell him I'm leaving?"

He frowned, fidgeting with his own cookie. "Do you want to keep your courtship with him?"

"I *want* to, but now, I don't know if it's possible. I'll be in Philotheum, five days away, and he'll be here. Probably angrier than he is now, with all of us gone." Now she was picking apart one of the berries that had been inside the cookie, getting red goo underneath her fingernails, but she didn't care.

"Well, it can work. I courted Linnea for seven months while I was there and she was here."

"Yes, but you knew you were going to get married at the end of it. Thomas isn't old enough to get married."

Finishing the last bite of his cookie, he reached across and took the cookie plate out of her hands, setting it down on the table beside him. "Mia, I realize how difficult it is, and I understand your reservations. I get why you're having trouble talking to him, but … I don't believe this will be impossible to work out, if it's what both of you want. But I do know that not talking never solved anything. Whatever happens, you have to talk to him."

"And what if doing that ends our courtship?"

"That would be devastating. I'm not going to lie. I've ended a courtship before and it was one of the hardest things I've ever gone through. But after a while, ending it isn't worse than staying in one that isn't working, and where you can't talk to each other. *Talk to him.*"

"How do I do it, Ben? Help me out here."

He smiled. "How about you go to the kitchen and request a picnic dinner for the two of you, with your favorite foods. Then, go prepare one of the empty guest suites with a fire – maybe some candles, whatever you'd like. And later, take the dinner up there, just the two of you and *talk*. Start off with telling him your feelings for him – tell him that you *don't* want to end your courtship; he needs to know that part. And then tell him your news. Perhaps the two of you can figure out the rest of it together."

"And if that doesn't work?"

"Well, you'll always have me, little bird. There will be lots of new guards to meet in Philotheum. I'll introduce you."

Earned

Mistle River Valley, Eirentheos

ZANDER WAS STILL pleased with himself when he climbed into the back of the wagon to return to the castle from Mistle Village. Telling Bryce Ragland that his dog would most likely be fine had been one of the most satisfying experiences of his life, even if it had come at some personal cost.

His whole body was aching now – from the experimental rabies vaccine, from the fierce cat bites and scratches running up his arms and deep in his left hand, from the antibiotics William had dosed him after the cat attacks. Getting the wild animals out from under that porch and into a bag so they could be taken to the clinic had turned into a treacherous task. But he'd accomplished it.

If he'd known they were going to have to kill the cats to test them, he might not have gone to such extremes, but he didn't really care. It would have been nice to save the cats, too, but he understood the circumstances – he was lucky enough to have probably rescued Digger.

He contemplated all of that, drifting half in and out of sleep – the day really had wrung him out – watching the scenery as they rode in silence for a while. The area was all farmland mixed with patches of heavy forest; from the road he could see down to the wide, rushing river that must irrigate the area.

"Whoa, what is that?" he asked, as a large structure came into view on an uphill slope of the river. Water rushed from it, creating an enormous waterfall. "Is that a power plant?" he asked William and Thomas.

"Our electricity has to come from somewhere, right?" He was surprised when Thomas signaled to Marcus and Nathaniel and then turned the wagon toward the river, taking the horses down the slope all the way to the edge.

Maybe they'd been traveling for longer than he'd realized, and it was time to give the horses a break. Or maybe – judging by the grin on Thomas' face – he just wanted to show off the incredible architecture here.

The river was breathtaking here as thousands of gallons of water flowed through the concrete dam above, breaking into whitewater caps on the rocks below. They had a right to show this off a little. The sight captivated him. "How did you do all of this?"

William jumped down from the wagon seat. "It took nearly three cycles just to build it, after Nathaniel and my father researched it for several cycles before that."

"That would be like thirty *years* in my world."

"Yes. We don't have the same level of production of the raw materials you do in your world, either. It all had to be done from scratch. The goal was just a start of electricity, enough for lights for the capital city and some of the outlying villages, without a huge disruption to the flow of the river, and we actually managed it. It's definitely one of our biggest accomplishments here, ever."

"Can you store electricity and everything?"

"No. It's a run-of-the-river power station only. There's no reservoir and no electricity storage. We use it as it's generated."

Marcus and Nathaniel were off their horses now, leading them to a spot where the water collected in a small, calmer pool. The temperature felt even lower here, near the spray from the massive waterfall. Zander pulled his jacket tighter. "What happens if the river freezes?"

"It doesn't usually, but if it does, then, yeah, no electricity until it thaws again." Thomas said.

"What do you *do*?"

William shrugged. "Use candles and lamps. The same thing Quinn and Nathaniel and I do at home in Philotheum. We're not dependent on the electricity for heating or cooking, the way you are in your world, and we don't have plans to change that anytime soon. The lights are nice, though, especially in the clinics."

"Are you going to do something like this in your kingdom?"

"Yes, but it will probably take just as long as it took us to do it here. None of the people who helped work on this project are in Philotheum. Most of them are working now on surveying the land around a different part of the river to start building a dam that would serve some other communities here. My brother Maxwell is very involved in that project, along with two of my father's brothers. Thomas, too, has been drawing up some of the maps."

"I have to do something productive with my time," Thomas said, shrugging.

"Well, I have an idea about that," William said. "I wanted to talk to you about it today."

"Tell me it involves finding Tolliver myself and giving him what he actually deserves rather than waiting for the army to find him and arrest him again."

"You know it doesn't."

This didn't feel like a conversation Zander should be part of, but walking away from them in the middle felt just as awkward as staying, and besides, he sort of wanted to hear about this. He was with Thomas. Actually, if Thomas wanted to take off right now and go searching, Zander would probably follow him.

"Oh come on, Will. At least if I caught him and killed him, Quinn wouldn't have to worry about the consequences of ordering the execution of a prince who also happens to be her half-uncle. Everyone could blame me."

"Blame Eirentheos, you mean. And that's *if* you succeeded in the attempt without getting killed yourself, which is unlikely in the extreme. We don't know where he is or who helped him get out of prison. Whoever it was had no problem murdering three guards on top of getting in and out of the prison undetected – well, undetected by anyone who survived."

Zander hadn't heard that part. He hadn't heard *anything*, actually since that first night. Everyone seemed to be keeping the problems quiet – or at least behind closed doors. He knew Quinn had been spending the bulk of the last couple of days in meetings.

"I'm not actually going to do it, Will. But I'm not happy about waiting around here while two armies go on a wild goose chase. He could be anywhere."

"We got some intelligence from Philotheum yesterday that suggests he could be in the Mousike River region."

"Close to Dovelnia."

"Yes. Which makes sense. We believe he still has a lot of support in that area."

"Of course he does. Hector was building support in that area for half a generation. Quinn should be having people arrested and questioning them."

"Yeah, Thomas. A lot of potentially false arrests would be fantastic for Quinn's cause."

Thomas kicked a rock that went sailing into the river, though the resulting splash was insignificant compared to the force from the raging waterfall.

"Quinn and I are as angry as you are, Thomas. But anger isn't the right way to resolve this. We don't know exactly who we're dealing with besides Tolliver. If we jump on this too quickly and start accusing people of being involved, we risk alienating the people who support Quinn. We need to do this the right way and recapture him without setting off any more political difficulties than we already have. So right now, that means waiting, and letting the armies do their jobs. Quinn and I actually have reason to believe that it may not be anyone from that region anyway."

"What do you mean?"

"I haven't had the chance to tell you about this with the way things have been the past couple of days, but we recently found out that Hector may have had an accomplice who traveled to the other world. It may have even been him who actually killed Samuel."

"Who?"

"A man named Rahas. I'll explain more about it later – show you the letter that we found. But if he's still around, and he easily could be, then he might be the one who is helping Tolliver now."

Zander knew he'd never heard that name before, and yet, a strange sense of familiarity washed over him when he heard it – almost a feeling of *déjà vu*. He knew, suddenly, that he was supposed to tell William and Thomas something – something important – but he couldn't remember what. As he listened to the conversation, he struggled to remember.

"And he knows about the other world."

"Yes, he's been there. So right now, the most important thing we can do is get Zander and Owen safely back there and get the gate closed before *anyone* finds out it's open. That means staying here and doing what we need to do while we wait to hear from the armies."

"Not like I have any choice anyway, William. I'm here in Eirentheos, and he's probably all the way over on the other side of Philotheum. I'm still sixteen, and I'm stuck here."

Zander stared out over the water as he waited for William to say what he was going to say. "Well, actually, this whole

Eirentheos-Philotheum thing is what I wanted to talk to you about."

For a moment, Zander forgot that he wasn't supposed to be listening and he glanced over at them. Thomas was frowning, but there was a tiny gleam of hope in his eyes – Zander wondered if this conversation was going where he thought it might.

"Back at the castle today, Quinn is going to be speaking to Mia. She's going to officially offer her the position of baby nurse."

Good for Quinn. It was about time for that, Zander thought.

"Now, before you react to that on a purely emotional level…" William put his hand on his brother's shoulder. "Mother, Father, and Quinn all know that sometime today I was planning to ask you if you'd consider coming to live in the castle in Philotheum with us."

"As your…?" Thomas' voice had an edge to it. William should have led with the second bit if he didn't want Thomas to react on an *emotional level.* Really not wanting to get caught eavesdropping *now,* Zander stared purposefully at the white caps breaking against a jagged boulder in the middle of the river.

William was impressive as he rose to the challenge in his brother's tone, though. "As our brother, Thomas. As a friend and confidant. As whatever you want to pursue in Philotheum. We're not asking because we feel sorry for you. We're asking because it's what Quinn and I both desperately want, and because, quite honestly, we need someone there with your range of skills, and your knowledge of so many of the things we've done here with the clinics especially, but also the power."

"I'm not an adult, William. Have you forgotten that?"

"I don't believe that's a designation that relies solely on a number, Thomas. And Mother and Father agree. You've earned the right to be called a man, and to either live here in Eirentheos or to come with us to Philotheum as an adult. It's your choice, of course, what you want to do. This is a sincere invitation, not a command."

That finally managed to crack through Thomas' armor. Though he didn't turn to look, Zander could hear the smile in his voice. "You're serious."

"Quinn is sitting on her hands to keep herself from writing to Ruth and asking which apartment has the best view."

"You're not going to let me pick my own?" He was joking – the audible grin was so big now he was nearly laughing.

Zander heard a soft thudding sound – perhaps a friendly punch on the shoulder –and he turned around in time to see the two of them hugging.

The feeling that filled him now was so unexpected that he forgot everything else. Although he'd already realized sometime in the last few days that he was actually enjoying himself here – that he found the whole world fascinating and the people were beginning to grow on him, too – he'd never felt like this. For a moment, he almost wished that he were over there – that someone was telling *him* he'd earned the right to be called a man and inviting him to go and live in a faraway castle, to help rebuild a kingdom torn by recent strife.

Back in his own world, he'd just been told he wasn't enough of a man to choose what he wanted to study in college. And maybe he wasn't, he thought, swallowing hard as he watched the brothers. He'd never really done anything for anyone except himself. Never made any hard choices – heck, he hadn't even made a choice about what he wanted to study, and there he was asking for someone else to pay for it.

No, maybe he hadn't earned anything at all.

WEEDS

Rosewood Castle, Eirentheos

"I'LL PULL THE wagon in front of the clinic," Thomas said as they entered the castle grounds. "Then it will be easier for us to get this stuff inside."

William nodded. "Yes, I don't want to risk breaking any of the vials of vaccine."

He looked in the back when he brought the horses to a stop right at the base of the clinic steps. Zander was sound asleep against a stack of blanket-wrapped crates. "Should I wake him up?"

"I'll do it," William said. "I need to take him inside and check his vitals again anyway – make sure he's not having a reaction to the vaccine or anything."

"Okay, I'll start unloading the stuff."

After opening the tailgate and offering a hand to Zander, Thomas worked slowly and carefully pulling the crates down from the wagon and organizing them up on the porch, and then began tending the horses, hoping that if he took long enough William would come out to check on him.

He was right; after about ten minutes, William appeared again – at exactly the same moment Nathaniel appeared on the path. Thomas sighed. "How's Zander?" he asked.

"He's fine. Exhausted, and he has a low fever, but otherwise good. I was looking for the file with the vaccine data."

"It's here." Thomas pulled it out of a crate on top of one of the stacks.

"Thanks." William was just opening it when Nathaniel finally reached the top of the steps.

"Hey, Will, how about I take a look at that and at Zander and you can get inside to Quinn and the baby? We've been gone for a long time." Nathaniel held out his hand for the file.

"I don't want to leave you with all of this." William nodded toward the crates.

"It's fine. Take advantage of it while my fiancée is still far away and I'm bored. Jared and Arthur are coming up from the stables to take care of the horses, so really, the two of you can go." Nathaniel shot Thomas a knowing look – somehow, he always knew when there was something going on.

"So … I have a question," Thomas said, once he and William were out of earshot of the clinic.

William stopped walking and turned to face him.

"This whole being considered an adult thing – does that mean really having all of the privileges of adulthood?"

His brother's eyes narrowed just slightly. "Yes – and the responsibilities, too."

"*All* of them?"

"Which privilege are you specifically referring to, Thomas?"

"Marriage."

"Oh. You want to ask Mia to marry you?"

"I'm thinking about it."

William nodded but his lips pressed into a thin line. Thomas cringed as he waited what felt like a long time for his brother's response. "The short answer is yes. I discussed with Mother and Father that if you were going to come and live with us as an adult then you would be treated as one in every way."

"And what's your personal opinion on it?"

This hesitation was just as long as the last one, and William's chest rose and fell twice before he answered. "Have you and Mia ever discussed the idea of marriage?"

Thomas bristled. "Had you and Quinn discussed it before you proposed to her?"

"No." William was calm, unaffected by his tone. "My proposal to her was a surprise to both of us, you know that. But nothing else was unspoken between us, Thomas. We weren't arguing, we weren't keeping things from each other – each of us knew what the other one wanted, because we'd both talked about it. Even if she'd said no right then, we would have been okay – we'd have been able to talk about it still, and laugh about it, and revisit the topic at another time."

"And you don't think Mia and I would be."

"I have no idea. I'm obviously not there when the two of you are alone together. It doesn't matter what I think anyway. Do *you* know what would happen if you asked her that question?"

Thomas closed his eyes and gave a single shake of his head.

"I'm not going to tell you what to do. If you were to ask her to marry you and she accepted, I would be thrilled to host a big wedding for you in Philotheum. But … if you want the honest truth from where I'm sitting as your older brother … I think the two of you have some serious weeds in your garden right now, and if you don't take care of those first, they'll choke out any life you try to plant."

Thomas kicked at a rock on the path, sending it deep into the nearby bushes. "When did you get to be the one who knows what he's talking about when it comes to girls?"

"I'm not," William said, chortling. "I don't know what I'm doing ninety percent of the time, and then I even mess up the other ten percent. But I talk to her, Thomas. About everything. And I've been at it just long enough to learn what happens when I *don't* share my thoughts and feelings with her. It crushes both of us. And that's what I see you doing with Mia. That is not a good place to start."

Thomas knew William was right. He had to talk to Mia. He didn't know what he'd been thinking, considering proposing to her. The two of them had barely talked in the whole last moon.

And now, an entire moon – or maybe longer, if he was honest – of avoiding a necessary confrontation had brought them to this – to both of them making separate decisions about a future that, ironically enough, seemed to be taking them in the same direction.

How he hadn't seen it happening, he didn't know, but he knew at least half the blame belonged on his shoulders. Just as their paths were coming together, *they* had somehow diverged.

"You're back." Ben's voice broke into his train of thought and Thomas looked up to see him coming up the hallway toward him. "How did it … is everything all right?"

Great. His distress was visible to everyone. Thomas forced himself to smile. "Yes. Everything is fine. Nathaniel and William think the vaccine is going to be a success, and we're hopeful that the dog didn't actually have rabies, so we didn't have to kill it. At least not today."

"That is good news." Ben's mood was the polar opposite of Thomas' – he was happy and relaxed, no doubt a product of a day spent with Linnea.

Thomas had never imagined the stoic guard could be as happy he'd been ever since he began courting Linnea. Smiling for no reason in the hallways, finding little treats and ways to surprise her, taking off entire afternoons so the two of them could go on picnics....*That* was all Thomas wanted with someone. How could it be so difficult?

"Do William and Nathaniel need any help?" Ben asked.

"They're fine – and you only have a couple more days left in your honeymoon. Really, Ben, go enjoy the time."

Once Ben was gone, Thomas headed for the wing of the castle where the household servants lived. Halfway there, though, he realized he should probably wait until evening, when she was finished with her work and they had real time to talk.

Well, Mia rarely spent any time in her room during the day anyway. She probably wouldn't be there, and *then* he could wait until evening. He knocked twice, already backing away from the door to wait until later, when he was startled by the sound of the knob turning.

"Thomas!" Mia said, stepping in front of the door and pulling it mostly closed behind her. *Odd.* She sounded happy he was there, but he suspected she was carefully controlling her voice. Her expression was closer to terror than joy.

"Can I come in?"

She hesitated – only for a second, but it was enough for him to see she didn't really *want* him in her room right now, and her cheeks flushed pink as she pushed the door open and stood there, waiting for him to enter.

He almost used her hesitation as yet another excuse – almost offered to come back later at a better time – but then he made himself just take the steps, walking past her and over toward the couch.

"There's nowhere to sit down, I'm sorry," she said, looking more flustered by the second as she closed the door behind her.

Both the couch and the chair were covered with piles of clothing and her other belongings, books, sewing projects she'd been working on… A wooden trunk stood open on the floor over by her bed.

"You accepted the job. You're packing."

Her whole face and neck were glowing now, and her voice wobbled when she answered him. "Yes. I meant to talk with you about it later…"

"Did you? Were we ever going to talk about it at all, Mia? Or were we just going to keep avoiding it and pretending like everything is fine when it isn't?"

"I was … wait." She frowned. "You know about it?"

"What do you mean? Yes, William told me when he asked…" A cold, sick feeling slithered through him. "You don't know what William asked me today, do you?"

She stared at him, her confusion obvious. "Was it something about me?"

She didn't know. She had no idea he was going to Philotheum, too. She'd accepted the job without even *considering* him. He couldn't look at her. Staring down at the floor, he had to swallow several times before he trusted himself to speak. "You're planning on leaving without me – without even telling me."

She didn't answer. When he finally glanced back up at her, there were tears streaming down her face, landing in big drops on the front of her dress; her hands were twisted too tightly in her skirt to do anything about it.

Part of him wanted to rush across the room, to take her in his arms, to wipe away the tears himself, to tell her everything was going to be okay. But another part of him – maybe a bigger part – didn't want to go near her at all. And he didn't know what she wanted. She was in here packing to move a five-day journey away from him, and she hadn't even bothered to mention it to him first.

He was only holding himself together just enough to know that he didn't want to do anything in anger. After taking a very deep breath, he said, "I don't think I'm up for dealing with this right now." And then he walked out the door.

GOING HOME

The Bridge, Eirentheos

ON THE NIGHT Zander arrived in Eirentheos, when Stephen had told him he was stuck here, ten days had sounded like a very long time.

Now that it was over, it seemed like no time had passed at all — or like he'd spent an entire lifetime here, he wasn't sure which. Whatever it was, the idea that two hours from now he'd be back in his own world felt strange.

"I told you if you kept up your questions about Quinn you'd wind up learning things that can never be unlearned, and you would change your life forever."

His fork full of food fell to his plate with an astounding clunk when he looked across the table and saw the man sitting in the spot Thomas had vacated only moments before. Alvin.

"What are you doing here?" he blurted out.

Alvin smiled. "Sometimes, the dinners Queen Charlotte arranges are just too wonderful to pass up. I just knew tonight would be one of those nights." Picking up his own fork, he took a bite of the meat, potato, and cheese casserole.

Zander looked around. Nearly everyone had abandoned the table already – they were all on the other side of the dining room, gathered around Owen. Zander could have joined them, but it had seemed only right to let Quinn and her family spend the last minutes they could with him. Ben, Marcus, and Luke were taking them to the gate right after the meal.

Quinn was mostly successful at holding back her tears, but Zander had seen her surreptitiously pull out a handkerchief twice while she was supposed to be eating. The plate at the place where she'd been sitting was still full.

"Nobody even knows you're here," he said to Alvin.

"You do."

He rolled his eyes.

"Was it worth it, Zander – finding out the answers to your questions?"

Did Alvin enjoy playing games with people? "What if I said it was?"

Alvin didn't react to that at all the way Zander expected him to – instead, his half-smile turned into a blazing grin. "That would be excellent. Truly an accomplishment. I might even have to say I was proud of you, Zander."

"Proud of me? For what? Running off to another universe just because I thought I knew better than what people were honestly telling me?"

Alvin's grin didn't fade. "Yes, definitely proud."

"I don't even know what you mean."

"So what did you think of your time here, Zander? Without your car and your phone?"

"I'm ready to be able to drive again, if that's what you're asking. But actually, horses aren't so bad once you get used to them."

"I heard you rode quite well yesterday – that you even beat Alex in a race."

"He's eight."

One of Alvin's bushy eyebrows arched up. "And he's been riding a fair bit longer than you. You don't seem to be limping after all of that, either."

He considered commenting on the fact that Alvin couldn't possibly know that, since he was sitting down, but those kinds of details didn't seem to matter to Alvin. Besides, it was sort of a point of pride for him – that he was riding well enough now to not get so sore so quickly. "Ben's a good teacher," he said instead.

"Yes." The look in Alvin's eyes switched to a very fond one. "Ben is very good at many things. Horses, swords, teaching…" he glanced over to where Ben was standing behind Linnea, his arms around her waist, his head resting on her shoulder, "and very loving. For such a young man, he has already lived deeply and well."

"I'll bet you wouldn't say the same thing about *me*, would you?"

"Since when do you have any concern about my opinion, Zander?" Despite his words, Alvin's expression was kind.

"I barely know you."

"Exactly. I would think the much more important question is whether you would say that about yourself."

Zander shrugged. "Until I came here, I never even thought about something like that. I was just … *me*, doing normal things. Like everyone in my world."

"And now?"

"Now I see a different side of it, I guess."

"Well, don't be too hard on yourself Zander. You're young. Much younger in many ways than the young men here appear to be. Ben, for example, has lived the equivalent of two hundred years in your time. He's had more practice. From what I've seen of you these past ten days, I think you have more going for you than you give yourself credit for."

"I don't think I'd ever be able to sacrifice everything the way Quinn did, or the way Ben does every day that he works as a guard."

"No? I wouldn't place my money against it, Zander – that you'd be *able* to, anyway, if you made the choice. But choice does trump ability, every time. Now, if you'll excuse me, I'd hate to miss my last few moments with Prince Owen."

Zander was still contemplating his conversation with Alvin as they mounted the horses.

Quinn had finally given up the pretense of holding back her tears. They flowed freely down her cheeks as she hugged Owen for the last time before Ben lifted him into his saddle, and then climbed up behind him.

"Thank you," William said, coming to stand beside Zander's horse, "for all of your help with everything. You have the money Nathaniel gave you, right?"

"Yes, although I still feel bad for taking it." Zander's eyes had nearly popped out of his head when he'd seen the bills in the leather pouch. There was more than enough to get the rabies vaccine in there – far, far more.

"Don't. We don't have any use for it, and neither does Quinn's family. Owen's and Annie's college educations are already well covered. Quinn told us about your situation with your father – hopefully there's enough in there to help you make a decision about what you really want to study for yourself. Or whatever you want to do with it. It's yours. Thank you again."

He walked away before Zander could even respond – not that he was even sure he *could* respond. He was still stunned a few moments later when Marcus began leading his horse in front of them, through the castle gates and toward the road.

The money – he didn't even know what to think about that. It surely wasn't enough to take care of college completely, but ... it did mean he could make his own decision about what he was going to do without worrying about his father.

A couple of nights ago – after they'd come back to the castle from rescuing Digger – he'd had a startling revelation. As angry as he'd been with his father, it was possible that he wasn't entirely wrong. Wrong about making Zander go into business, maybe – he knew he didn't want that – but maybe it wasn't so awful that he didn't want to pay for Zander to mess around in college when he didn't even know what he wanted to study.

Or hadn't known, anyway. After spending time looking at the hydroelectricity dams and the maps that Thomas and Maxwell were working on, the idea of building things that could help people appealed to him. Quinn's dad, Jeff, was an engineer – maybe he'd talk to him when he returned Owen tomorrow.

"Did you have a good time, buddy?" he asked, riding up beside Ben and Owen – and marking off the accomplishment of having that much control over his mount.

"Yes, I had a very good time. I like it here."

"Are you sad to be going home?"

"No. I want to see my mom and dad and Annie. I don't like leaving Quinn and William and Samuel, though."

"I know you don't."

"I'll see them again, though."

"Yeah, I'm sure you will," Zander said, exchanging glances with Ben. He'd never been less sure of anything in his life, but he wasn't going to say that to Owen.

"Alvin said I will for sure."

That made Zander raise an eyebrow. If *Alvin* had said it, then maybe…

All of a sudden a memory came back to him in a vicious flash, sending creeping chills down his spine. The man – the strange man who had been sitting on the riverbank … in that instant, Zander knew exactly who he was.

"Zander! What's wrong?"

He looked up in time to see Ben and Marcus turning their horses around and heading back toward him – he hadn't even realized he'd stopped. Luke stayed ahead of them, but he, too, had turned around and was watching in concern.

"I think I saw Rahas on the other side of the gate."

He realized, after he said it that if Ben and Marcus didn't know what he was talking about, he might sound crazy, but the reaction was immediate.

Ben's eye's widened, but Marcus' reacted almost violently. His entire body went stiff, and his hand went instantly to the hilt of his sword. "What do you mean?"

"I don't know for sure, but, I think I saw him in Bristlecone." He actually *was* sure – he just didn't know how he knew, and he didn't want to explain that.

Marcus only grew more tense as Luke rode over and Zander told them the story of the strange man on the hillside near the river in Bristlecone. "I wish we'd known about this before," he said at the end.

"I wish I'd remembered enough to tell you. What do we do now?"

"We go," Ben said. "It doesn't matter that you didn't tell anyone, because there's nothing else we could have done, anyway. The three of us are the only guards who know the gate was opened again – we could have brought Simon or Maxwell, perhaps, but that might only have added to the danger. We don't know if he saw you use the gate or if he knows it's open. The important thing now is to get you and Owen through it. Do you have any way to get help on the other side if you need it?"

"His cell phone is charged. It worked with the same charger as my camera."

"I don't know what that means," Ben said, "but I'm assuming that's a yes?"

"Yes."

"Here," Ben reached behind him, unlatched one of the saddle bags and withdrew a long knife, in a stamped-leather sheath. "Take this."

"To *Bristlecone?*"

"Yes. I don't want you to be unarmed."

If he used that knife on someone in Bristlecone, he was going to need the money for something other than college, but if he'd learned one thing from Ben during his time here, it was not to argue with him.

The rest of the way to the bridge, everyone was overly cautious; all three guards scanned the area repeatedly, noticing every small movement. Marcus' hand moved to his sword for a moment when a rabbit scurried across the trail in front of them.

But they made it without incident. The trail curved close to the river, and then they rounded a bend, and there it was – the long stone bridge stretching across the river. The last reflections of the setting sun glinted along the moving water – the short delay while they'd talked on the trail had eaten up some of their time.

All three guards dismounted in incredible synchronicity as soon as they reached the base of the bridge. Marcus and Luke were wary, walking around the area, their eyes searching behind every tree and rock. Ben pulled Owen down and set him down gently before reaching into the saddlebag again and taking out his backpack.

Their load was much lighter going back. The cooler and duffel bag had been left behind, along with most of the contents of the backpack – Zander wasn't even sure what else had been in there. Now it contained a few things Owen was bringing back with him along with the money and a letter Zander had spent the last two nights writing to his parents. He didn't know if he ever planned on giving it to them, but it had felt important to write it, helping him organize his thoughts for some of the difficult conversations ahead.

Although Owen could have easily carried the backpack himself now, Zander reached for it as soon as his feet hit the ground beside them.

"Thanks, Zander," Owen said.

"Of course, little man." He ruffled the boy's hair. "You and I will have to be friends forever now, since we're the ones who have the secrets together."

"I know how to get to my house and how to get inside with the garage code," Owen said suddenly.

"That's … good," Zander said. "Do you want to go back to your house instead of mine to wait for your parents? I have a key, too."

Owen nodded. "I know how to call my mom and dad, too. And there's enough food and stuff at my house if I need it."

"Okay, buddy. We can go straight there, if you want." One more night away from his house wouldn't make any difference to Zander. "We can even order a pizza if you're hungry again. I don't know what time your parents will be back, but I'll stay and take care of you until they get there." Something wasn't right with Owen right now – probably it was just the transition, and the fact of leaving his sister.

"Not straight home," Ben warned. "The gate needs to be closed immediately, if you can."

"I can close the gate," Owen said. "I know how."

"Owen," Ben crouched down next to him, looking in his eyes. "You can't *ever* open that gate again. You know that, right? It doesn't matter what happens, or if you miss this place, or even if you think Quinn needs you. You can't open it."

"I know." His voice trembled a little. "I'm going to throw the magnet in the river."

Zander set his hand on Owen's shoulder. It wasn't going to be easy, but they would get through this.

"Zander," Ben said, holding his hand out. When Zander took it, the guard squeezed it tightly. "It's been a pleasure."

366

"An honor for me, Ben. Really. Thank you for everything."

Ben smiled. "On to new adventures, right?"

"Something like that."

"Well, it's almost sunset."

Zander slung the backpack over his shoulder, and reached for Owen's hand with the other. The weight of the knife was awkward at his belt, but he wanted Ben to see that he took the warning seriously, so he kept it there.

They were nearly to the top step of the bridge when he heard it – a sound that was terribly out of place in this world, but that he would have recognized anywhere. The cocking of a gun.

He whirled around at the same time all three guards did.

"Now this – this is interesting," said the man standing there. One of the men, Zander corrected himself, because there were two of them.

He recognized the black-haired man from the riverbank immediately – Rahas. The man who'd killed Quinn's grandfather – and possibly her father as well.

Zander had never before felt the kind of cold, raw anger that slammed through him when he saw Rahas – he didn't even know where it came from – perhaps it was flowing out of Rahas himself, from his dark, lifeless eyes.

But it wasn't Rahas who had spoken.

There was another man there. He was shorter, also dark-haired, but not the strange midnight coloring of Rahas. And though Rahas was the one with the gun pointed right at Zander, the other man was smiling.

"Queen Quinn's top advisor and his son, the guard – along with the head of King Stephen's guards, sneaking off to another world." He shook his head. "I do wonder what Her Majesty's people would think. Whoever are your friends?"

"What are you doing here, Tolliver?" Marcus asked.

Tolliver. Even the name set Zander's skin crawling.

"I could ask you the same thing, *Marcus Westbrook*. Your little party here wouldn't have anything to do with the gate not working properly these past several moons and my guard here being stuck in a different world, would it?"

"Go," Ben hissed, pulling out his sword. Zander pushed Owen up onto the step above him and moved his body in front of the little boy's.

"Oh, I wouldn't do that if I were you."

To prove Tolliver's point, Rahas pointed the weapon just slightly to the side and fired a single shot.

Owen jumped at the noise, but nobody else did. The guards were apparently as aware as Zander was of the weapon's capabilities. While Tolliver and Rahas were focused on the bullet's path into the water, though, Zander nudged Owen up onto the last step, and climbed up one more himself.

Zander could see that Rahas' shot had gone just slightly wide – while he'd clearly fired a weapon before, he still didn't handle the kickback perfectly.

"You need to get it," he whispered under his breath, hoping his voice would carry far enough for at least one of the guards to hear him.

He knew they needed to get their hands on the weapon, but he didn't know what to do. Getting himself and Owen through the gate was the top priority, but he didn't want to leave the three of them alone here until they had that gun – and it wasn't just that. Tolliver carried a sword, and he was probably even better with it than his partner was with the gun.

Somehow, he also needed to keep them from following him – to keep Owen safe.

Ben still hadn't put his sword away, and now Marcus and Luke were drawing theirs.

"Drop your weapons," Tolliver said.

As surreptitiously as he could, Zander slid the backpack from his shoulder to Owen's hand, still twined in his. "Go," he whispered. "I'll come in a minute."

"No, Zander. He might shoot you."

That's better than him shooting you, Zander wanted to hiss, but Tolliver was listening to everything.

He dropped Owen's hand and pushed the boy a little further behind him.

But Tolliver noticed the movement. "Stay right there."

The sky was growing dimmer by the minute. Much later, and Owen would have been able to sneak away in the dark – except the gate would be closed then.

For several seconds, time stood absolutely still.

Just as Zander was considering how fast he'd have to run to catch Rahas off guard and get that weapon out of his hands – Rahas *probably* wasn't good enough with the weapon to hit a quickly moving target – Ben glanced up at them and then turned back to Tolliver. In horrified fascination, Zander saw what he was going to do before he did it, but before he could yell at him to stop, Ben swung his sword and advanced.

Zander turned and shoved Owen backwards, apologizing to him just as the crack of the gun filled the air.

Two things registered in Zander's mind at once – first, that Owen was gone, safely on the other side of the bridge. Second, that Ben had been hit, enough to knock him to his knees. The information was secondary to the motion of his body, though. Grabbing the knife at his belt, he bolted down the stairs as fast as he could move, heading for Rahas – the man wasn't skilled enough with the gun to get off another good shot quickly enough to stop him.

He didn't know what the guards were doing behind him. There was motion, and there was noise. Something heavy hit his side, but his goal was singular.

The knife made contact exactly where he wanted it to – the soft spot at the base of Rahas' throat at the same time Rahas brought his hands to Zander's neck, one of them still holding the gun.

The weapon fired, but the bullet flew uselessly into the air. Zander's ears were ringing so badly he couldn't hear anything.

It took all of his anger – his *rage* – and his determination, but he did it. With a sharp thrust, he shoved the knife in as deeply as he could before jerking it sharply to the side.

The gun fell to the ground, but Rahas didn't give up. Both hands now free, they closed around Zander's neck, gripping tightly.

With the man's fingers choking him, he almost panicked and lost his resolve. But with a final burst of fury, Zander managed to tug the knife in the opposite direction, finally causing the man's grip to loosen, and Rahas to fall beside his weapon.

His relief was short-lived, though, as a different sensation hit the side of his neck – the tip of Tolliver's sword. *Crap*. Zander's knife was still in Rahas' neck.

"Who are you?" Tolliver spit through his teeth.

Zander didn't acknowledge him, didn't even worry about the weapon touching him – he was more worried about the gun still on the ground. Tolliver was edging toward it, but Zander's foot was closer. He kicked, hard, at the gun, sending it flying away from them and toward Marcus.

The tip of the sword pierced the side of his neck, but by then, Marcus had the gun. "Drop it, Tolliver. Now."

When Tolliver didn't drop the sword immediately, Marcus fired. Tolliver fell; blood immediately pouring from his lower leg.

Zander scrambled away, back toward the guards and the bridge. Ben was on his feet again – relief washed over him a fraction of a second before terror struck again, in the form of movement in the trees.

Tolliver and Rahas weren't alone. A third, enormous, fully-armed man was walking toward them.

Marcus pointed the gun and shot again.

He missed. The man kept coming.

"Zander, GO!" Marcus yelled.

Running up the steps of the bridge in near darkness now, Zander couldn't help but watch. The man stopped when he got to Tolliver, kneeling down.

"Don't shoot again," he hissed at Marcus. "There's only one more round." If he discharged it, they'd know he was out of ammunition.

"Just *go*, Zander."

He almost did, almost took the last two steps to safety, but he looked back once more, just in time to see Ben sway, and take a stumbling step forward to catch himself.

"Sorry Owen," he whispered.

The sun disappeared completely as he ran back down the steps toward Ben.

Marcus still had the gun trained on Tolliver.

Zander reached Ben, steadying him and helping him down to the ground, putting his body between Ben and Tolliver. The gunshot wound was in Ben's abdomen; blood already covered the front of his shirt.

"I'm fine," Ben whispered, "albeit a little messy." Beads of sweat pooled on his forehead, and his features were turning a dusky gray.

Zander wished he believed him. He looked around, but he didn't have anything – the backpack had disappeared with Owen. Shrugging out of his jacket, he pulled off the shirt he was wearing so he could press it against Ben's wound.

"I have more men, Marcus. If you shoot at me again, you're going to find yourself outnumbered quickly. You'll never get your son out of here." Even injured and on the ground, Tolliver's voice was mocking. "If you let me go now, I'll leave you alone.

The man who'd come to assist him stood over him now, his sword at the ready, and Tolliver was likely still capable of inflicting damage.

"He's lying. He's a coward. Now that he doesn't have Rahas, he knows he needs to get out of here." Ben said, even though it was now clear that just the effort of saying it was painful.

"What difference does it make if he's lying?" Zander tried to make his voice loud enough that Marcus could hear, but not enough to for it to carry to Tolliver and his new accomplice. "We have one bullet. If we miss with that, all that's left is direct combat, and we don't outmatch them by much. In the meantime, we don't get you to help."

"Leave me. Go after him."

The blood had already soaked through Zander's shirt. Ben was growing weaker; he could barely lift his head.

Across from them, Tolliver was on his feet again.

"And what if he's not lying?" Marcus asked.

Suddenly, behind Tolliver, there was a crunching sound in the trees.

"Make your decision, Marcus," Tolliver said, sneering at them.

Marcus fired the gun.

Hope surged inside Zander as Tolliver went reeling backwards; the man with him scrambled to catch him.

But when Tolliver righted himself again, they could see that while he had been hit, it was only in his left arm – not likely a fatal blow. His right hand was still wrapped around the hilt of his sword.

A second man stepped out of the trees, making Zander remember every curse word he'd ever used in his life.

"Now are you tired of your little game, Marcus? Your son is going to die if you don't get him out of here – your hesitation may have killed him already."

Ben was right. Tolliver was a coward. As soon as Marcus and Luke lowered their swords to their sides, he slunk away, supported by his comrades. They didn't even attempt to take Rahas' body with them.

"There aren't any more of them!" as weak as Ben was his anger was stronger. "They could just come back and ambush us! This is your chance to kill him!"

"With what?" Marcus asked, dropping to his knees on the ground beside his son. "They're better armed – we didn't come here prepared for a fight. He won't come back. He's too concerned about his own skin – he just shot a royal – and his men are too concerned about losing him."

A few feet away from them, Luke had already summoned a bird and was furiously scribbling a note.

"You're better than them. They're cowards. They'd lose."

"*We'd* lose, too. I'm not going to leave you here to go chasing after him. He's not worth it, Ben."

The look Ben gave his father was one that Zander wouldn't be able to get out of his head for the rest of his life – it was a look that shredded something deep inside of him.

"You're going to lose me anyway," Ben said, his voice still stronger than it should have been. "I can't get on a horse, I can't even get off the ground."

"I've sent a message," Luke said, coming over to them, "asking for help. Someone will come."

Ben shook his head. "It won't be in time. I don't have enough time."

"Don't say that," Marcus said, his voice growing desperate. "Nathaniel and William will know what to do."

Ben closed his eyes for a second, then opened them again. "I could use some water," he said to Marcus who got up immediately to retrieve it.

"I have some bandages," Luke said, following him.

"You shouldn't drink water," Zander said, still pressing his blood-soaked shirt against the gushing wound.

Ben ignored that, and Zander suddenly understood that he didn't actually want the water anyway. "Thank you for killing Rahas," he said. "You sacrificed everything for that – if you hadn't … this would have turned out much worse."

"What's worse than this?" he asked.

But Ben's thoughts had shifted. He had a faraway look in his eyes. "Linnea's pregnant," he said. "She doesn't know that – I didn't know that until just now. Don't do it tonight … not for a little while yet … but will you tell her for me that it's a girl? A perfect little girl – just like her – and that I love them both so much?"

Zander couldn't remember having cried since he was young, but he couldn't stop the tears that flowed down his face now as he nodded. "I would, if you were going to die, but you're not going to die."

"Don't, Zander, please."

For a moment, he almost continued, almost told Ben to keep fighting, to wait, but then he realized the arguing would be a waste of the precious time left. Though Ben was bleeding profusely from the front, there was no blood underneath him – the bullet hadn't gone through. He wasn't a doctor, but he knew that was bad news.

"Fine. But what if it's a boy, and I've lied to her, then?"

Ben gave him a weak smile. "She won't be mad – she'd love him just as much, and so would I. But I see my girl pretty clearly."

"I'll tell her, Ben. I will."

"Good. And I need you to please make sure she doesn't spend her life being sad and alone forever. She can grieve, but if she takes it too far, then someone needs to talk some sense into her. Wherever I am, when I look at her, I want to see her smile. Can you do that, too?"

"I can try," he said. "I think you overestimate my ability to get her to listen, though."

"I think you'll manage. Thank you, Zander. I wish I was going to be around to see the great man you're going to become, but I'm glad I got to be here at the beginning." His voice was growing weaker now and his hands were trembling from the pain.

Marcus was back with the water, and Luke had the bandages. The water was abandoned, but they worked together for a moment to get the clean cloth against the bloody mess without taking pressure off of it for a second. Once Marcus was holding the bandage, Zander and Luke backed away, leaving him to be alone with his son.

Zander headed for the river to wash his hands and face and continue his cry.

The thundering of hoof beats roared down the path much sooner than Zander expected. Some of the castle guards must have been perpetually equipped to leave instantly if they were needed.

Luke walked over to meet them.

"What happened here?" one of the guards asked. "What were you doing, Luke?"

"I don't have time to answer questions right now, but the men who attacked us – Tolliver and at least two of his soldiers went that direction," he pointed. "We need to find them."

"Do you need help here?"

"Yes. But not the kind you can provide right now. Just … find Tolliver."

Nathaniel came riding up only moments after the first set of guards disappeared, with several more guards behind him. He dismounted while his horse was still moving, running over to Marcus, already holding his large leather medical bag. "Who is it? What happened?" he was yelling.

But it was too late.

Zander was still curled in a ball at the edge of the river when Nathaniel came over to him.

"You stayed."

"I thought I could help Ben." He swiped angrily at a belated tear that made its way down the side of his nose.

Nathaniel just nodded and sat down next to him, resting his hand on Zander's shoulder while the two of them stared out over the moonlight reflecting on the black swirling water. Nathaniel was unapologetic about the flow of tears down his own cheeks. "You're bleeding," he said after a few minutes.

"Yeah." He pulled back the hand which had been pressing another of Luke's bandages against the gouge on his neck, at the same time using his other hand to peel back his bloodied jacket, revealing another long cut on his side. "Tolliver's sword," he said. "At least on my neck. I'm not sure about the other one. It's all just a blur. I didn't even notice the blood until after I came over here to clean myself up. It didn't even hurt."

"Does it hurt now?"

"Yeah."

"I'll bet. It doesn't look very serious, but I want to get it cleaned up and get the bleeding stopped." He was already digging around in his bag, pulling out some kind of leather pouch.

"I'm fine," Zander said. "Don't we need to get Ben back to the castle or something?" Most of the guards had followed the first group, spreading out into the woods to search for Tolliver and his men, but three of them had taken places around the little clearing, standing in uniform next to their horses, their swords drawn, their stances protective.

"No. They'll send a wagon. Ben is officially a royal as well as a guard. He'll be given his proper due. We've got some time; let me take care of you."

FIRELIGHT

"COME IN," ZANDER called when there was a knock on his door. The sound had startled him – everyone was so preoccupied, he hadn't expected anyone would need to talk with him tonight.

"Hey," Quinn called from the doorway.

"Hey."

"Can I come in?"

Though he stayed where he was, he held out his hand toward the couch across from him.

"It's dark in here," she said once she'd closed the door behind her.

"You can light some lamps if you want to." Even as he said it, he knew he'd prefer she didn't. The low flickering of the fire in the grate was enough for him; it was comforting – and dark enough to hide the random tears that had occasionally been escaping. That hadn't happened in a while, though. Now he was mostly numb.

"I like it like this," she said. He couldn't see her face very well as she sat down across from him, but the rough sound in her voice and the white cloth clenched in her hand told him that she'd done her fair share of crying tonight.

"Did they send you in here?" he asked.

"I'm a queen, Zander. Nobody 'sends' me anywhere."

He half-smiled to himself. She was still capable of indignation.

"I did tell them I was coming to talk to you. William asked me to bring you this." Withdrawing an object from her pocket, she stretched her arm to the little table between them to set it down. It was a little brown glass bottle. Or it looked brown in the firelight, anyway. "For the pain."

"The physical kind, anyway," Zander said, sighing and reaching for the bottle. Pills rattled against the glass.

"How are you feeling?"

He ignored the deeper meaning in her question. "The numbness is starting to wear off in both my neck and my side."

"Want me to get you a glass of water so you can take some of those?"

"I'm all right. I'll do it in a little while." Truthfully, he sort of welcomed the pain – it was real and there, and it reminded him that tonight's events had really happened. Pain was better than being completely numb inside and out.

"Okay." The tone in her voice told him she understood.

"How is Linnea?"

"Thomas and William are with her. I think she's in shock. All of us are; it doesn't seem like it could be true."

"It doesn't seem like it could be true, but it is. I saw the whole thing." He'd ridden behind Marcus and Ben in the wagon all the way back to the castle.

"I heard you were a hero. That you killed Rahas, and you tried to save Ben."

"I didn't do anything for Ben. I couldn't help him. I was useless. Worse than useless. This whole thing is my fault."

"Your fault *how?*"

"If I hadn't come here, if I could have just let things be, and not insisted that I had to have answers that were none of my business, then Ben would be alive right now."

"Don't be stupid, Zander."

"Excuse me?"

"Seriously. If I wasn't a queen, and you weren't injured and a hero, I would walk over there and physically knock some sense into you. This isn't your fault. You didn't kill Ben. Rahas and Tolliver did."

"They wouldn't have been able to if I hadn't come here."

She paused, the silhouette of her head looking down toward her lap, wiping at her eyes with the white cloth. "Learning to take responsibility is a powerful thing, Zander. But you have to be careful to only take the amount that actually belongs to you. You didn't kill anyone by coming through that gate. If you'll remember correctly, you saved at least one person's life – and you possibly saved Ben's, too."

"All for nothing. I jumped down off of that bridge thinking I could do something – he said I did, you know, Ben, before … that if I hadn't killed Rahas…And now, what? Rahas is dead, but so is Ben and I'm homeless in another universe." There were the tears again.

She was quiet for several minutes before she spoke. "You're not homeless, Zander."

"Where am I going to live, then?"

"That's up to you. William and I would be happy to have you in Philotheum, if you want. We have plenty of room in the castle."

"You'd be happy with that, Quinn? Your husband would be *happy* with you inviting your ex-boyfriend to live with the two of you?"

"This isn't a situation anybody planned for. I'm sure it's not an offer you ever considered in any way. If you're really uncomfortable with it, then you should know that Stephen has offered the same to you here. He would come to you and tell you himself, but he figured tonight wasn't the best night."

"He offered that, really?"

"Yes. Of course, you are an adult. You're free to live and work wherever you'd like – in either Eirentheos or Philotheum. But neither kingdom has any intention of turning a hero out onto the streets. We're all more than happy to provide for your needs until you get settled – or beyond."

"I'm not a hero, Quinn."

"Do you have another word for someone who would sacrifice his entire life in defense of a kingdom? Because I don't."

He didn't know what to say for that; he ended up settling for rambling. "The money was in the backpack with Owen – everything of mine was, except for what I'm wearing. I don't even have a shirt."

"We'll get you clothes, Zander. And everything you need. Nobody here is going to let a hero run around with nothing. You're entitled to full military benefits for your service to the kingdom tonight. We have more cash from the other world, but the money is useless here anyway – we have plenty of other kinds of paper if you need some."

He chuckled, which surprised him. It didn't feel like he should be able to react with any emotion at all. "What was Nathaniel doing with that kind of cash here then, anyway?"

"Traveling between universes is risky. He always had enough money with him to be able to cover an unexpected emergency in case something weird happened. At some point, someone could have figured out that his birth certificate wasn't real, or who knows, so he didn't want to leave everything in a bank – and leaving that kind of cash in an empty house is probably a bad idea, too, so… Plus, there was always enough here for someone else to have cash in case they needed to make a trip to the other world."

He nodded, not really interested in the topic anymore. It didn't matter. "I can't ever go home."

"No. At least, not in the foreseeable future."

"Not in the 'foreseeable future', Quinn? We just told Owen to close the gate permanently. I'm sure he did, even when I didn't show up. He better have."

"I'm sure he did. There are rumors, though, of other gates that existed and people knew about in the past. Even Alvin admitted the other gates are real. It's always been our hope that we would find one."

"So Tolliver could go through one of those ones instead? Fabulous idea."

"You're right. We have to take care of the Tolliver problem before finding another gate."

"Yeah, you could call it that – the *Tolliver problem*. Did they catch him?"

"No. They're still searching." She stood and began pacing the room, casting long shadows up the walls as she passed the fire. "The only good thing – not good, but … I don't have the right word for it – about Ben's death is it gives me a solid crime for which I can have Tolliver charged. When we catch him, he will be executed for the murder of a royal. I really don't care what anybody else says."

"Good. Because if you don't have him killed, Quinn, I will find a way to make it happen. And I'm not the only one who feels that way."

"Trust me, I've had the same thoughts. I've lived in fear of something like this for eleven moons. But it's hard to execute a prince who is also your uncle when he hasn't actually committed an executable crime. Particularly when you're the first queen to ever be the ruler of a kingdom, and a good number of your people still support him. But now he's done it – he's given me an iron-clad reason."

"I was personally hoping he'd make it through the gate just in time to be run over by a semi."

"Well, if we ever find another gate, you're welcome to push him."

"I just might."

She sat back down and they were both quiet for a while, staring into the fire.

"Do you think Owen is okay?" he asked. "There, in Bristlecone all alone? Nobody's there. I'm not sure when either of our families will be back – mine will before yours probably, but I don't know if he'd go there."

"I don't want to think about it," she said. "He knows his way around, he knows how to get home, or ask for help, or something. It sounds like all of the danger was on our side, so I'm just going to have to believe he's okay. That somehow, somewhere, someone is watching out for him."

He nodded. "I'm the one the police are going to be looking for."

"Yeah, probably. But they won't find you. Nobody will. I'm sure Owen will tell my parents, and they'll figure out some way to tell yours. It sucks we're leaving them to do that, but … if I've learned anything in my experience of leaving that world and trying to live in this one, Zander – you can't worry about it. You just have to believe that everything will work out how it's supposed to there, and live your life where you are."

"And that's here now."

"That's here. And we have enough of our own troubles and worries here."

ANSWERS

Rosewood Castle, Eirentheos

"THERE YOU GO, little man," Thomas said, fastening the last pin on the diaper. "Does that feel better?"

The infant cooed in response as Thomas lifted him into his arms, carrying him over to the window. A light snow covered the grass outside the castle, which seemed appropriate for today. "Someday soon, Uncle Thomas is going to teach you how to throw snowballs," he whispered to the baby.

The creaking of the half-open door behind him made him look up. "Mia."

Her whole face went white when she saw him. "I'm sorry ... I was looking for Quinn and William ... I ... I have the baby's outfit." She held up the tiny green velvet jumper, embroidered in gold with the crest of Philotheum.

"Quinn and Will are with Marcus and Linnea, making some of the last-minute arrangements," he said, taking the outfit from her. He looked at it, shaking his head. "This was not supposed to be the first occasion we dressed him up for."

A shadow passed over her eyes, and she nodded and sighed. "At least Quinn got to have a say in this one. Lady Sophia messaged that the one for his Naming Ceremony is ready and waiting."

"Well, Lady Sophia is going to have me and Linnea to contend with over taking decisions from Quinn like that from now on."

"While you're there for the ceremony, anyway," Mia said, her voice shaking and her face going several shades paler.

Thomas closed his eyes for a long moment, calming himself and the baby at the same time by rocking slightly back and forth. "Mia, where have you been for the past week?"

"What do you mean Thomas? We've been planning a funeral, and I thought you were mad at me." A tear was already sliding down her cheek.

"So mad that I didn't want to see you? That I didn't want to hug you? Do you think I don't know how close your family and Marcus and Ben were when you were growing up? How hard this must be on you, too? I wouldn't have minded being there for you – or to have you there for me. Or was your telling me that you're moving to Philotheum your way of breaking things off between us without actually telling me?"

The tears were dripping off her chin now, and he almost felt bad, but he didn't – he was angry now.

"I didn't *want* to end our courtship, Thomas. I was going to tell you – I meant to tell you everything, and then, that afternoon, you walked into my room, and you saw ... I didn't mean. I just don't want to *fight* with you anymore, Thomas. I can't. This is too hard."

"*Not fighting* seemed harder to you than trying to avoid me while we're packed in carriages together for five days, Mia? You'd rather leave me hanging out here alone dealing with this than have me be mad at you?"

She looked down at the floor.

"I don't understand."

Her eyes stayed down, and the tears just kept going. "I didn't think you would want to have anything to do with me after what I did, and since I'm leaving anyway…"

And then he knew. She'd already ended it without saying a word to him. "Let me see your wrist, please."

Her shoulders were shaking, but she did it. She lifted her sleeve enough for him to see that it was empty – she wasn't wearing her courtship bracelet.

"Mia…"

Still not really looking at him she walked toward him, putting her hand in her pocket and then pulling it out again, the silver chain dangling from her fingertips.

Shifting the baby into the crook of one elbow, he stretched out his other hand to accept it, and then watched, horrorstruck, as she turned and fled from the room.

After he'd had a few moments to compose himself, he leaned his head down and kissed the baby on the forehead. "Just don't ever ask me for advice about girls, Samuel. Stick with talking to your father about that one."

"And just what is it you think William knows about girls that you don't, Thomas?"

The voice surprised him so much that he jumped and whirled around, jostling the baby a bit. The infant screeched his disapproval.

"Why don't you let me hold the baby for a moment, Prince Thomas?" Alvin said. "I haven't had the pleasure yet."

"You never fail to surprise me, Alvin." Thomas handed the baby over, and he quieted immediately, staring up at Alvin's bushy eyebrows.

"Glad to know I'm not losing my touch already. So, you didn't answer my question. What makes you think your brother is better at relationships than you?"

"Well, for starters, he knows how to get Quinn to actually talk to him."

"No he doesn't. Nobody can *make* anyone talk to them, Thomas. I'll admit he does a nice job most of the time at letting her know that it's safe to talk to him – and he's even getting halfway good about recognizing and apologizing to her when he's made it hard."

His jaw dropped again. "It's *safe* for Mia to talk to me! What do you think I would do to her?"

Alvin shrugged, seeming to only give him half his attention as he focused on the baby. "I don't know. Ask difficult questions she doesn't know how to answer when she's already feeling guilty and lost? Expect answers to those questions without giving up any of your own secrets? Demand she talk to you without first establishing where each of you is emotionally?"

"She's been hiding from me, Alvin! And she hasn't been talking to me at all! Don't you think I have a right to expect some of those answers?"

"If what you want is to feel right and justified in your own actions, Thomas, you don't need me. You're already there. You're right. She messed up and didn't talk to you, and then she handled it wrong. You win – and you've got the medal to prove it. Or the metal, anyway." He nodded at the courtship bracelet still in Thomas' hand.

He rolled his eyes and threw the bracelet onto the nearest table. "She made it sound like I was being unreasonable for wanting her to tell me she's moving to Philotheum. That's not fair."

"*Fair?* Have you told her *you're* moving to Philotheum?"

"She didn't give me a chance!"

"She didn't give you a chance, Thomas, or you didn't make sure to make one?"

"How do I *make* a chance when she's been avoiding me? I don't even know where she's been half the time."

Alvin raised an eyebrow. "There's another half of the time, though, isn't there? But she's not the only one who's been avoiding a fight. Really, Thomas? Where have *you* been? You're not upset because you didn't know where she was – she's been in the castle. She's been busy – which is convenient for you, because you can look around for five minutes before you give up and blame it on her – and leave her with another question you can demand an answer to next time."

Thomas swallowed hard. He knew that was at least half true.

"You're upset because she didn't tell you that she was considering requesting a job in Philotheum – did you ever tell her that *you've* been having the same thoughts and desires to move there for the past eleven moons?"

"I didn't think it was something that could actually happen, so I didn't see the need to upset her."

"So, your intentions are good, because you didn't want to upset her – and yet when she avoids the conflict and doesn't know how to tell you about wanting to leave…"

"I just think it's ridiculous that she wouldn't talk to me when I came to her."

"Feelings are often ridiculous, Thomas. Yours included. Look, I'm not going to say she's right in everything. I know you're frustrated that she didn't come to you and talk to you, and yes, she carries much of the responsibility for that. But I think you might want to consider what your goal is when you are in the same room together. How did you start this conversation? Or the last one? Did you even ask her how she was or tell her you missed her before you launched in with, 'Where have you been?' or 'What are you doing?' Do you need an *answer* from her so badly that you'll miss connecting with her?"

Thomas closed his eyes. He knew Alvin was right. He *had* done nothing but demand answers of Mia when he hadn't been willing to give up his secrets, either.

"You can't *win* a relationship, Thomas. You can't withhold answers of your own just to get hers first. So, yes, she was wrong, too. And, yes, she has, at the moment, found it easier to give up than to face the tough questions from you. And she's hurting right now – even more than you are. And you are not being gentle. What's left is for you to decide what's important to you – being right, or being with her."

"Does it matter?" he asked, looking at the table where he'd thrown the bracelet. "It's too late now, anyway."

"No, dear one. There's only one circumstance in which you can be too late to work out your issues and tell someone your real feelings for them. Somewhere else today, I know someone who is quite glad he didn't wait to show love and compassion to those he cared about. And your sister, for the rest of her life, will reap the benefits of knowing she showed hers as well. You're not too late."

Throat thick and heart heavy, Thomas wiped at the single tear that had dripped down his cheek. "I don't think I've ever had this long a conversation with you before, Alvin."

"No, you haven't. But there are times when it's important to take just a bit more time, and listen just a bit more carefully. This was one of those times." He patted Thomas on the shoulder. "Now, I'm going to give this one back to you – I'm afraid he's going to need a fresh diaper again before you get him dressed. I have a ceremony I need to finish preparing for."

Thomas glanced at the clock after Alvin left – it was getting close to the time he'd told Quinn and William he'd meet them downstairs. He hurried to change and dress the baby, and remembered to grab the bag of extra diapers and supplies.

He was halfway into the hall, about to close the door behind him when he stopped. He turned around and went back into the room, over to where he'd dropped the bracelet. Picking it up, he slipped it into his pocket before heading downstairs for real.

WELCOME

QUINN, WILLIAM, MARCUS, Thomas, and Linnea were the last to arrive back at the castle for the reception after Ben's funeral. Zander looked up as they entered, watching as William's older sister, Rebecca, came to take the baby again.

"Drink, Sir?" a servant asked, standing next to him with a tray of glasses.

"Thank you," he said, accepting one. He had no idea what it was, but it tasted okay – sweet, but not overly so – and he sipped on it as everyone rushed to greet Marcus and Linnea.

He shook his head, wishing everyone would just back off from her. Sitting through that ceremony had to have been hard enough. And if she was...

"Yes, Zander, she is."

The glass went clattering to the ground, yellow juice splashing everywhere. "How do you do that *every time*?" he asked, spinning to face Alvin.

"It's a gift," Alvin said, smiling and stepping to the side as a servant rushed to clean up the mess.

Zander sighed and rolled his eyes. "And where's the justice in that, Alvin? She's pregnant, and her husband is dead." He spoke the last part in a low voice so no one would overhear.

"There is no justice in it Zander. Not everything is about justice. Some things just are."

"Well, I want some justice for this. Four days later, and we still don't know where Tolliver is."

Alvin put his hand on Zander's shoulder. "Patience, young one. They've captured one of his men. Rahas is dead. That's a start."

He closed his eyes and shook his head. "Killing Rahas didn't stop Ben from dying. Even finding Tolliver and killing him wouldn't bring Ben back."

"No. It did bring you here, though."

"You could have just picked me up and dropped me in the castle if you wanted me here so much Alvin. I don't think you needed to go to these extremes."

"I didn't bring you here. If you'll recall, I specifically warned you that you were treading in water past your shoulders. Owen was pretty clear on that point as well."

"And in the end, it was all for nothing."

Alvin sighed, reaching for two more glasses as another servant came by with a tray. "I'm sorry you feel that way, but someday soon, I think you'll come to realize that no effort made in true love or true sacrifice is ever for nothing."

"Sure." He took a long drink of the juice this time. It was so silent for a moment that he assumed Alvin had disappeared again while he was drinking, but when he finally pulled his glass away again, Alvin was still there, blinking at him. "What?" he asked.

"Can I ask you one favor?"

"As long as it doesn't involve walking over any strange bridges, I suppose so."

"You know that little feeling of doubt you've been having – about something that's not quite right?"

Zander narrowed his eyes.

"Usually, if something doesn't feel right, it's because it isn't. Don't be afraid to speak up about it."

"I'll get right on that."

"Wonderful." Alvin smiled, and then his expression grew more serious. "Also, I haven't had the chance to tell you … I know this doesn't mean much to you, Zander, at least not yet, but you have no idea how proud of you I am. You took on this situation, which was very difficult for you at the outset, and you made the best of it you could. You not only found a way to put aside your own misgivings, but you were able to stop and put the needs and interests of others before your own."

"I think you can give Ben the credit for that."

"No. Ben was an excellent mentor to you, Zander, but no alchemist. You brought the raw materials. Also, you need to learn to accept a compliment."

He sighed. "I'll get on that, too."

This time when he went back to drinking his juice, Alvin did disappear – though not completely. A few minutes later, Zander saw him talking to King Stephen and Queen Charlotte.

Linnea was over by the long food table, dishing up a small plate. For a second, he was annoyed that nobody was getting it for her, but then he realized she'd probably snuck away, wanting a minute to herself.

He hadn't talked to her at all since it had happened, and he didn't intend to now. Staying away seemed like the best plan as she had so many people to take care of her, and she didn't seem to like him much anyway, but when she quickly set the plate down on the table and took a step back, resting her hands on the table to steady herself, he rushed across the room.

"Linnea, are you all right?" he asked as he reached her.

"I don't think so." Her voice was wobbly, and beads of sweat were collecting on her temples.

Just as she gagged, he grabbed a large bowl of apples from the table, dumped them unceremoniously on the tablecloth and got the bowl under her chin just in time.

By the time she was finished, William, Thomas, Quinn, and Charlotte were there, forming a protective circle around her; her two brothers supporting her whole upper body in their arms.

A servant immediately whisked the bowl away and disappeared. Zander thought he could get used to that part of living in a castle.

Although he wasn't invited, he followed as William and Thomas quickly helped her out of the room, into a little alcove to the side that connected to one of the main hallways.

"I'm fine. You don't need to carry me," Linnea said as they helped her to a cushioned bench.

"Oh, try and stop us," Thomas said, kneeling down in front of her. "What was that, Nay? Just the day getting to be too much for you?"

"I don't know. Maybe. I thought I was doing okay, but I did throw up early this morning before breakfast, too."

Quinn raised an eyebrow.

"You were still asleep. I didn't think I needed to announce it. I feel better now, anyway. A lot better. I think I could even still eat something."

"Drink something first," William said. "I'll go get you some water. If you keep it down for a while, then I'll get you some food."

"No," Zander said, feeling his face go red. "I'd feed her if she's hungry. I don't think she's sick."

Four heads whipped around to stare at him.

He held up his hands.

"Is that possible?" Linnea asked. "Will? Could I be sick already from…?"

William frowned, looking up like he was trying to count. "Six weeks is long enough for sure, sweetheart. I mean, I don't know how long…"

"She is," Zander said, walking over and bending down near her, looking her in the eyes.

"You are, Linnea. Pregnant, I mean."

"Are you psychic now, Zander?"

"If I was psychic, do you think we'd be here?"

She rolled her eyes.

"Look … I didn't mean to do it like this. It should have been more … something. But I guess this isn't the kind of news that can wait forever and there hasn't been any other time I could talk to you." He paused, his ears growing warm; he knew everyone was watching him. "Ben knew. The night he … when I was sitting with him, he told me that he knew you were pregnant, and…" he wiped a tear out of his eye. "He was so happy about it, Linnea. It's what he was thinking about when he…"

She was crying now. Thomas sat down next to her and put his hand over her belly. "A little Ben," he whispered.

"Actually, Ben said to tell you it's a girl, and that he loves both of you."

He didn't have to hide any more of his crying in *this* room. Even William and Thomas had wet, red eyes as they hugged and held Linnea. After a few minutes, Stephen came looking for them, and he joined in, crying as he pulled his daughter into his arms, all the way off the ground and held her.

Zander backed away slowly, not wanting to draw attention to himself as he left to give them more privacy, but just when he'd almost made it out of sight into the hall, Quinn followed him.

"Thank you for that," she said, pulling out a handkerchief to dry her puffy eyes.

He shrugged. "I really didn't want to do it like that, but…"

"But it worked out. Did Ben *really* tell you that?"

"Yeah. And then Alvin just confirmed it a little while ago. I guess peeing on a stick is passé here, huh?"

She cracked a grin. "We make do with what we have."

"Premonitions made by dying men and proclamations from mysterious prophets?"

"Welcome to Deusterros."

He laughed out loud. "I guess. So," he glanced back toward the little space where they all were, "I take it it's good news?"

"It's very good news. Linnea didn't really want to be pregnant when we traveled, but I think she'll be okay. I guess Ben will get to come back with us to Philotheum in a way after all."

"Benjamina?" he guessed.

She chortled. "Yeah, I wouldn't suggest that one if I were you."

"So, is Linnea still going to go to Philotheum, then? Even though…?"

"Yes. She and Thomas both are. It's what she wanted anyway, new adventures, something different. Being with her brothers. She's going to need them now more than ever."

"Good for her, then."

"What about you, Zander? Have you decided if you're going to come and live with us?"

He shrugged. "Are there warm showers, at least?"

"No. Not in most of the castle. You can warm water over the fire for a bath."

"Whatever." He sighed. "I guess it's going to be an adventure for me too, then."

She sighed, reaching out to take his arm, squeezing it gently. "You know, I never thought it would work out like this Zander, especially after thinking I'd never see you again. I know it's not going to be all sunshine and rainbows for you – for any of us, really – but even though it probably sounds strange to hear this, I have to say I'm glad to know you'll be along."

"I don't know if I can say the same just yet."

"I know," she said, sounding both sad and hopeful at the same time.

"I guess we can just keep moving forward and see what happens, though, right?"

"Yeah." She smiled as William came to stand next to her, putting his arms around her waist.

"Linnea's doing better now," he said. "We're all going to go back into the reception."

"Okay," Quinn said, swiping at her eyes one more time with the tissue.

William looked at Zander. "Walk with us?"

Zander nodded. It wasn't what he'd planned or expected, but already this world was growing on him. As he stepped aside to let the two pairs of monarchs go in front, Thomas and Linnea came up beside him. This time, he didn't flinch when Thomas patted him on the back.

EPILOGUE

Bristlecone, Colorado

THE YOUNG BOY turned as the man approached. In front of him, the dark river raged, overflowing with heavy snowmelt from the mountain peaks above.

"Zander's not coming, is he?"

"No, Owen. He isn't. He'll be staying on the other side for a while."

Owen nodded. "I knew it was too dark now. It's been almost ten minutes."

"I know. I'm sorry it took me a little while. I came to walk you home, but there was someone else I needed to walk home first."

Looking up, Owen nodded solemnly, absolutely silent for several minutes.

"I was all right," he finally said. "I got the magnet. I was going to throw it in the river, but then I just knew that I shouldn't, so I decided to wait. Was that wrong?"

"No. It's never wrong to listen to what your gut is telling you. The river is still too close to the gate. Throwing the magnet there wouldn't have closed it. You need to take it somewhere else and break it, so it can't be used again."

"My dad has a hammer in the garage."

"That sounds perfect. Shall we go and find it?" Alvin held out his arms and scooped Owen into them, carrying him up the path.

ACKNOWLEDGEMENTS

Writing this series has been an amazingly fun and heartening undertaking. The best part of it has been meeting all of the amazing readers who have shared the journey, and have sent me notes, and made me smile when opening my inbox. It means more than you could possibly know.

I also have to give some very sincere thanks to some of the special beta readers and others without whom these books would not be what they are. (These are in NO particular order!)

Janene Silvers
Michelle Patrick
Kristy K. James
Mallory Rock
Danni Menard
Jennifer Simmons
Lori Dees

OTHER BOOKS BY BREEANA PUTTROFF

The Dusk Gate Chronicles
The continued adventures of the Rose family in
Eirentheos and Philotheum

Rumpelstiltskin's Daughter
A new take on an old fairy tale

COMING SOON
The Gatekeepers
An all-new adventure featuring some familiar characters

Visit www.BreeanaPuttroff.net to find out more!